SARDANA ENCORE

Book II

Ray Harwood

Matador
9 Priory Business Park,
Wistow Road, Kibworth Beauchamp,
Leicestershire. LE8 0RX
Tel: (+44) 116 279 2299
Fax: (+44) 116 279 2277
Email: books@troubador.co.uk
Web: www.troubador.co.uk/matador

ISBN 978-1784623-319

British Library Cataloguing in Publication Data.
A catalogue record for this book is available from the British Library.

Printed and bound in the UK by TJ International, Padstow, Cornwall

Matador is an imprint of Troubador Publishing Ltd

MIX
Paper from
responsible sources
FSC
www.fsc.org FSC® C013056

Followed by others in the series:
Sardana Renaissance
Letters to Peter
…and the Sun did Blush

To follow:
Sardana Shadows

Also by the same author:
Last Sardana

Blokes, Jokes and Forty Stags
On the Left Hand Side of the Axis

Cover Design: Jacqueline Abromeit
at www.goodcoverdesign.co.uk

Welcome back!

Thank you for returning
to the Sardana "sagas".
I hope you continue
to enjoy.

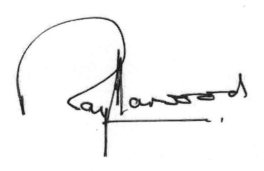

THE SARDANA TRADITION

Little did I believe that when I set out to put my thoughts on paper, to become *Last Sardana,* it would be anything other than my first and last book, and not follow in the footsteps of those stars who make surprise comebacks, having said they have hung up their boots.

However, in penning the *Encore,* it comes as no surprise that the encouragement and support I received first time around has not waned. More to the point, as I watched the lives of the Martinez clan extending beyond what, in truth, was merely an introduction in the first book, I found that sticking with it has been fun, and has stretched my imagination to new horizons.

My private Sardana chain of those who have inspired or performed in editorial or keyboard roles seems to have remained firmly intact and fully linked, despite several re-writes and changes of mind from yours truly.

Again, the support of my wife Dean, Alison Clarke and Kristina Tang has remained to make the most out of my manuscripts, which are mainly put together in Jolly Harbour, Antigua, Pelangi Beach, Langkawi, Hotel Arts in Barcelona and Hotel Golf Santa Ponsa, all of which seem to provide conducive surroundings in which to play around with the fate of the Martinez family.

I would have been particularly lost again without Linda Lloyd's constructive criticisms and smoothing, which come with her considerable editing skills.

INTRODUCTION

Who can really tell what influence there is on an unborn child by the activity of the mother prior to releasing her offspring into the hard, tough world? But there is, undoubtedly, a relationship – usually built for life.

In Rosas, on the north-eastern coast of Spain, Pedro 'Peter' Martinez's lifestyle certainly replicated the passion, creativity, bonding and fun generated by his greatest fan and most severe critic, his mother Maria. Through her hereditary love of joining the swirling circles of the Sardana with her fellow Catalans at the Saints' Day celebrations in her Spanish village, Peter's roots were permanently implanted.

The reality of the life Peter was born into was taught to him not only by his mother and father, but also by all those around him as he passed through adolescence. The discovery of his manhood and natural compassion for his fellow inhabitants of the planet, and the freeing and nurturing of his super-creative talents, were part of a pedigree for success.

Peter's architectural ability removed him from his Spanish homeland and its gypsy influences, spiriting him off to career success and wealth in London and Malaysia; yet he was always magnetised back to the biggest love in his life, Maria, his doting mother… and the early promise of a young gypsy girl, and all the love and hatred she embraced.

Passing on through marriage and into early middle-age was no less eventful than all the formative years preceding this element of his more dignified life.

And thereby continues this tale.

CHAPTER 1
1955

When they arrived by the beach, Jaimé was beside himself. He got out of the car before Peter told him to, or allowed him to, and like a gazelle he ran into the distance. Almost out of sight.

Peter was at first concerned, if not worried. Jaimé had stopped at the end of the bay and perched dangerously on the high point of rocks. He then performed as would a bookmaker's runner or, in Marcia's parlance, a turf accountant's one, by talking with his hands and arms. He could have been the conductor of the Seville Symphony Orchestra in the emotions he expressed.

Peter caught up with him.

He was fascinated, even infatuated, with the story Jaimé was telling. His arms stretched out to denote, "All this," as he pointed to the sun and indicated the route it would take before it set. Sunrise to sunset, was, "One day." Both hands held to his chest, below his chin and suddenly thrown into the air was, "Will reveal, or will be revealed." He individually illustrated a number of things in that way. He did drawings in the air above his head of houses, with roofs and rooms in which to eat and cook, and areas in which to sleep and play. When he pointed towards Peter from a distance and rubbed both his hands together graphically, it signified the making of money. Pointed directly at Peter, it meant the making of money for Peter. In this way, the pair were able to communicate, and Jaimé passed on to Peter what his father had explained to him as being an opportunity for Jaimé to provide an assisting role.

"What you're going to be helping with is the measurement of an area of land that'll one day be developed with houses… and will make Mr Peter a great deal of money. But for you it is a generous opportunity." That was the experienced assessment by the father.

Peter knew so many people who could talk and hear. Tania, Meribel, Marcia, Marco, his mother. But none could express themselves like Jaimé. What a courageous young man.

Peter sent a message back as he got closer to the boy. One pointed finger: "You,"… the beckoning of arms indicating, "come back,"… the pointing to the ground below Peter's feet, "here," then a turn sideways on and a slap across his own backside, meaning, "you naughty boy."

Jaimé did as he was told. He came back to Peter with his head bowed in admission that he was the naughty boy he had been accused of being.

It was not long after that Peter had explained they were going to set up some bamboo stakes in line as ranging rods, and then gradually measure the lengths between them in an absolutely straight line, that Jaimé was off again like an antelope being chased by an imaginary tiger, charging down the length of the beach, only to be told again to come back; he had been a bad boy because they would need to do it in stages of about 100 yards. Not metric, because Peter could only borrow a measuring tape sixty feet long, which must have originated in the UK, where they were still working to imperial measurement. So it would, as Peter explained, be a slow job, but very exact and they would transpose the measured lengths together with marking pens on the decorators' lining paper, brought for that very purpose.

By pointing down his throat, and then to his temple, behind which he knew was his brain, Jaimé signified, "I understand." Peter responded, "Good," by lifting the thumb on his right hand into the air. The rest of the morning Jaimé still ran everywhere, each five uses of the tape then making up the 100-yard module.

When they had reached the magic marker at 100, it was Jaimé's job to move the ranging rods, used as pace makers, which meant an 80-yard dash to the furthest. Jaimé then changed gear to become a Jesse Owens, with a medal to achieve, and put his heart and soul into this, his first day's work.

The result of Jaimé releasing all this energy meant that Peter was making excellent progress. He had guessed at the length of available land for his intended development. 'Intended development' – what a precocious, even preposterous idea for a young man not yet 20! Somehow or other, he'd gained years of experience in life far greater than his birth certificate would allow one to believe, and the amazing thing about Peter was that he put every day of learning to work. Marco had told him that he should set out to learn something new every day. Peter amended the idea by endeavouring to view his day as two halves and to have learnt one thing by midday and another by the time his head hit the pillow.

His rule was that his discoveries did not necessarily have to be things he could find answers to in an encyclopaedia at the library, or from his mother's dictionary, which bore many of Peter's thumb-prints. His learning could be about emotions, his own feelings and thoughts and how to deal with them, or lessons in life gleaned from studying the reactions of others, or observations of what he found attractive, or out of place, symmetrical or untidy… his brain was attuned to design. He would shape his moods by what he saw and then in his mind interpret those moods on to paper, or into the gut of a tennis racquet to shape the way he applied the bat to the ball, as it were.

A gentle conversation with Michelle would produce a calm, less aggressive style of play or coaching. An early morning contretemps with an irate lorry driver intent on making his own day, and that of others he encountered during it, a hell on earth, would arouse a tiger in Peter, causing serves and smashes and drives that would be almost unplayable on a tennis court, where Peter vented his feelings most frequently.

Jaimé's rushing here and there had a happy effect on Peter. Here was a young boy whose infirmity could hardly leave him with ambition to rise much above a supervised gardening job, and even then, with a restriction on the use of anything too mechanical, for fear that he might not hear the dangers that could be lurking in his path. But despite the handicap of being a deaf mute from birth, Jaimé was a totally happy soul. At least he was on this day.

By 1pm the sun was very high and Peter felt the need for refuelling. He'd slipped the kitchen staff a few pesetas for a couple of the hotel's packed lunches and thrown in a couple of beers and bottles of Coke for the lad.

Peter put his first proposition to Jaimé.

"We," – illustrated by an imaginary hug between the two of them – "stop," – a passing of one flat palm over the other as if a ground controller was giving the captain of a landed aircraft the order to cut the engines – "and eat," – two fingers pointing down the throat with a spare hand rubbing the stomach – "for an hour." – a finger pointed at his watch and a 360-degree tour of the watch face.

Jaimé's return conversations were invariably short. That was a compliment to Peter's method of explaining to his young assistant. Jaimé gave a single thumbs up sign. They spread a groundsheet out under a tree, round about Avenue 7, in Peter's mind.

Jaimé gave him just one moment of anxiety. He stood in front of Peter, pointing at the flies on his jeans and, for a few split seconds, Peter thought he was indicating that he needed him to help with his zip, or were they buttons? But what Jaimé was asking was for permission to go behind a tree to urinate. Peter gave a relieved thumbs up, indicating how much of a good idea that seemed, and joined him behind a neighbouring tree.

Explaining that the water from the bottle Peter was trying to get Jaimé to splash onto his hands was not for drinking was a little more problematical. But he got the message through, although Jaimé was still left with a perplexed look on his fully rounded face below his shock of black curly hair, as his family background did not have an essential wash of the hands after a pee as part of its culture. Peter laughed as he thought, "It does now." So that was one of very many things that Jaimé was learning that day.

After the picnic, Peter indicated that a short siesta was in order. The idea got a thumbs-up from his young companion.

Peter closed his eyes. When he awoke, Jaimé was gone. Still a little dazed by his reawakening into the bright sunny world beyond the shade of the tree, he thought, *where the hell could he have run off to?* No use calling out Jaimé's name because he wouldn't hear it.

He stood up and scanned the near and progressively more distant horizons without a sign of Jaimé. The fields were quite densely covered; that was why Peter had packed a scythe into the car, in case they needed to clear a path, which until then had not been necessary. He had a bright idea; he could shin up the tree, something he hadn't done since a kid, and see if he could spot Jaimé from his higher lookout position. His ribs still ached from his recent beating but after some difficulty and a few expletives, Peter was in command of all around him.

"There's the little bugger," he announced to all the surrounding flora and fauna. He descended with care, hoping to God that Jaimé would not do one of his runners.

Jaimé was totally unaware of Peter's presence as he stood some 20 feet back from where the young boy was crouched on both knees, with a couple of feet of decorators' lining paper laid out and pinned down onto the surface of a trodden path with a stone at each corner. He'd got one of Peter's valuable marker pens in his right hand and was drawing frantically onto the paper. Peter moved closer and as his feet hit the firm path, Jaimé picked up the vibrations, transmitted via his sensitive knees into his body and brain.

Looking over his shoulder furtively, Jaimé waited anxiously to see whether a, "Slap on the butt, you naughty boy," remonstration was forthcoming. Instead, Peter moved even closer, towering over the pavement work of a would-be street artist.

What he saw amazed him. It was a black and white illustration of the sky, the gentle hills and the deep shadows formed by the trees covering the slopes, with a growing crop of sunflowers veritably turning their heads to say hello to Peter's gaze from above. The foreground was exact in every detail, yet it was captured and expressed in a flowing artistic way, but without the benefit of tones and texture from brush strokes. The boy had painted with a pen.

Jaimé was looking up at Peter, a little like a labrador who'd stolen a leg of chicken. Peter held his arms out, indicating a welcome, and that the boy was far from being in trouble. How was Peter to get over the joy and amazement at discovering he was in the presence of a genius? Rodin sprung to mind.

After giving the lad a huge hug, he stepped back and steadied him by holding both his shoulders, as if to say, "Don't you bloody run off now." He stepped back and pointed at the boy. "You," and then clenched his fist, turned sideways and placed it on his forehead, ensuring it was on a part that didn't hurt, and arched his back. "A genius thinker," is what he implied.

Jaimé at first looked a little puzzled and then seemed to recognise the image Peter was portraying.

The boy pointed a finger at his own chest – "I" – and then drew a square of canvas in front of himself, took out an imaginary brush from his hip pocket and painted. "I am an artist." Peter gave the thumbs-up, confirming that indeed he was. Jaimé pointed a finger at Peter's chest, and then at both his feet. "You wait there." He turned and ran a zigzag route through an effective path back to where they had been picnicking. Peter could see he went to his duffle bag, which he had proudly paraded with when reporting for duty earlier that morning. It looked as though he was taking out a baton. He did a swift about-turn and ran at greater speed on the return leg. Peter felt inclined to turn away himself and extend a hand behind his back, as though performing the next leg of Jaimé's intended relay, but didn't. He stayed firm, not moving, as instructed.

Jaimé pulled up in a cloud of dust and handed the baton to Peter. It was a roll of paper. Jaimé rolled one hand over the other, saying, "Unroll it," which Peter duly did. Tears appeared in his eyes. He held out both his arms and the boy automatically took a step forward. Peter held him as tight as he thought he had ever held anybody before. He didn't move for as long as it took to swallow back the tears. It seemed an age, but the otherwise overactive Jaimé didn't try to wriggle free. He was enjoying the exclusive comfort and security that Peter offered to him, unlike the lad's parents, who shared their affection equally amongst their four children.

When they parted, Peter knelt down with the unfurled paper now gently stretched between both his hands. "Brilliant!" Peter said, referring to a sketch Jaimé had done of him while he was asleep. But to call it a sketch didn't do justice to it. It was little short of a portrait. Obviously Jaimé had a couple of pencils in his duffle bag, and Peter could tell that he had created the shadows and form by rubbing the pencil 'ink' with his fingers. Unfortunately, Jaimé hadn't yet realised the rules about artists' licence. Peter pointed to the two stitch marks Jaimé had pencilled accurately into his brow, then at the lad, and indicated that they should be rubbed out.

The boy said, "No!" and they both laughed.

Suddenly the enormity of what had just happened hit Peter. The boy had said "No." He hadn't shaken his head negatively. He had brought up a guttural,

"No," from deep down in his young stomach.

Peter pointed into Jaimé's throat and put a hand on his solar plexus. He indicated, by placing his open left hand in front of Jaimé's chin, that he should let something come out of his mouth. He then shook his head in a negative way and pushed the boy's stomach.

"No!" It was a little less guttural this time, and a more consistent tone.

Peter stuck his tongue out. So Jaimé did the same. Peter shook his head; it was not what he had in mind.

The boy said, "No."

Peter made signs as though he was rubbing out something on a blackboard, with an indication to start again. He stuck his tongue out. Jaimé did the same.

Peter indicated: *hold it there.* Then, with his right forefinger, he pushed his tongue back into his wide-open mouth, but showing Jaimé that he was pushing it up into the top of his palate, not just anywhere in the cavernous opening. He then used the same forefinger (having wiped it first on his shirt) to push Jaimé's tongue up into his palate. He told Jaimé to hold that position and then lightly pressed his chest. He shook his head, indicating the negative. Whilst holding his open hand under the boy's chin, he put gentle pressure with the other on Jaimé's rib cage and squeezed out, "Non!" as clear as a bell.

They both jumped around with joy, linking arms, quite without warning or rehearsal. It was their own personalised Sardana. Peter stopped suddenly. Jaimé followed suit. Peter put each of his forefingers into the extreme edges of his mouth, making himself look more like a wide mouthed frog than his usual self. He put his tongue out. Jaimé copied. Peter this time pushed his tongue into the bottom of his mouth, behind his front lower teeth, but with his lips widely stretched from side to side. This time he placed a hand on Jaimé's throat with a light pressure.

Peter said, "Si!" with the emphasis on the 'S'.

He made sure Jaimé was set in position and nodded his head up and down.

With heavier pressure on his throat, Jaimé oozed out a "Si!" Somewhat guttural, but it was there, and furthermore it came out of Jaimé's improvised voice-box. Or was it that Peter had inadvertently provided a key to this previously unopened treasure chest?

The two leapt into the air and repeated their Sardana of joy. They became over-exuberant and fell into the long grass.

Peter went back to the spot where both Jaimé's works of true art were lying. As he started picking them up, he saw Jaimé was at his side. Jaimé pointed at himself, and then at Peter. "Me to you," he was saying in sign language. Peter said, "No, they are yours," pointing towards Jaimé, who was now engrossed

6

with Peter's mouth. Suddenly he put his hand to his chest. Fiddled his tongue into the top of his palate.

"No!" he said emphatically.

Peter pointed to his own chest in reply. "For me."

Jaimé hesitated. Screwed his face up, trying to remember how this one worked. He tried forcing his tongue down into his mouth, grimaced to widen his teeth, which took his lips with them. He put his hand on his throat.

"Si!" he said emphatically.

Off they went on another joyful spin with bags and bags of laughter. Not only did Peter have to suffer Jaimé running everywhere for a further four hours, albeit with considerable joy, but each time Peter gave him an instruction, the boy would reply, "Si," or, "No," not caring whether he had got the sense right or otherwise.

Jaimé even ran the few feet between the car and where Peter had collected up their day's gear and picnic containers. Peter started his mother's car and began pulling away, satisfied with the day's work. He was overjoyed with the two presents and the discovery of a genius artist who now, in the space of only one day, could speak two words.

What a good day it had been. Peter leant across and patted Jaimé just above his left knee. There was no reflex. Not even a twitch. It felt dead to his friendly slap, with which Peter wished to say, "Well done." He quickly checked the road ahead and then looked at Jaimé's face. The lad was sound asleep. He was out for the count, completely clapped out.

"Well, old son. You don't surprise me at all," Peter said affectionately.

Peter ate in the restaurant later that evening, wanting to be just by himself. He was happy to wave in acknowledgement to his fellow diners, or to those on their way in or out; but so much had changed in his life in a limited number of hours or days that he just wanted to be alone with his thoughts.

He was due to leave for the UK in about a month, which would give him a couple of weeks when he got there to get orientated before real study began. So, as his principal priority, he really needed to get his survey work plotted in a form that would allow him to transport a master plan to the UK, where he could develop his thinking. He hoped to return to Spain with a pretty advanced development design for Christmas. That was a must, he'd worked out. It was a special family time when his mother would otherwise be missing him anyway, so he'd have to go home, and he ought not to go empty-handed.

So in the very short term, while he was still in Spain, he needed to get onto an as yet non-existent drawing board.

He also now needed to have a discussion with Marco, and Jaimé's father. He'd found something out that was probably more emotionally disturbing than how shallow his relationships with Laura and Meribel had turned out to be. Spending time resuscitating Jaimé's life was surely more worthwhile than any involvement in Tania's. As she had put it, after all, her culture went back centuries, so who was Peter to get involved in that?

Then there was Marcia, with whom he was infatuated, without a doubt. That surely spelt trouble too. Bob was clearly something of a street fighter and, in any event, given the attractions of an older, richer man – albeit one maybe unable to light a fire under his young wife's cauldron – any thought of Marcia giving up all that security was preposterous. At least Peter thought so, so any designs he might have on her did spell disappointment, if not trouble.

Michelle was now in the hands, perhaps literally, of Miguel, who certainly had the experience and benefit of a decade on Peter, which would enable him to help her. So Peter felt his direct responsibility there had been usurped.

All in all, he was on the brink of a new beginning, but with a few current situations to sort before he selfishly concentrated on himself. He began making all sorts of plans over his meal. He'd ask his mother and Marco if he could borrow an unused room for a couple of weeks so that he could lay out his development plans.

He'd have a talk with Bob about the site, because Bob had said he wanted to find out what Peter had been up to before they could talk positively about the development. He'd have to risk allowing Marcia to input her ideas, as she'd sidelined Bob, somehow. But then that was not Peter's problem, it was hers. He'd made notes on the back of the menu as to his priorities.

The next morning Peter, Marco and Maria had their regular review meeting. Having established the fact that within a week the hotel would go from 100 per cent occupancy to a new Thomson/Lunn Poly/Thomas Cook cheaper deal scenario, filling about 80 per cent of space, they had agreed to try and effect savings in overheads of about 20 per cent, while retaining quality. That, Maria and Marco agreed, would effectively mean they would make a higher percentage profit leading into the leaner times of the autumn. They would virtually then close until the spring season, re-opening officially in May.

"… Right, anything else?" Marco said to Maria, Peter, the head chef and Sñr Martin, who made up the Executive Board of the hotel.

Peter said, "Nothing to involve anyone other than you and my mother." The other two were discharged back to their duties.

"So, what's burning with you, Peter?" Marco asked, feeling he knew his nephew so well by now that he could tease ideas, opinions and problems out of him.

"I think you ought to be concentrating on the welfare of staff now that you're building the basis of a well-run and successful ship. The hotel has worked well in its first season, and you… well, we really, must build on that for the future. A sudden turnover of staff could spell disaster."

Marco flashed a glance at Maria. "Tell him, Maria," he instructed.

"Well, Pedro, Marco and I have already had this discussion. We actually agree, but short of paying staff not to work through the winter, we're a bit lost as to how we can accomplish what you're saying."

"I've got a particular idea on the gardening, housekeeping and administration fronts. I've half an idea in the kitchen area and I think the rest will hang together."

Marco laughed. "Maria, let's brace ourselves, the boy is about to preach."

Peter told them all about his experience with Jaimé and said he felt his father Carlos had no idea how to handle his son's fate. If the hotel did something to secure Jaimé some treatment, of a very much more advanced kind than the local quack could provide, then Carlos would be won over, as would the remainder of his team, who would follow his leadership. Jaimé's art should definitely be developed.

"The boy's a genius and perhaps copies of his work – not the portrait, of course, but the sketch of the bay and some commissions of the hotel itself – could be sold to raise money for some special treatment for him." Peter felt he could deal with the instructions for hotel sketches, but help would be required for the treatment. Maria thought automatically of Miguel.

Peter then went on to explain that he felt Tania was either off-balance, unbalanced or just walking a tightrope, and should she fall it might impact on the hotel's reputation. Marco was silent on that one. Peter then said he wanted them both to know that he felt he was being 'stalked', and they should note the unreliability of Tania's emotions. He had no wish to be a part of the life she was acting out.

"Oh, come on, darling, you're big enough and ugly enough to be able to handle that one, surely!"

"Mother, she's a witch! I tell you, if she wanted something badly enough she'd kill for it. It's in her blood, I reckon."

"OK. We understand what you're saying. Keep out of her way for just a few weeks and then when the winter comes and we lay off the staff, we'll try and replace her."

Marco was fidgety.

"Anything else?" Maria asked.

There were a couple of mumbled nos.

"Well, I've got one," Maria announced. "The damn Admiral wants an impromptu end-of-term dance on Saturday night. An 'Au revoir Calella Olympics Fiesta' is what he's calling it."

"What the hell does he want to do that for?" Pedro summed up all their views.

"Well, what he's asking for is just the normal hotel dinner, but a small band out on the terrace under the area covered by the storeys above; he reckons they'd develop a 3D sound from under there. He thinks the extra drinks we'd sell would easily cover the cost of the band but he wouldn't rule out a surcharge of 1000 pesetas per head, if we wanted to charge."

"Too true," Marco said firmly. "Any extra drinks will have to be served by somebody. Then there's all the clearing up to do. No, not free. We'll go for the 1000 pesetas. I'd think we'd only break even."

Peter added his opinion. "I suppose that'll coincide with most people leaving the next day. Bob and Marcia Hunt, the Admiral, Guy and Philippe, I'm presuming Michelle stays on, the Browns, the Cooks, the Guibaud family, they're mostly all going home. I suppose it would be rather nice actually to see them leave on a high. At 1000 pesetas I reckon it's a good idea. By the way, they've still got one of the Hunts' tunas in the freezer. Can't chef do a salade Niçoise, or something like that? We could make it a festive four-course dinner and music for 2000 pesetas a head. And maybe we put a jug of sangria on each table."

"You men! You'll make money out of anything…"

"Tell you what," Peter intervened – a little rudely, his mother thought, "I'll get Jaimé to do the impressions of bits of the hotel and beach, perhaps the pool and the village, and we'll have a little art display. People could order copies and we'll mail them on and we might raise enough for him to see a consultant in Barcelona or Madrid or somewhere… now there's a good idea."

"Would his parents let him stay up to be here? He's a good-looking little chap, if he sits there all the girls'll fall for him and the prints'll sell like hot croissants…" Maria's suggestion went down well.

"Well, if that's that," Marco said, "I'd best go and tell Virginia she's on social duty on Saturday night. She'll hate that… so I might as well get it out of the way."

Peter's schedule suddenly became all the more hectic. They arranged a discussion with Carlos for the next day, and for him to bring Jaimé with him. Peter would go into the art shop in Palafrugell that afternoon and get some proper sketch blocks and drawing pens with black Indian ink and a couple of watercolour washes. He had ideas of his own as to how he could enhance Jaimé's paintings. He was quite excited by it all.

Maria and Marco had acceded to Peter's request to borrow a room, so all was fixed. He'd invest in a 'T' square and set square for himself. He'd worked out he could improvise for a drawing board by using one of the unused flush doors from the store. He could lay that over the dressing table unit in the room Marco and Maria said he could use. It was the one that looked over the kitchen courtyard, which had been a bit tricky to let on account of the early morning deliveries waking people up, plus the smells wafting up from below.

He'd best get on, he was busy, and now he had to contact those guys he was at school with who had formed the band to see if they were free for Saturday. "God knows if they're any good," he'd said to Maria and Marco. "But they'll be cheap and I reckon they'll be OK. Somebody, I can't remember who, said they'd heard them and they were very good at replicating. They're apparently good Beatles soundalikes, and Simon and Garfunkel, and a girl joins them for some Carpenters stuff… yes, it should be alright if they're free."

They were, so that was another problem solved.

Maria went straight to the office from the meeting in Marco's room. There was a message left by Sñr Martin, who had started especially early to allow the meeting to take place. It was marked all over 'Urgent', with a scribbled note asking her to contact Mrs Hunt.

Marcia answered the phone. She was not her chirpy self.

"Marcia, hi! It's Maria. I got a message to contact you urgently. What's the problem?"

"Oh, thank God you've called! I wasn't sure if you were working or in town. Listen, Bob's got pains in his chest and upper arms and insists it's the 'bloody fishing'. But I've been rubbing in some stuff that usually puts his rheumatics right, it's called 'Deep Heat', but in three days, that and paracetamol hasn't seemed to make any difference. I wouldn't worry except his breathing's dreadful and he hasn't had a cigar or cigarette since Monday night after the tuna. He ate far too much of the fish, and I wondered if that was having an effect on him. Anyway, you know what he's like, he'd go mad if he thought I was talking to you about it, but to put my mind at rest I think we ought to get a doctor. Can you help? Do you know a good one?"

"Well, the old family retainer Marco swears by is Dr Gomez. He's an older man, a bit short on English, but if you wanted a younger man I think you'd have to go to Barcelona, which is a bit of a drag. Alternatively, you could take him to the hospital in Palafrugell, which is quite small, or Gerona – very modern with the latest equipment."

"Which would you say would be the lowest profile? Bob's likely to slam the door in the face of most medics, especially if they preach any change in his lifestyle."

"Without a doubt Gomez. He'd come from Llanfranc to the hotel. They're probably about the same age group too. He's a bit of a rebel… he told an acquaintance to carry on his existing lifestyle and he'd live well into his 70s."

"What happened?"

"Well… I'm only telling you so that you can keep your own spirits up, you sound low for Marcia Hunt. He died a month later."

"Cheers, Maria. That does keep my spirits up. How old was he?"

"When he died, 76. He'd had his birthday three weeks before, but the doctor, when he made his forecast, had omitted to ask him how old he was."

"Oh, Maria! There's a bit of a funny side to that, isn't there."

"That's better. That's more like our Marcia."

So it was fixed between the girls that Dr Gomez would be called. He'd come about 11, he said. Maria told him all the symptoms and the history, and about the fishing trip.

"I expect he's strained his rib cage and a few muscles he's not used for a while. But I'll come and have a look at him. It'll be 4000 pesetas, plus prescription, is that OK?"

"Yes, I'm sure, Dr Gomez."

"Right, I'll be there soon."

Ten minutes later the phone rang in the office. It was Gomez.

"Sorry, Maria. What's the patient's name?"

"Robert Hunt."

"OK. I thought I'd make the invoice out before I came, to save time."

When Marcia told Bob what she'd planned for the morning, he took it all very calmly. While she was surprised, she also wondered if there was an element of relief in his reaction.

"So! You've been fishing and pulled a muscle," Dr Gomez said to Bob through Maria, who had offered to translate. Bob trusted her completely since they'd done the deal on the fridge, which had been good for his insulin, great for his beers and not bad to freeze up the odd ice lolly he made with orange juice, bottled Perrier and a dash of whisky.

"Yes, I think you're right," Bob said.

"Ask him to take his shirt off, please. Could you also ask him if he knows what his last blood pressure count was? And what did his father die from?"

Maria asked the questions.

It was, "Yes," to taking the shirt off, "160/90," on the blood pressure and, "old age," as the cause of his father's death.

Marcia whispered to Maria that she thought he'd died from choking when in an advanced state of drunkenness. Did she think that was important? Maria said she didn't.

Gomez took Bob's pulse, then put a stethoscope on all recognised pressure points around the chest and back, and tapped him with his hard-knuckled bent forefinger. He took his blood pressure and then got Bob to move his arms up above his head, over to each side and then behind his neck with fingers of each hand entwined. In that position Gomez redid the stethoscope, did some extra tapping… and then went into thought mode.

"Ask what his mother died of."

"Bob, how did your mother die?"

"Screwing her boyfriend."

"Bob!" Marcia said firmly.

"Well, look, that's bloody silly, my dear old mother hadn't been out bloody fishing so it was either normal heart failure or, for all we knew, screwing her boyfriend who did a runner at three o'clock in the morning, because she died peacefully in her sleep at 78 years old."

Maria translated. "Natural causes, old age."

Dr Gomez said he was pretty sure it was muscular, but would Bob go and have an ECG at Palafrugell hospital anyway?

Bob asked through Maria what Gomez's treatment would be for the pulled muscles, if that was his diagnosis. She asked the question.

"Probably paracetamol, up to eight in the day and half an aspirin in the morning and another half at night." He didn't add that that was to hedge his bets in case it was a heart problem, as the aspirin would thin Bob's blood as well.

Gomez also expressed concern about his patient's breathlessness. Maria translated that across to Bob.

"Look, tell him on a good day I smoke 50 Dunhills and a couple of good cigars. So my breathing's not going to be as good as a two-year-old's."

Dr Gomez said, "Alright then. We'll go for the muscular solution but I tell him I want him to cut out the smoking." Maria obliged.

"Cut out!" Bob shouted. "That doesn't exist in my vocabulary. Cut down does."

The doctor was told the patient's views.

"Then ten cigarettes, and that will become 20," he explained to Maria, "but no cigars."

"… And drink?" Bob said when he heard about the rationing, as he called it.

13

"A limited amount of whisky, and a glass of red wine."

The doctor started getting his gear together and took the pre-prepared envelope from his inside jacket pocket.

"Is this for the young lady?" he asked Maria.

"I'm sure it is," she responded.

The doctor thought for a couple of moments. "Good God," he said, "I should have asked. Is this Mr Hunt's daughter?"

"Goodness me, no! It's his wife."

The doctor put his hands to his head. "Then I should have said, I think they shouldn't think about being intimate until we're certain it is muscular. I think it is, but we have to be careful. Can I leave you to tell them?"

"Muchas gracias," Maria said in response.

"What was all that bit about?" Marcia insisted.

"Oh dear. In a nutshell, he said he hadn't realised you weren't Bob's daughter, and once he knew you were married he's advised no sex."

Marcia screamed with laughter. "Hear that, Bobby? I'm more dangerous to you than 20 fags, a few glasses of whisky and a run round the block. Now there *is* a compliment!"

Bob remained sullen. "I'll go down to the pool and get sunstroke," he announced, and left before the doctor.

"Is he a stubborn man?" Gomez asked Maria.

"Oh yes, I think so."

"I'd like him to have the ECG, could the two of you work on that? Give me a call and I can arrange it at short notice."

The good doctor acknowledged Marcia's payment in pesetas newly drawn from the bank. He bowed in a gentlemanly fashion and said, for her benefit, the only few words he had so far attempted in English – "Sorry, no sex" – accompanied by a gentle male smile.

"Don't worry on my part," Marcia said, making no allowance for his poor English. "You're doing me a favour, you'll get me a break. I think that's why he's so breathless anyway."

Maria crossed the room and, without a word, put a strong right arm around her shoulders.

"There!" she said. "You're worried, aren't you?"

"Only worried because he's so fucking stubborn. I don't want him ill."

CHAPTER 2

Although Maria wouldn't have wanted to admit it, when the Admiral organised something he certainly got the whole place buzzing. She sensed that the absence of guests sitting up at the bar on this particular evening for their pre-dinner Camparis, gins and tonics, Bacardis, etc was because they were all getting dressed up for the occasion. Indeed, the Admiral, by networking round the whole hotel to get every guest to make a booking, which he'd actually achieved, was the real catalyst for this becoming a good evening.

Peter and Jaimé had done brilliantly in setting up the lad's work and the graphics giving the reasons for the display in four languages. Jaimé's sketches and enhanced watercolours were truly excellent. Maria thought there would be plenty of takers for copies.

She had heard Peter's newly discovered trio practising along with its female singer, and they too were a find.

José had said he'd come and join Maria, Marco, Virginia and Peter at least for the dinner part of the evening. It was sad that Peter didn't have a girlfriend at this time, though it was probably better in many respects. It was one extra attachment he didn't have to either consider leaving or taking with him.

Maria hoped Tania wouldn't become a nuisance. She was short on waiting staff, anticipating that most people would be sitting down within 15 or 30 minutes of each other. There were choices of food too, so Maria had doubled the service team for the evening.

Chef had put a lot of time into his tuna dish. He'd done it before to good effect and, rather like a sculptor or artist who likes the materials they are working with, he had produced what Maria termed as one of his little masterpieces of filleted tuna steaks marinated in a delicious teriyaki sauce. The recipe he had perfected depended on him skinning tuna cutlets into a steak without bones and each portion weighing about 100 grams. He made a superb marinade of 1/3 of a cup of reduced sodium teriyaki sauce and, unusually, three cloves or so, with crushed garlic. All that was for each portion so he measured out enough to supply, at a guess, possibly 50 per cent of those expected to dine. His trick was to use a jar with a tight-fitting lid as a makeshift cocktail shaker so that he could mix the ingredients to be poured into a casserole dish. He then simply dipped the steaks on both sides into the marinade and barbecued for five to six minutes on each side. Some further marinade he added during cooking but then it was all drained off when his practised fork told him the fish would flake easily. Each serving was accompanied by al dente vegetables.

There had been a lot to think about in the build up to this unscheduled attraction. Now Maria relaxed, knowing that everything was under control.

The lighting, she thought, looked much improved as a result of the local electrician's efforts. It was a lovely fine night, and they had everything to play for.

In the rooms above, the ladies were making their final adjustments. Judging by the amount of perfume they were piling on, the dining room would be like a parfumerie. The heat and humidity had played tricks on most of the ladies' senses and all were over-doing the scent, as it was hard to judge when they had reached the level of allure they were seeking.

Bob knew that if he brought his white tuxedo he'd have a use for it, and the bright red bow tie that went with it. Most men were light-weight suited or jacketed, with Farah trousers and those naff but fashionable leather shoes with holes all over them.

Marcia had asked Bob to choose what she should wear.

"White," he'd said. "Virginal white, but with those stunning red stiletto sandals."

How bizarre, she thought, *people will know we're matching.* His white tuxedo, her white dress, his red tie, her red shoes… but she'd do as he asked, he seemed better, more like himself. Dr Gomez had called in for another 4000 pesetas and a few comforting checks and words.

Through Maria he asked Marcia, "Have you changed his mind about the ECG?"

"No. No change," Marcia said.

"… And his chest pains?"

"Only occasional, apparently," Maria translated back.

"Good," Dr Gomez diagnosed. He looked playfully at Marcia. "Soon," he said, wagging a mischievous forefinger. "Tell her soon," he said to Maria with a smile.

The bar area filled up quite quickly once the first guests arrived, and some spilled out onto the terrace. Maria loved the buzz of people and didn't like the thought of how quiet the coming winter months would be. Still, she would be back at the library helping out and, in her mind, she was planning a trip to London, probably in November. Sñr Martin had an absolute passion for the English capital at that time of the year. He said there was a strange crispness about the mornings, often a cool fog swirling around the tops of the lamp standards along the Mall and near St James's Palace. The ducks on the lakes in the park had their extra coats of feathers on and you could buy roasted chestnuts from the street vendors hanging around to serve the tourists. She'd shop for Christmas and grab some speciality foods from Harrods and Fortnum and Mason in Piccadilly. Moreover, she would see Peter in his new environment. She wondered if it would change him.

She also had an open invitation to stay with the Hunts: "At least a couple of nights or, better still, for a weekend," Marcia had insisted.

Maria was whisked back to the reality of her current environment. Somebody dropped a glass in the midst of over-excited conversation. She moved across to where the sound had come from. Peter was there too; he'd heard the crash, which in the hotel trade spelt danger and the risk of an insurance claim. The small gathering, standing by looking helplessly at the glass, which had fragmented into an area about a metre across, was suddenly parted by a low-flying body.

By the time Maria reached the potential danger area, she realised it was Tania who had thrown herself into action, semi-crouched as she swept the offending crystal into a pan with a hand-held brush.

Peter recognised Tania's backside and the long gypsy legs revealed by the tailored split in her black mini-skirt. Her semi-transparent black blouse was stretched to its extreme across her back as she leant low to sweep. That revealed the outline of the thin straps of her bra. A lump came into his throat as he realised it would not take much more revelation to stimulate him into an involuntary grab of her backside and a rushed bunk in the laundry room. But he didn't want that to show.

He looked for his mother, who was opposite him in the surrounding circle. She recognised his glare of anger. He pushed towards her, stepping over Tania's now semi-kneeling body as he went.

"What the hell is she doing here?" he demanded.

"We needed more staff. She and her sister can clear tables and deliver drinks... look, already she's following her natural instincts and clearing up... none of the regulars got here in that time."

"Well, Mother, just you listen. I don't want that girl within a metre of me. Alright? She's trouble and you'd best not let her near Virginia either."

"What do you mean by that?"

"Never you mind. That's Marco's problem."

"Marco's?"

"Look, I've got to get back to Jaimé's display. I left him with quite an audience. I don't want him to get stressed out."

When Peter got back to the temporary gallery he'd set up, partially under the stairs and on the walls leading to the lift, there were 20 or so guests, all focused on one area. Not one painting, just one central point of attention. Peter raised himself up onto his toes to see what had attracted them. He could see Jaimé's head and the side view of his face. He was clearly in deep concentration. There, sitting on a chair, was the Cooks' second daughter, head tilted down towards the floor, hands crossed into her lap.

The boy was doing her portrait with his own special pencil. He was working at immense speed, smoothing out shadows with his now grubby fingers. The final touch was to give life to the pupils of her eyes. He stood back like an old Master and appraised his portrait. He was clearly OK with the result. The girl's father started clapping and within ten seconds, all 20 or so onlookers had joined in. "Bravo!" were the shouts, as though José had just killed his first bull. A couple of guests even threw some peseta notes on to the marble floor below, where the girl was sitting.

Peter gently pushed through the impromptu gathering. He heard words of appreciation in the four languages mainly spoken by the guests: "Bon", "Excellent", "Super", "Magnifico"… Jaimé had the acclaim of his first international audience. Sadly, they were not words he was able to hear.

Peter held a stern forefinger out in front of Jaimé's face. Jaimé knew that sign. He'd done something wrong, but what?

Peter pointed a finger at his own chest, then an expansive wave indicating a flow of words coming out of his mouth as he pointed at Jaimé. "I told you." This was followed by a complex long wavy sign to indicate, "Always," then a motion denoting a signature. "I told you always sign your name. You haven't done that." Jaimé looked up and smiled broadly and, with the assistance of a hand on his throat and a bit of structured breathing, he said "Si."

As one, they all clapped and the money went rolling in. The portrait with its proud signature now had a more total credibility. During the course of the evening, Jaimé did about 15 sketch portraits. The one he did of Marcia was overwhelming and Bob, admittedly with a couple of whiskies under his belt, but in total passion, put down ten ten-pound notes and asked if he might have the painting. Peter, the young artist's self-promoted manager, said of course, and then showed Jaimé how to write the words, 'To Marcia, with love, Jaimé', which Bob reckoned would make it worth at least £1,000 when the boy was hanging in the Academy Summer Exhibition, about which he had no doubt.

During the last couple of courses, couples got up from their tables and went out onto the terrace to dance. Bob Hunt was getting a bit carried away, as was his wont, with his turf accountant mate John Jones. Marcia had already given him two eye-contact warnings and one verbal, which didn't seem to calm him down. The trio were playing some gentle Carpenters stuff, so Marcia went across to the other side of the table, put both her arms around Bob's neck from behind, and whispered, "Slow down on the drink, darling. I'll want you to undress me later. Come on, I want to dance now." The promise of undressing his wife always meant something of a treat, and Bob hoped he'd be allowed a fresh attempt at satisfying his young bride in a conjugal way. He knew it would happen one day.

He didn't really like dancing but tonight was the end of a basically very successful holiday and he felt happy to 'chuck' his feet around, as he called it.

With the activity and massing of people, not to mention the intake of food and wine and the evening having now shifted into 'dance yourself silly' mode, it was hot.

Peter was uncomfortable. He could feel Tania's piercing eyes burning into the back of his head, and almost permanently locked on to his eyeballs when he was facing her. He pondered the fact that if he'd had a female companion with him, he would have felt less exposed. He hadn't, so that was that.

Occasionally, when she was busy, he glimpsed her and kicked himself that his thoughts again turned to that body beneath the blouse and skirt. He must be crazy on two fronts. Crazy because he knew he could have his way with this gypsy girl any way, or anywhere, he chose. More crazy to think he was allowing himself such thoughts. After all, he still had a couple of stitches to remind himself of the dangers of any association with her.

Marcia took his mind off Tania. Now there was a beautiful young woman who also, he felt, amused herself with his emotions but, deep down, he felt was unavailable. Certainly she and Bob were letting their hair down now. Bob was going through an attempted flamenco on the dance floor, with a lot of clapping and stomping of feet, while Marcia obliged him by pretending to be some sort of wild bull, with fingers for ears, who was prepared to rush at Bob's large frame, and skirt by his rib cage as he subtly side-stepped her charge.

Bob had now given up using his tuxedo as a cape. His shirt was open-necked and very wet with perspiration, and goodness knows where he had thrown his clip-on bow tie. Maria thought to herself that he seemed to be over the muscular problems he'd got from hauling in the tuna. Maybe he'd just needed to re-exercise his strained muscles.

Meanwhile, the Admiral and his wife were showing everybody else that they had obviously indulged themselves in formal dance lessons at some stage. It was probably a winter pastime for them. They danced very properly around the edge of the floor, carefully navigating away from each crash course with other pairs of passing vessels.

Peter was pleased to see Maria and José bopping jauntily to the band's

Beatles set. He was sure his mother was singing the words. They were happy anyway. He felt Maria was happy, too, that she had shared with him the fact that they were an item. It couldn't have been easy for either of them to be living secret lives.

Peter felt an arm link into his.

"Hi, Peter!" the owner of the arm greeted him.

"Hi, Michelle. How's it going?"

"Not great," she said with a grin.

"Why?" he asked in a concerned voice.

"I've got no-one to dance with."

"Are you asking?" Peter said, with a deep smile.

"No. But I'm free if asked."

"So would you like to dance?"

"Only if you get your mates to play something very slow and extremely sexy."

"I reckon if we get on the floor they'll automatically do that."

"Then let's."

Almost as they stepped onto the dance floor area, the music stopped, ending that set of dances. They had taken no more than three steps. They stood apart, laughing together.

"Well, that was terrific," Michelle said. "What did you do? Nod your head to let them know you'd had enough of this female liability?"

"Not at all."

The break was hardly long enough for the musicians to change their sheet music and before Peter and Michelle had left the floor, the music broke into 'Guantanamera'. They danced closely but silently, which restored Peter's confidence to bounce back Tania's stinging rays, sent out to pierce his body armour but now ricocheted straight back, like needles into an effigy. Tania found it hard to accept the sight of Peter in the clutches of another young woman, whom she knew was more his style.

"You know how you rejected me?" Michelle suddenly said to Peter, making him feel deeply uncomfortable as she pressed her body into his. How could he answer that?

"Well, I wouldn't say I did that exactly," Peter replied. "I'd say more correctly I wasn't prepared to take advantage of your low and complex state."

"You're the sweetest guy who's ever turned me down."

"I'm not sure if that's a compliment, or you telling me that I'm a bit of a fool for not taking the opportunity."

"Because of all that, Saint Peter, I want you to know that I'm head-over-heels in love."

"If it's with me, we'll go back to my room right now and make up for lost opportunities."

"Of course I love you. But it's not the head-over-heels kind."

"Don't keep me in suspense. Who's the very lucky guy?"

"Miguel."

"Ah, Miguel! Was it anything to do with him borrowing my swimming trunks?" Peter suggested with a smile. "Anyway, isn't he a bit older than you?"

"Of course he is. That's one of the attractions. Those ten years or so – and who's counting? – give him the stability that guys I've dated before haven't had. He's Mr Calm, Mr Steady, Mr Loving and Caring. He's actually my Mr Everything. He'll be here shortly and I hope he'll be very jealous of us holding each other. But I wanted to tell you before Guy or Philippe blurt it out; they're leaving tomorrow. I'm staying on to do your tennis course and Miguel's going to continue to rid me of any craving, as well as strengthening the security he brings into my life."

The music stopped, then started up again with the smoochy tempo of 'Amigos Para Siempre', appropriately meaning 'friends for life'. Peter and Michelle danced on, each with their separate thoughts. But they were close.

The romance of the moment and the calm that surrounded them was suddenly disturbed by a shrill scream from just inside the doors to the terrace. Peter stepped back from Michelle's warm clinging body. The real world had once again intruded, and his fantasy one had to be put on the back burner.

There was a sound this time of serious breaking glass as another scream was emitted. He recognised it was Marcia's horror-stricken voice that had sent out the panic call.

Peter stalked back into the restaurant, to find Bob's large frame spread face down on the table set for the eight people who had dined on it some couple of hours before. His head had fallen sideways, exposing one side of his face. He was groaning and his eyelids were fluttering like butterflies over his glazed eyes. He was clearly in pain.

What possessed Peter to do what he did next, he would never know. He rushed to the table and, with total command of whatever the situation was, he quickly arranged two empty chairs alongside the one from which Bob had plunged forward. John Jones was there watching, frozen with fear, obviously with no idea as to what might be a remotely useful contribution. However, as in his army days, he'd do what he was led to do.

"Here, roll him off the table and lay him along the chairs," Peter directed. "He's crushing his chest as he is."

John did exactly as he was told, the task eased by the restaurant's regular waiters, Diego and Santi, who had rushed to the scene and now took part of Bob's weight between them.

There was suddenly a pushing and shoving through the gawping small crowd, the type of gathering that always seems to form when two cars thud together or an elderly person falls on a pavement. Dr Guibaud, one of the hotel's French guests, was there, and immediately went into emergency mode. He took one look and said, "Coeur." Then, "Vite!" indicating that the three men should get Bob onto his back. He looked up at Peter. "Magnifique!" he said, praising the wisdom of having laid Bob out flat.

The doctor's practised hands moved deftly across Bob's chest. He looked over his shoulder and up into Peter's face, now knowing where his best support would come from. "Ambulance. Rápido. Rápido." Peter turned and ran into reception.

He shouted at Sñr Martin, "Llame una ambulancia! Sñr Hunt está muy enfermo. Su corazón."

Maria and José appeared from Maria's back office, drawn by the noise. Maria read the panic in her son's face. He looked really scared.

"Mother, Bob Hunt, I'd say he's had a heart attack."

"Are you sure?"

"Pretty sure. That's Dr Guibaud's view anyway. He looks dreadful."

"I think Dr Guibaud is, in fact, a cardiologist. Oh, poor Marcia. Is she alright?"

"I really don't know. We concentrated on Bob."

"I think we ought to screen the area off and move all the people out onto the terrace," said Maria. She looked at Peter. "Any idea how long an ambulance might take?"

"On a good night, ten minutes… on a bad one… forever."

"Pray for it being a good one," José said sympathetically.

Peter took total control. Suddenly Tania and her sister were no longer threats. They were serious helpers. He instructed them to bring the screens over, which had until then prevented guests from the restaurant area seeing into the kitchens, and to place them around the table next to which Bob was lying. The doctor was giving what was newly termed the kiss of life. Bob's groans receded and he looked calm. His breathing was steadier.

Marcia was crouched on the floor, holding one of Bob's hands. She was as ashen as her dress was white.

"Where's that bloody ambulance?" Peter said as, almost in response to his question, a distant siren grew louder, and then stopped. It was probably in the forecourt of the hotel now.

"Here," he shouted to Tania, "go and open the doors into the hotel! Make sure the ambulance crew can get straight in with their trolley."

Tania was totally submissive, a professional helper. *Christ,* she thought, *how wonderful to be under his total control!*

The ambulance men set to work. Oxygen was clamped over Bob's face, he was lifted on to a stretcher and covered with a blanket. Marcia had kicked off her shoes and was holding them in one hand, with Bob's hand in the other, as she ran alongside the stretcher strapped to the trolley. Peter found himself at the other side while the crew pulled and pushed professionally from each end. Bob was now in through the open rear doors of the ambulance with Marcia alongside.

Suddenly a cold female hand grabbed Peter's arm and pulled him into the back of the ambulance. One attendant stayed alongside the stretcher-borne Bob; the other drove out of the drive and towards Palafrugell, which could not be close enough for any of them as they had each rightly assessed the level of emergency attaching to the journey.

Marcia held her hand out to Peter. "Help me, please, Peter. Help me, give me strength to get Bob better."

"He'll be fine," Peter said commandingly.

"Is it bad?" she said.

"I really don't know. But we'll have him in the right place before long."

"I'm scared, Peter."

"Bob wouldn't want you to be."

"He's never listened."

The trio of musicians hadn't actually seen the diversion that had interrupted their act. They'd felt the gig was going well but something very dangerous had erupted, which had scared the pants off everybody.

By this time the Admiral was on the small rostrum where they were playing. He was flicking his fingers, not in time to the music but indicating that they should stop. They played a few final bars, then tailed off.

"… Merci, après quelque chose de trés rapide, mais heureuse. Malheuresement, mesdames et messieurs…" he said, having taken the microphone from its stand.

He explained that a guest had been taken ill, but a French doctor had attended to him (the Admiral was fiercely patriotic and competitive to the last), and it was forecast that he would be fine, though he'd been taken to hospital as a precaution.

"We have 30 minutes left in which to dance our farewells to the Hotel Playa. May I take this opportunity to thank all the management and staff for their attention during our stay. So, until we meet here again next year, we must all soon say au revoir."

The Admiral turned back to the trio, indicating, "Play now," which they dutifully did. 'Viva Espana' enabled all the frustrated matadors to encourage their partners to become charging bulls, with fingers for ears, as Bob and Marcia had done just an hour or so previously. The floor was again thronging and one might almost have said poor old Bob Hunt's plight was, if not forgotten, at least covered up.

Maria couldn't get back into the restaurant; the doors to the terrace had been locked from the inside. So she went back through the reception to get into where Bob had had his attack, intending to sort out the mess and breakages.

Marco, looking serious, was with Carlos, Jaimé's father, and was remonstrating with him as Jaimé looked on.

"Everything OK?" Maria said to Marco, looking also at Carlos.

"Not really," Marco said. "But I'm sure it will be."

"What's the problem?"

Marco pointed at Jaimé. "This young man must've done about 20 sketches of guests during the evening. He's been paid various sums, which he's put into that shoe box where he's got his pencils. Other guests have ordered copies of his hotel sketches, so he's got together a real little hoard of cash. Carlos was about to take charge of it, and if some doesn't get spent on a few brandies and some of the rest isn't spent on clothes for the other three kids, I'd be very surprised. Peter intended the money to be put towards special medical treatment for the boy. So I'm suggesting we put all the money into the safe overnight and Peter can sort out what to do with it in the morning. Carlos doesn't agree and says it's his son and he should be in charge."

Maria turned to Carlos. "Carlos, my dear friend, Mr Marco is right. Please agree that we take charge of Jaimé's enormous success. It's him we want to benefit. Surely you must agree."

Suddenly, Jaimé went through his essential preparatory moves and said, "Si!" He knew very well what was happening and equally understood that in his father's hands, money was not safe.

Maria threw her arms around Jaimé's neck. "Bless you," she said. "No, Carlos. It's going to happen like we said, OK?"

"Si, Señora Maria."

The matter was closed.

Maria went into the corner of the restaurant, to be confronted with Tania's rear high in the air, as she knelt on the floor picking her way through bits of cutlery and carefully sweeping the broken glass into her dustpan. She hadn't heard Maria approaching.

"Thank you, Tania."

Tania jumped. "Oh… Señora Maria! I'm sorry, I didn't know you were there. It's OK. It's my job. It's my place to do this."

There was a sadness in her words, a sense of inevitability in her voice.

Maria picked up on it straight away. "No, Tania, this evening you're employed as a waitress, not a chambermaid, that's why you've got a pretty skirt on, and a nice blouse. Tomorrow, perhaps a little like Cinderella, you'll be doing your other important job, one that's essential to us. So what you're doing now is beyond your call."

"Waitress, chambermaid, what difference? I won't change my league. I'll always be in the back room, except when it suits Mr Peter to come and find me at the fiesta, and then he wants me in the street, but not in the grandness of the hotel."

"Tania! What are you saying?"

"Señora Maria. You have a wonderful, beautiful son. I watched him with Mr Hunt. If anybody saved his life, Mr Peter did. He is a Saint. But I also had to watch him dance with Mademoiselle Michelle. She's his type. I watched Mrs Hunt show everyone in the hotel who she wanted to share her pain and suffering with – it was Mr Peter. She too is in his league, and he's in hers. I have to accept that I'll have to go unnoticed because of my parentage… but I can't hide…" She started to sob and stifle her words. "… I can't hide my desire to be held by him, and for me to be able to share my grief with him."

Maria, for the second time, it seemed, in a very few minutes, put her arms around the neck of someone in need. She patted Tania's back, as if comforting a crying baby.

"Tania, stop crying and feeling sorry for yourself. Let me tell you something."

Tania seemed to pull herself together. She thought perhaps she was going to be let into a secret as to how to win Maria's son's attention.

"Look, it's like this. I feel exactly the same way about Peter. But I'm his mother. I get some attention but not all his attention, yet I of all people am in his league. Michelle's the same. The one you were jealous of him dancing with. OK, Marcia's temporarily in favour, getting his time and attention. This morning it was young Jaimé being encouraged to draw and paint, tomorrow it'll be someone learning tennis. Peter… is just not a single person's person. He's not rejecting your constant stares, which I have to say are very noticeable and you should stop them if you want him to even look in your direction. But he's not protecting our culture, or his parentage, or class; he's simply moving through his life towards an ideal and I believe he'll allow very few emotional distractions until he gets there. Michelle will find her man, Mrs Marcia's husband will, I hope, be repaired, Jaimé might get the attention he needs and I shall wallow in the memories and joys of motherhood and pine for Peter while he's abroad."

"Abroad?" Tania said, concerned.

"Yes, you probably don't know he's got a place to study in England."

"England! Oh well, that's it. He'll meet somebody over there. I'd best put my dreams out of my silly gypsy head."

"Don't ever shed your dreams, Tania. Cherish them. Dreams often come true in other dreams. It's reality at times that it's better to put out of our minds. Reality can sting and hurt. There are times that it doesn't, and the fact is that somewhere on this planet there's bound to be somebody waiting for you. He'll turn up when you least expect it. But burning the back of Peter's head with those laser beam eyes of yours will scare him off… then you'll have to fall back on your dreams."

"Señora Maria. I've always thought you're lovely. Mr Marco is very fair too. Thank you for explaining. My mother and father left me quite a lot short on the facts of life."

"Are they still alive, Tania? I don't know."

"My mother died giving birth to her sixth child. I have four sisters. She so wanted a son and it was he who died with her. My father… well, who knows? He left us and then came back and then left us again. He'll either come back to surprise us one day, or he's gone forever, or he's died. If it's the last case, then it would be that he's been murdered. That was in his stars, for sure.

"Look, I've still got some glass to clear up and then I said I'd help with the washing up. There's a lot to do, and many hands make light work."

Maria had her handbag slung over one shoulder. She opened up her purse, took out a 2000 peseta bill and knelt down beside Tania.

"Here, buy yourself a little present. That's for being helpful, and being a member of Peter's great fan club."

Now, if that had been Marco with an appreciative gift for services received, she would have merely tucked the money into her bra with a not too emphatic, "Thank you," principally because Toni always said she didn't charge enough. If it had been Peter she would have been mortally offended and reminded him she had offered herself to him for free. With Maria, she just didn't know how to react.

"Oh, Señora Maria. No! No thank you. I'm happy with what I'm being paid. This is just an accident that somebody needs to clear up. It's included in my night's pay."

"It's not pay. I've told you. It's for you to buy yourself a present. Please just take it without further question."

The reception at Palafrugell Hospital was smooth and professional. Name-taking and family history was restricted to the bare essentials, Peter doing the translating as none of the emergency staff spoke English.

Bells were ringing around the admissions area and Bob was transferred from a stretcher onto a casualty bed. A young doctor appeared, a little dishevelled and looking slightly rushed. He made no fuss, went straight to Bob's side. He ordered a continuation of oxygen, spoke some sort of prescriptive language to the nurse, who rushed away and returned quickly with a hypodermic and a glass vial, which the doctor scrutinised carefully. In the interim, one of the other nurses had cut Bob's shirt off him and asked Marcia's permission, through Peter, if she could take his trousers down. He was left bare-chested but in his underpants.

He seemed to be sleeping, his breathing steady.

Another nurse wheeled in a trolley bearing an ECG machine. She started shaving small areas around Bob's chest and stomach. Wires were stretched across and around the passive body in a practised, skilful way. The sensors on the ends of the wires were adhered to Bob's body. A paper roll started turning in the machine and pulse lines appeared on the paper from an inkjet, which jumped up and down as though recording a reading on the Richter scale.

The young doctor, who did speak some English, directed his words towards Marcia.

"I suggest you go and get some air. I'll need about 30 minutes. Your father is stable. I'll ensure he won't come to any harm."

Peter quickly put him right that it was not a father and daughter situation. They were a married couple. The doctor apologised profusely. It was as well that Marcia didn't understand what he then asked Peter.

"So were they, well, you know, in bed when this happened?"

"Good God, no!"

"I see. Usually at this time of day a heart attack, which I'm pretty sure this is, is brought on by over-zealous sexual activity for an older man."

"No. They'd been dancing, but last weekend..." Peter told him about the fishing trip and how Bob had been attended by Dr Gomez, and, as he understood it, about the paracetamol and aspirin treatment.

Peter and the doctor agreed the best thing was that he and Marcia went out to get some air. Marcia took Peter's arm once they were in the corridor, making their way to the entrance and to a bench placed outside in the hospital forecourt, usually frequented by visitors needing a cigarette break.

"If Bob lives, and please God he does, it'll have been your actions that saved his life in the hotel, I really believe that. I can see now that he fell forward onto his chest, compressing his rib-cage and then all the bits and pieces inside him that pump the blood around."

"Oh, you can't say that," Peter responded, "the French doctor was the hero. He'd been there before… no, I just think it was a combination of events. Oh, and by the way, be positive. He *will* live."

"Do you know, I've almost seen this coming, but Bob's a stubborn old stick. *You* try and change his lifestyle."

One hour later, the diagnosis was complete, as far as it could go. The doctor thought it was an arterial clot, which had dispersed before it blocked the valve into Bob's heart. He prescribed rest and then X-rays and scans the next day.

"No, he's not on a danger list," he answered Peter in their native tongue. "Seriously ill, yes. Just in case there's another clot cruising around that hasn't manifested itself yet, we've put him on warfarin, so that will thin his blood, and we've already reduced his blood pressure to 130/80, which shows that's capable of reacting to a cocktail of atenolol and diltiazem, which is good news."

Then he turned to Marcia. "If you like, you could spend the night with your husband. He'll probably wake wondering what happened to him. He won't know a lot about it, but he will remember the pain he experienced. It would have been extreme, and a lot of his problem was initially a faint to counter the pain."

Marcia thanked the doctor and said she would like to stay.

Peter checked if there was anything else he could do for Marcia, who said he'd been an absolute brick and there wasn't anything else he could do at that moment.

"I'll call here in the morning to see how things are."

Suddenly, Marcia put her hand to her mouth. "Christ!" she said, looking at her watch. "I'd forgotten! We're leaving today!"

Peter explained what she had said. The young doctor looked puzzled, as if she should have known.

"Say her husband is likely to be in our care for two weeks, please."

Peter told her and Marcia paled.

"Look, get some sleep yourself. We'll sort that out in the morning."

Peter had called a taxi to get him home and Marcia waited for that to arrive. She squeezed his hand and kissed his cheek, her Chanel No. 5 ultra-potent at such close proximity. She waved him off down the drive-way as Peter slumped in the back of the taxi, as much as anything because he just did not want to engage in conversation. He was more tired than he imagined he could ever be, but then it had been a long, eventful day. He looked at his watch. It was 12.30am. He'd been at the hospital for about an hour and a half, he reckoned. He wondered how Bob would fare during the night.

The driver was a bit haphazard, but taxi-driving, or any driving at all, was a reasonably recently practised art in Spain. Coaches were worse. They crashed all over the place and tipped over the sides of hills with regularity. The driver drove with dipped headlights all the way, even though the lanes were quite suitable for full beams. He wasn't sure, he said, where the exact entrance to the hotel was, so Peter told him it was another 150 metres on the left. Yet the driver seemed to be making no allowance for the fact that he was to turn very soon, and hadn't changed down a gear, which Peter would have done.

"It's here," Peter said loudly. The driver turned the wheel to the left, but started braking on the turn. Peter was thrown across the back seat of the taxi. There was suddenly, above the noise of screeching tyres, a metallic thud. Peter glimpsed a bicycle being thrown into the air and a dark body projected with it into the hedgerow.

"Oh shit!" he exclaimed. "You weren't bloody looking! Oh, what the hell now? Who have we killed?"

The taxi driver stopped his vehicle. "What was that?" he asked.

"I'd say you hit a cyclist. I'd also say you were going too fast."

Peter climbed out of the rear passenger door. The bike was lying on the ground with its back wheel still spinning. It was a dull night. Clouds had drifted in to hide the summer moon.

"Mr Peter," came a young voice from within the hedgerow.

Peter tried to follow where it came from.

"Mr Peter! Please don't kill me. It's me. I know I'm a nuisance."

"Is that Tania?"

"Yes."

"Where?"

"Over here."

"Keep calling out and I'll find you."

"Mr Peter, Mr Peter, Mr Peter…"

"Are you alright?" Peter could see this black-covered body embedded in the hedge.

Suddenly the engine of the taxi was fired and, from a standing start, it accelerated. It passed them both in reverse gear, just brushing the bike on the ground. It now had no headlights on at all. The tyres bit into the driveway as the driver braked, threw the car into first gear and spun the steering wheel to the left, accelerating into the main road, then into a locked right turn once on the tarmac road. He then sped off at a rate of knots into the night.

"What the hell!" Peter said.

"He won't have insurance," Tania said, in a controlled voice.

Peter held out a hand. "Here, do you think you can walk?"

"I hurt a bit."

"Here, hold both my hands." He lifted her from the bank and into an upright position.

"I'm fine," she said. "If you could pick up my bike, I'm OK. I can get home."

"I can't let you do that," Peter said.

"I'm OK, really." She looked down at her left leg, which was now visible as the clouds cleared, allowing the moon's rays as headlights. Some light shingle had adhered to her soft, moist skin.

Peter picked up on the outline of her shapely knee in the grey light.

"Look, we'll get back to the hotel and I'll get the car and drop you off to your village."

"Are you tired of living, Mr Peter?" Tania queried.

"Not at all. Of course not."

"Well, if you get seen dropping me off anywhere by my cousins, it'll be at least broken legs this time, and you'd find it hard to explain how you did that walking into another tree."

That made Peter laugh, despite his body reminding him he'd had a hard day.

"Mr Peter," Tania said in a serious tone of voice. "You were marvellous with Mr Hunt. You saved his life, if it has been saved. Everybody thinks you're a hero."

"Oh, come on, Tania," he said modestly.

"Everybody thanks you." With that, she stepped forward and took his head into her open palms and lightly kissed his lips. "You are sent from God. That's a thank you from Mary."

He was sure he was out of control. He must be on somebody's autopilot or radio control. It was not him speaking. Yet he still spoke the words.

"I'd, of course, thank Mary for that. But I'd rather receive a thank you from Tania. Tania, the wild gypsy."

She had retreated a pace after her acknowledgement on behalf of the world. She stepped forward again. Put a slowly moving left arm around the left side of his strong neck and finessed the hold by linking both forearms into a caress that pulled his head towards hers, and her lips onto his. She closed her eyes and kissed him passionately. His hands fell onto her waist, and then around to her buttocks, which he gently pulled towards him. The night was suddenly electric. His adrenalin pumped, as it would in any young man given an identical situation. The body against his was soft and warm.

He had kissed before with Laura and Meribel. Kisses he had thought were meaningful. But this was a warmth and dimension he had yet to experience. Their lips together were as he had imagined intercourse would be. Involuntarily, his tongue was sucked into her as it forced its way through the outer lips into the chasm beyond.

She winced. Not in pain, more in prospect of experiencing a great happiness. Simply a dream on the brink of coming true. Reality suddenly hit her. She moved her hands from behind the back of his neck, down onto his masculine chest. She pushed gently as he tightened his hold. She strengthened the leverage and at the same time pulled her hips away, allowing her stronger right hand and arm to push firmly against his waist. Their lips had parted moments before. Her eyes were wide open and piercing. Suddenly, this tearaway vixen was in control, in command, and Peter was submissive.

"Dear Mr Peter, we are not to be."

He was speechless. Should he say, "But you said…" and remind her about her promise of availability? Or should he respect the lady's change of tune?

He hardly believed that what had been the promise of an easy conquest was now forbidden fruit.

"Lo siento," she said, "es verdad."

She adjusted her skirt and top and knelt to pick up her bike.

"Tania, you need lights," Peter said, from a purely practical point of view.

"My God will shine upon me. I feel he has already," she said finally, and rode into the darkness of the night, initially swerving before she built up momentum.

Peter watched her outline disappear out through the entrance and onto the tarmac road.

"How the hell am I expected to sleep now?" he whispered up at the racing clouds.

He eventually did, but not until after Maria had heard him come home. "How's Bob?" she called out.

"I think he'll be fine. The night will be the test, but he's calm and he's got instant treatment and medication. It looks as though it was a heart attack brought about by an arterial blockage."

"Oh dear," Maria called back thoughtfully. Then: "Peter?"

"Yes, Mother?" he responded wearily.

"I was very proud of you. They're saying your prompt reaction saved Bob's life."

"Oh, come on!" *And there,* Peter thought, *hangs another tale.*

When Peter arrived at reception the next morning, it was beginning to resemble a busy railway station. Both Maria and Sñr Martin were running out final room bills and suitcases were gradually taking over the floor space. The Admiral had a large trunk, there were some designer matching sets and other heavier 'been around the world' containers. Soon they would be on their return journeys to their countries of origin, with well-tanned owners.

Peter interrupted his mother for just a few moments. "Any news of Bob Hunt?" he enquired.

"I rang at about eight and he was stable."

"Is that OK news?" Peter asked.

"I'd say so. The better news is that I spoke to Marcia and she's given me a list and location of a change of clothes she'd like, plus a spare change too. She feels she's overdressed for the occasion. She said Bob's getting excellent attention and that he opened his eyes around about dawn, smiled and squeezed her hand and went back to sleep. They've apparently put him on a drip and he's now monitored by some dreadful machine, which, according to Marcia, beeps like a young child the whole time."

"Will you take the clothes," Peter asked, "or would you like me to?"

"We could go together if you like. I think the major exodus should be over by 11.30. The bills will be run by then and Sñr Martin should be able to cope. What d'you think?"

"Seems a good idea. By then, you never know, Bob might have turned a corner and be awake."

"Don't expect too much, dear," Maria said in a comforting way. "A slow recovery is a more solid one."

"I'll come back about 11.30… by the way… is Tania working this morning?"

"No. Why?"

"Well, I got a taxi back from the hospital last night or, to be more precise, this morning. The driver wasn't the best in Spain. He swung into the hotel drive as, as I later discovered, Tania was about to leave the complex on her bike, with no lights."

"Goodness! What on earth are you going to say happened?"

"Well… my man, I think, hit the back wheel of her bike, which threw her into the hedgerow."

"Was she hurt?"

"She grazed her knee. I think that was the extent of it. But she was shaken."

"Well, poor dear, she would have been, wouldn't she."

"The taxi driver did a runner, scared of a huge claim on his non-existent insurance."

"Really? So how did she get home?"

"She insisted on cycling."

"Should you have let her do that?"

"You try and tell her. She's a strong-willed young lady."

"She was very helpful at the dinner last night. Actually, I think she's a nice girl. She's just not been blessed with parental guidance."

"So you're not expecting her in?"

"No. I said because she was so late working she should take the half-day off, which she'd normally have worked. She'll be in tomorrow, I'm sure. Must go. Look, they're getting agitated, they want to pay their bills so much."

"See you about 11.30."

Michelle was doing her early morning teaching stint. "Hi," she said as she came off the court. "Hi, hero."

"Hero? What's the hero bit?"

"Well, word is that if it had been Marcia, you would've delivered the kiss of life yourself, but I've been telling everybody you're saving that for me. But it seems the common opinion is that you saved Bob's life, if it *has* been saved."

"Oh, come on!" had become the frequent reply from Peter, who was beginning to be embarrassed by the previous night's drama. Particularly because each time he received what appeared to be the common accolade, he just spoke these same words, which even he could see were meaningless.

CHAPTER 3

Peter's target of leaving for England in three weeks was on schedule. There were plenty of flights for just one single fare by the third week in September, when most tourists with children had already left for home.

He had set up his drawing office and laid out the skeleton dimensions from his day's work with Jaimé onto a huge length of lining paper. He had never been confronted with this sort of task before, but did have the odd moment of thinking perhaps he was four or five months ahead of himself because surely the first thing he would learn in architectural college would be setting out a site on a drawing. In the event, however, when he did get to the opening weeks of college, it was to deal with an imaginary project to build one house in Hampstead, north London.

He followed his own logical approach to get his much larger scheme into being on his paper. He drew one spine line, as he was later to explain to Tania when he let her into the secret of what he was doing. He'd seen her on the Monday after Bob's attack. She'd been a little withdrawn when they met in the corridor leading to the kitchen, where they so often seemed to bump into each other.

She'd put her head down when she'd first realised the inevitability that their paths were going to cross. She wasn't on an unlit bike this time, though.

"How's your leg?" Peter enquired.

"It's fine, Mr Peter, thank you. But I'm sorry I caused you the problem on Sunday morning."

"Problem?"

"Well, yes. You must have been tired, you were almost in bed and then you had to sort me out again."

"I think it was the other way round, that you caused me an even bigger problem. First you gave me a message from Mary, then one from yourself that stopped me going to sleep for at least a couple of hours."

How very pleased she was with herself. She knew he was joking, but had learnt that when he exaggerated something to the level of being preposterous, the base point behind it was seriously meant. She, too, hadn't found it easy to sleep. Usually if she kissed it was as a prelude to being fucked, which was always the way she felt about it, if she was to be perfectly frank with herself. Toni would certainly kiss her at some stage of satisfying his needs with her, as, in fact, did her father, but with a more paternal emphasis than a pseudo-passionate one.

But she had never kissed, or been kissed, tenderly. Nor had she ever been allowed to free herself from the panting and powerful male clutches of such an embrace. So, as much as she had left Peter stupefied (although she did not know to what extent), she too felt her legs had gone weak on her, and she had to push herself hard to pedal home.

"Mr Peter, I'm always saying sorry, and I'm saying it again. You looked so tired and exposed. I wanted to thank you on everybody's behalf for your efforts with Mr Hunt. I suppose that's no excuse. I should have just shaken your hand."

"Tania. Just keep looking out for things to thank me for. You can show your gratitude like that any time you're passing."

She laughed. "No! Mr Peter, I promise I won't do that again."

Why, for God's sake? he thought. He'd love some more of that and then to be able to remind her of her early offer. This girl knew emotion and, he imagined, if she could pretty well bring him to a climax with a kiss, what would she be like laid across him on a bed?

Now, however, she had made her announcement that it would never happen again and he had to presume all earlier deals were off too.

The following day, Tania went to the bike rack after work. She had done the evening shift because a party of guests were on late flight arrivals.

She had taken what she thought to be her bike out of the rack but, seeing a light on the front above the basket, which certainly didn't look like hers, she put the bike back. She was sure that was where she had left it, though. Then she saw the dynamo on the back wheel, which had a label on it. That would be the name of the owner, so she looked to see.

She read: 'Necesitamos luz en nuestras vidas.' She smiled. The lights in her eyes, as the message said, were not associated with getting home safely on her bike. To her they were for seeing Peter with.

So it was her bike, modified, and only one person could have been that kind. Peter must have fixed it up. She knew how to switch the dynamo on to the back wheel so that it illuminated the front and back lights. They all worked as she rode proudly down the drive to get home. She felt more confident, stronger… more visible and, though she didn't remember it until later, she sang every pop song she knew the words to on her way home.

So it *was* the next day, the Wednesday, that, not having seen Peter the day before, she plucked up courage and, when she saw Maria on her daily inspection round, asked her if Peter was going to be around. She needed to thank him for something.

"He's in room number 212."

"Oh, is he ill?"

Maria laughed, "No, goodness me, no. He's working in room 212 on a project of his."

"Oh, I see. Well, I ought not to disturb him. I'll wait till I bump into him."

She wondered what the project was.

Tania had been vacuuming the second floor corridor carpet, perhaps extra zealously, knowing Peter was behind one of the closed doors. She was now bending down to dust the top of the skirting board when she heard heavy male footsteps running up the stairs. It was unlikely to be anybody other than Peter. She kept moving along the corridor, back towards the staircase, rear end first, dragging the duster over the painted timber as she went.

Coming from the other direction, Peter recognised Tania's approaching bottom in a split second. If he had thought more deeply, he would have held back on his initial instinctive inclination to strike it firmly but playfully with his large open palm. Nevertheless, he did not hold back and delivered a firm but stinging slap to Tania's right buttock.

She was upright like a shot from a starter's pistol, and as quick. She too did not hold back on the intention to clout whoever it was for doing that, as she would have done to her cousins in years gone by. But as her left hand swung round to strike her assaulter across the side of his head, Peter reacted instinctively again. He managed to grasp Tania's flying left wrist and slowed its momentum to zero before it landed on its target.

"Hey, young lady. If that had landed I reckon you would have opened up my cut and I would have been back to the hospital for re-stitching."

"Well, frankly, Mr Peter, you'd deserve it. I bet I'll have quite a bruise on my bum."

"Did I slap you that hard?"

"Well, yes, you did."

"Do you want to come into my room and I'll put some witch hazel on it?"

She laughed. "I can see your uncle in you. No, I don't, but thank you all the same. I'll survive, but I doubt I'll ever be able to ride my bike again."

At that Peter suddenly looked very concerned. He supposed she would have seen the bike with its lights, but perhaps she had gone home by bus, as she often did.

"Do you really mean that?"

"Oh, come on, Mr Peter. How could I ever not ride my beautiful bike again, now that God created a miracle and fixed lights on the front and back and… a real dynamo."

"And God really did that for a wicked girl like you, did he?"

"Well, it was either God or it could have been you in one of your softer, kinder moments."

Peter put his hands in the air. "To get an accolade of being kinder or softer from you, I give in… I surrender. It was me. I didn't want you to get knocked off your bike again."

"Mr Peter, thank you. It was very kind. You *are* very kind." She leant forward and brushed his left cheek with her right one, but then stepped back very quickly. "My butt still stings like crazy," she was quick to say. "Anyway, what are you doing with a room up here?"

"I've set it up as a lair where I can bring all the young women in the village one by one and devour them."

"I don't believe you for one moment."

"Do you want to be the first?"

"No. Because I know my cousins'll find me."

"Come on, I'll show you… you'll be perfectly safe."

Inside the room, and after Tania had said he shouldn't have taken the door off, Peter showed her the rolled out paper he was using as creative material, with the single spine line, which Tania asked him to explain.

"This is my project." He had invested in a roll of tracing paper, by way of moving his aspirations up towards success and riches, and left the lining paper to do a back-up job.

"You take this end," he said, indicating the beginning of the roll of tracing paper, "down to the other end of the door. Lay it over the lining paper, which is pinned to the door with drawing pins. Yes… that's right. Good. Now, just put these drawing pins lightly into the board. Perfect."

He pinned the end he was holding to the end of the door where he was standing. He picked up a blue marker pen from a vase he'd set up to contain his drawing gear, and strained his eyes slightly to pick up a faint line he had already put on to the paper he had prepared for his full schematic drawing. He traced that faint line with the blue marker pen, providing a thick wavey line the length of the makeshift drawing board.

"OK. So you're a seagull. Do you understand? You're up in the air looking down and here…" indicating the blue line, "… is the sea."

He then took out a red pen and drew a thick line around both ends of the tracing paper, roughly parallel with the sea.

"Now that's an existing field of vines and sunflowers. I've arranged to buy that from one of our cousins. Ours don't go round beating up people who dance with their girlfriends. They've got on with life and created their own static industry. They haven't had to move around the countryside to find a home or make a living. Anyway, I'm going to develop all this area behind the blue line and within the red ones for housing. Housing that I think tourists will buy. Now, what do you think tourists would want most? Apart from you?"

Tania had moved round and was kneeling intently on a chair overlooking the plan and immediately next to where Peter sat. From time to time he'd walk around the site, making sure Tania knew which was sea and a band of sand, and where there were trees and jungles of sunflowers.

Tania thought about what tourists wanted and if she'd heard Peter's comment about herself, she'd certainly matured enough to ignore it.

Yes, in fact, Tania thought the whole time Peter was excitedly explaining his project that it was very much a one-to-one performance. He hadn't treated her as someone of low intellect, or skirted over issues he felt were too complex or detailed for her to grasp.

"The sea and the sand," she said.

"That's right. Excellent. Now you see this spine line?"

"Yes."

"Well it's about a kilometre in length and that's the amount of sea and sand each person on the development can not only use, but is able to look at as what they're going to use, as their base for swimming or building sandcastles or just sunbathing. So if they can look out of their windows and see the sea and sand then that would sell houses."

"That's right."

"OK, so if a house is 20 feet wide, about six metres, then you could only get 60 houses down the site with that desired view."

"That's a lot of houses. That's OK, isn't it?"

"Watch this." Peter then drew four or five tributaries coming out of the sea and into the land. They were tapering tracts of water, he explained to Tania, wider at the entry to the sea than at the furthest point inland. He then drew a line of houses on both banks of the tributaries.

"Now you see each of these houses has a mooring, in fact, at the end of a 20-foot decked patio, behind each house. Decked. Strip timber. So no grass to cut while they're on holiday and the bonus of a view of the sea from ground and first floors. Now there are 88 houses on each tributary. There'll actually be five inland waterways so, hey presto! 440 houses in prime locations. In fact, but it's a bit of a complicated story and hard at this stage to explain, there'll be some land used for flats. Although everybody probably doesn't want to cut grass, not everybody wants a boat. So there'll be some flats and we'll get to build overall 500 homes, with a few shops. Maybe, and I say maybe, the farmhouse there," he said, pointing to a brown square under the tracing paper, "will become a hotel… and I tell you what… you've got first option to work in it."

"As a chambermaid?"

"It's up to you. Get yourself some ambition and who knows what you might be able to do by the time the development's built."

She flushed with excitement.

"So, what do you think?" Peter asked.

"Brilliant… absolutely brilliant…" She really was excited. He could tell the odd little giveaway sign, which always made him smile.

Tania put her hand across to his. "Thank you for… shit! Look at the time! I've been here a whole hour… I'll get the sack! Oh, Mr Peter… I'm sorry, I must go… but thank you for two more things in our time together."

What philosophy is this going to be? he wondered.

"Thank you enormously for treating me as a person and sharing your excitement and enthusiasm with me… and thank you for being the only real man in the world who's been in a bedroom with me without either asking, telling me, or forcing me to get into, on or even under the bed to have sex… despite your erection, which I find flattering!"

She roared a gypsy laugh. Kissed the side of his cheek and rushed to the door. There she opened it slowly and stood partially the other side of it, curved the most curvaceous of lovely legs around the opening edge of the door with a hand above her head, held high towards the top of the frame. She exited stage left, leaving Peter in absolutely no doubt that, given the opportunity, she really knew how to handle herself to good effect. She slid out of her pose, waved a cheeky left hand at him and closed the door.

"Remember there could also be an audience behind you," Maria's voice stated loud and clear from the corridor, as she focussed on Tania's posterior leaving the room.

Tania wished the world could have opened up and swallowed her whole. "Señora Maria!" she gasped, and then, sensing that Maria was not exactly fuming, she laughed and went into girlie mode. "I was just taking my leave of your son. He's been showing me his project and I realised I'd been ages. He's so intense about it. Isn't it brilliant? I'll make the time up this afternoon. I'll put in an extra hour."

"There's no need. Can you get down to 114, one of the kids has upset a vase of flowers and the guest doesn't know how to mop up water. Is Mr Peter in one piece?"

"Yes, of course."

"Then I'll see how he's doing myself."

As Peter heard the door open, he looked up, still in a state of arousal, hoping it might be Tania returning to complete her mission.

"Mother!" he said, with a tinge of shock in his voice.

"Did you think it was Tania coming back for more?"

"More! More what?"

"More explanation about the project. How's it going, anyway?"

Maria had seen the beginnings the day before, so she hadn't expected much more drawing development. "Oh, you've put the sea in, and some trees. Well, that makes it easier to understand."

The bed was uncrumpled, the en suite light was off and the fan wasn't still running. No. That was all OK. Quite harmless. It was as Tania had said. Maria's assessment would have done her justice alongside any detective struggling with a murder inquiry.

"I'll leave you to get on," she said.

"The morning's raced away again, are we still on for a 2.30 visit to see Bob?" They had been told on their previous morning visit that now afternoons would be better all round.

"Yes, dear, that's fine. Marcia rang and said she'd probably come back to the hotel tonight. Bob's pretty well conscious the whole time now and last night had a normal night's sleep. He wants Marcia to get some rest. So she may get back here tonight."

"Good news," Peter affirmed.

The next ten days or so flew by. Peter worked hard on his layout but still supervised Michelle's tennis coaching. He'd had a call from Meribel to thank him for dropping off her bits and pieces.

"By the way," she said, as if it was something of an after-thought, "was the letter from the UK of any significance?"

Why not meet her and tell her? he thought. After all it was she who'd inspired the application and acted as a mailbox.

"Well, I was going to ring you and tell you actually."

"Don't make excuses. I know you've been busy. I heard about Bob Hunt and your involvement. Quite a hero, aren't you."

"Look, would you like to meet up for a coffee or a drink? I'll tell you about England and you can catch me up with your news."

"Well, I'm pretty busy. But when are you free?"

Oh here we go, Peter thought to himself. *Now we'll play 'Who's available when' poker,* which needed a damn sight more bluff than the game itself.

"You select an evening and I'll make myself free," he challenged.

Now how would she get out of that one? she thought. He'd got her. Clever bugger. But then he always was.

"Friday?"

There was silence as Peter hypothetically re-juggled his arrangements.

"Great, OK. But couldn't do before eight."

"That would suit me fine. I won't have to make any alterations."

"Shall I pick you up?" Peter enquired.

"Yes, but just park outside. I'll see the car and come out. Mummy and Daddy wouldn't be too welcoming. They think you ditched me."

"Your mother seemed OK, but yes, that's fine."

Bob was on the mend, although he would have to be referred to a heart man in the UK. Currently he wasn't allowed to drive and he and Marcia were looking into all sorts of arrangements to get home. Peter was due to see them both in hospital on the same Friday afternoon as he had fixed to see Meribel in the evening.

Tania was around and always bouncing. She had taken Peter a coffee one morning. Rushed in and rushed out in definite 'can't stop' mode. Beyond that, her purposeful putting herself out of general circulation had worked to the extent that their paths had not crossed, so her willpower remained intact. This way she was able to retain the belief that they weren't good for each other, weren't intended for each other. It wouldn't be good for those theories to be put to any certain test… because she knew she would weaken.

Anyway, Peter's time left in Spain was rushing by, as was Maria's time with him, moments to savour her boy before he went to England. She seemed to have come to terms with the prospect fairly quickly, Peter thought. In fact, without the other knowing it, both he and his mother didn't quite know what filled their days. Peter, the planner, would get to the end of each day of that first week, wondering what he'd accomplished and whether he was on target to get through what he wanted to do, and more particularly what he needed to do. So he made a list of essentials, and pencilled in the day he aimed to leave for England.

He did that the morning after his date with Meribel. The evening had started strangely, really. She was clearly acting like the jilted party and had a definite aloofness about her. They went to a bar they had frequented quite regularly in Palafrugell. He had fully expected she'd have coffee. He usually only had, at most, a couple of beers when he was driving. He'd offered her coffee but part of her attitude seemed to be non-agreement with any of his suggestions.

On the phone he'd asked, "Would you like to go to Nino's for some tapas and a glass of wine?"

"No, I'm happy with a coffee at Il Terrazzo. Thanks," she'd counter-proposed.

So when the coffee was suggested, Peter was surprised when Meribel said no, she would have a glass of wine. Knowing that she only ever drank white wine, Peter ordered that, but she put out her hand, placed it on top of his and said, "No Peter, I'm more often drinking red now." And so it was to be.

She'd had three glasses of red during the early part of the evening as she listened to all his news. Hers hadn't really changed. She was still going to Madrid in October to take up her place, which would lead to medicine. There seemed lots of ifs and buts, though, which might change that plan.

"I've been thinking about a year out. Perhaps in England, to broaden my language."

"Really?" Peter had responded instantly. Was that, he wondered, a way of her saying would he like her company? So it seemed to go on most of the evening. Would he like her to look over his plans? Could she organise a little au revoir party out at a nice restaurant for his mother and uncle and aunt?

"Incidentally," she said, "I'm having a cultural weekend in Barcelona the weekend after this one."

"Going with somebody I know?" Peter asked.

"Absolutely by myself, but a friend may come with me."

She was reaching out to try to patch things up. The wine didn't help her case and, as hard as Peter might try, the paternal genes took control. Like Paco, once Pedro had put something out of his mind, he didn't know how it felt to reverse it.

"Let's get you home," Peter finally suggested. Meribel was too tired, and bordering on being too tight, to counter that suggestion.

He pulled up in the lane where they'd usually said their fond farewells in the good days, rather out of habit than design, he now realised.

"Well, it's been good to see you. We'll see if we can get together before I go," he said, although he knew there was no sincerity in that statement.

Meribel put her left hand across on to Peter's strong thigh. He was sure she had never ever had three glasses of red wine before and, who knows, probably a sherry or a glass of wine to give her Dutch courage before they met. She looked across at him through slightly dulled eyes.

"Peter, my sweet. This is a hard one for a girl. But how would you think of us going in the back, just for old times' sake, you know, like we used to? You'd like that, wouldn't you?"

"Meribel, my sweet. You've had just one glass too many to drink. If I took up the invitation you'd have every reason to hate me in the morning." He placed her hand back on her disappointed thigh and got out of the car, moved around to the passenger door quite quickly and opened it.

"Let me get this tired young lady home, eh?"

The drink had locked in as she leant heavily on him. She was beginning to cry.

"Hey, doctor. Come on. Have you got your key?"

"In my purse," she managed to get out.

Now, a fellow doesn't go into a young lady's purse. "Here, I'll hold it, you get the key."

"Why are you always so fucking practical?" she said, by way of a critical statement. "I hope when you're in London you'll learn to loosen your tie. If you're not careful you'll grow into a boring old fart. No-one, no-one in their right minds, wouldn't go into the back of a car with me."

"Meribel, it was good to see you. Here, you're home."

He put her key in the door and unlocked it. He kissed her lightly on the forehead and gently guided her inside. She hardly noticed. She was on autopilot. He waited in the lane for her bedroom light to go on. Her blinds were already drawn. Within seconds of that, the bathroom at the side of the house was also illuminated. *There goes the wine,* Peter thought. He hoped she wasn't too bad, but that would cure her of red wine without food for a while.

What a soppy fool I'm being, he thought as he drove home. He'd declined Meribel, he had missed his opportunity with Tania. Was he mad or something? He needed sex, surely, like any other man. Even Marco was accepting more of it than Peter was. Perhaps a bike with a light on it would swerve in front of him and toss its rider into the hedgerow for his harvesting. There was no such miracle.

Nor was Tania, or Michelle or, in fact, any female except perhaps Maria there waiting in bed for him when he got home. Why did he exclude Marcia from his thoughts, for God's sake? After all, she would surely be the best. Probably because he'd feel guilty about Bob. *There you go,* he thought to himself, *Peter Martinez, you are going mad. Get into bed and if any of them come in and climb alongside, thank God for the favour shown, and take it.*

Suddenly Peter nearly jumped through the roof.

"Aren't you going to say goodnight, darling?"

Shit! It was only his mother. "Of course. Sleep well. See you in the morning."

"Was Meribel OK?"

"Well, not really. She drank herself stupid… made herself look a bit silly."

"What a pity. Goodnight. Sleep well."

Saturday's plan was to see Carlos Sanchez at the library in the morning and show him how the project was coming along. Carlos was extremely impressed, he said he could see a tremendous contribution to the region's tourist industry and how welcome 500 residences would be. That was potentially 500 boats, 500 cars… all drinking petrol and diesel, bringing income and taxes into the province. Five hundred families who no doubt would be able to afford to spend more in the markets for food and fruit than the locals could. In the winter, 500 more families perhaps wanting to borrow books… and with that, Carlos went into deep thought.

Peter didn't want to interrupt so left him to it for a minute or two. Eventually Carlos said, "Peter, do you know me to be an honest man?"

"Yes, of course. Without a shadow of a doubt."

"Then if I say something, would you assure me you wouldn't take it as a request for favours?"

"Look, of course. I wouldn't dream of such a thing."

"OK. It may seem a crazy idea. But as you know, my wife's health isn't excellent. Given four or five years, I'll need to retire, but I'll still want something to do with my time."

He pointed to the small cluster of 'centre shops' Peter had now illustrated to serve the needs of the new community.

"You see that small one on the corner? It would make an ideal newspaper and bookshop. Maybe selling stamps as well. Could I take an option on renting that unit, and buying…" he thought through what he was about to say, pondering deeply over Peter's plan, "…buying that house?"

"Of course, that's done. If we build, these are yours."

"But at full market price. You'll understand."

"At full market price. I, and the world, would want to understand that. I tell you what, I'll get you an option drawn up legally by the solicitor."

Carlos got up from behind his desk and shook Peter's hand.

"Your mother has done well to bring you up as a fine young man. Don't let her down. The ideas you've shown me have a touch of genius about them. Look through the library, the place is full of references to works of art produced by geniuses who often cut their ears off, or die early of syphilis, or booze. Try to stay as the Peter we all know, and care for. By the way, I heard about how you saved the life of a guest at the hotel."

… And missed out on screwing at least three or four young ladies recently, Peter thought as he thanked Carlos and took his leave. In fact he left to keep on programme for his Saturday plan by seeing Bob, at Bob's invitation, in the hospital that afternoon.

He hadn't really seen Marcia to speak to all week. She'd get back to the hotel absolutely whacked, take a small room service meal and then, apparently, sleep. Spending a lot of time with Bob and the tension of seeing his slow progress was taking it out of her.

Bob was out of bed when Peter got there. As he parked he had expected to see Bob's car, which Marcia was now throwing around the lanes of Calella en route to her daily visit to the hospital. There was no sign of Marcia's presence in the private room that Bob had apparently 'bought' for himself now that he was not wired up to the essential diagnostic lifelines, which had been monitoring him to recovery.

On seeing Peter, Bob got up briskly from the chair, then quickly sat back down again.

"Peter! I was so pleased to see you I forgot, I can't rush about at the moment. I got up too quickly then and my old legs nearly went beneath me. Do me a favour, old mate, no need to tell Marcia about that, she's become a worrier. Christ knows why. For God's sake, she should really be getting me to run round the block after her in a little pair of those hot pants she wears so well, because if I snuff it, she'll inherit the lot, plus a couple of useful insurances."

Peter had heard from his mother that Bob was going through a cynical phase, peppered with a bit of phobia about the inevitability of dying. The doctors said this was not unusual in somebody who now knew that they had knocked on death's door and, while the lock had apparently jammed and they'd been refused immediate entry, they saw their survival as a mere remission, and a loan of time.

"Come on, Bob," Peter retorted, "I'm sure that's not fair. The last thing Marcia wants is to become a rich young widow. She's absolutely dedicated to getting you well enough to go home, and to get you treatment there and recovered enough to at least walk beside her at pace, hot pants, mini-skirt or jeans and all that."

"You're OK, aren't you Peter? I can tell you now, and it's not the warfarin bringing the rat instinct out of me, but I can tell when somebody wants me to turn my back so that he can make a pass at my young missus. Oh, and there are plenty of them who do. Some call themselves best mates. But you. Well, I suppose you can have anybody you want anyway. The guys behind the bar at the hotel reckon you had that Michelle, some chambermaid and your nice little girlfriend all within the same week and could still beat most of the blokes at tennis too.

"So, Peter, there's a couple of things to say. Firstly, I gather I've got to thank you for saving my life, that's what they say. That gives me the option of dying again and making Marcia a rich widow, or fighting on to get over this new hurdle in my life and seeing it through for a few more years." He held out his hand. "So there's a very genuine thank you for all that you did. I'm just sorry I wasn't alert enough at the time to know exactly what you did do… but if it was you who gave me the kiss of life, I want you to know I didn't appreciate you tonguing me in front of all those people… but seriously, Marcia and I can't thank you enough."

He drank a glass of water. "Secondly, and I'd best warn you there's a third thing coming up… secondly, though, Marcia's washed up. I'm about to say the plan is to go home in about two weeks from now. The quacks say they'll have had enough of me by then. Now, when we get home, I don't want Marcia looking as though she's done in and needs a holiday. So I'm going to say that as I'm having physiotherapy here in the mornings, I don't want her interfering. So I'd like to put a regimen in place for her. She needs to get up and run in the morning. Get some regular breakfast inside her. Some more exercise with maybe tennis with yourself or Michelle, some sun on her body, it's faded already, a salad lunch and then she can get to see me from about four until 6.30. That way I'll rest up and get fit for the journey, and she'll be recovered by the time we get home."

"Sorry, I don't understand. What's my part in all that?"

"Look, mate. I've said I trust you. I'd like to hire you to make the lady run before breakfast. I remember her saying on the first day she'd come across this rampant stag on her morning run, and that she'd set her sights on him as a target to run the legs off. She pointed you out later. She does that to make me jealous, but over the weeks, as I've said, I don't reckon you want to have your legs run off by this committed lady. So I'll hire you for that at whatever your coach rate is. The same for the tennis to either you or Michelle, and then for you to ensure she listens to you and rests up for a bit of sun. She'll sort herself out from there on for a sensible lunch and then to get herself dressed up to impress me."

"Bob, I'd do all that willingly. I don't want paying."

"Oh no, old mate. You get paid and then I know you'll get her sorted, but with no strings attached. So we'll agree a price. Leave that to me." He looked at his watch. "We've got ten minutes for the next bit. Before Marcia's due. One thing she is, she's always on time."

"Where is she? I expected she'd be here because the message I got was that you both wanted to see me."

"We do. That's the third point. It's a joint request. But I sent her off to get some clothes as a treat and then on to a hairdresser and a bit of a pampering. I upset her by saying she looked washed out. Well! You know how girls don't like to hear that. Enough to say she explained in graphic expletives that it was my bloody fault that she was drained. The fags, the cigars, the booze, the diabetes, and now… well, she did intimate that she didn't even know I'd got a heart until it nearly conked out… so that's where she is. We understand you've got a change of plan and you're now coming to England to study."

"Yes, Westminster Polytechnic."

"Get used to calling it 'Regent Street Poly'. I had a lot of mates go through there. Bloody good it is too. OK, so how do you get to England?"

"I fly in a couple of weeks' time."

"You're not using your loaf. Why don't you cadge a lift?"

"Loaf? Cadge a lift? Sorry, I don't understand."

"I'm suggesting that you ride in our car. Loaf is a funny English expression for brain, and to cadge is a strange way of saying 'grab at or catch' a lift, lift being 'ride'. Strange old language, isn't it, mate!"

"What, you mean with you and Marcia?"

"Broadly speaking, yes, except to be honest, you do the driving."

"Shit. That's got to be about 800 miles, hasn't it?"

"Thereabouts, but we make two overnight stops, and we pay for the hotel. I pay you £1,000, about a quarter of a million pesetas to do the driving… and in case you think it's the rat poison they're dosing me on, if we were to fly, we'd have to go up-front first class, then we'd have to repatriate the car, flying could kill me off, they say, and it's a sodding long way by boat. So we'd be in pocket at £1,000. Besides – and I don't know why you make me tell you the truth, but you do – we've got a holiday insurance that pays for all this medical treatment plus any help I need to get me home.

"And there's a bonus for you, too. We would take a little nurse along with us who's been looking after me some of the time here. The hospital would hire her out to me and, if you approve and would want me to, I could insist she looks after you too, that would save the insurers an extra room for a couple of nights. You've got a minute to make your mind up. Herself will be here then, and besides, you've exhausted me."

The thought of three days or so of breathing in Chanel was reason enough to say yes. If the money wasn't Bob's (but in any event he could obviously afford it), then that was certainly a further reason to take the job.

"It's fine with me," Peter said, just as the door opened.

If they had been sitting in a box at Ascot on Ladies' Day and Marcia had walked in, she would have done justice to any haute couturier, save that she wasn't wearing a hat. She was clad in a white suit with black polka dots. The jacket had wide shoulder pads and tight-fitting three-quarter-length sleeves. Her Rolex and simple wedding and engagement rings added sparkle to the tailoring. The lapels were cut to show a respectable amount of cleavage, giving any interested onlooker a hint of what could be revealed later, perhaps. The jacket flared over her shapely hips and fitted down snugly around the top of the matching pencil skirt, which shortened her normal stride by at least half. The hem was about two inches above her knees and her legs tapered down into black stilettos with solid front and open heel. She carried a bold red leather bag and her hair was piled high with a matador's lady's comb holding the sculpture in place.

"Hi, darling," she said, strutting across to Bob's chair. As she did, it was patently obvious she had emptied a whole bottle of perfume over herself.

She had almost ignored Peter during her grand entrance. Now she kissed Bob's forehead, and then turned to Peter. She dangled a limp right hand, which stiffened once held, and leant forward to brush his cheek with hers. She stood back and placed her hands on her hips.

"Bob was grumpy and said I looked washed out. He couldn't see any point in saving his money up just to make me a rich widow. So what do you think?" She executed a sex-oozing 360-degree spin before parading again with hands on the areas Peter knew were wrapped in lace and silk which was black and beautiful. He could never forget that.

"I'd say not washed up beyond redemption. Perhaps a few pounds up on weight, where your muscles are being ignored. You're a bit pale so you possibly could do with a little more light tan, but overall you're close to a pass."

"What did you fucking say? I'm overweight and white?"

"Well, not those words…"

"You bastard! You're worse than he is and I don't have to take it from you. But… in a professional capacity… what would you do about it?"

"Are you serious?"

"Oh yes. More serious than you would ever imagine."

Bob started to laugh. "Now, now, children, this can't be doing my health any good. So… what *would* you do, coach?" Bob enquired.

"At 7.30am, a gentle jog, then 8.45 to 9.00, light breakfast. Ten – tennis for one hour, 11.15 to 1.30, relaxation. Swimming. Sun, then 2pm, a light lunch. That's all I'd need."

"… And that, dear Peter, is what you have frigging got! You're on!" Marcia ruled.

Bob couldn't believe how clever this young lad was.

"Have you asked Peter about sharing the driving with me?" Marcia asked aggressively.

"No."

"Oh, why not?"

"Because I asked him if he'd drive all the way."

"That's over 800 miles, isn't it?"

"Yes!"

"Well?" demanded Marcia.

Peter interrupted. "I'd be delighted."

"… And you'll stay with us in Dulwich for your first week?"

Peter looked at Bob. Bob shrugged. "Sorry, mate. That's Marcia's idea. She's all maternal about you being alone in a foreign land and wants to keep an eye on you… for your mother."

"Well, I expect I'll need to continue a bit of coaching once you're back," Peter countered.

"Bloody cheek!" Marcia concluded. "I'll be fit and sleek by then, by all accounts."

CHAPTER 4

When Peter and the film The Graduate eventually caught up with each other, he could see the resemblance between his own position and the one Dustin Hoffman found himself in, certainly from the point of view that neither had wanted to turn up to their own party. Dustin Hoffman's had the benefit of seeing him welcomed home; Peter's was a farewell do, and it was steeped in a downcast atmosphere for a variety of different reasons.

Maria. Well, Maria was temporarily, maybe, losing a son. A son, indeed, who had virtually become her life following Paco's accident. She would try to remain philosophical and look forward to his welcome home party, but at the moment, during the 'adiós' party she had arranged, she was having to force herself to appear cheerful.

She could see Marco's unhappiness about the break in his relationship with Peter because, when he was really stressed, he quietly overdid his drinking allowance. It only showed to her and Virginia, but tonight that seemed to be the intended route through which he would be drowning his sorrows. Marco had also come to rely on Peter's balanced male input to a number of issues: maintenance, future development, handling male staffing problems were just a few of the areas in which they were jointly involved.

Peter had no idea who his mother had invited. "Just a few old friends who'll miss you," she had said.

"Oh, Mother! I'd rather not have to face that. I'm bound to miss them, too, so it's going to be bad for all of us."

"Darling, just leave it to me," Maria had promised.

So why the hell was he going to miss Meribel? You'd have thought she'd have developed a tactful bout of flu or some such reason for not coming. But she did come, although, probably because Peter did not share a great deal of his time with her, she was an early leaver.

Carlos Sanchez, the librarian mayor, was likewise an early bird. He arrived sufficiently early to see Peter's final site layout.

"Very, very impressive, young man. When will you submit it for approval?"

"I'm told I can get good copies made from my final traced overlay in the

UK. I have the parish application forms to fill in. It would help if I got a letter of sponsorship to the scheme from you and then, as you know, it gets onto the faster route to approval. Anyway, by Christmas it'll be in."

"Well done," Carlos said, patting Peter's broad back.

Just then, young Jaimé came bounding up to Peter with a rolled-up piece of parchment; in fact it was watercolour paper, tied with a red ribbon. He thrust it into Peter's hand.

"Can I open it?" Peter asked by pointing at his chest with one finger and signifying slitting the bow with a knife and unrolling the paper tube.

There was lots of breathing and posturing by Jaimé's to encourage the word, "Si," to flood out on an outward thermal from his lungs. Jaimé couldn't keep still and even helped Peter unroll the paper tube.

"Wow!" Peter exclaimed. He looked at Jaimé, who was now quiet. "Wow, Jaimé!"

It was just brilliant. Jaimé had only seen Peter's layout once, a few days earlier and, in Peter's opinion, even then he had not had a really good look at it. Certainly not too surprisingly, because of the communication factor, there had not been any questions at the time. Yet Jaimé had produced a black pen and ink perspective, as though from the cockpit in an airliner about 100 feet up before landing right in the centre of the development. Every detail was present and Jaimé had introduced a couple of daubs of watercolour just here and there. A little blue in the sky, some hint of green trees and orange sunflowers, a few red roof tiles and pastel shades on a couple of walls of the little houses.

A tear ran down Peter's cheek. He moved across to show Carlos and then his mother and Marco. They were all taken aback.

Bob Hunt insisted he would not be in a wheelchair at the party. He had a couple of sticks he didn't use very well, but which made him feel secure. He stood upright now, to make a point that he was well on the road to recovery.

"What's that, mate?" he shouted brusquely, not wanting to be left out of something that was obviously getting some attention around Peter.

"Well, you've yet to see the plans of Girasol," said Peter. "We were close to looking at them when you decided to take yourself off to the hospital. It didn't seem appropriate to bring them in there. But what all the fuss is about is that this young man, who you've not met yet in depth, has produced a perspective of how he thinks the development might look."

Bob sort of grunted with disdain in a wild judgement of what he had yet to see. However, when he saw the actual drawing, he pulled back.

"He didn't do this!" he said knowledgeably. "He couldn't have. This is the work of a trained architect turned artist. He's nicked it!"

Peter was offended. "Bob! You'll have to take that back. Jaimé *did* do this. I've seen him do it before, and I have to say he's improving with very little training. I have a view. I feel he may be autistic beneath being a deaf mute. God gave him this talent to make up for the mistakes or malfunctions of birth."

Bob turned to the boy. "Sorry, son. OK, I give you the benefit of the doubt."

'The boy' didn't react.

Peter explained. "If you want him to understand, try this." Peter pointed to Bob, then indicated a hypothetical speaking sound coming from Bob's mouth: "He says…" then, pointing at Bob again, with a finger mimicking an invisible tear, "… he's sorry."

Jaimé gave a thumbs-up sign. Took a deep breath and out came: "OK." Peter was gobsmacked. He laughingly looked at Jaimé and said, "Yes, no and now OK."

Jaimé laughed with him. "OK," he said again.

Suddenly Peter's attention was ripped from his immediate surroundings. He was Dustin Hoffman personified. Here was a guest he did not want to encounter. Well, less of a guest, more just somebody there.

"¿Te gusta beber algo?" It was the tantalising Tania again.

Peter's face broke into a smile. "How did you wangle your sweet little butt in here?"

"Mr Peter!" she replied in shock, dropping her face to the ground with accentuated hurt. He did not react.

"Your mother said would I do her a favour and pass drinks round and tapas for overtime."

"Do you have a red wine?"

"Si, Señor."

She spun her tray of mixed drinks round and Peter collected his request.

"I want to say good luck and adiós while I can, Mr Peter."

He was touched. "Look…" he started to say, when he was interrupted by Marcia.

"Waitress, do you have a very dry martini?" she enquired.

Tania explained that she didn't but could go and get one.

"Please," Marcia said, "I won't move while I discuss our journey with Mr Peter."

Tania shot off to the bar. She wanted to be quick.

"You know, Peter," Marcia said, "it shows that you fancy a little bit of rough."

"Marcia! That's unfair."

"Well, it's up to you. That girl – it's Tania, isn't it? – she is a little bit of rough, but it shows that you feel safer in her company than in mine. You'll run your backside off to make me sweat behind you, but with her you're won over

52

without her having to do anything more than encourage you to look down her gypsy cleavage. Take one long last look. Here she comes, fortunately with a martini. You've got quality cleavage to look down for the next three days."

As Tania returned, Marcia ruffled Peter's hair in fun, and said in a loud voice, "Don't you make a pass at me. Otherwise I won't share the driving with you for the next three days."

Tania worked out what had been said. Her stomach churned. But she had come to terms with the situation. She had nothing other than a bike, now with a dynamo, and a body with which to gain Peter's attention. Mrs Marcia had style, money, a Bentley and an ailing husband, and, in Tania's inexperienced view, a body, if need be, as available as her own, except, if it was used or abused, it did not have the backup of Toni and the cousins to teach lessons.

So Tania moved away to do the drink rounds.

Bob needed bed and commanded that his wife join him on their last night in the Playa. They both instructed Peter that they were to leave by 9am the next day at the latest.

The three had rehearsed the route, which was finally determined to be Calella – Leave 9am. La Jonquera (Spanish border) – 10am – allow for traffic – say 10.30am. Le Boulou – say 11am. Perpignan/Narbonne – say midday. Light lunch in Narbonne. Narbonne/Carcassonne/Toulouse. Cahors approximately 5-6pm. Stay over. That, hopefully, would be day one. "See you bright and early in the morning!" Peter shouted happily.

Miguel and Michelle, now very much an item, said their fond farewells and said they reckoned to go and see Peter in the UK. José was clearly looking after Maria's emotions but Marco, somewhat worse for drink, was certainly not dancing attendance on Virginia.

Virginia gave Peter a tearful hug and asked for a promise that he would look after himself. As Peter returned her cuddle, he could just see Marco giving Tania something of a dressing down on the other side of the patio.

One by one they left.

Maria and José made up the appropriate quartet of a family circle, with Marco and Peter. Maria took the lead.

"OK, Pedro. One kiss now and that's adiós. You'd better bloody write though."

It was one kiss and a hold to eternity. Then she turned and said, "… And you'd better come home quietly. I'm tired." As she broke away, Peter noticed the front of his shirt was soaking wet from the silent tears Maria had shed.

José shook Peter's hand and put an arm round his shoulder. "I'll look after her," he said securely. He followed Maria away.

Marco was furtive. "Listen, son. I'm not going to be into all this emotion. Good luck. But I bloody want to see you before Christmas." And he scurried off, Peter presumed, for a secret cigarette down on the rocks.

All had gone.

Peter turned round. He'd felt eyes burning into the back of his head. Tania looked radiant in the moonlight. A tear ran down her cheek.

"Tania."

"Mr Peter."

Peter leant forward and offered his cheek.

"Beware of the witch in Mrs Marcia," she said.

Peter laughed. "I can look after myself. You're a funny complicated thing, Tania."

"I've nearly finished. Can I just say goodbye to you once? Could I meet you on the rocks in five minutes? I promise I won't be trouble. I swear Toni won't be around."

It was exactly what Peter needed. To cast some oats in what had become his own home territory.

"In five minutes," he agreed. "But a minute later, and I'll have been whisked away by the demons sweeping me into England and the New World."

A couple of other members of staff bade their farewells. Peter was a popular chap.

Damn it, he said to himself. *Condom!* He dared not go to the cottage just for that. His mother would be full of questions. Tania would have one. Yes, he was sure she would. He would slip into the hotel, though, and have a quick freshen up.

He used the urinal and smiled about his mother's influence as he washed his hands. He splashed water onto his tiring face and took a little of the house cologne, which he rubbed around the back of his neck.

He'd got a couple of minutes' walk to the rocks which, according to his watch, would make him that much late. She'd wait. She wasn't under the threat of demons to sweep her anywhere in a hurry.

A couple of minutes earlier, Marco was about to throw the butt of his cigar into the gently swirling water on the edge of the rocks when he heard hurried footsteps coming down the path beside the pool and towards him. They were female steps, determined and coping well with the slight feminine heels that ricocheted off the flag pavings. As the sound of the steps got nearer, he used the benefit of the moon behind him to identify first the form, then the face. It was Tania. Come to find him, no doubt.

She had not picked out his normal bulk as she knew it. He was camouflaged in his black evening suit against the rocks he was leaning against. So when he grabbed her right arm, she jumped.

"Tania!"

"Oh! Mr Marco!" she said, first in surprise, then shock, and then in horror as she realised the suddenly changed situation.

"Have you come for your pocket money, my dear?" he enquired.

What could she say? "I'm on a promise to screw your nephew"? or... "I'm just out for a walk."

"Oh, Mr Marco..." She repeated the words to give her thinking time. "Tonight's not a good night."

"Huh! Be careful I don't choose your payday not to be a good day, my girl."

"No, Mr Marco. You have to understand. It's female. I really don't feel like pocket money."

The drink in Marco gave him enormous strength, dampened his brain and took any gram of compassion out of his body. He grabbed Tania's wrist firmly, and pulled her forcibly towards the changing room. It was still unlocked. Marco could hear footsteps crunching the gravel higher up on the path leading to the pool.

"Rapido, rapido!" he insisted, pushing her into the changing room. He took the key from the lock on the outside of the door. Let go as she semi-fell inwards in front of him, but was able to twist and land lying on the floor cushioned by her right arm. Marco locked the door from the inside.

"Listen, you silly girl, you owe me from the time I treated you to money in the girls' locker room, but I won't make too much of a point out of that." He put his hand into his hip pocket where he kept a roll of notes. He never used a wallet. He peeled off a 1000 peseta note and clumsily sat her up, undid the top buttons of her black blouse and pushed the note into her cleavage.

The footsteps that had disturbed the gravel at the higher level were now close. He put his hand over her mouth and leant forward and whispered in her ear: "Shut up! Be a good girl. Do what you're told... what you're paid for and you won't get hurt. Make a fuss... and you will... what's wrong with you? You usually can't get enough of me or my money."

"I've told you. I've got my girlie problem," she now whispered. Actually she was scared.

The footsteps had stopped. There was now the occasional shuffle. A slow walk up and down. Someone waiting. The changing room had been built with no windows. The footsteps suddenly became alive again and got louder as they approached the door between Marco and Tania and Marco's unwanted intruder. Marco's hand was firmly across Tania's mouth.

The tension and excitement that been aroused in Marco caused him to slide his left hand inside Tania's bra. She bit the palm of the hand across her mouth. He raised that hand with a clenched fist, as though to plunge it into her face. She did not move. She knew the sort of pain that would inflict. Toni had done that before and broken her nose. She didn't want that again.

God entered her world. He gave her the vision of Peter outside. Counting the seconds. He'd made it clear he was not going to wait around.

If she did deliver to Marco, which seemed inevitable if she was to remain conscious, then she couldn't just walk out of the changing room and say, "Hi! We've finished with each other now, here I am free to say one last goodbye to you!" God's message was she was not to be in Peter's world. He kept making that clear.

Marco was turned on by this ironic situation. He lowered his fist and cupped her chin in his strong right hand. He could break her jaw in one vice-like grip. He took his left hand from out of her bra and moved it down onto the buckle of his belt, which he undid. He deftly undid each fly button until his unsupported trousers fell to the ground. He took Tania's right hand and placed it round his left buttock and then the same with her left to his right thigh. He placed one hand behind her neck and guided her soft chin downwards. "You know what we like… give me a nice kiss and you might get a bonus, but only if you're good."

There was no emotion in Tania's performance of her duty to her patron. She was sickened by the inevitability of the situation. There'd be a bonus for her, no doubt. She was good. But then there would be no loving farewell to the man she really wanted to please, and in turn receive pleasure from.

She carried on silently, the silence broken only by the odd grunt of pleasure, like a pig finding an extra truffle in an otherwise barren, cold and unemotional wood. Certainly there was silence enough to hear Peter's sudden determination to leave the spot, where he had stood, to be fair, for a full eight extra minutes, to allow for the young lady being late. Almost like a guard outside Buckingham Palace, which Tania had seen once on a newsreel at the cinema, he sounded as if he had stood to attention and marched in quick time, passing the door to the changing room, up the flag path and, with diminishing sound, into the gravel leading back around the hotel complex.

They had both obviously worked out that whoever had been outside was no longer there. One final outburst from Marco indicated Tania's job was done. She stood up and put both arms around his neck and kissed him affectionately on his lips. However abused she felt with any of the men in her life, she could never ever complete her tasks and leave without a weird feeling inside her that they had paid her a compliment by choosing her for their pleasures. She normally rid herself of that strange feeling of tenderness with a thank you. When the money rolled in, the thanks were even more genuine.

Peter, meanwhile, was furious. The little bitch had played one final game with him.

"Good night, chiquito," his mother called out, "I'm missing you already."

Peter hesitated in his reply. "Mother, don't miss me, because on every night of every day I'll kiss you as I go to sleep and ask God to bless you and keep you safe… and I know that he will."

She choked on her tears.

"… Oh, and by the way, what more do I have to do to get you to drop this wretched 'chiquito' thing?"

"Become a millionaire and produce a grandchild I can call chiquito. Now go to sleep, you've got a long drive in the morning."

CHAPTER 5

'Adiós' seemed to echo around the courtyard in front of the hotel. Marcia had brought the Bentley round earlier and had overseen the careful stacking of all their luggage into the boot so it wouldn't rattle and make Bob edgy on the journey. Peter and a couple of cases, along with the cardboard tube containing his site plan, which he was now beginning to guard with his life as he had yet to make a copy, were almost squeezed in as Marcia's many cases had taken prime space.

The nurse, Gina, promised to Peter by Bob as part of the deal, had arrived at about 7.30am as arranged. The hospital had highly recommended her. Although she was only 21, she had done two years' nursing in the UK, so could communicate adequately with her charge. She'd been hired for the planned three-day journey and the first couple of days back in England, at the end of which she would have a ticket for her return flight.

Maria was cheerful, under the circumstances. She had already exchanged adiós with Peter. It had started with her going into Peter's bedroom at about 6.30am and announcing that she was awake. As then was Peter. "Give me a big hug," she had demanded. They held each other like figurines produced in quality porcelain by Lladro. Then, as if fuelled by the comfort she had gained from that close contact, she changed gear into maternal lecture mode.

"Buy Marcia some flowers to thank her for their hospitality… open a bank account to put Bob's payment into… where's your passport…? Don't rush into bed with the first English girl you meet… they're a bit quick at taking that opportunity, I understand… get plenty of sleep… work hard…"

"Mother! Give it a break. The one thing you haven't told me to do… I need to do… it's a long journey and I need to make sure I've been to the loo… so… if you'll excuse me… I need to go." As he got out of bed, he softened his sternness with another big hug and a kiss on Maria's forehead.

"Y no laves ese lugar antes yo vuelvo para darte otro beso," she chided him.

Peter knew what she meant but was bound to wash the spot on his forehead she had kissed. But he'd remember that farewell kiss and assured her he would not, in fact, wash the trace of her kiss away.

Bob was not the man he had been when he arrived, and Maria was sad about that. He was no longer confident and jaunty, but then he'd had a near miss, so he had been told by the doctors.

"Anyway," as Maria said to him hopefully, "they know the problem and they'll put you right when you get home. And I've reserved you the same three weeks here for next year... so you'd better work at getting very right by then."

Marcia appreciated Maria's tone and optimism. They had built up a great understanding relationship, despite the years that separated them. "And we'll look after your Pedro, and when he's in his own bed-sit I'll go across and push the harem girls out every now and again and give the place a clean up," she promised.

Peter heard that. "You keep your hands off my girlfriends. They're like sofas to me – move them around a bit but clean around them... that's unless my mother's coming to do some shopping... then maybe you could put them into storage somewhere for me."

They all laughed, though for Maria it was a little strained.

"Are you driving?" Peter eventually said to Marcia.

"Could you get us over the border into France as the first leg? I'll watch Bob doesn't get too worked up. He's had a tablet to keep him calm. Besides, it looks as though Gina wants you to look at her knees for a while. She was wearing white trousers when she arrived this morning, now she's met the chauffeur and she already looks like something out of the King's Road."

"King's Road?" Peter enquired.

"Oh, you'll find it, that's for sure. A hunk like you won't get 20 metres away from Peter Jones without finding a young lady on your arm."

"Hookers?" Peter asked.

"Good God, no! You won't need hookers. These'll be debutantes, young ladies of fashion looking for the final necessary accoutrement – a young stag!"

"Oh, come on... I'm not easy!"

Marcia paused. "So you actually know that, dear Peter, do you? I'd thought I'd never hear you admit to that... so you're human after all."

She did laugh as she completed her verbal undressing of Peter Carlos Martinez, but there was more than a hint that she actually meant what she said. Not in spite. In fact.

It was eventually Bob who summoned up all his old reserves. "OK, folks. Let's get this show on the road."

Peter looked good behind the wheel. He was relaxed. A few blown kisses, and his sights, and those of his passengers, were set on La Janquera.

Figueras was upon them in no time, with its sign to Rosas to the east about 21 kilometres away. That had seemed such a long way back from there, that day with Uncle Marco, after Paco's death. He'd thought it a real journey, but here he was now with a much longer one facing him, and one under his control.

The first leg, with a number of stops for varying reasons, went generally according to plan. Even to the extent that about as far as Marcia got to the steering wheel was sitting next to Peter during most of the afternoon, while Bob snoozed and remembered to wake just a sufficient number of times to get a peep at Gina's lower thighs.

Peter could see Marcia was concerned about getting Bob home. She would joke occasionally to break some ice, or comment if she saw an advertising hoarding with a product worth a mention. But her hands fidgeted. She'd already worn her deep red nail-varnish off her right thumb, where she kept picking at it with her forefinger. Her left hand seemed to have nowhere to go. She slid it up and down the seam of her left trouser leg and let it stray at any given opportunity onto Peter's right jean-clad thigh, which she patted to give herself some reassuring comfort, rather than as a mark of affection, which Peter's body interpreted it as being.

Peter would say, "Petrol station coming up with toilets, café and fuel. Who'd like to stop?"

"Oh, good idea," Marcia would say on every occasion, sealed by a pat on his thigh or knee. The hand would linger for the security it seemed to gain, but would then be withdrawn, back to do its insecure wandering. Peter thought how well Marcia looked, back in trim. He'd worked her hard, and it showed. As he'd expected, her Chanel went straight to his nostrils.

Marcia had enjoyed the route through the Pyrénées Orientales and then the flat plain with occasional glimpses of the sea through Perpignan. Peter got them all navigating as they approached Narbonne.

"If we miss the Toulouse turn-off we're in for a longer, busier journey, so keep your eyes peeled for any sign saying Limoges or Toulouse."

Almost as one they had picked out the road as it came up and Peter was safely on course.

"Well done!" Marcia said, with a comforting rub of his thigh.

It was dusk as they arrived at Cahors. They found the Chateau that Marcia had researched and chosen for this first stop.

Bob had travelled well enough and certainly kept his humour. "So we're going to check in here, guys," he announced, then eyed Peter and Gina. "Now, do you two young things want to do an old man a financial favour and share a room, or are you going to be prudish and expensive?"

Peter had caught Gina's eye as Bob had said it. He was used to such humour; better still, he knew that Bob actually meant it.

Gina had a soft look on her face.

"Well, we'll give it a try," Peter announced.

Her expression changed. "Prudish and expensive please, Mr Hunt."

"Oh!" Peter said, with feigned sadness.

"Well, OK," Bob said. "But in the morning I'll get Marcia to check if both sets of sheets have been used and, mark my words, if they haven't, you'll get one room tomorrow night."

Gina laughed. "Then in that case, Mrs Hunt, we'll make sure we crumple up the linen as soon as we arrive. But the idea is anyway, Mr Hunt, that I do spend some time in your room through the night, so that Mrs Hunt can get her own quality sleep. That's what the doctor's instructed. So when you wake you'd best ask which one of us is there if you want anything."

"Won't be bothered about that," he said firmly. "I'll want the same from both of you."

"He's feeling better," Marcia announced to the chauffeur and nurse.

Bob was to have a light meal in his room and Marcia said she would join him and then perhaps have a coffee with the others. Then Gina could do a short stint and they could share some sort of rota. Marcia had had many disturbed nights, constantly either worrying about Bob when he was in hospital, or semi-nursing him in the week that he had been allowed back at the hotel. So if she had four or five hours at a stretch, she was sure she would feel like a new born baby.

As they shared dinner together, Peter apologised to Gina for joining Bob in their earlier male banter over the sleeping arrangements. They got on well and Gina gave him a number of hints about London living. How to use the tube, when to go to Horse Guards, not to miss this and that. She'd enjoyed London but thought she would gain more freelance work in the tourist area of her homeland where, as on this commission, she could earn well. She didn't know why but the English particularly were prone to the odd serious illness once they got abroad.

After the drive, Marcia had showered quickly and changed into a smart red skirt, which Peter thought he'd seen before, and a matching chiffon blouse. Peter thought that was probably for his benefit, to tantalise him, but in fact it had been Bob's request when she'd asked him what she should change into just to pop down for a coffee.

"Depends," Bob said. "Am I well enough to watch you dress?"

Marcia was really pleased to hear Bob say that. He'd been so low for so long. It was probably the relief of being on his way home that had relaxed him.

"Of course you are." She knew that would signify she'd be looking a bit tarty by the time he had chosen. She bet to herself it would be one of her red and black combinations.

"OK," he said. "High black stilettos with a red skirt. Then a red blouse… is it chiffon? I mean, you know, a bit see-through… ? Yes, red chiffon blouse and I'll leave the rest up to you."

"All black, I think. Don't you?"

"Yes. I'd suppose so."

Now here she was, presumably having tucked Bob up, with Peter, who was still thinking the get-up was for him. Gina took her leave. Peter and Marcia together were always relaxed. Bob sometimes made her spiky, and that rubbed off when there were three or more of them together. Just the two, they got on like a house on fire.

"Thanks for doing all the driving."

"That's OK."

"Thanks for getting me in trim."

"That's fine."

"Thanks for saving Bob. You know I can't thank you enough for that."

"Rubbish."

She talked and talked. There was no scratching away at nail polish. Eventually Peter said he needed to get to bed.

"You must be tired," Marcia agreed. "What about me coming and giving you a goodnight story?"

Peter laughed. "I'd love it, but then I might stay awake all night."

"So don't you want that… if I was by your side?"

Of course Peter did, he was only human. But he'd keep his guard up.

"Of course I do," he eventually admitted, "but tomorrow I'll be driving a good 500 miles if we're to hit Fontainebleau by the evening. So I'd best not take the risk."

"You know you're a very unapproachable young man, Peter. I couldn't be more fond of somebody, or want to show my gratitude more but… well, you'll see for yourself when you go to the Tower of London, where a number of young ladies have lost their heads. You're like a knight in shining armour. But in your case you never drop your guard or take off that steel front to allow a person to come in. I'll see you in the morning."

She got up. He knew she was fairly seriously disturbed, definitely frustrated that he wouldn't let her break down his defences, and slightly insulted by the fact he did not find her irresistible.

"Marcia." He called her back.

"Yes, Peter."

"Do we run in the morning?"

"Oh yes, Peter," she said sarcastically. "I want to be in trim for all the other guys, for when they drop their guards."

Peter stood up and put a strong arm around her slightly trembling shoulder.

"You've had a bad time. Get some sleep. We'll have a slow jog round this estate as soon as you're ready. You can go ten yards in front of me, and I'll fancy your every stride."

"You, Peter, are the world's greatest bastard." She lifted herself onto her toes and kissed his cheek. "And I hope you die of an erection during the night thinking about it."

"I could well do," he said with a smile. "But what a way to go, eh! See you in the morning. Knock me up as you go by."

"Gosh, your command of English is really improving! Who taught you that?"

He looked quizzical. He would ask Gina if it was a double entendre.

God, now he was tired. Peter smiled as he climbed into the king-sized bed, wondering if Gina, for fun, would rough her sheets up so much that it would appear the bed had been shared. He had followed his usual wash and teeth routine. Why, he didn't know, but he always combed his hair before climbing into bed. He selected his preferred number of pillows and lay for a while studying the elaborate cornices and moulded ceiling. It was a lovely room with, he did not doubt, a great history.

He closed his eyes and as he did, he had visions of the road before him and the trees in the avenues flashing past, and the constant athletic groan of the Bentley's tuned and honed engine. He hoped that would not stop his sleep.

"God bless Mother," he said silently, "and Dad, wherever he is, Marco and Virginia, Marcia…" he paused on Marcia, "… and Bob, and Gina, Tania…" (What had happened to her, he'd really thought she'd meant it) "… Michelle, Meribel… Laura." Laura lived somewhere in these parts, perhaps he should have looked her up. Bless Jaimé, he prayed, so that he might produce wondrous artistic results with brush pen and vocal cords…

He never did remember how he ended his own way of praying. He usually fell off to sleep midstream. This night was no different. But then he'd had reason for that. The emotional disturbance of leaving and the 'Adiós' with so many, and then the drive.

Bob slept fitfully but Gina came into her own professional self. Each time he awoke she let him know she was there and on every occasion soothed him back to sleep. Marcia had returned after coffee and stayed till about one, then moved into the second room in the suite. That had given her a long, for her, five hours of sleep by the time she woke at six, nowadays her normal waking time.

It took her a few moments to work out where she was and that Bob was only through the adjoining doors. She gazed at the ceiling, recalling that Bob had begun making all sorts of innuendo about sharing beds, and how she had not wanted to be a party to Peter and Gina having the luxury of sharing space. She had a memory of spilling out her anger at Peter's lack of interest in the body he was so anxious to keep in trim. Bob was certainly in no state to do anything other than look at the goods in the window. Peter, she was sure, was well able to go in and buy, but was doggedly resisting.

Frustration apart, she felt really good. She put a light robe on and went in to see how Bob was.

Gina was asleep, curled up on a chaise longue, and Bob was propped up in the middle of about six pillows. He opened one eye as Marcia approached.

"Did I wake you?"

"No. Your perfume did. I knew you were here."

"What sort of night have you had?"

"Good, I think. What's the time?"

"Just gone six."

"You're up and about."

"I said I'd run."

"Can't you give it a miss? Stay and talk. You're nice and trim now."

"No, I think I'll run. You have your early morning tablet, it'll make you sleep a bit. Gina'll hear you if you want anything, and when I'm back and showered we'll go to the restaurant for a light breakfast. How's that?"

"Sounds good."

"You've got water?"

"Yes, here."

"Here's your pill."

She watched him take it. Both his eyes closed. She leant over and kissed his forehead. She left the curtains closed and tip-toed out into the outer bed area, then went straight to the bathroom. Dropped her robe and splashed her body with light warm water. It seemed to enliven the Chanel shower wash from the evening before. She brushed her hair and returned to the bedroom, where her Adidas hot pants were waiting to embellish her body. Unusually, she always ran bra-less, relying upon her matching black running top, which fitted her like a glove. The inside of the zip was cold against her cleavage. It would soon warm up. She slipped into her running shoes and slid out through the door. Gina's room was next, then Peter's.

She crooked her forefinger to knock on his door, as she had threatened. Sure, she'd knock him up. Oh yes, one day she would! But something stopped her. Her hand dropped to the circular door knob, which was brass with a smooth enamel bulbous surface that was cool to the touch. She turned it to the left, fully expecting it to revolve only so far, with the door locked from the inside. Then she'd knock. But the knob kept turning and, with a little pressure from her left shoulder, she found the door opening before her.

What a silly lad, she thought. He could have had everything stolen. She quietly entered the outer lobby, closing the suite door gently behind her. The door to the bedroom was about a quarter open. Peter appeared to be still asleep. The light bedclothes were pushed down around his waist. He was on his back with head turned slightly towards the open door.

He had a lovely physique and, asleep, looked even more handsome with all his face muscles relaxed. He had a strong early morning beard. Marcia realised how groomed he always looked when shaved.

The sun was just beginning to shine onto the bed. *A film director couldn't have made Peter look more beautiful… enticing,* she thought. She slipped out of her trainers, closed the bedroom door and tip-toed across to the bed. She had no idea how to cope with the intimacy of this situation. She could jump on top of him and scream, "Now take me!" But that somehow was not how she'd wanted it to be.

No, none of that was to be. She would simply surprise him, drag him out of bed and continue their brother-sister relationship. She was not one to impose on anybody.

So this will shock him, she resolved, lightly taking a corner of the sheet and duvet covering the lower part of his body.

With one great heave, she pulled it back and at the same moment said loudly, "Get up and run, you lazy bugger!"

He was awake in a split second, to find her staring down at his face. Instinctively, he started to sit up. He didn't say a word. He looked down the bed and she followed his gaze.

"Shit!" she said, and paused. "So at last, my darling Peter, you show me some emotion, a welcome. You're pleased to see me."

They were both staring at the evidence that he didn't wear trunks in bed, and at his manliness.

Marcia held her hand out for his, and his fingers were drawn towards hers as though magnetised. She sat on the edge of the bed, and took his hand to the zip to her top. His involuntarily unzipping exposed everything he had always secretly had such a yearning to hold, to mould, to kiss… oh, for them to be his, for a rationed period of time.

She leant towards him. He had no resistance to offer. It seemed the most natural thing in the world and so he kissed her breasts fondly and with enormous artistic appreciation.

What followed was a veritable impromptu erotic ballet, the strength of the one party complemented by the honed and trained body of the other. There was more longing than animal lust, just an entwinement until both bodies expired with explosive joy.

They lay side by side, looking into the depths of each other's eyes.

Marcia broke the silence.

"Christ! Peter, that was the most beautiful 20 minutes of my life."

"Who was timing?"

"I counted each second and divided by 60."

They laughed.

Marcia took both Peter's hands into hers. "Can I tell you a secret?"

"I think you're going to."

"You really want to hear it?"

"Go on, I can't wait."

"OK. Cross my heart and hope to die. I've never made love before."

"Sorry? Do you mean never had intercourse before?"

"Yes. Yes. I've never ever done that before."

"But there's Bob."

"I'll explain some day, but there's never been Bob, or anyone else. Just you. You're my first."

Peter lay silent, then: "Do you want to hear my secret?"

"Oh Peter, you're so sweet. You don't have to... you won't make it any better... it's how we've just made love that counts."

"I'm not just saying it. What's the expression? Cross my heart and hope I die. But you're my first, too."

"I can't bloody be!"

"Really and truly, cross my heart too."

"Meribel?"

"Oh no."

"Michelle."

"No."

"Nobody?"

"Nobody."

"Then how did we both know what to do?"

"We're animals."

"Oh, Peter! We'll never forget each other for that then."

"I don't think we could."

In Peter's bathroom, Marcia fluffed her hair up as she looked in the mirror. "Well," she said to herself, "I can afford to look a little dishevelled, I've just been on a three-mile run. Shit! It feels like it too."

They'd agreed on the story that they had done a three-mile circuit around the grounds and adjoining forests, if asked by Bob or Gina.

Marcia passed Peter still lying in bed, now with the covers pulled right up and over his head.

"You alright under there?" she enquired.

"No, I'm dead, and I've been laid out to be embalmed."

She pulled the covers off his face. "Don't joke!"

"I'm sorry. I didn't think. But I feel dead."

"Serves you right for not being more fit."

"I'll see you at breakfast. Remember, three miles."

"Fine. Do I get one more kiss?"

"Just one light one, otherwise I'll be back in bed." He paused and looked at her. "What about the future, Marcia?"

"Let's just remember the stolen present. The future'll look after itself. Everything in this life is pre-determined."

She walked into the outer lobby of her suite, making out she was winding down after a hard run. She opened the door into the room Bob was in with Gina. He was awake.

"I'm back," she said. "How are you doing?"

"Gina's running me a bath."

"Do you want me to give you a hand or can I clean up my hot sweaty body?"

"You do that. What will you wear?"

"Whatever you ask."

"A skirt… and happy colours."

"So it shall be. But I'd like to wear a blouse as well, I'd catch cold."

They laughed. It was a world, and a day and a time, in that universe when she thought everybody was laughing.

It appeared nothing had changed between Peter and Marcia. The same amount of leg-pulling. No long, lingering glances (or perhaps they always gave each other those anyway).

Breakfast was light all round – that is, until Bob suddenly turned to the other three.

"I'm going to pay the bill. Did you check their sheets, Marcia?"

"Oh, Bob! You really don't want to know."

"I bloody do."

"Well, you'll be cross. Gina's hadn't been used…" they all looked shocked, "… on account of the fact she slept with you all night."

"Then we'll still only need three beds tonight."

"… And a chaise longue… and that also means Gina didn't have a good night's sleep, so she's allowed to drop off in the car."

"Then she's travelling next to me," Bob said chirpily.

CHAPTER 6

Peter kept his promise and, despite Marcia insisting he make a phone call home as soon as they arrived in Dulwich to say they'd had a safe journey, he found the notepaper Maria had said he would need to write to her on. He quickly developed a style of cramming in as much news as he could using the fewest words, and without too much emotion. Maria, on the other hand, wrote two or three lines a day in her responses, so Peter got amalgamated stories back rather than staccato, to-the-point memoranda.

Dear Mother,

Great journey. Drive not too strenuous. Bob did really well. Marcia was fine too. (He didn't like to say just how fine Marcia was.) She's worried about Bob. Gina was helpful to them both.

Dulwich house is nice. Pretty big. Lots of other houses around it. Nice garden with pool. All neighbours are pretty near, though.

London's big. Dulwich is in London and Bob says there's another seven or eight miles beyond us till you get to anything like fields or farmland. Seems London stretches from Calella to Rosas in the North and Barcelona in the South.

It's really big.

I've seen the Poly. Right in centre of London. Looked at some digs. More to look at. Been introduced to a chap called Max who's doing same course and in similar circumstances. Might flat-share with him.

Got copies done of Girasol at a place Bob knows. So not so worried if I lose the original now.

Not much other news. Just settling in. Love to you, Marco, Virginia and anyone else. Hope José's well and still mopping up the tears.

Love you. Pedro.

He knew she would like the Pedro touch.

Peter and Marcia really hadn't had a lot of time to talk alone. The second night stopover hadn't been as relaxed as the first. Bob was suffering a bit from fatigue (so was Peter, come to that), and Marcia had sat with him most of the way. There was less joking about crumpled sheets, which allowed Gina to chat away to Peter in Spanish whenever she felt he was tiring. Two couples with different agenda making the same journey.

Bob said he didn't really want Marcia to run the next morning. "We're quite close to home now. It would be dreadful for you to rick an ankle." Peter had heard that part of the conversation coming from behind his head, and lip-read it in the rear view mirror. About the closest he and Marcia got to talking about that morning was Peter's reply, focussing on Marcia's reflected eyes: "Oh, you should never worry, Bob, I pick her route with, what do you say… with a fine toothcomb… she's in very safe hands with me."

The bastard. Surely he knew it would make her quiver. Her stomach did churn. *Oh God*, she thought… *yes, those very safe hands please… but please guide me and help me to put Bob first before my own pleasures.*

Gina broke the silence. "Pardon me overhearing, but what fine comb do you use on your teeth?"

Peter couldn't work out what she meant. Marcia was too deep in thought to have heard and it was Bob who finally worked it out.

He said, "When we've sorted this one out, let's play a game… we'll come up with English expressions and try and work out what they mean. Gina, the words are 'fine toothcomb', the spikes on a comb are called 'teeth'. Some combs, for dealing with thick hair, come with large firm teeth. Others come with fine teeth for dealing with the more delicate strands of hair. So when one uses a fine toothcomb, it means it picks things out carefully. In the case Peter made, he picks the route for Marcia to run, making sure there are no little stones or rocks that she could rick her ankle on.

"Right, what about 'as pissed as a newt'?" Bob started playing his suggested game.

"Oh, come on, Bob. We don't want the rest of the day to be that academic. Let's play 'I Spy'." Marcia firmly gave her opinion.

In fact they did neither, as Bob was asleep in minutes.

"Can we stop at a lay-by?" Marcia requested. "I just need to stretch my legs and ease my back off a little. That was a hard run you put me on this morning, coach."

They changed seats, she and Gina. Peter noticed she was back to nail polish removing but with more tender tapping and stroking of his thigh. After that they got ten minutes together on the deck of the ferry. Marcia had said she was feeling a little seasick, and Bob asked Peter if he would take her out and get her some air. Peter was concerned that she was going to be sick, but as soon as they left the saloon she said, "I'm fine. We need space. We have to talk."

"Thank God for that," Peter said. "You made it look very genuine."

They leant on the rail overlooking the English Channel.

"Peter, darling, you've just hit the nail on the head. You said to thank God for me not being sick. I've been getting some similar messages to thank God for his influence on my life – impulses, you might call them too. Firstly, to thank him that he helped us to choose the Playa. It was he who brought us together. Thank God, secondly, that you saved Bob's life, and then thank him for you making my life. If we never make love again, that memory will be with me until the day before I die."

"'The day before I die'? What do you mean by that? Isn't it 'until the day I die'?"

Marcia laughed, as she always did when she knew she had the upper hand in their relationship.

"No, I meant what I said. Because if I get the hint that I'm going to die the next day, I'll get you dragged from whichever bed you're in at the time and have you brought across to be screwed, so that I die a happy, contented woman, satisfied and with a smile on my face the next day."

"Marcia, you're dreadful! I only hope you won't have got anything too contagious!"

"Joking apart. God and I are agreed that as a thank you to him for allowing you to enter our lives, and for saving both Bob and myself in two different ways, and for allowing you and me such enjoyment and satisfaction in just those 20 minutes, I'll dedicate myself to getting Bob through his health problems and try to be a dutiful wife. If you said would I move out and become an item with you, it would be the easiest thing in my life to do, but God has been too kind to allow me to do that, so I have to stick with Bob. As for us… if invited, I'll be where you want me and when… and that's a safe promise, knowing that it won't be every hour of every day. For one reason, that would kill us both; for another, you don't drink the finest wine in the cellar every day of the week… it begins to taste the same each time and the cheaper, more common wines you try in between seem to have more flavour and intrigue. So we're for 'very special occasions'. Can you see what I'm saying?"

"Yes, of course."

"Can you accept what I'm saying?"

"I think I have no alternative, but my God I'll want you out of the cellar all the time."

"Then in the meantime, you'll be allowed a taste of cheaper, more common, more available lovers, just so that you can keep your hand in."

"You're amazing, Marcia."

"We're both amazing, my sweet... and if we don't get back to Bob pretty quickly, he'll guess we're up to something and I'll have to feign travel sickness or something. That would take all the pleasantness away from this most memorable day."

CHAPTER 7
TIME FLEW BY IN LONDON

Peter went cold when he got Maria's first letter. OK, so it was good she was well and mentioned José often, talked about Marco and Virginia, how Michelle and Miguel were now a serious item. How Meribel was keeping in touch and that, out of the blue, Laura had called in at the hotel with her mother. Of course, Peter was interested to read all that news, and enjoyed his mother's art of attacking the detail.

But the point at which he went cold was when she wrote:

… had another problem again on the housekeeping front, no, not Meribel this time, but Tania.

The day you left, in fact we'd hardly waved you off down the drive, there was a call in the office from Beth, Tania's sister. She informed us that Tania wouldn't be in, which was really annoying. Beth said she herself could be with us in half an hour and so she would cover.

I asked Beth what was wrong with Tania. Well, you know what she's like, she said she didn't want to say. So I said I had to know. She started crying, but it seems when Tania got home from work here, and Marco said he saw her leave just after ten, she had a date with her boyfriend. Not somebody from the hotel, I think, because I didn't know the name. A chap called Toni from her village. Well, according to Beth, he's a very jealous boy and he didn't believe she'd been working, which we could verify if required, but accused her of having been with another man, and beat her up because of it.

Tania's apparently got a broken nose and a cracked rib… not a very nice boyfriend, eh! Beth thinks the police arrested him on a grievous bodily harm charge and apparently he's a drug runner as well. Anyway, Beth is doing the job and is prepared to skip school. Marco says that's fine. The new blood will do us good.

Saw Jaimé on Tuesday, he's still talking about 'his fortune' from the sketches and little portraits he did. It was about 50,000 pesetas, which Marco is looking after…

The letter was full of news. Peter would never compete with her storybook. But Tania… that was a shock. Had she not turned up to save his bacon and then taken a beating on his behalf? It would be hard to find out what happened. He walked over to a mirror and checked out the scar on his eyebrow.

Max had a habit of walking into a room and illuminating it with his sheer exuberance of personality.

He had arrived back. Peter had heard his key in the door and the bang as Max threw the door shut behind him. He could never do that quietly, even at two in the morning. This time it was mid-evening.

"Time for a beer," Max commanded.

Peter said, "In the fridge," still ploughing through to the end of Maria's letter.

"No. Not here. In the pub. Got somebody you should meet."

"Oh, come on, Max. I've had a hard day. It's 9.30. I've got bed in mind."

"So have I," Max replied. "I've told you about my twin sister. Well, she's hit town with a couple of friends and, according to her, they're looking for a good time. Now, they're the sort of girls I want you to meet."

Dear Mother,

Thanks for all your news. If you speak to Tania, say sorry to hear about her fight. Tell her it's time to give up that boyfriend.

Don't like idea of all these ex-girlfriends coming home behind my back. Tell them we've now moved into superb flat… new address is Cyril Mansions, Prince of Wales Drive, Battersea Park, S.W.11. – Posh, eh!

It's very big. Max and I have a bedroom each overlooking Battersea Park and the River Thames. We guess there's room for two more, we've got bedrooms up in the roof. Max says we shouldn't hurry. We'll probably find a couple of girls, nurses or something looking for rooms. Useful to do the cooking, although Max is a good cook and I'm getting more adventurous.

Met Max's twin sister… actually quite lovely… but then so is Max. She's nice. You'd like her. Sort of girl who wants to settle down and have grandchildren.

Bob's alright. He's going to have heart surgery. He'll be a bit ill for a while, but he should be OK. You'd be proud of Marcia. Have you heard of Florence Nightingale? Well, that's her. Absolutely dedicated to getting Bob right, which is rather nice.

Done a month now at Poly. Enjoying greatly. Learn, learn, learn, all day and some evenings. But it's good.

Bus goes straight from flat to Poly, about 20 minutes, so that's good.

Doing an environmental study called 'Save the Earth' – all about solar heating and using natural energy, windmills and the like, so I'm using the plans of Girasol as a basis and then sort of laying over how it could become energy efficient and not damage the ozone areas around the planet… all a bit too heavy for you and Marco, I expect, but if my thesis does well it gets entered for a world energy conference somewhere in the Far East… so I'm trying hard. Max too.

Not long to Christmas. Need to fix an evening with Carlos Sanchez's Parish Council Committee. Fancy doing a presentation to them before I submit for consent, formally. Do your stuff, use your charm. Could you fix a date? Maybe use the hotel á la carte restaurant and ply them with some cheap wine. Save the good wine for very special occasions. (He thought deeply about Marcia as he wrote that.)

I'll give Marcia your love, and I'm sure from her to you.

Write to you soon. Missing you.

Love you. Pedro.

Peter had indeed met Max's sister. She and Max were both originally from Argentina, though educated in England, and both spoke fluent Spanish. She was as striking a girl as Max was a man. God had been pretty generous when he allocated their genes.

She was tall, very slim, with jet-black hair cut in a fringe. Piercing blue eyes, as clear as aquamarine. Max looked identical, which made him a bit of a magnet to girls.

The first night Peter had met Anna was on the occasion that he was dragged, almost from his bed, ostensibly to meet her friends, who wanted some action. He and Anna clicked immediately, principally because Peter had been courteous towards her, wanting to include her in the late evening meet-up, whereas to Max, she was purely a sister who was quite used to supplying him with girl friends to flirt with and to whom he gave little attention.

After that evening, Max had enquired which of Anna's two friends Peter was interested in.

"Neither," he had said with great honesty.

"What?" Max said. "They were lovely, and Claudia said she had the hots for you. You're in there, amigo. We could invite the two of them round and do them supper."

Peter didn't seem keen on the idea.

"I liked your sister."

"What, Anna! Go on! She's a bit of a bore, you know. She's into serious things like art, and classics, music, ballet. Come on, amigo, she's only going to suit some professor or other. Anyway, you can't ask her to dinner if one of

74

the others is coming for me because, whatever I do, she'll report to head office, and that will be the end of my fun."

"Head office?"

"Mother and father. She always spills the beans. Tell you what… maybe it would be a good idea for you to take her out. It's OK with me for you to bed her, providing I'm not around to hear the screaming… and then I'll have something on her to report to the parents, if she splits on me. Good idea, amigo!"

"Max. Let's get one thing clear." Peter had picked up a number of useful expressions from Bob. "We get on like a flat on fire, I enjoy your company and couldn't have hoped to have found a better flat-mate. The main difference between us is that I'm not intent on bedding every female I meet."

"So it wouldn't be your main objective to get into bed with Anna, then?"

"No."

He held his hand out to Peter. "Place it there, amigo." They shook hands. "That's the sort of friend I'd get pleasure from having introduced to my twin. Welcome to the family."

CHAPTER 8

Peter could hardly believe he was nearing the end of his studies. Three years had absolutely flown by in London. So much seemed to have happened. It made Peter cross with himself for finding Maria's letters a little 'villagey', but it made him realise how little went on in Calella compared with London. Yet when he was there, he had felt he was rushed off his feet. Plenty seemed to go on.

London, though, was so different. There were bags of shops, coffee bars, pubs, cinemas… it had everything. He'd told Anna that he knew little about art and had never been to a ballet or opera. He had never heard of the Proms… there was so much he needed to discover.

In return, Anna said she didn't understand the first thing about architecture, and felt she'd like to share in Max's chosen career if she somehow could. So Peter had taken her to a number of prominent buildings in London and, by way of further explanation, had introduced her to Girasol.

"You're a genius," she had said. "All this you're prepared to create."

The topic of bed had not really entered Peter's mind, and in any event, he felt he didn't want Anna to be a cheap wine.

His notes home were still full of what he had done, been to, seen, and Maria noted the more frequent mention of Max's sister. She'd surely have a name before long. He was still in touch with Bob and Marcia; Bob had had the operation and was recovering.

She was proud that Peter had been shortlisted for an interview on the energy-saving project he had been working on for so long, but was worried about the prospect of him winning a place to the conference, like any other caring mother.

Of course she'd be proud, but she knew little about the 'Far East' and feared Peter might pick up malaria, or be bitten by a lethal snake, or kidnapped into some slave trade or other.

Still, he might not make it, so why worry too much in advance? He'd be home in December, because she'd fixed his meeting with the Parish Council. While some children in Spain had their advent calendars ready for the countdown to Christmas Day, Maria had annotated her desk calendar to record how many days it was before she would pick her Pedro up from Gerona airport. How she missed him, and how disappointed she had been that she had not yet been able to arrange her shopping trip to London. She'd just been too busy. However, she now planned to go in the spring.

The lead inquisitor on the energy project panel, a Professor John Rich, was an absolute fool, in Peter's view. He'd asked a whole load of questions but put them in such a way as to telegraph the answer he expected.

"So your new village development scheme you've highlighted… would you provide cooking facilities based on imported Calor gas, oil, or a timber burning oven?"

"Not Calor gas," Peter responded confidently, "because that has to be manufactured, and apart from the gas itself, the container construction, the rubber tubes, the valves, all require industrial processes using up man-made harmful energy."

"Oh, yes! Good," Professor John Rich had responded.

"Oil, in its turn, again has to be 'farmed' and it's those processes that will soak up the world's energy resources."

This time it was, "Interesting, Mr Martinez."

"So, on balance," Peter continued, "I'd specify timber-burning ovens."

Professor John Rich grimaced. "But surely…"

Peter interrupted. "… But to burn a particular type of timber."

"Really? What particular type of timber?"

"Well, as we farm fish from the sea, so there are vast quantities of driftwood to be farmed from the sea. Then there's the waste, the bark, and the small branches resulting from essential forestry, industrial tree felling for the production of paper and telegraph poles, railway sleepers and the like. All that waste could fuel the amount of energy my village would require."

"Really? Interesting," the Professor said, looking above his energy inefficient glasses to his fellow interrogators on the committee.

The interview process had gone on for a long time.

"… And finally… Peter, if I may… what would the greatest energy-saving influence be in your village?"

"Small double-glazed windows."

"Small double-glazed windows. Really?" the Professor said, with some disappointment. "To what effect?"

"Well, they would retain heat in the cooler seasons, and remove the need for air-conditioning in the summer, as the heat intake would be restricted."

"Really?" came the academic reply.

"Yes, really," Peter said emphatically. "Take time out, sir, and go to any cathedral at any time of the year and fill it with thousands of worshippers, or, at worst, tourists. It remains at a constant temperature, season on season, and for that reason it needs no energy-using heating in winter or air-conditioning in summer, whether in Moscow or Seville, Italy or Westminster. It's about the thickness of the walls and limitation as to the size of the apertures therein."

The Professor was silent. Peter actually thought the rest of the committee was going to applaud.

"Thank you, Mr Martinez. That's been very interesting. Tell me, could you put what you've said into a 30- or 40-minute presentation to a larger committee – say of 200 or 300 people?"

"Yes. I think so, sir, because I believe in what I've been saying."

"OK, Mr Martinez." The Professor turned to the rest of his committee. "Any questions?" (Not that they'd dare.)

"Thank you, Mr Martinez… Peter. You're a very interesting young man."

As Peter was hoping to get that conference opportunity in Malaysia, Honey Yim Lam had no idea where Westminster Polytechnic was, though she knew that England was 6,000-odd miles from Malaysia. Her interview to be sent to the Save the Earth Conference the following January was very different from Peter's.

Firstly, she was to be judged, alongside her fellow prefects at the Barjong Secondary Modern School on the tourist side of the central city in Penang, on her walk and deportment. The selection committee of mistresses and a 'visitor' had to choose only those girls who could 'walk and be noticed'. Secondly, their English language should be excellent, with some knowledge about English heritage. Thirdly, they needed to have a figure to suit a traditional sarong and have knee joints that did not crack when they knelt in the traditional style of servility to their guests.

They needed to know nothing about the environment or what was happening to the ozone layer but, if they did, it could be an advantage if there were two candidates the judges found to be equal.

Honey Yim's walk was astounding, and she knew it. She'd developed it by practising for hours in front of her grandmother's full-length dressing mirror. She realised now that the 'visitor' who was bound to influence or sway the opinion of the mistresses was, in fact, a gentleman from the Energy Conference Committee from Kuala Lumpur, and she had to win his attention.

She had learnt how to walk to impress, but only as an extension of how she walked naturally anyway. Her English, all the mistresses knew, was excellent.

Nobody actually did know, however, that her blood father was English. Not that that made any difference, because he had returned home with his army unit in 1946 and they'd never spoken a word together. Something in her genes, though, helped her with that foreign tongue. Her father's role in her procreation had also given her a greater height than most of her contemporaries. At 5 foot 8 she was tall, although not the tallest, and that helped her to impress.

Looking good in a sarong or a toga, a bikini or even some sailor suit out of her grandmother's dressing up box was absolutely no trouble at all.

Mr Han Ho, the said gentleman from the Energy Conference Committee, couldn't take his eyes off Honey Yim, and she knew it. She'd inherited that judgement ability from her mother who, although now a seemingly ordinary lady working in the Regional Government Offices, where the pay was good enough to enable her to send her Honey to a good school, could still command the attention and affection of any hot-blooded male who dared glance at her. She had married to provide Honey with a secure family base, as with her other children, but her husband, though kindly, was a bit staid and overprotective.

Honey had learnt how to hook with her eyes where others needed their entire Malaysian bodies.

"A question, Miss Lam," said Mr Han Ho. "If the delegate to whom you are seconded were to be English, and you found yourself in a one-to-one situation, lost for conversation, what would you be likely to say?"

"Sir, is the delegate male or female?"

Thrown by the girl's intellect, he played her game back.

"Either."

"Then I'd ask him or her if they had a golliwog."

"Why on earth would you do that?"

"Well, because in all the books you read about English children, and all the adventures they get up to, they always take a golliwog with them when they go on picnics in the sun."

"And if he or she says they did have a golliwog, what would you then say?"

"I'd ask why they always take their golliwogs on picnics… and tell them that we Malaysians don't."

All the mistresses giggled at her apparent naivety. Mr Ho was heard to mutter, "Lovely." Inwardly, he wished he was young enough to be a delegate and to draw the lucky straw that allowed his stay to be hosted by Honey Yim Lam. He wrote 'chosen' against her name and then debated the merits of the others with his co-selectors, to decide who would make up the remainder of the hosts for the conference's 200 expected attendees.

Honey was to spend the next four months practising her walk, talking to as many people as she could find who spoke English, and watching her diet. She was 18 and her principal criticism of herself and the maternal genes she'd inherited was that she was small-chested. She found a single spring-loaded dumbbell in her grandfather's 'box of junk' and practised for about 15 minutes each day, pulling in her tummy muscles and flexing her upper torso, which she could see in the mirror had the effect of lifting her breasts. A week before the conference, it looked as though she might achieve an enhancement to a 34-inch bust, up a full inch from the day of her selection.

On training day, she and the five others selected from her school set off for Langkawi, an island about two hours away by steam ferry. She felt bubbly, confident and excited. They'd have a week's training before the delegates arrived.

Peter's last letter before he arrived home for Christmas and his final presentation to the Parish Council portrayed his new confidence and maturity, developed in the months away from his family apron-strings.

Hi Mother (which had replaced *Dear Mother*). *Guess what! Yes I'm off to Malaysia to save the world from blowing itself up.*

He passed on the news of how he'd been selected, and that he'd been asked to deliver a paper, which he explained was an academic term for reading an essay on 'Saving the Environment', and how the basis of his thesis had been that condoms should be banned in order to save the destruction of trees in the rubber plantations of the Far East.

Maria asked José if she was right in thinking that rubber was bled from rubber-producing trees and that extracting, milking or farming it didn't kill the trees. He'd said yes.

"Then why would Pedro's thesis be based on banning condoms to save the destruction of rubber trees in the Far East?"

"Because he's a young man who's obviously intent on pulling his dear old mother's leg."

"Well, I thought what he said wasn't true, but from the way he so confidently wrote about it, I had second thoughts."

"Then make sure you get you own back."

"Would you help me?"

"Yes, of course, as long as you still let me use condoms and risk impacting on the earth, instead of you!"

"I'll break your leg if you don't."

Peter still wrote about Anna (whose name he had now divulged), but then as much about Max… how busy he was with his studies… how he'd seen Bob and Marcia, and how Marcia had been turning herself inside out to keep Bob from the office, and getting him to exercise more… and to relax… how he'd prepared his presentation to the Parish Council… and how Bob was still a bit sore that he hadn't been cut in on the deal… but if it came off, in terms of getting consent, how he and a consortium of mates might help Peter to develop the complex. Marcia was so pleased with the end to that letter.

Mother, I'm so looking forward to seeing you and José, and, of course, Marco and Virginia… is Jaimé around…?
   Love you.
Pedro.

The reunion was as good as his pre-emptive message had been. It was he, Maria was sure, who would not break the hug at the airport when she picked him up. José had watched with delight. Peter could get more emotion out of Maria than anybody in the world, of that he was now convinced; and in terms of inheriting her love, he knew her Pedro was some competition – competition to which he was delighted to succumb.

At the appropriate moment, José had finally made his presence known. He was thrilled when Peter's right arm went round his shoulder, and, with his left arm round Maria, they had rushed to the car park, an excited trio delighted by this great home-coming.

The presentation to Carlos Mendes and his cronies showed how polished Peter had become in that short space of time. His delivery was now not far short of perfect. He turned to Carlos, whom he of course knew well – and with whom he had his private deal anyway – and, in a single word, removed any hint of sponging that people might interpret from their association or taking him apart from his pack of colleagues.

"Señor," he said, leaving a poignant silence before repeating: "Señor!"

He then went on to thank them all for coming, and to explain that what he was going to present was a replacement for decaying, non-profit-making vineyards and sunflowers, which were not of a quality from which to produce good wine or oil. He spoke of how his family would have no reason to worry about the land or the wine, or to worry about its future preservation for the purposes to which it had been put through generations. He explained how, therefore, the development would be conservational. Instead of benefiting just his family's coffers, as in the past, 500 households, some of which would produce lettings of two weeks at a time, would bring economic wealth to the itinerant community for a number of miles around. His audience heard how the design, he believed, would bring international interest to the area, and if it was extended out to sea as a marina, it would be the talk not just of the Costa Brava, but of all of Spain and Mediterranean Europe, and would hit the fashion magazines of the world.

Peter was a master chef who knew how to finish the meal with an exotic *bombe surprise*, rather than a simple local *crème Catalan*. "Finally…" he said, still holding the attention of his gathered critics, by natural instinct, "… it's something of a secret but as I'm the one involved, I can tell you that the prototype in front of you will be the subject of my own presentation at the 'Save the Earth' conference in Malaysia next February, where I've been invited to present a paper on energy conservation."

Maria was absolutely speechless. Marco wiped a tear from his eye. Virginia, although not doing her part to preserve energy by eating an entire plate of almonds, burst into applause which, bless her, they all followed. José stood apart. *Very, very good,* he thought. *How like his mother.*

Permission was granted for the development just before one of the happiest Christmases the Playa had ever seen. With Peter on the planet, there would be no future limitations.

Maria had come to terms with the fact that there would be many more bienvenidas and adiós until Pedro put his roots down in Spain again. She even contemplated whether that would ever happen again in a final sense. Peter was a much broader man than the boy who had left just three years earlier. He was prepared to take on any conversation piece and talked incessantly about art and films and trendy shops… even politics.

Maria noticed how people almost queued up just to say, "Welcome home," and to hear Pedro's opinion on Real Madrid, Barcelona, Chelsea or Arsenal, or on the latest film or fashion.

Opening the hotel on Christmas Day had been a major decision. It meant that José could bring his parents and son to enjoy a large mixed gathering of Martinez family and friends, with paying guests and their families too. Carlos Mendes was there with his wife and her sister and brother-in-law; cousin Carlos and his wife were dragged down to the celebration, and some of Marco's business acquaintances had in turn brought their family together. So, overall, Maria was able to put together a day of activity and variation that Pedro could get his teeth into, as opposed to a quiet boring festive one with perhaps a family game or two to pass away the time.

January 12th sadly dawned for Maria. The downside was that Pedro would be leaving. The upside, she saw, was that without him being around, José could come and go at the cottage as she and he pleased again. They were not dependent on the boat alone for whenever they felt the mutual need. José could leave Barcelona at six, after a hard day's work, drive for two hours or so, and spend the evening and night with Maria; then, by leaving at 6.30am, he could be in his executive office by 8.30am, ahead of the rest of his staff. He may have felt exhausted for the rest of the day by Maria's exuberant desire for his company, but they were having a wonderful time together in what was becoming a deep-rooted relationship.

Peter had spent the break polishing his presentation for Malaysia. He'd even lined up Maria and José, Marco and Virginia for one evening's dummy run of how he intended to make his points in support of his evolving opinions on environmental survival. At the end, Maria had stolen the show, showing in a very personal way a continuing closeness with her son.

"Shouldn't you mention the survival plan for rubber trees?" she'd questioned.

Initially, Peter was completely thrown, so full marks to her. But he quickly illustrated his ability for instant rational thinking.

"In that regard," he explained, "I'll be advocating a policy whereby it'll be illegal for couples to sleep together unless they do it back to back... in that way the world's temperatures will be kept down and the existence of rubber trees won't need to be challenged."

Maria and José found that both funny and original. Marco and Virginia did not understand the point.

Peter had under a month back in the UK before he and the British contingent of delegates flew to Kuala Lumpur and then on to the island of Langkawi in the north west, across the sea from Penang.

Seven days before their arrival, Honey Yim Lam was in Langkawi being measured for sarongs and saris, and checked out by specially flown-in consultants as to hair and make-up arrangements. She was being well trained in the agenda for the three-day conference and the support the hosts were expected to give to their allocated charges.

Mr Ho's experienced conference organising team explained that the girls should all be prepared for their delegate being either male or female, and stressed how their hosting skills should ensure that each attendee went back to their own environments recommending that the opening up of Malaysia to tourism should be the next big thing. The task of the hostesses was to ensure they built in enough Oriental allure to do just that... but with their smiles, their expressive hands, their gentle subservience and over-riding charm, not with their bodies. Bodies, and a shared use thereof, were out, and anyone breaking that rule would be sent straight home.

Honey's mother knew her daughter would not let herself be misled during such a wonderful opportunity to widen her knowledge of life, and to mix with people, some of whom would be coming from the western world. Her father, or at least the man she thought was her father, would not have such confidence, her mother thought, and so mother and daughter had agreed that they would simply tell the dictatorial head of the family that Honey Yim Lam had been chosen to go on a geography field trip to the neighbouring island of Langkawi. At that news, her surrogate father was pleased that her academic education was going to be extended in such a way.

Boys and Honey were banned from getting together. Eddie Yum Yam had had his wedding arranged with his now wife, which had led to the immediate provision of a daughter, and he saw that as the pleasure which Honey would one day have in store too. In his own generation, the bride was usually no more than 18 at the time of marriage, but he had been prepared to modernise his thinking after concerted pressure from his wife, to allow Honey to complete an advanced level of education, and he had granted a stay of execution to the prospect of an arranged marriage until she was 21. That concession was only obtained by Honey's mother's clever persuasion – that is, her rationing of her husband's conjugal rights until he saw reason and allowed Honey to get a better education than they themselves had been allowed.

Honey's mother had then decreed that they would make love once a week during the three years of Honey's education. From the day of her marriage, they would abstain from lovemaking, and the task of enlarging the family could be left to the younger generation.

"Do you want to abstain? Have you had enough for a lifetime?" her husband had asked meekly.

She had lowered her head and sobbed. "I'd prefer not," she blurted out amidst her crocodile tears.

"Then your suggestion is a good one. We'll defer the marriage and continue the arrangement on a weekly basis. Besides, we'll get Honey a better groom if he knows she's fully educated."

Part of the preparatory procedure by Mr Ho's team was to try to paint a picture of the composition of the delegates before they arrived. By then it would be hectic and, while each girl would certainly get to know their own charge, the other attendees would merely be blurs of personality, to be gossiped about during meal breaks, when each would be compared with the others by girlie chit-chat behind their backs.

Mr Ho made the presentation himself with the assistance of a slide projector. That was why Peter had had to send a recent photograph of himself along with his acceptance of the invitation, although he had had no idea his face, in a glorious one square metre image, would be projected on a screen for all to see.

"Peter Martinez, born Spain, now studying at Westminster Polytechnic, London and presenting a paper on his views as to how to protect the environment."

Peter had always been mature for his age, probably due to the loss of his paternal influence, and once he'd reached his teens, he had upped his age by a couple of years to anyone who was unlikely to see his passport or birth certificate.

It was a moment when most of the girls showed their age. It was temporarily like the adulation at a Beatles' concert when the girls let it be known that their favourite, at whom they would even throw their underwear, was Paul McCartney or George Harrison. In the case of Peter Martinez, most girls squirmed a little and giggled at the exposure of their thoughts that they found him really dishy.

Not the same reaction to Joe Thompson of the USA, John Locke from Scotland, Pierre Jordan, France, etc.

As Mr Ho explained, when he tapped the rostrum to bring the girls' attention back to where it needed to be, "You must all dedicate your time and efforts to whoever is allocated to you. That will be done by way of a draw of names and numbers by the management team, and their selection will be final."

Honey had a strange feeling that she would be deeply disappointed not to draw Peter. The age, the deep eyes, the beautiful shaped lips, all those things were implanted into her brain, even once the slide show had moved on. The odds of drawing Peter were, she realised, extreme. So she'd have to be pleased with whomsoever she got.

On the eve of the conference, Honey lay awake, still with that vision in her mind. She'd know who her charge was by 8am tomorrow morning, in anticipation of the arrivals on the 9am flight from Kuala Lumpur, which was specially laid on by the conference organisers.

It was a hot night. She was excited and couldn't sleep.

She looked through the open window, which was only intended to be shut during heavy storms or strong winds. The complex was quiet. There were cleaners and a few odd job men providing finishing touches around the footpaths. Others were adjusting the signage pointing to the conference centre. It really was too hot to sleep. She'd slip on a T-shirt and jeans and go for a walk, she thought, perhaps a refresher on the orientation front so that she never mislead her charge during the busy timetable.

After she'd crossed through the gardens and as she approached the main complex, she saw the conference suite doors were open, leading just off the vast structure that served as the large reception area. It was quiet. There was nobody around. Impulse led her to poke her head into the inner lobby, where she imagined the delegates would be mingling tomorrow morning.

Ahead of her was the conference hall itself; all the lights were dimmed apart from those above the now elongated rostrum, where the officiating body was to sit the next day.

Honey wandered up to the raised platform. She would never get to that position during the actual proceedings. Maybe her charge would be one of the presenters, and it might help them if she was able to describe what it looked like from that height, looking down at the delegates. So she walked calmly up the three steps and turned to face all the empty conference seats.

She surveyed the view. It gave her a great feeling of power to be looking down at the emptiness, so what it would be like when there were people sitting on the seats, she could not contemplate. She sat in the Chairman's chair, in the middle of the rostrum. Wow! That was a powerful chair. The arms gave her a tremendous feeling of security. She sank into the thick leather. She glanced all around her and at the open topped shoe boxes with their rows of envelopes below the rostrum. What were they for? The boxes were merely marked with letters of the alphabet.

She knelt down, which meant she was then actually below the height of the conference tables. Deftly slipping her fingers into the first box, she pulled out the first envelope. It had on the front a name, 'Joanne San Ang'. Then the next, 'Sally-Anne Anam'… and so on. She worked out they were the names of the chaperones.

In the second box, fourth one in was Honey Yim Lam. She took it out, making sure to pull the one immediately behind it up a little so that she readily knew where to put it back. As she did so, she realised the flap of the envelope was only tucked in and not sealed. She lifted the flap out and the piece of card thus exposed bore the name 'Mr Toni Perrera – Italy'.

That was it. They were the allocations for their charges for the next morning. Her heart sank. She couldn't remember Toni Perrera's slide projection but he was not going to be particularly fashionable, otherwise she wouldn't have forgotten him. She was so disappointed. She'd desperately hoped to read 'Mr Peter Martinez'.

Oh well! At least she was there. Perhaps God would bring them together. She tucked the flap back in and put her envelope back.

An impulse suddenly overcame her. Who was the lucky girl who had drawn her Spanish prince? She had made up her mind that was what he was going to turn out to be.

It was not her doing it, she was sure. It was God's hand guiding her as she went back into the first box, took the flap out of the first envelope and checked the name. Not Peter Martinez. She'd got through about 20 envelopes when she heard voices. She understood the Malay patois. They were security.

"All OK in here. No need to search. I did that an hour ago…"

The voices receded into the distance, but she heard the doors into the conference hall slam shut, and a key was turned in the lock.

So what, she thought. At least she was locked in with the prospect of finding Peter Martinez, or his name at least. But she didn't need all night. 'Sandra Lieu', about the 30th envelope, contained the magic card 'Mr Peter Martinez'.

Honey looked hard at the print and the name. Instinctively she lifted it to her lips. She kissed it. God had determined they should be one… "And so we will," she resolved.

Sandra Lieu would be perfectly happy with Toni Perrera, in fact they might fall in love and get married and have children and buy them golliwogs, and they might grow old together in an Italian Palace. Honey found her own envelope again… and switched the cards. Her heart was racing. She would never sleep now. She had to get out, before she was found by the security guards. She looked around her.

There was a window open but she had to unlock the shutters. She eased them open. She could make out a flower bed below the window sill. There were now no external lights. It must be well into the night. She thought, *Every sensible chaperone is getting her beauty sleep.* She eased herself up onto the window sill and swung herself down into the flower bed. It was only about a metre's drop. "No problem," she whispered as she stood up, brushing the light soil from where she thought it might be clinging to her jeans.

She hurried back to the villa she was sharing with three others. She found her way to her allocated bed, slipped her clothes off under the duvet, and put them into a pile beneath the steel framed divan with its creaky spring base. Her heart was heaving. "Thank you, dear God. Thank you. That will be our secret."

CHAPTER 9

Peter had flown for the very first time on his pre-Christmas return trip to Gerona. He'd been a bit worried by the prospect. The older you are when you take on such an experience, the worse it seems, probably because you can understand the practical aspects of a plane losing power and crashing, and the terror it would evoke in you as a passenger.

Max hadn't helped things by joking about how he hoped the captain knew it wasn't flat all the way to Spain and he'd have to gain height over the Pyrénées. So when Peter had announced he was flying to Malaysia, Max came up with many more options. Coping with the cold air currents and snowstorms over Switzerland was an obvious one. Saying they'd be alright if they did have to crash in the desert, on account of it being flat and soft. That didn't comfort Peter too much.

Re-checking that Peter could now swim brought a cold chill to his back. Well, yes, he could swim but it was, without a doubt, his least favourite activity. He never knew quite why but even in the Latchmere Baths, round the corner from where they lived, he felt haunted by the thought of Paco drowning, and the now interminable wait for him to come home. Maria's promise to him as a boy – "He will come home one day. You just wait and see" – was about the only one his mother had failed to keep. So with flying, the promise, "Of course it won't crash," was something he just about believed, and a more realistic comfort, it seemed, than, "Of course your father will come back."

Anna was good about explaining how to understand the changes in pitch of the engines on a long haul flight. She seemed to know, from her return trips home, no doubt, that it was the extremes of engine tone that caused inner panic to the uninitiated.

"You'll take off at full revs, and then the captain will put the fear of God into you as he trims back the engines when he's reached his initial required cruising height. He then might take on more power to cope with turbulence, especially over the Indian Ocean, where my friends say the thermals off the sea will toss the plane all over the place. Then there's the extreme of flying into land with hardly any power at all, suddenly to be panicked into thinking the worst when the captain throws his monstrous beast into reverse to stop you falling off the end of the runway. Tell you what," she continued, "pay my fare and I'll come with you and hold your hand, if you'd like."

He actually thought he would like that. Paying the fare would be a bit of a stumbling block, though.

Anna was disappointed he didn't give her a reply. Perhaps he should have done.

The flight was very much as Anna and, come to think of it, Max too, had described. They flew in daylight over the Alps and dusk across one of the Arab countries. He didn't know which. He had a major fright as the plane lost height some eight hours out. He plucked up courage to call a hostess across and ask her if she too had noticed the drop in altitude.

"Well, it's either this, or we'll run out of fuel," she explained calmly.

"Is it expected?" he asked.

"Oh yes. Every trip. We refuel at Bahrain. You can get off and stretch your legs if you like, and buy a really expensive watch quite cheaply."

They landed in what appeared to be a veritable sea of lights in the middle of a desert. Quite why it was so light Peter did not know. There weren't many buildings and it wasn't, at least he thought it wasn't, that Bedouin tribes needed to be guided to the lights to pick up their returning relatives, as nobody actually disembarked there. It was, in those days, a refuelling stop only.

They lost height again to land at Kuala Lumpur, gained it again in a little plane that got thrown all over the place flying north up the coast of Malaysia, and finally lost height once more to come smoothly to a stop at the new grass runway strip the authorities of Langkawi had built, almost straight from the edge of the sea to the beginning of a range of hills covered in cedar and other trees.

At Kuala Lumpur they had picked up one of Mr Ho's team. Peter was beginning to realise that there were different looks attaching to what he had otherwise thought would have been a Chinese face. What he had taken to be the standard Chinese face was the one he had seen in a couple of restaurants in Soho and at Choy's in the King's Road in Chelsea. In fact, he was to come to learn, they were of the Hong Kong variety, circular and slightly plump.

The serenely beautiful girl he was looking at was on board to do a PR exercise, explaining, during the one-hour flight, what the delegates should expect. He listened as she explained that he and others were welcome to, "Our beautiful country and the culture of Malaysia, produced by centuries of interbreeding between the Malays and Chinese." He thought that nothing as beautiful as this bone structure and the figure that supported it could have been bred overnight. It could only have come about as a slow process, as with the evolution of a beautiful dish of food: a little tweaking, generation by generation, and the addition of some extraordinary oriental herbs.

He was fascinated by her highly decorated lips, unblemished, wrinkle-free skin, long neck, slim artistic forearms and a body so wrapped in a sari as to show it contained the finest goods available to man.

He was just about able to listen to what she was explaining and focus on her beauty at the same time. The latter took most of his attention, which, in a classic standoffish way, she seemed to have recognised. But instead of dropping her guard, she seemed to raise it as if to say, "Don't look, otherwise you'll want to touch… and thereby will have a disappointment, as there's no way your eyes will get beneath the gift wrapping."

She still smiled at him, but equally at her other temporary dependants. She'd said something about how they would each have a guide allocated to them to assist them during their stay, and that they would be introduced at the Langkawi resort on arrival.

Mr Ho's organisation was exemplary, but then he was one of the best conference organisers in the Far East. Some said he had had some experience in America.

The delegates had checked through customs at Kuala Lumpur and so walked straight off the plane and in to waiting coaches, after being assured their baggage would be at their hotel rooms before they were. The coach swung in to the Pelangi Resort opposite the remaining paddy-fields, which had escaped the development, unlike those on which the complex had been built.

The cobbled access road passed through cultured strips of imported grass lined with clumps of bougainvillaea and hibiscus bushes, and frangipane trees bearing their candle-white wax blossom, with hints of splashed pink watercolours. Smiling human faces popped out of the bushes, as though part of the planting arrangement of some hugely orchestrated grand welcome. Hotel staff, who in fact were cleaners with an important job to do, strolled along the paths, getting to where they were going on time, but at their own pace. Each held their hands together and reverently nodded their heads in an unforgettable welcome to the staring new arrivals.

Peter had never before been part of such surroundings. An enormous calm washed over him. He felt secure and, although it could not possibly be, because he had yet to speak directly with any one of this beautiful race, he felt he was among friends.

The coach now pulled up under the vast umbrella provided by the huge king post roof trusses, honed out of enormously heavy and long hulks of teak.

The canopy over 'Arrivals' was merely an extension to the great structure over the reception area where Honey Yim Lam had been the night before.

She and the other chaperones were waiting at the top of some six gracious steps, which the delegates would climb to reach reception level. Their brief had been to usher the new arrivals into the air-conditioned outer lobby and ultimately into the conference area, but not until late that afternoon, when the official welcoming ceremony and address was due to be made.

Mr Ho had explained… well, possibly it was more realistic to say he had ruled that the girls would usher the arrivals into the lobby, without feeling that their personal charge was to be their only responsibility. The first smooth rounding up of their sheep was to be a collective responsibility. In the lobby, a welcome drink would be served and each delegate was then intended to look at the table to locate their own name tag, which would be laid out for them.

"Help anyone to pin on their name badge. As they're mainly men, they'll be inclined to put their badges on upside down. So they'll need help."

There was to be a general informal welcome by Mr Ho, who would explain that each delegate would then be taken to their room and settled in. The girls would leave their charges to unpack for about an hour, and would then give them a tour of the resort. They'd all meet very informally for lunch, which the girls would eat with their new-found 'buddies'. The afternoon could be a relaxed swim, or some delegates might want to re-read and polish their presentations. Then there would be the formal conference opening and a grand first-night dinner to set the conference off on its proper footing.

Peter had been sitting midway down the length of the coach, so he was about the 20th person to alight. Honey's heart was racing. She had no idea why. It was just her first experience of anything so organised, such an adult function. It was the real version of the type of pretend thing they had been brought up on at school, in case one day they experienced the real thing.

"Today," they'd sometimes been told, "you are to imagine we have a visit from a VIP. It may be the King of Malaysia, or the Queen of England. Maybe the regional Head of Police…" And so they would have their welcoming parades, and practise singing welcome songs, but the only person ever to arrive was the local plumber to attend to a blockage in a drain or some other problem.

Now it was not a dream world of wild preparations with no end result. Here was Honey Yim Lam, waiting to meet and greet her Spanish prince – not that she dared say she knew to whom she'd been allocated. In that early morning briefing, some of the girls had confessed they were hoping to be allocated Mr Peter Martinez, because his slide made him look beautiful, and he was young too. Honey said she really didn't mind who she got. "Whoever he or she is, I have a job to do. That I will do to my utmost."

One of the organising committee had heard her say that and applauded her sentiments, making a point of condemning the others for expressing a preference.

Honey looked down from the vantage point of her raised position as the somewhat crumpled travellers filed out of the coach one by one. As Peter moved along the aisle, he was able to crouch a little and look upwards at what he could only initially fix in his mind as a line-up for one of Mecca's Miss World contests, which he had once seen on television in a café. They were not, though, wearing swimming costumes like the Miss World contestants would have been. These girls were wrapped. The fact that they were beautifully covered was neither here nor there to him. The overlying impression was that under the saris, in all their varying exotic shades of batik design, there were warm-skinned maidenly bodies of extreme beauty.

Peter's mind had always been an analytical one, and was not likely to change. In a flash, he recollected the first time he had seen Laura, Meribel, Marcia, even Tania and while he could remember those first split seconds and a definite attraction, for whatever reason, this was a completely different experience. Each waiting guide exuded a style and magnetism he had never encountered before.

There was a sudden break in the line, which allowed a slightly taller girl to move forward. The deep blue of the material enshrouding her was enough to make most heads turn, but it was the girl herself who left the delegates, and most of all Peter, breathless. She had a neck like a swan and the arms of a ballerina. She had a soft young face with well-defined cheekbones, above which there was a pair of topaz jewels, which in her case acted as eyes. She had hair woven out of silk, piled high with a hint of a wispy fringe. Even at a distance, her ears looked the most beautiful ears Peter had ever seen. Her earlobes carried blue stones, which must have been there the day she was born, they looked so much an essential part of her.

The head was turned to Peter's far left, scanning the arrivals like some remote-control movie camera, not missing a face or an impression. It was intent. Peter remained with a fixed gaze focused on her. Their eyes met, and rather than dart around to see how his face was formed, or to scan up and down his casual blue trousers and white, now substantially creased shirt, her head stayed still and her eyes burned into his. Her glistening lips began to part, slowly revealing firm, white perfectly arranged teeth. Those pearls became dominant as the lips grew wider and rounder as they stretched and opened fully. Lights were turned on in her eyes. It was as though she had been looking out for Peter, but that was impossible, he thought. It seemed that her greeting was almost a reunion, and that they had known each other intimately in a previous life.

Peter normally was able to control his senses, but he suddenly felt the discomfort of the sort of level of heartbeat he experienced at the end of a run. Quite naturally, he found himself smiling back. He fully expected her scanning process now to pass him by, to take in the other 20 or so chaps to his right. But that didn't happen.

Their reciprocal gazes were suddenly disturbed. The second of the four coaches from the airport pulled up amidst a hissing of air brakes and hydraulic doors puffing to open. The wretched driver had seen his opportunity and parked closer to the pavement than the driver of Peter's transportation. The image of Miss Malaysia was blocked. Honey Yim Lam was no longer able to focus on her prince either. He who had arrived on a flying carpet, just as they used to in the books that had taught her so much about life beyond the paddy-fields and rubber plantations of her home.

Peter instinctively pushed his way through to the front of the coach to get a full view back to the line-up on the top of the steps. She had gone. Soaked up in a flash of light out of his life.

One of the young guides approached him. "Let me show you to the reception area, sir," she said.

"I'm OK," he replied, with his normal independence. "I'll find it."

"Please, sir, I will lose my job if I let you do that. Please follow me."

By any standards she too was beautiful, though he would have thought shorter than 'Lady Blue', who was still in his thoughts. Her smile was a mile wide, with teeth any orthodontist would be proud to have produced. Yet probably hardly a ringgit had been spent by her parents on anything other than bamboo shoots, or a range of nuts plucked from the jungle surrounding their home, to strengthen and whiten those teeth. These young ladies used fingers, rather than expensive toothbrushes, to greater effect than any young girl advertising Macleans or Colgate in Western fashion magazines.

Peter dutifully gave in and followed his guide's gentle Malaysian strut. By the time he reached the reception area, there were a lot of visiting delegates already assembled, as well as the array of Miss World geisha girls rushing around and giggling as they approached the mainly male attendees. They looked at those badges which had been pinned to shirt or jacket... read the name and, if not recognising it as being their allocated charge, rushed off to read another label to find their dependent partner for the days to come.

"Here! Follow. Name tag here," the young lady demanded, as per the instructions from the morning briefing. Behind the third table, bedecked with safety-pinned plastic labels, were three young sari-clad ladies, again capable of getting at least a second glance from any young man passing by the shop window in which they were placed.

"Name, sir, please?"

"Peter," Peter replied mischievously.

"Mr Peter, sir. First name, please?"

"That's Peter."

"Mr Peter Peter?"

"No, just one Peter. Just Mr Peter."

It suddenly dawned on the three that he was playing a game with them.

"Please, sir. Do you have brother called Paul?"

So suddenly Peter was on the back foot, as the three giggled as though they had just caught their local priest with his trousers down.

"No!" Peter broke into pigeon Malay. "Me no brother called Paul. Me no brother at all. Why you suggest I have?"

They shrieked with laughter.

"Because, sir, we say 'Fly away Peter, fly away Paul, come back Peter, come back Paul.' If you are not that Peter, then you must have another name."

Enough leg-pulling was enough. "OK ladies, I am not fly away Peter, I am Peter Martinez."

As quick as a flash, as though all the girls were champions at Pelmanism, and could remember each strategically placed label, one produced his tag. "Peter Martinez, sir."

She stepped forward and suddenly was close. The closeness of Marcia just before he returned to Spain for Christmas was nothing compared with this. Yet, at the time, he remembered, he really had had good reason to think Christmas had come early.

Marcia always phoned at least twice a week. But for a time, she'd been busy nursing Bob through his operation and was undergoing all the post-op moods which went with that.

"Peter, darling," she'd said in one call in early December, "when are you going home?"

"About the 16th, I'd planned, I'm doing a presentation to Carlos and his cronies on the 18th."

"Let me just have a look. The 14th. Would you be free on the 14th?"

Of course he would be, he thought. "What sort of time?"

"Midday plus half an hour or so."

"Until when?"

"Say about seven."

"Looks fine. I've got a final morning lecture at ten, and Max is having a boring drinks party, which won't start till about nine. He's related to an owl."

So the plan was a light lunch at L'Ecu de France in Jermyn Street, maybe the cinema, and, "I'll buy you tea at the Ritz. Oh, and I've got a Christmas present for you, which you can have early."

"Oh, hell, Marcia. Don't say things like that. What on earth can I buy a lady who not only has everything but who can, in fact, afford to buy anything?"

"Your beautiful body," she said.

"Oh, come on, Marcia."

"No, I actually mean it. The 14th will be our three-month anniversary. You'd best get it into shape!"

They had met. They'd certainly had a light lunch, over which they frantically caught up with each other's news. She'd got tickets for 'The Graduate'. The very early afternoon showing. To him the opening was reminiscent of his farewell party and, to an extremely limited extent, the seduction of Dustin Hoffman was reminding him of the presence next to him. In fact, the close-to-him-holding-his-arm-in-the-cinema Marcia. A sort of promise of availability was often scary yet, to a young man, confidence-boosting. They reached tea at the Ritz, and Marcia leant across. Now in public and in a fully-lit environment, she was a little more reserved. Perhaps even cautious.

"I need to call Bob," she announced.

"Of course. Should you be going?"

"Good God, no. I'm on this reunion with the girls from the Bluebells. Happens every year. Bob wouldn't let me miss it for anything. I'm going to make a call. Come up in 15 minutes."

"Sorry," Peter said. "No comprendo. Come where?"

"It's your Christmas present… actually to both of us… I have room 307."

"Room 307," he said, with some anguish in his voice.

"Well, my darling, if I'd left these things to you we'd still be scratching around on the ground floor. This is level three." She brushed his hand with hers. "Don't be late. It'll take you four minutes by lift."

He knocked on the door of room 307 exactly 15 minutes after the announcement of her departure. It was already 'her' room. It oozed a Marcia Hunt aroma as the door opened. Within, it was dark apart from the glow of lights from the Westminster area, which penetrated the darkness now shrouding St James's Park. A hand reached out and guided him into the room. The same hand was removing his tie as he was sat on the bed. Then his shirt, the belt of his trousers, his shoes… this was a proficient undressing… and then the gentle push forcing him onto his back, as he realised, and appreciated this was to be an exchange of Christmas cheer. The exchange was indeed close and a special type of loving, expressing mutual needs. But in the confines of that room, he'd had little hint of the secrets and girlish fun of the Orient, which he was now experiencing.

"OK. You now know me," he said, pointing to his name tag. "I am Peter Martinez. There's a girl who is part of your team. She wears a blue sari... and is tall... is she a chaperone?"

"Sir, Mr Martinez. There are a number of us in blue saris. It is the luck of the draw if one hands out labels, or papers for the meetings, or if we are to be seconded to the guidance of any delegate. Mr Ho has taken our names out of a box and matched them either to support our visitors, by name, or to perform the other duties. The young colleague you refer to may be 'backroom back up', as Mr Ho describes it. But why do you ask?"

He was too shy, and felt too juvenile to answer.

Not that Peter could count exactly, or needed to, but he would have guessed there were now about 20 men left standing with their empty welcome drink glasses in their hands, still being peered at by a lesser number of girls. Perhaps the great organisational abilities of Mr Ho had gone wrong.

There was suddenly a change in the calm atmosphere outside the main conference venue. First one head turned to the entrance door, which had opened to the elements, allowing a draught of warm air to enter the lobby to be chilled by the overworking air-conditioning, then another, and another.

Peter's was one of the last to follow the other heads, which had turned like meerkats following their leader to pick up a scent.

It was the statuesque beauty in blue, flanked, or so it appeared, by her two maidservants, who had done a wonderful job grooming the young lady to be presented to her waiting world. The two rushed away and went on a peering-pairing exercise. It appeared lady in blue wasn't bothered about finding her match.

A few heads blocking the clear sightline between Peter and Honey Yim Lam parted, as if reacting to some laser beam about to link two people or objects together. Peter's eyes met with Honey's for the second time. *Dear God, please don't let some chap in his coach get in our way this time,* he thought.

The meeting of the eyes forced her lips to part and her teeth gleamed again. He reciprocated. He was now certain they knew each other from another world. He made his way across.

"You don't seem to have a delegate to watch over."

"Oh I do, sir," she said.

"Then shouldn't you be rushing around and reading labels to find your charge?"

Honey giggled. "You don't seem to have a chaperone."

"No, but it's not been for want of beautiful girls coming and reading my badge and wanting to cheat and change the name in their envelope."

She bet that was not far from the truth, but was he showing overconfidence in his popularity?

"Why would they want to do that? Mr Ho has drawn lots for the pairings."

"Ah! You haven't even bothered to read my badge. It says my name, and under it I've added the words… 'who wishes to meet a beautiful Malaysian princess, and for them both to live happily ever after'."

Her legs positively weakened. What humour! Could he mean it? There was a quiet pause between them.

"Now why don't we open your envelope and we'll go together to see who's been selected and I'll offer him, or her, a million ringgit to let them have my chaperone in exchange for you. What do you think? Shall we open the envelope together?"

"I've no need to," she said behind a broad smile, which this time exposed a soft, beautiful, rich purple tongue, curling and skimming behind her teeth.

"No need to?"

"No. God has chosen my charge."

"And who may I ask has God chosen?"

"It is bound to be you."

"How can you be so sure?"

"There's a chemistry between us."

"You're a sweet beautiful young lady, but life is not like that."

"If you have a God, it is."

"What's your name?"

"Honey Yim Lam."

"Mine's Peter Martinez."

Of course, she knew that.

"Now let's have a pact. If my name is not in your envelope, you are to smile at me whenever we're within smiling distance."

"And if God has put your name in my envelope… ?"

"Then you must smile with me all day."

Honey leant forward and read his badge. "It doesn't say about the princess and you taking her away with you."

"You don't believe in fairytales, surely."

"Yes I do."

"Honey, you're lovely. Please give me the envelope."

"I've no need."

"Here. Give."

"Oh, alright. But I shall cry if my beliefs are wrong."

"… And I shall wipe the tears from your eyes."

He took the envelope and opened it.

"Mr George Banks, America," he read out.

Honey burst into tears. Had she got it wrong? Had it been re-switched? Peter held his arms out. She fell into them amidst a number of staring faces from the surrounding delegates and their guides.

"Here, wipe your tears. I'll read it again. Mr Peter Martinez."

She stopped crying instantly. "Here. Please. Let me see." She read the card. "Mr Peter Martinez. Thank you, God," Looking up into the heavily beamed ceiling and into Peter's face, she whispered, "… and I do believe in fairy tales. Listen, sir, I have some guiding to do with you… we've got to see your room… show you the beach… both the pools…where the restaurants are… the nursery gardens… the gym…"

He would never have been able to stop the excited exhaling of the pre-prepared agenda… so he put a large hand over her beautiful mouth, stifling her words.

"It's one step at a time. Slowly," he said.

"Of course. You're right. I'm just so excited I have 'Mr Blue Eyes'."

"Me too. Miss Topaz Ones."

CHAPTER 10

Honey took charge, as she was expected to. She ushered Peter around the lobby, principally to display her delegate to all her other colleagues, but without him knowing it. "Bound to be you," was the general consensus of opinion. Girls will be girls and there was little doubt that Peter's photo slide had caught their imaginations, and confirmed to them what a young Western man should look like. They giggled as they got a real-life view of what he was in the flesh. Arguably, Honey was the most beautiful of the Malaysian team of chaperones, so there was more than one thought that the pairing might just have been made in heaven.

"Now the shuttle," she said, telling Peter to follow her through the lobby back into the vast reception area and out into the pool of sunshine, which illuminated the buggy collection point. The shuttles were a fleet of enlarged golf carts, some capable of taking three plus a driver, others five and some up to 11. They were open-sided with plastic shields rolled into the overlap of the roof, which were let down during tropical rain. They moved silently around the complex, fuelled by their electric batteries. Honey explained you could always call for one from the room or take pot-luck and hitch a ride if one passed.

Honey and Peter shared a smaller buggy with the young Malaysian boy driver in his traditional batik shirt and smart imported light brown chinos. As they drove between the bougainvillaea and hibiscus and other exotic oriental palms and prolific orchids, Honey pointed out places of interest. "Children's club,", "Breakfast salon,", "Video lounge,", "Swings."

"Swings?" Peter asked. "Why are you telling me about swings? They're for children."

"I'd like to go on the swings with you, sir, while you're here."

"Why on earth do you want to do that?"

"Because I've never been on one, and I'd be scared by myself."

She had a child within bursting to get out, Peter thought, but outwardly she was calm, very organised, and becoming more beautiful as she relaxed in his company.

"Villa 3107," she reconfirmed to the driver.

The villas were two-storey and built in Malaysian style, mainly of timber below a clay-shingled, steeply-pitched roof. There were filigree facings to the shutters and around the eaves detailing, and on the external teak balustrading alongside the staircases and around the balconies.

The buggy stopped outside a carved teak sign, which had the number 3107 burned into it and hatched in with a black vegetable oil. Honey jumped out and rushed to the baggage shelf on the back. She had begun to lift Peter's case before he got there.

"Hey! Young lady. That's my job. I shift cases."

"No, sir," she countered indignantly. "It is indeed my job."

He moved across and put his hand over hers on the handle of the case and lifted it off. "When I say it's my job, OK, it's my job."

"But sir, we are told to do it."

"… And are you told to call me 'sir'?"

"Yes, of course, sir."

"OK. So here are the new rules. You don't get to do your job of carrying suitcases, OK, and you drop the 'sir', it's too servile."

"But sir, I have to."

"Are you also told you must do everything to make your guest comfortable?"

She hesitated. "Yes, but we are told we must not have any body contact. So if you are asking can I make you comfortable in that way, I am not allowed."

Peter roared with laughter. Almost guffawed.

"Have I done something wrong?" she said. "Is that not what you were asking?"

He peered at her badge, and the gentle mound of femininity it was set upon. He read her name precisely. "Honey Yim Lam, my friend. There are normal everyday ways of making someone feel comfortable. It makes me feel uncomfortable that a young lady of very nearly my age group is calling me 'sir'. So I'm going to ask you again to break a second rule, apart from me doing the bag-carrying. Would you call me Peter, please?"

"I don't think I'd be allowed. Perhaps I could call you Mr Peter."

"Well, I suppose that's better than 'sir'. So it's Mr Peter from here on."

"Yes, and you carry the cases, providing Mr Ho is not around to punish me. May I still be Miss Lam?"

"No! You become Honey."

"But if Mr Ho is within earshot could it be Miss Honey… otherwise I might be in trouble."

"Do you know, Honey, they say in the West that the East is 30 years behind."

"Do they say that in a spiteful way?"

"No, not at all. Sometimes I believe it's meant in an envious way. It's now getting so casual in Europe, probably since they stopped compulsory military service and women started burning their bras."

"Burning their bras!" Honey positively blushed. "And, sir, do men and women talk about those?"

"Those are good questions… oh, Honey, I can see we're going to have so much fun! Me trying to explain Western ways, and you taking everything I say literally. In modern Europe, men and women talk about everything whether it's really a male or female topic. It's called equal rights."

"Mr Peter, Malaysian girls will never burn their bras, and we don't want equal rights." *And so the princess ruled and they lived happily ever after.*

Honey invoked her unequal rights by unpacking Peter's case and hanging everything up neatly. She clearly expected to attend upon him all day. He bet his bottom dollar with himself, though, that as soon as the clock struck nine o'clock, she would be off on Mr Ho's instructions, back to wherever she was expected to get her beauty sleep. Not, Peter thought, that she needed any more as she was already so staggeringly beautiful.

Honey went into the bathroom and was in there for a good ten minutes. Peter had heard water running but presumed she would not just go and take a bath without his approval.

She reappeared.

"Mr Peter. You have had a long journey, and you have a busy schedule. The welcoming address is at midday, and after that there is a lunch, then some relaxation and then the beginning seminar at six this evening, and then a welcome supper. I've run a bath for you. I don't know how you like it. But it is warm. Not hot, nor cold. I've dressed the water with some invigorating herbs and spices of the Orient. I must not be here while you bathe, though."

Peter interrupted. "… Because Mr Ho, who is turning out to be a complete spoilsport, wouldn't like it. Honey. That's fine. Thank you. I shall love it just warm. Where will you go?"

"I shall sit on the steps outside in the shade. Will you call when you've finished?"

"Honey, my back aches from being cramped up from flying. Would Mr Ho permit you to give it a massage? Or is that not allowed?"

"He hasn't said."

"In that case, I'll give you a call and if he hasn't made any rules about this, it will be part of my demands that he's told you to fulfil."

Honey thought she would be able to trust her Mr Peter. After all, he was Western. She wouldn't trust a fellow Malaysian under similar circumstances.

He duly called. She equally duly returned to find him with a white bath towel tied sari-fashion around his waist.

"I think on the bed," she said. Words that conjured up some beautiful sexual exploitation, but he would respect her trust in him. Her natural talents worked a treat. He felt a new man, now able to slip on a T-shirt and jeans and tell Honey she could now commence whatever tour she was programmed to give.

How she was relieved by his attitude. She'd never had the experience before of being turned on by a male body. Even just the shoulders, rear ribcage and waist, and to top it all, Peter's strong neck.

She'd had this insatiable desire to roll him over and remove the towel. She'd really had to fight that impulse. She'd noticed things that had never happened to her before, although she was well into puberty. Her breasts had tingled, and it had felt that all her otherwise well-honed thigh and tummy muscles, which she tensed on her walks to school or as she washed, were released in some sort of pleasurable expectation.

So she was happy when Peter replied, when asked whether she had relaxed his tired back: "Yes, it feels wonderful. A minute more and I'd break Mr Ho's golden rule."

"Which one?" she asked.

"Oh, dear sweet Honey, all of them in one moment."

"I see," she said, hesitantly, wanting to give Peter the impression of her naivety, although knowing full well what he meant.

She waited on the steps while he put on his T-shirt and jeans… and off he was rushed. They had a light lunch and relaxed in hammocks strung between the casuarina trees.

"Won't we be killed by falling coconuts?" Peter asked.

Honey laughed. "Mr Peter, don't you know that coconuts have eyes underneath them and they can see people, and don't ever fall on their heads."

"Really?" Peter said convincingly. "Now that's something we didn't know in the West."

The opening of the conference was quite solemn. All the chaperones sat at the back of the hall while the delegates got down to outlining the serious stuff, a bit like a synagogue on a festive occasion. According to the programme, Peter was due to deliver his paper about midday the next day. It was billed as 'a much merited appraisal as to how design and architecture could play its part in environmental protection'. He didn't need to rehearse it. If he got stuck, he could follow his notes. But Honey Yim Lam was advising him to have a rehearsal of his delivery from the actual rostrum.

The benefit of her first-hand experience enabled her to advise. "You may feel different looking down on people, rather than as equals on the same level."

So, in accordance with her recommendation, they would have a dry run at seven the next morning.

The supper after the opening was relaxed. The guides were included, so it became all the more colourful. The pitch of the decibels generated became higher as the oriental beauties excitedly enjoyed the food and the fun of trying to teach their charges how to use chopsticks.

Mr Ho had no fears thereafter about body contact. The Australian and New Zealand contingents were now behind their natural time-clocks, while the others were generally ahead. The Americans really didn't know whether they were coming or going, so for each of their various reasons, all delegates were happy to lay their heads on their own uninterrupted, unshared pillows. The girls, too, were exhausted and it wasn't just one who skipped stripping off their makeup in favour of a desperate desire for sleep.

Friday was another day.

Peter would probably have slept through the morning if he had not been awakened by a gentle tapping on the outer door, which at first he could not understand. He certainly wasn't in Prince of Wales Drive… or Calella… Then it dawned on him, he was in Malaysia, and that was probably his wake-up call.

He opened the door, a little casually holding a towel around his lower half by just grasping both ends in his left hand, which was acting like an accountant's bulldog clip. Honey bowed her head with dropped eyelids and, with both hands held together at chest height in the formal Malaysian greeting, did a little curtsey.

"Good morning, Mr Peter. Did you sleep well?"

Peter couldn't return the head-bowing, hand-clasping compliment for fear of dropping the towel.

"What a wonderful first sight of the day," he said, in all sincerity. "My Honey. I did sleep well… and you?"

She'd hardly slept, in fact. She had lain staring up at the ceiling, it seemed, all night. Her body was still tingling, and she did not know quite how to cope with that. She'd had a doting boyfriend since third year at school. He was the son of a friend of her father's and both sets of parents were trying to arrange their marriage, or so she thought. But, although he was a boyfriend, they talked about schoolwork, not about growing up and emotions and things that Honey's body was reporting back to her brain now.

"Fine," she eventually answered.

She was wearing a pink, mauve and green sari. Her face and eye makeup were impeccable. She was bright, awake and smiling.

"How long have I got?" Peter asked.

"It's just after six. We get a 15-minute slot at seven."

"Right. You wait on the steps to please Mr Ho and we'll leave here at 6.30 precisely, and we'll walk."

That's what they did, and when they did it. Then they had breakfast and after that, Peter put on his presentation suit to attend the conference proper for 9am. After the earlier presentations, the Chairman of the conference went to great pains to explain what input Peter was due to deliver... all about design... materials... in fact he made it all sound too boring.

So there were two qualities of ovation for him, by way of pre-delivery encouragement. The one was the formal conference type, which acted as a preamble to most of the presentations throughout the three conference days. In Peter's case, there was a sort of fan club unleashed and all the hostesses showed again who was the most fashionable of delegates. Their clapping went on far too long for Mr Ho's liking. He'd need to have a word.

Peter stood up, knowing exactly how his paper started. Honey inwardly panicked because she recognised his extreme hesitation about starting his set piece. He'd been so good at the earlier run-through. Peter turned the papers in their neat pile in front of him, face down.

"Chairman, ladies and gentlemen, delegates all, supporting teams."

He started, still with a hint of his native accent: "Your words, sir, made my contribution, in terms of the built environment, seem most terribly boring... almost as though I had nothing to suggest for each of us to action in scientific terms to overcome the environmental problems. But there is an onus on individual effort, which all of us here could think about adopting to help the planet out. Other delegates, I believe, intend to put their cases for energy production, how to keep the seas stocked with fish and prevent icebergs from melting, but those will be contributions from recognised experts of high repute. I'd like to put this conference in perspective in a slightly different way but before that, have a couple of things to say.

"We are here courtesy of the Malaysian Government, and none of this would have been possible without their initiative."

There was instant applause. Perhaps he had it right.

"What is more, none of us would have gathered into this conference hall on time without all the beautiful young ladies sitting at the rear of the hall..."

More appreciative clapping.

"Now could I just illustrate the point I wish to make by asking them all to stand up." There was much impromptu giggling as first two young ladies stood up, followed by a hesitant half dozen or so.

"Come on, ladies. Please don't be shy. You are about to become the subjects of a very serious experiment… now, I'm going to count to three. I'd like you all to stand up quickly at the end of the count. One, two, three."

Amidst nervous Oriental laughter, they all dutifully stood.

"Perhaps the delegates would show their appreciation for the guidance these young beautiful ladies have given us collectively and individually."

The delegates warmly followed his suggestion by clapping vigorously. Peter waited for silence to return.

"Now there, Chairman, ladies and gentlemen, lies the real problem. A hundred or so young ladies carrying out a normal body function of standing up generated so much energy, as in the heat source type, that the air-conditioning in this conference hall attempted to go into overdrive to reduce that sudden increased temperature. The clapping you all generated produced wind currents that would counter the flows of chilled air. So those two natural actions generate enormous energy requirements.

"Now my subject is about the built environment. We as architects and designers can make a major contribution and it will be part of my submission to suggest that where we, as developing humans, went wrong was to leave our predecessors' caves and seek sophistication.

"To make my point, if the previous experiment had been carried out in a cathedral in Europe or a temple in Malaysia, there would have been no need for air-conditioning because the buildings, when constructed, dealt then with environmental control… hugely thick walls in Europe… no outer walls in Malaysia, allowing the wind to be its own environmental conditioner. I put it to you all, in whichever field you practise, to show concern for the damage you might be creating, for the changes in climate and global warming; to pause and, in the interest of self-preservation, turn the clock back for a while.

"Young ladies, our fears are for your generation and the generation your children will represent. Our greatest fear is, in three simple, non-technological words: your own contribution…"

As Peter continued, Honey again felt the pangs of yesterday. This man was like a guru. He had knowledge and he was on a mission to impart that.

"… Your own contribution would be to recognise that, although it may help you to feel beautiful, it is as important for you to give up using, for example, hair lacquer… not to smoke cigarettes… to resist manufactured makeup… you do not need it… your grandmothers were as beautiful as you are without modern, polluting cosmetics… take a warm bath…" Honey again felt the hairs at the nape of her neck bristle. "… Not a hot one… continue to wear traditional cotton based fabrics made on the loom the old-fashioned way…

avoid nylon and other man-made materials which consume oil and electricity in the manufacturing process… eat uncooked foods, salads and drink spring water, not purified water in manufactured plastic bottles.

"If you all make that contribution… if we all pull together in that, we will be well on the way to protecting the environment… but let me revert to my set piece and tell you what architecture can do, and is likely to do, to supplement your initiatives."

He looked down at the lectern, turned his paper the correct way up and took the delegates through the salient points.

"And so… my fellow friends of the Earth, together, and in the knowledge of how our forefathers ensured we have reached this generation… let us combine together, to keep the world we all so love spinning on its axis. Thank you."

There was tumultuous applause. Delegates and chaperones alike stood as one and clapped for several minutes. Peter, with enormous panache, beckoned with his palms downwards for the audience to quieten. He leant forward to the microphone and whispered, "That's precisely what we shouldn't be doing… listen to that air conditioning humming!" There were hoots of laughter.

He left the rostrum to the left. He could actually have equally taken the right-hand route but, there, waiting in the wings on the left, was his Honey. She had tears rolling down her cheeks.

"Oh, Mr Peter, I was so proud. You were brilliant. You're a star. All the girls love you."

"Go on!" he said, as he so often did when he was embarrassed. "I only said what needed to be said."

"I will never, ever use hair lacquer again," she said, with purpose. "It's a pity we just can't get a car to take us away to swim," she added, "but you must listen to the other speeches."

"Unfortunately, you're right. It would be very rude not to."

From then on Peter became something of a cult figure. He was invited to go to America by one delegate and Mexico by another, once it was realised that he spoke fluent Spanish.

The final session was on Sunday, when the conference formally closed. Peter's flight was at 9pm. Langkawi to Kuala Lumpur, and then the midnight flight back to London via some dreadful desert outpost to refuel. A semi-formal lunch had been arranged. Honey had been quiet all morning.

"Will you just leave after lunch?" she enquired, as they walked towards the open-air restaurant.

"I've got till about 8pm, when I have to be at the airport. I had wondered, as presumably you'll be off duty after the lunch, if we could get that car we talked about and go off for a swim?"

"Could you hire a jeep, Mr Peter?" she said excitedly.

"I guess I could. Why?"

"I've heard there's a waterfall almost 45 minutes' drive away, at the end of some rough terrain and there is a magic about the water."

"What sort of magic?"

"Oh, it's only silly young girl talk. Far too silly for you to even hear about."

"OK, let's say we get away from here at about three. I'll have said adiós to the people I've met, and liked, and not bother with those I haven't."

"Your girl fan club will all want to say goodbye. Please don't forget them."

"To kiss them all goodbye would take up the time we have to swim. What do you think?"

"I think you just say a few words to all of them and wave one big goodbye," Honey suggested.

Peter networked around the tables after he had finished his lunch. Yes, of course everybody was bound to meet in the future. They always said they would. He did say a global adiós to the chaperones. It was noisy, colourful and very alive. Something about the excitement of the Far East really appealed to Peter. It all seemed so genuine, so real, there was no pretence. If they didn't understand something they said so, and proceeded to find out the answer. They were emergent in a big way.

It was now 2.30pm. "I've got a couple of things I have to do. I could meet you in the lobby at five to three. The jeep will be there," Peter said to Honey.

"May I come to the room and pick you up from there?" Honey asked.

"Sure. But I carry the cases. The conference is over."

"I know," she said, and allowed a tear to run from her left eye.

"Come on now, Honey. We have to stay happy."

"I know," she said, and this time tears ran from both eyes.

"You're a terrible softie." He had an overpowering instinct to lean forward and touch cheeks… and that is precisely what some outer force encouraged him to do. Honey stepped back and looked around them furtively, as if they had been caught and lightning would strike them both dead.

"I'll be at the room," she said.

Peter made his way across the lobby. He wanted to buy something for his mother, and maybe Max, and he supposed Anna. He hadn't got much time and it seemed convenient that they had a display of Selangor Pewter – but then it was a tourist shop. His eye was immediately taken to a prettily carved letter opener. He thought his mother would like that, and what was more, she would use it in her office at the hotel. He hoped she was OK. He felt guilty that he'd hardly given her a thought in Malaysia. He'd phone when he got home. There was a chunkier version of the knife, presumably for a male. That, and a little jewel box for Anna, would be fine. He started to settle up.

"We have perfume, sir."

Peter hardly heard what the young lady said. "Sorry. Could you say that again?"

Before she did, he knew exactly what she had said, and was going to repeat. His senses were obviously playing tricks with him.

"Perfume!" he said. "Do you have Chanel?"

"Of course, sir, no shop could say they sell perfume if their stock did not include Chanel No. 5. We have perfume or cologne, sir."

"Perfume. Could you wrap it?"

"Yes of course. A special paper?"

"Do you have a really deep blue colour?"

"Yes, sir."

"With a pink bow, please."

"Would you like a label to write to the young lady?"

"How do you know it's a young lady and not for my mother?"

"Because you've taken so much care over the choice, the paper, and it shows that you can smell it on the young lady already, in your mind."

He could. Did it really show that much? When he got to the room, he literally threw everything into his case. Toilet things went into an overnight bag. His conference notes and the copy of his paper went into the briefcase his mother had bought him for Christmas.

There was a knock at the door of room 3107. He now knew that gentle knock so well. He opened the door. He'd changed into shorts and a T-shirt. Honey looked absolutely beautiful. She was wearing a simple pink cotton blouse with a pretty stand-up collar, a deep blue pleated mini-skirt and high-wedge blue shoes. He surveyed her from tip to toe.

"Honey, I've never seen so much of your body before. Those saris aren't fair to a young man. You're beautiful."

"You say that as though you're surprised."

There was now a maturity about her. She'd changed out of her young girl mode into an experienced all-woman one. He pondered, wondering which he preferred. He felt safer with his emotions with the young girl, but would have confessed to being turned on by the woman standing before him now.

"Mr Peter. Your stares are embarrassing me. Come on, we have to go."

She was taking control.

The jeep was white and spotless. Honey threw a beach bag into the back.

Peter had an audio tape and a bulge in his shorts pocket. At first glance, out of the corner of her eye, Honey thought it was like Ben, the one her parents were going to try to get her to marry, when he sometimes got a bulge. They'd never talked about it but some of the girls at school said it happened when boys got aroused. She'd rather hoped Peter was showing such signs. She couldn't look too closely but it wasn't like Ben got. It was possibly a box of some sort, and that made her laugh inwardly.

Inside the jeep, Peter put the tape into the cassette player. It was his unwind and relax classical tape, which Anna had introduced him to as part of what she called his 'further education'. Elgar's Adagio cello concerto was followed by one of Mozart's piano ones. By the time Bizet's Adagietto came on, Honey had slid down into the adjoining passenger seat, had tilted it back a couple of notches and was listening intently to the music, which she had never encountered before. Peter glanced across. He'd had an inkling earlier, on his first impression, of a look he hadn't seen before. Honey was probably not wearing a bra.

They'd only driven about four miles but there was a sign indicating a lay-by coming up. He stopped the jeep. She opened her eyes slowly and turned her head to look at him. Her hands were in her lap. Her whole demeanour said, "You're invited."

He leant across and took her right hand into his and lifted it to chest level. He slid his hand around inside hers, so that she now had his hand cupped inside hers. He laid both his and her hands on her right breast, which firmed appreciably at his light touch. She made no attempt to move his hand away. She smiled, one of her wide smiles of welcome.

"You're not wearing a bra," he observed. She just smiled. "What are you up to, Miss Lam?"

"I had an accident, Mr Martinez, I was ironing it and I burnt it. Don't you know all the girls do that nowadays?" She lifted her left hand from her lap and, although appreciating Peter's attentions enormously, felt it was right and proper that she should remove their combined right ones from her now aroused body.

"Honey, I've got a little 'thank you' for all you've done for me." He fumbled in his pocket and brought out the blue and pink wrapped box.

"How did you know I'd wear blue and pink?" she asked, her words reflected by the amazed look on her face.

"I could lie. But I find that difficult. So the truth is, the colours happen to be right by chance."

"Do you find it difficult to lie?"

"I can't lie."

"Neither can I, Peter. Thank you for whatever is in the box. Thank you, thank you, thank you. I've never had such a romantic present before."

"How do you know it's romantic? It might be a car puncture repair kit."

"No. I know it's romantic. It's the way you've given it to me. Could I open it now, please?"

"No. When I'm on the plane."

"Why?"

"Honey, I'm finding you incredibly beautiful and we've got something special between us. The present might just be like a time bomb."

"Then, if you've given me such a present, you can't stop me from blowing us both up. It might be the safest solution. I'm going to open it."

She reverted momentarily to being a little girl at her birthday party. She very carefully peeled the Sellotape from around the shiny paper and then opened the various overlaps. She suddenly saw 'Chanel' in its black lettering on the white background of the box. She drew her breath.

"Peter, that's really, really so wonderful! How did you know I've never ever wanted any other perfume apart from Chanel? I've never actually smelt it but somewhere or other I saw an advert for it in a French magazine and I've longed to have some ever since."

In a couple of twists of her hips, she was up on her knees with her arms thrown round Peter's neck, her left cheek planted hard against his right one.

"Peter, Peter, Peter, oh my lovely Peter! Thank you." She appeared to think deeply, then said, "Peter, let's pretend we've got three hours to live."

"Oh, come on, Honey. That's not only morbid but it won't be true."

"Peter. Please. Let me have a last girly fantasy before I grow up, and fight back the… I think the word you've been using is 'inevitable'… yes, the inevitable tears. So that's done, my darling Peter. Three hours from now…" She leant back over him and put her forefinger to his beautiful lips so as to stifle a response. "May I open the time bomb, please?"

"Yes. Fine. I'd love you to."

She gently broke the seal and carefully removed the glass stopper. Peter's lungs were already choking on the wondrous fragrance. She dabbed a little on the insides of both her wrists, then a light forefinger's worth behind each ear. She then spread the faintest amount on the palm of her right hand and smoothed that down her neck, dangerously, Peter thought, close to her cleavage and then up to the nape of her neck and just into her hairline.

"Now get me fast to this magic waterfall. Let's go. OK." She now took on a very commanding role as she unfurled a homemade map and placed it on her lap. She leant forward and turned up the volume to Verdi's Chorus of the Hebrew Slaves.

"What is the music, Peter?"

"It's called 'The Slave's Chorus'… and here I am, a slave to your charms… well, I can't lie… a slave to all of you."

The Chanel now was to remind him of Honey, and only Honey. It was different from when Marcia and Meribel wore it… maybe it reacted differently to skin types… but it was only Honey who could fill his nostrils and lungs like this.

They bounced on rocks once they had turned off the road and only just squeezed between boulders on each side of the rough track, which seemed to be going downhill. They manoeuvred round a fallen tree. They could hear rushing water but the overhanging rain forest was making it quite dark. There was suddenly a downward shaft of light as if from a helicopter trying to pick out some escaping convict with its piercing searchlight. There, ahead of them, was a pool of water which in her Malaysian imperial upbringing was about 50 feet across. The surface was deeply rippled and it was part blue and part green in colour, apparently reflecting some blue sky and the verdant green of the overhanging foliage.

Honey said, "Peter, look." And she pointed upwards. There, as far as the eye could see, was a huge shaft of water, about ten feet wide, majestically falling from the opening cut in the umbrella of trees, through which the light was penetrating and the blue sky above was gently receiving the odd puff of cloud and letting it pass by.

The waterfall was like a sheet of shiny steel.

Honey grabbed his hand. At first they had to shout but then reverted to sign language. She pointed to a rock formation over on the right. He was suddenly reminded of young Jaimé.

Finger pointed at Peter's chest – "You," – then towards the rocks – "go there." She crossed her arms and took the hem of her blouse, indicating, "And undress," by making as if to raise the blouse over her head.

She then reversed her finger into her chest, then pointed to rocks on the left: "I go there." Slowly, she undid three buttons, exposing half of the most beautiful cleavage in the most appealing formation Peter realised he had ever beheld. She was olive-skinned, with a hint of the warmness and allure of the black olive strain. He presumed that to mean that she, too, would get undressed.

Peter had surreptitiously peeped into the pool. It was about a metre and a half deep. *Thank God!* he thought. He didn't fancy practising his moderate swimming in that current. He worked out he would be able to stand. They went their opposite ways.

Honey slipped quietly into the water. She had let her hair down, Peter noticed, as she swam towards the middle of the pool. He sat on the rocks and slid in himself, making his way to join her. The water was crystal clear and he could see her body was totally nude, part magnified under the water. She, too, noticed Peter had thrown any hint of modesty to the wind. He felt her hand touch his as they stood looking up at the sheet of molten steel pouring down and hitting the water some ten feet or three metres in front of them.

Honey took a step forward, and pulled Peter alongside her. There was a hint of both courage and suicide about her determination to go further forward into the eye of the fall, as it were. Peter stopped and indicated the enormous weight pouring down from above. She made an image of a ducking dolphin. Peter held back. Prudence made him see the danger that could be ahead of them. He shook his head negatively.

Honey released his hand and stood in front of him. She leant her body towards his and, without hand or arm contact, kissed him fully on the lips. Their lips were parted by six inches, it seemed, into which was enough distance for her to spread her huge smile. Still smiling, Honey moved her head forward but held her body back, and kissed him again through her smile. As she did, she slipped her tongue fleetingly between his now slightly parted lips. Subsequently, she had never understood why that had been instinctive. She pulled away, turned quickly and dived under the weight of the cascade. Two strong pulls of breaststroke below the water and she was able to surface now behind the torrent.

There was so much emotion now charged into Peter's body. The over-riding one was panic and fear of what he knew he had to do. As for the rewards, he had no idea. Life was full of surprises to him. Other men might have anticipated when they were on a lucky streak and been prepared for such. Peter always seemed not to be and hadn't given a thought to raiding his toilet bag for a condom before their outing; it was now packed for the journey home and miles away anyway. He said a very quick prayer for God to travel with him, took an immense breath and dolphined under the fall.

He could make out Honey's exquisite form standing just beyond his couple of underwater strokes. His fear had caused him to take a very deep course on his way to meet the far braver Honey. His arms folded around her legs at about knee height. He'd never seen an unshaven girl before – not that he was that experienced, but that told him Honey had not played around with her body to court fashion and the new-found trends girls were following in their liberated pursuit of men.

Honey was light in weight anyway, but below the water her body was like a smooth bag of feathers as he collected it and made his upward push to find oxygen and recharge his failing lungs. Her arms clung around Peter's neck for security and her legs clamped firmly around his waist to cope with the surge up and out of the water, until Peter was able to stand firmly with both feet on the rock floor, raising himself to his full height.

She laughed as she saw how out of breath he was, and leant forward and blew mischievously into his open, panting mouth. That made him laugh too and their heads locked side by side as their bodies joined their laughter. Honey couldn't remember if it was the second or third time, or if she had always had the feeling that the pit of her stomach was empty, her thighs had lost their muscles... and the longing for a regeneration she felt was necessary. This time, without a doubt, Peter, like Ben, did have a bulge. She had a feeling that the girls who knew about such things were right.

Did Peter want her to behave like a slut? Would he have any respect left for her if she did? Surely she should save such feelings for when she was married. Perhaps it was God rehearsing them for marriage. She was now the one with fear. Behind the cascade, it was quiet. She whispered, "Peter." He heard her clearly.

"Honey," he replied. Her body was entering a trembling spasm. He turned her head so it was in front of his, and took the initiative to kiss her. He forced her lips apart. The kiss was out of control, she was somehow drawing his tongue into her open mouth and chasing it back into his with her own tongue, which then caressed his teeth gently.

Her trembling was receding.

"Peter. I'll never lie. I'm so sorry, but I love you."

With that, she raised herself by her arms around his shoulders, and gently lowered her body so they became one unit, formed together and entwined.

Twice, she remembered later, he had fulfilled the empty pit in her stomach and restored muscle to her thighs, to her shoulders and, she felt, even down into her toes.

This time Peter was not being timed, or allocated time. They had the remainder of three hours together before life came to an end. So they should never pass this opportunity. They found their way up onto a rock ledge above the waterline and lay there, no talk, no movement, just lay there... their bodies making intermittent contact with each other.

They dressed, and as they walked back to the jeep they held hands. They climbed in in silence. Peter clicked the cassette player on. They continued tightly holding a left hand with a right one as they navigated the rock path, as though to ensure a part of their bodies continued to be in contact.

Honey leant forward and turned up one cassette track. "What's this, Peter?"

"It's by a man who wrote beautifully sad opera, called Puccini."

"What is the girl saying?"

"It's in Italian, 'Oh mio babbino caro'. She's just saying 'Oh dear daddy' and goes on to ask if she can marry her boyfriend, who he doesn't really approve of."

Honey cried. She cried through Bach's Air Suite and wept solidly at Samuel Barber's Adagio.

What they hadn't taken into account when they discussed Peter's leaving time earlier that day was that Honey hadn't looked at her own itinerary. She had to report to Mr Ho's assisting team in the reception area of the hotel by 7pm. Mr Ho was not prepared to pay for another night's board and so the chosen girls who had come from Penang were going back on the 7.45pm ferry that evening. Two hours on the inter-island boat would see Honey back off her 'course', or so her father would think, to be picked up at the Penang ferry terminal about 9pm. At that time, Peter would just be beginning his long flight home.

Peter looked at his watch. It was tight for time, so they crammed in everything they had to say of a personal nature, now that the relationship had changed. Peter would write first; there was just a possibility he and Max might change flats so any address he gave might be out of date and the British Post Office were not good at dealing with changes of address. He couldn't write to her home, she said, because the family would soon twig there was something going on, as a letter from England or Spain would be a talking point for the whole village. So she suggested he should write to her best friend Sally Lau, who could be totally trusted. She'd write the address down when they got back to Pelangi.

Saying 'au revoir', which Peter went to great pains to translate as 'until we meet again', they both agreed, gripping hands, was going to be painful. They were both suddenly confused yet elated at having found each other, albeit, as Honey never failed to stress, with God's help.

They kissed goodbye at 6.50pm, according to Peter's alarm clock, which he could read over Honey's shoulder as they stood clinched, neither one of them wishing to make the final move until Honey broke from Peter's arms, turned, looked back once, then rushed out through the panelled teak door leading out of room 3107.

Peter had never knowingly had a lump in his throat before. What he had had was the feeling of an impending and substantial loss. He'd had that taste in his mouth, he remembered, when he realised his father would never return from the deep. Now he suddenly felt his legs running aimlessly, as he had on that tragic morning; yet this time, he was riveted to a square footage of locally woven carpet, not moving at all.

He could not hold back his tears.

"Dear God," he whispered, "not again. Please not again."

CHAPTER 11
ENGLAND – 1987

All Josephine 'Jo' Smith had ever known about Peter's trip to Malaysia was from the framed newspaper cutting he cherished on the side unit in his St James's office.

"Young Spanish student sets the 'Save the World Conference' on fire," was the headline, always there to stare at her, and his many visitors, along with the framed design awards, photographs with VIPs, and an always unexplained photograph of a high waterfall, somewhere in the world.

Jo was sorting papers in Peter's office as he arrived. He was usually on the dot of nine, which didn't fit in with Jo Smith's usual working lifestyle at all, although after ten years of being with Peter as his PA, she should have got used to it. If she'd had her way, she would have started at the more civilised hour of ten, and that thought was constantly bugging her, so that psychologically she was never really in work mode until that time.

"Morning, Jo," Peter said in his usual confident way. Certainly he was never fazed by any time that he started, or indeed, finished work. Some would have called him a workaholic but he didn't see it that way. He just intended to earn a lot of money, which inevitably meant he'd have to work hard and long hours to achieve that. So that's what he did, and that's what he was used to.

He sat down in his black leather swivel chair. Jo always took a chance on him not being delayed by putting a cup of freshly brewed coffee on his desk. He'd said at her interview, "I like a cup of coffee on my arrival," and she hadn't realised how serious he was about that.

"Where's my coffee?" he'd said on her first day.

"I'm sorry, I thought you'd like it freshly made and hot once you arrived."

"No. You can be pretty sure I'll arrive at nine, so I'd be pleased if you'd have it ready." Thereafter his command was obeyed.

"So, what's on, Jo?"

"Your post is there as normal. The only urgent stuff is from the bank. They've got the bond to be sorted out on the Washington deal. All you need to do is to approve it and Bryan Thompson can do the rest." Bryan was the company secretary, and like all Peter's selections, was first-rate at his job.

"… And what's in the diary?"

"You've got Jan Roberts at ten."

"Oh shit, I'd forgotten, although I know you reminded me. How long does she need?"

"How long is it going to take a lady like Jan Roberts to get over 20 years of your life into her notebook for Gordon's mega PR release for September?"

"So, how long?"

"You'll go mad."

"Jo, you're beginning to aggravate me. How long?"

"Well, she said could I book two days…"

"… And you said, 'No bloody way, you'll get a morning and the rest you'll have to make up', didn't you?"

Jo had been there before. Providing Peter liked Jan, she'd no doubt get her two days, and more if needed.

"If I'd known becoming the CEO meant having to pour out my life history to be sent around the business press of the world, just to boost confidence in the group and the share price, I think I would have passed up the opportunity."

One thing that could always be said of Gordon Jones was that if anybody knew the whole PR industry, he did. Jan Roberts's reputation, too, stretched out ahead of her. One of her coups had been her interview with Mandela as he left prison. She'd shown her versatility in a business profile she'd done on the Duchess of somewhere or other, in which she had made an amazing but apparently fully supportable accusation that she was using her position within the Royal Family to promote her own PR company. The media took the fact that the Duchess had walked out of the interview as a guilty plea.

Peter cleared some essential phone calls and OK'd the Washington bond. That was good news. It meant they were nearer the green light on a £30 million development deal in a fashionable part of that great American metropolis, right under the feet of the American competition.

Peter's internal phone rang.

"Jan Roberts is here. The boardroom or your office?"

"My office would be a little more relaxed."

"May I show her in?"

"Yes, get it over and done with. If there's anything going on, I want you to interrupt."

"Of course," Jo confirmed confidently. Although everybody saw Peter as a confident person, he still had fears about the type of grilling he was about to get. He remained a very private person who truly trusted very few of his work colleagues.

The left leaf of the pair of panelled doors, linking Jo Smith's outer office and his, opened. Jo led the way.

"This is Peter Martinez. Mr Martinez, Miss Jan Roberts."

Peter's immediate impression was that she was soft-natured, early 30s. Judging by her clothes, she was making a lot of money, or else she had a very generous sugar daddy. She wore a tailored light grey pinstripe jacket and skirt, a bright pink work shirt, probably sheer natural tights (unlikely to be stockings), and high stiletto court shoes in an imaginative blue colour. She had jet black hair cut in a bouncy bob and her only jewellery was a pair of neat pearl earrings.

"Gordon's told me you're going to be cruel to me," Peter said, with a Martinez smile.

"Surely not," replied Jan Roberts, holding on to Peter's hand with a strong grip. "It's your life I'm here to get into. There won't be any need to be cruel to get you to tell me where you were born, if your mother was enthralled by the experience, how childhood was for you… you know, little happy experiences like that."

So she had a sense of humour, or at least Peter thought that must be meant as humour.

"Coffee?"

"No, Josephine's getting me some water. I'm on a caffeine-free stint. You know what we girls are like about harmful foodstuffs these days." It was her style to lull a client into a false sense of security.

Peter suggested she should sit on the white damask couch and he would take one of the two armchairs. Jan assessed the armchairs as being higher than the couch.

"Oh, I'd be lost on that. I'll have to make some notes, I'd prefer something with arms." (And she prayed that Peter wouldn't fall into the trap she'd laid and, like almost every other guy she had previously set up, reply confidently, "Won't these do?", holding out his own unwelcome open arms.)

He passed the test. "Then we'll both sit like teddy bears in armchairs. Would you like to begin?"

"Fine," Jan replied. "OK. What's taboo, off-limits… what's secret to you?"

"People asking me what's taboo and what's off-limits and trying to wheedle out my secrets," he said with a smile.

"Well, if you're going to be evasive, you'll just have to shout if I touch a sensitive spot. So, Mr Martinez, let's find out what's been the biggest thing, event, in your life and we'll work either side of that."

"Miss Roberts, I'm not being evasive, but you ought to know, if you haven't been briefed to that effect, I'm a bit of a precision engineer. Take your last question. In 40-odd years, there have to be so many biggest things and events that one can't single one out. I'd say my father and mother, in their strangely different ways, were huge influences, then an uncle, my introduction to the arts, making my first million… Malaysia… you asking this unbalanced question… and others to come, I suspect… that painting." He pointed to his first painting from Jaimé. "Now take your choice. Every one of those and dozens more have been the biggest single event."

"So there you are. I now have the complete answer."

"Then how do you record that in your obituary of my living life?" he said with a slightly mocking smile.

"*Peter Martinez believes in allowing strong family ties to influence his life and rates the enjoyment of art alongside that of his own affluence and the cultures outside his native Spanish background…* That painting, though. On that I'd need a bit more background information. So how did I do?"

"Very well," came the reply from a slightly surprised Peter. "Tell me what you see in the painting," he said, standing up and beckoning her to follow as he walked across his office for a closer view.

"I'm loath to say, because I'm sure I'd be wrong, but initially I would have said it was a Monet. But then it has a hint of Van Gogh in some of the brushstrokes. To be precise, it's an impressionist piece of sunflowers. The tones and the subtlety are wonderful. I like it very much indeed."

"Good. And that portrait?" Peter said, pointing to the painting of a teenage girl hanging on the wall opposite, which had taken Jan's eye on the way in to his office.

"Forget the fact the girl's amazingly beautiful, the painting is almost of the texture and quality of a photograph."

"By the same artist?"

Jan thought and didn't rush her answer. "No."

"OK. So one of the greatest influences in my life has always been the belief that the disadvantaged should not be put out of one's life, but that something is found in them that can be brought out to advantage. The biggest example of that is that artist. In fact, he did both paintings. He's Jaimé. That's pronounced 'Himey', if you didn't know. J-a-i-m-é" he spelt out pointedly.

"Jaimé. Is that your son?"

"No, but he's my biggest inspiration. He was a very young man when I first met him, he helped me in the preparatory work for my Girasol development. He was a deaf mute, but I learnt to communicate with him through the attributes God had given him, to make up for the components he was born without. We've developed a love for each other and each other's work."

"Are you using 'love' in a homosexual way?" Jan posed.

"Miss Roberts! That's neither taboo nor sensitive, it's bloody outrageous. OK, you've touched on a very sensitive area. Your generation. Your generation are losing the art of appreciation. You've got everything you want that a pocket full of credit cards can buy, but when something comes along which is a summation of what life should really be like, as the Bible tries to tell us, you find it hard to recognise. God wants us to be loving and appreciative, and when there are chasms of ability between two humans, those can be bridged, though not in some seedy sexual way…

"You know, as a kid it was my father who taught me two huge lessons in life. One was when we used our combined strength and superior firepower to put an end to the life of a little defenceless wild boar, because we'd already killed its parents, and that's the way the food chain works. The other was to show me that even a small tree in a forest, in the shadow cast by its giant relative, can still survive and grow, and that all the trees of the forest can do their growing and expanding together, whatever their size or ability or handicap. They don't have to stick their tentacles of branches up the trunks of other trees in order to co-exist. So no, I'm not gay. Or homophobic. Those private areas of other people are for them, male and female."

"Mr Martinez, I understand and actually agree with everything you say, so we can now get on. We've had our little abrasion. I'm not gay either but, and I do apologise for the cliché, I do have to say some of my best friends, male and female, are. So… tell me about Jaimé…"

"Tell me about… what's your view on… ?" And so it persisted, like the slow but constant shots delivered from a line-up of gun barrels at a pheasant shoot.

Peter realised the questions were all different but he could see that the answers, if pooled, would become her storyline. What Jan extracted from him was detail of his happy days at Westminster Poly, as opposed to his intended ones at Madrid.

She even surprised him by saying, "And what about Malaysia?"

His heart sank. This was either to be news or taboo.

"What… about Malaysia?"

Jan fumbled through her papers. "It must be in my case," she said, and leant across the arm of the chair. The effect was that she lifted one buttock off the down feather cushion and pushed her right breast hard against the top of its adjoining arm as she leant her left hand over into her case. Her hair fell loosely to one side.

Peter stood up and walked across to his unit. "Do you mean this? Is this what you're looking for?"

It was the newspaper clipping about the World Conference. He looked at the frame. If only he had been able to say, "Now, if I'd been truthful, the greatest effect on my life ever has been Malaysia and Honey." Sometimes he could just not believe the way fate had intervened in that encounter.

Saying goodbye, or the intended au revoir, to Honey had hit him very hard at the time, as he remembered all too well. As hard as the news of his father's accident, in fact. He had hardly slept on the plane, although his body was beginning to ache from the pummelling it had received crossing beneath the cascade of the waterfall.

By the time he had landed at London Heathrow Airport, his mind was made up. He'd find a course, maybe in public relations, which he felt Honey could benefit from, possibly at Westminster, he thought they had them in their curriculum. He'd invite her across and she could have one of the spare rooms. Max would love that, he was sure. That had been still in his mind as he got out of the airport bus in the King's Road and walked over Albert Bridge to the flat. Dear old Max, and Anna, come to that, had been thrilled to see him back when he let himself into their shared home. All he could talk about was the conference. He dared not mention Honey, Anna would be upset, he thought.

With the homecoming over, and the promise of, "A cup of coffee when you've unpacked and got yourself together," Peter went to his room and straight to his briefcase. He intended to get his address book out, to write straightaway to Honey via her best friend Sally in Penang. But he couldn't find the book. Then it came to him: he had put it in the hip pocket of his trousers. It was not there. He resolved to start again and go through every piece of paper he had gathered together in his hurried departure. It had not become wedged in between clean or dirty washing in his suitcase.

After two hours, he could only come to the one conclusion. It was lost. It had either fallen out of his pocket on the plane or he had been pick-pocketed. It was gone.

In the next two or three months, Peter tried everything he knew to find either an address for Honey or something positive to lead him to her.

Mr Ho, to whom he spoke very expensively on the phone, and his whole organisation, were shits. All they kept saying was that the young lady seconded to Peter was one Sandra Lieu. Beyond that, they were not to divulge even the names of the other chaperones.

"You'll have to understand," Mr Ho explained, "at these conferences there are frequently young men away from home and they get fixations about one of our pretty girls and bother them in the future. We have contractually promised to protect the young ladies from any harmful experience brought about by working with our organisation. That is from real or potential harm."

Honey would be too proud to contact him. She'd put the whole thing down to a painful lesson in life – her first experience of man at his worst. Anyway, her only point of contact would have been through the Poly. Peter resolved he'd go to Penang and try to find her. But he didn't have a photo, or any idea where to start…

Jan found her own newspaper cutting with some notes in red biro scribbled here and there.

"Yes. It was in Malaysia…" that stirred Peter from his thoughts, "… that you expounded the theories you've now travelled the world promoting… perhaps I can come back to that. How do you rate the very first development you were a party to?"

"Brilliant. It was all down to a perfect client/designer freedom of exchange."

"Were you not the client *and* the designer?"

"Oh, sorry, then you must mean Girasol. But my first input into development was a hotel complex on the Costa Brava. The clients were my uncle and my mother. They were very generous in allowing me to make suggestions, which they then took time to think about and usually allowed to be put into effect. They're still there. A Roman set of columns as an entrance, the driveway, the pool… they still look good."

"You're… what, now? How old?"

"Can we say mid to late 40s?" Peter smiled. He was nowadays reversing his previous habit, and knocking off a few years when he felt he needed to.

"You mention your uncle, mother, father… your roots were in a family, yet it appears you're a lone driving force."

A lump came up in Peter's throat. "Who does your research?"

"I do some, we use bureaux to supplement what we know. Why?"

"It's not very good."

"Really?" Jan said in an embarrassed tone.

"Yes, really. I've only been a lone driving force since my wife died."

"I am sorry."

"So was I."

If the floor could have opened and swallowed her up, Jan Roberts would have helped herself on the way. Sensing her embarrassment, Peter stood up, crossed to her chair, put his large tennis coach's hand on hers and said, "Why don't you buy us lunch?"

"Because that would be too inexpensive a way for me to apologise for my clanger. But I'll willingly buy lunch anyway."

Over a light lunch at Langan's Brasserie, with a glass of good Montrachet each, Peter explained that he had married his best friend's twin sister when he was 24. She was from Argentina and one of the motivating factors in his earlier career was to be able to afford to send her and the children back to her parents for a month in the summer.

"Children?"

"Yes, I have a boy who's now 25 and a beautiful daughter of 23 who married young, probably influenced by the loss of her mother and in search of her own space and security."

"How did your wife die? It seems to have been well before her time, in terms of the Biblical entitlement?"

"She was killed in an accident. She went home to South America as usual and was driving her father's car along a mountain route she knew well, on the way to her sister's. A lorry came round a bend, out of control. She was killed, we're told, instantly. So was the poor lorry driver."

"How can you say 'poor' lorry driver?"

"Well, he was guilty, or so the pathology reports showed, because he'd got alcohol and drugs in his blood. 'Poor'… well, I still feel sorry for somebody who kills another human being. He'd feel tragic if he knew what he'd done."

"The children?"

"They had a rough time. It was 11 years ago, so they were both at an age when they needed a mother to help them grow up."

"I'm sure you did both jobs very well."

"Actually I didn't. I got them farmed out, they spent their holidays with my mother and stepfather in Spain. While they were looked after, I ran away to Malaysia to look for sanity, development, opportunity… and something special."

"Something special?"

"Sorry. Taboo, off-limits. Not for discussion."

Lunch over, they walked back to the office behind the Haymarket Theatre, chatting as they went.

"What about the 'Miss' in your title?" Peter asked Jan. "I really can't believe you haven't been snaffled up."

"Thank you, if being snaffled is a compliment! In my early years learning the trade, I worked for a local newspaper. I had a childhood sweetheart who demanded my attention when I wasn't working, but didn't seem to want to work himself towards setting up a family home.

"I got to about 25 and couldn't see that going anywhere, so I applied for and got a job in a PR company, and loved the work. I became addicted to it. Now I meet lots of very interesting people, but most men see me as an available proposition, forgetting the fact that they're usually not. So I have a number of good male friends but none are the marrying kind, at least to me while I'm still at the top of my career."

Back at the office, she went to powder her nose.

"Is she leaving now?" Jo asked Peter.

"I'll give it the afternoon," he said nonchalantly. "Oh, and Jo… do me a favour, could you? Can you ring Dan Askew and see if he can get me two good seats at the ballet tonight."

Jo had all the rotten jobs and was rarely on the receiving end of any favours, unless Peter got blown out and was left with a couple of tickets, or had to pull out himself to go abroad.

"Just slip me a note if you can get them with time of performance, what's on… you know, sport, you've done it before…"

Jan re-entered the office, looking as fresh as she had earlier that morning. They went straight back to their respective chairs.

"How about we continue on a Jan and Peter basis?" said Peter.

"I'd be pleased to join that," Jan said, in a very matter-of-fact way.

"So after Girasol, how did you become part of Bob Hunt's organisation, Peter?"

"Well, I'd had dealings with Bob and he became a minority shareholder in Girasol. His health wasn't so good and by that time I'd left Westminster with a BA, but decided not to go on and qualify totally as an architect."

"Why was that?"

"Oh… it was bow-tie stuff and who you knew and if you were successful, unless you were Sieffert or Messrs Piano or Rogers, you'd always be on the fee end of things. Ten per cent of the development costs was likely to be top whack whereas, at the sharp end of development, you could chase 25 per cent with quite small overheads. Bob Hunt offered me a ten per cent stake for a four-year contract, and a pretty good salary. I knew his family well, and although Bob sadly died about 14 years back, and that was an extension of at least a decade on what he was aiming for, I'm still very much in touch with his wife. She still feels I'm looking after her interests and providing the housekeeping money, as it were, although we've moved Hunts, the company, on a great deal, and it doesn't exist as it at one time did.

"Hunts were building 5,000 housing units in the early 80s and with Bob's two original driving forces tiring a bit, it was left to me to decide what Marcia Hunt's 65 per cent and my ten per cent should become. Organically, if we grew ten per cent per annum, that would be slow.

"Anna's accident held things up a bit, but once I got my feet back onto the ground we started talking about selling out. Cash seemed to be of interest for

Jeff Hodson and Don Christie, and shares for the Hunt family and myself. The deal agreed that if we sold out I would want an improved position. Yes, you can say it if you like: I was a bit power-conscious. Anyway, we sold to Relko, where with us on board they ousted the Chairman and his cronies and made me Chief Executive. That way we had the world as our oyster and it enabled us to think of expanding abroad."

"You said you were looking for an opportunity in Malaysia."

Peter's thoughts suddenly went into overdrive. He had in fact, only been looking for Honey, but using a development opportunity as an excuse bought him time to establish his connections at the Gensing Highland Government sponsored opportunity. He managed to have weekends in Penang and, in camouflaging sunglasses, a T-shirt and jeans, he tried to look through all the directories and registrations, to trace births in the Yim Lam line. It was, he discovered, probable that Honey had taken her mother's names at birth, which were likely not to be recorded as such, but could otherwise have officially been registered in her father's name. Whatever the case, he drew a complete blank.

"Yes, we went into a government-sponsored consortium… basically we took a fee to teach them what we knew."

Jan eased one buttock off the cushion and again stylishly dived into her briefcase. As she did so, Jo entered the office. She coughed tactfully and handed Peter a note. It said, "Yes, 2, Royal Ballet, 7.30 – Sylvie Guillem – Loads of Swans – Enjoy."

Jan seemed oblivious. She pulled out a photocopy of a major Malaysian Daily. There was a headline: 'ENVIRONMENT PROTECTOR TO DEVELOP GENSING.' Below was a very flattering article about Peter Martinez. "Impact on conference now returns" was the sub-heading.

Peter said, "You know, I hadn't seen that," and thought, poor Honey, she'd surely have read the write-up on the conference she had played a part in. And he'd have thought, anyway, that she would have seen the article featuring him, complete with photo, and made some effort herself to find him.

Peter looked at his watch. "Let's give it an hour, and see where we've got to then. But look… I've got a couple of tickets for the Royal Ballet this evening, Sylvie Guillem and loads of ducks or cygnets… something like that, anyway. Would you join me?"

"They're swans, I think. But I'm sorry, no thank you."

If Peter had been stood up, she didn't see why she should help him out.

"Why?" Peter asked, a little surprised.

"Peter, you don't just have tickets like that hanging around in your wallet until you decide, at the last minute, who you'll invite. You must have bought them with a purpose and you've been let down, probably quite genuinely…"

He didn't let her finish. "Look, I only organised them after we got back from lunch. That was the content of the note Jo gave me. I bought them hoping you might have kept this evening free to review the interview notes. Could I put the invitation to you again, in that knowledge?"

"I can see why you are where you are. You're cunning, decisive, determined and very generous. I'd love to."

"Then let's try and get this inquisition of a Spaniard over and done with," Peter said, with sudden determination.

"I don't think so. The Spanish inquisition went on for years. What we could do is agree to close today's chapters on an anticipated new beginning tomorrow. And then perhaps this very grateful guest could rush home, freshen up and we could link up in beautiful ballet mood."

"Fine with me."

The Jan Roberts interview was making Peter focus on the point ahead when she might ask him about BCG. The name BCG in itself made his stomach churn. That was bound to have been a William idea, put to his father, who, in a typical moment of weakness and adulation for his elder son, would have said, "Good boy! Brilliant, lad. I like it." He'd never have appreciated the lack of imagination actually shown by simply cutting The British Construction Group down to its initial letters.

In just that way, some guy at the BBC had impressed his stroke of 'genius' on an inept board on a bad day. Likewise ICI, LEB and BR had been brilliantly re-branded, as had BOAC, MGM and all the others, portraying the enormous lack of creative thinking lurking in most organisations… or so Peter may have mused. He had in mind no masterstroke to make any changes. He'd probably go to an agency and get them to do a complete makeover. Renaming, logo, branding, the lot, yet not losing out on the '50 years since inception' factor. Perhaps Jan's agency did such things. Jan herself dug deep and picked up on most important issues. Her search into the Malaysian factor that afternoon was typical of that.

CHAPTER 12

There was not going to be a lot of time available between the interview and getting to the ballet, so Peter suggested that he would get Perry to drop Jan across to her home in Holland Park, which was not that far.

"Perry will get himself some food while he waits for you, which he always seems to need, and then come and collect me with you on board. If we get the timing right it will allow us to scrape in to the Opera House just as the overture's striking up!" He'd get a taxi from the office to his flat, he thought.

That became the agreed plan.

Peter didn't know why but, as he fumbled his key into the double lever mortice lock of the apartment, which he always thought was less to keep burglars out than let those entitled get in, a feeling of emptiness swept over him.

He'd sold up the family home after Anna's death. In fact he'd added it into his land bank and developed the site. He moved on to a smallish town house where he had an au pair/housekeeper to help him manage the children's needs, even though they were both put into boarding school. Then, as they became more independent, he moved up the property ladder.

He had realised only a couple of months previously that nobody else had ever slept in this current apartment.

Any meeting with Marcia, which had become his only basis of company with the opposite sex since becoming a widower, had been hotel related. "That's safest," Marcia had ruled and, if between them they had wrecked the bed linen or duvet, all they needed to do was tip the chambermaid, and ensure not to return to that venue.

Mrs Brown, the housekeeper, had put the day's post on the usual hall table, propped against the artificial flower arrangement the interior designer had insisted on him having. There was nothing of consequence. Peter threw his jacket onto the bed and took his tie off. Really, he thought he should shower and change straight away but he was sure he had time just to sit for a few minutes in his favourite chair in the lounge, and switch off after his day of stimulated autobiography.

He had collected a glass of chilled Chablis on the way through, which he sipped as his feet seemed to go into auto pilot and lift themselves up onto a footstool somebody or other had given to him and Anna as a wedding present.

He was sure it was Jan Roberts's 'clanger' that evoked the memory of the origin of that footstool. He took a generous gulp of his favourite nectar, as he looked around him.

It really was an empty apartment. Well, it had plenty of furniture, all of it quality, but it had no personality.

He realised suddenly what it was. Stirred by the earlier references to Anna, which he was sure had also led him to make the ballet booking, he began thinking about her. He forced himself out of his comfort zone and into the bedroom. He knew exactly where the white leather picture frame was. He only very occasionally looked at it, having found he couldn't cope with Anna's luminescent blue eyes always following him round the room in that excellent photograph of her, taken by herself on her wedding day. He had thought it would be best located in the wardrobe, the least intrusive place. Only twice before had he specifically collected it and taken it into the lounge for company, and as a reminder of contented memories.

He usually started by laughing with her, remembering how their fairly platonic relationship had developed.

Basically, Peter had not been a particularly nice guy when he first found himself thrown into Anna's company.

She had moved into the flat Max and Peter shared in Prince of Wales Drive, opposite Battersea Park. Max didn't really want his sister there keeping an eye on his activities, but the fact was, when he invited a girl back to the flat for the first time, he was able to explain that she would be quite safe because his sister would be there. It seemed to have become a very effective chat-up line. In terms of Max's score rate, which he always pointed out to Peter was high compared with Peter's own derisory achievements, his system worked.

Peter, however, was a little more subtle. His encounters were not, in his view, to be compared with Max's conquests. Honey had been a fairytale love affair, probably just minutes old, or an hour or so, when they'd discovered a soft reciprocal passion. Their union at the waterfall was not lust. No prearranged plan, but an entanglement that was as natural as the spring water around their bodies.

The aching feeling of loss when he failed to find her again had never entirely left him.

With Marcia, he knew now there was nothing to value. In terms of a conquest to match any of Max's, which by requirement had to be pretty silent so as not to wake Anna, he knew his own were enormously satisfying.

Marcia knew how to satisfy, excite and show her appreciation of his maturing prowess; a short-term liaison on top of the bed was good, it seemed, for both of them, as opposed to Max's sleepovers.

So Anna's presence around him in that flat was a friendship, not intended to be more. She was as satisfied to sit and talk as Peter was to listen, and bedtime for each of them was always a separate affair, even in Peter's male mind.

"Look, I've a busy day tomorrow, must get to bed… see you in the morning," without a touch of cheeks or a handshake, was a common seal to their day.

Living in the presence of Anna, and a variety of Max's friends, was an education for Peter. Anna was culture personified and when neither she nor Peter had much else to do on a rainy Sunday afternoon, they would take themselves off to a museum or art gallery and play a sort of game. "See if we can like the same things," Anna would say.

They agreed Picasso was a joke, Monet was a genius and some artists' work hanging on the railings alongside the Ritz, heading towards Knightsbridge, was crap, and possibly bought in some job lot somewhere. Other work was good… imaginative… entertaining, even though occasionally splashed by the rain of a seasonal Sunday.

Music was the same really. Anna said the only way to go to the Proms was to be in the pit with all the real people in the world. Ballet was special, Peter thought, as he sipped his wine and let the memories spill over once more.

It suddenly occurred to him that if he had been Max, he would have a pre-arranged campaign in his mind as to how to bed Jan Roberts. Her place? His? But Peter didn't automatically think that way – probably, he smiled to himself, because he had missed out on a public school education. He never had, not even on that memorable New Year's Eve of 1959/1960.

Peter had never had a sister to study, and from whom to learn. He had now come to recognise, from living in the same environment with a girl, that they had times when their normal personalities changed, sometimes for the worse; when they displayed a hurt and a bitterness that males found hard to understand.

He'd learnt that first from Marcia, on the odd occasion when he had phoned her to suggest meeting up and she'd pretty well slammed down the phone, saying, "Darling, don't even dare to think of coming near me again."

The follow-up call would be her phoning him. "Now what about us doing that meeting up you talked about?"

One thing with Marcia was that she had always brought out his confident boldness. "I thought you didn't want me to come near you," he'd reply.

Marcia would then laugh. "My darling, sweetest dear Peter, that was hormones talking."

He'd heard one of the site agents on a development once say that he was into his darts and snooker time. "She's throwing her hormones out of the pram at the moment," he'd said. So Peter hadn't really thought hard about it. It could have been just the excitement of New Year's Eve. It might have been that Anna was hormonal. In any case, Max had appeared that morning and said they all had work to do because he'd won the company raffle and had brought home the first prize case of Lanson Black Label, so they had to get a crowd round to help them drink it. Anna had looked at Peter and told her brother, "Don't let's invite too many. Peter and I can help with that."

Peter was surprised. Anna didn't like drink as much as her brother, but in her comment, unless he'd got it wrong, there was a hint of invitation.

"Too true," he'd replied, which produced a wink and a smile from his female flat-mate.

Then, just before people were due to arrive, she had appeared in a short black mini-dress with a deeper cut neck-line than he'd ever seen her in before, and black patent stilettos. He'd kicked himself for saying she looked nice, which prompted her to move towards him and put a hand on each of his shoulders.

"Darling Pedders, you've never noticed me before, have you? But let me mark your card when it comes to New Year resolutions – I've got the feeling I'm looking into 1960 with a different vision from ever before."

Peter had presumed she'd met somebody who had changed her perspective. But no new friends of hers arrived at the party. Peter's invited mates had shown an attraction towards her, which, in fact, he hadn't liked too much. Then, at five to midnight, he felt someone pull his shirt-tail out of his trousers. Thinking it was somebody who'd had more than their allocation of champagne, as he was beginning to feel he himself had, he spun round angrily.

It was Anna.

"What was that about?" he asked.

"Well. You've hardly noticed me all evening, beyond recognising early on that I'd wanted to look nice for you. All your mates are pestering me and I need some defence against their various approaches… I wouldn't mind a bit of attention from you."

"Anna. Have you had a bit too much to drink?"

At that point, the sounds of Big Ben striking bellowed from the flat's communal radio. The normal New Year havoc broke out and before other girls pushed Anna out of the way, she briefly kissed Peter full on the lips, then vanished to exchange greetings with others in the pack. Peter himself was not short of attention, but nevertheless was in shock. He'd suddenly seen Anna in a completely different light.

The next time they met, though, was after all but one guest had left, a girl in a red minidress, which Peter felt had danger printed all over it. She had stayed, it seemed, at the suggestion of Max.

"Alright darlings, we're off to see in the New Year," he announced. "If you're going to do the washing up, don't make too much noise. If not, we'll give you a hand in the morning." And off they went.

Peter and Anna stood facing each other in silence.

"Do you want to do the washing up?" she asked.

"Not a lot," he replied.

"Would you see in the New Year with me?"

A little taken aback, he said, "We already did, didn't we?"

She, being a female and two years older than Peter, was encouraged to take the initiative. She took his hand. "Then please, I'd like to do it again. Come and tuck me in. That would be a beautiful start to the New Year."

She's tight, he thought. He was surprised, although Max's supply of champagne had his own heart pacing a little. He'd best get her up the stairs in case she tumbled. She was unsteady on her feet. *Is it the shoes?* the ever-practical Peter wondered.

He'd never been into her room before, but now he needed to ensure that if she fell, she was home, as it were.

It was large and occupied the high point in the mansion block, the roof space. Everything was 'Anna neat and tidy'. The colour scheme was pastel and soft. The room oozed femininity, which was brought out in the limited soft lighting she had previously left on.

She had her own bathroom, which he knew about but had never seen. Her quarters, it was agreed, were out of bounds.

He remained just inside the door, which had somehow closed behind them. He let go of the elbow he had been supporting. Anna swayed a little as she turned towards him.

"Happy new year," she half-whispered.

She brushed passed him and locked the door from the inside, seemingly in reasonable control. She appeared momentarily to sober up.

"If you'd like the loo, pop in over there. I'm OK."

As it happened, it was suddenly one of the best ideas of the evening. It was psychosomatic; once the idea entered his head he needed the loo.

The small bathroom was pure Anna. All the towelling was Peter Jones quality white. It carried her perfume. Everything was again tidy and neatly laid out. She'd perhaps forgotten her robe was hanging on the back of the door.

He lifted the seat to the toilet. Hell, the water was deep blue. He'd never seen that before. Relieved, he tore off three panels of the much perforated toilet roll, wiped the rim of the porcelain toilet and flushed the cistern. He would work it out later but stripes of dark blue, presumably disinfectant, slid down the curvatures of the pan from under the rim around the top. *Mother would love this,* he thought.

He remembered Anna had a fetish about him and Max putting the lid of the toilet down when they had finished. So he did that.

Restricted by his trousers, which he had left down around his ankles on his way to the hand basin, he did a sort of penguin walk. As he ran some water, he glanced at himself and gave a cheeky smile and a wink in the mirror.

He splashed water into his hands and pulled his trousers up, deciding not to be over-presumptuous and take them off. Anna would decide, of that he was certain.

When he returned into the bedroom, the lights were dimmer. He couldn't readily see her.

"Silly Pedders, I'm here."

He followed the sound waves back to the source. He could now clearly make out just her head, surrounded by her short black hair, semi-sunk into the soft, puffed up pillows.

An inviting hand appeared from under the covers and patted the eiderdown.

Peter did as he was told. Anna giggled lightly as she had to shuffle across from under the bed-cover, to prevent him sitting down on the left hand side of her pelvis, as she was lying on her back.

Hand and arm number two appeared, slightly pushing down the bed cover, exposing her bare shoulders (but nothing more), which were dutifully performing their task of supporting her head and fixing the long neck to the remainder of her body. Peter noticed she was still wearing the slim gold necklace he knew her parents had given to her for her 21st birthday.

"Come on then," she whispered, touching her lips lightly with her left hand and extending the other, which he took. He was gently pulled over onto his side to enable their lips to reach. Her kisses were soft.

He lifted himself slightly, pulling back the eiderdown so he could slide in. He'd slipped his shoes off as he first sat on the bed.

Anna's eyes widened appreciably.

"What's all this move about?" she said with a funny little smile on her face.

"I'm getting in to wish you a Happy New Year."

"You're bloody not, my darling Peter. Your invite was to tuck me in, my sweet." She seemed suddenly as sober as a judge.

"But you didn't mean just that."

She sat up, pulling the eiderdown around her.

"I did. Any man might try to tell me how much they love me, but just be pretending to get me to lose my virginity."

"Is that so?" Peter said, ceasing to pull back the covers. He'd never actually ever said he loved anybody before anyway, apart from his mother.

"Look, I've never told anyone that before," he said, "but when I do, I'll expect it to be in the right circumstances, when there's a mutual feeling of love. Trust me, you'll still be a virgin in the morning."

Anna stared at him, partly in shock, with perhaps a tinge of disappointment as it seemed as though he was not going to try to push his luck – and then fall asleep, as she understood an ill-intentioned male would be likely to do.

As if she had been hit by an anaesthetic, her head fell back onto the pillow. She was comatose. Peter tidied the bed cover around her and decided to leave. No! He felt he couldn't. She looked so childlike and vulnerable. He lifted himself off the bed and moved round to the other side. He'd noticed earlier, and had been rather intrigued, that it was a double bed. He laid himself on top of the covers, and remembered no more. When Anna woke the next morning and found him still at her side, on top of the covers and not yet awake, her heart leapt. Her sudden stirring caused him to wake.

"Good morning! Thank you, Peter."

"For what?"

"Not taking advantage of me."

He laughed. "You wouldn't know if I had."

She lifted herself onto one arm, enabling her to lean across and kiss his forehead.

"Then neither of us will ever know." And she shrieked with laughter.

Neither of them, in later analytical discussions, understood how they'd been able to stick with her ideal that night, or on the others when Max was out late, or away, and when Peter said goodnight to her in her room.

If she was paranoid about remaining intact (although petting was gradually trusted and allowed), she was petrified about Max reporting to their parents at HQ that his twin sister was sleeping with the lodger, albeit occasionally.

The photo of Anna reminded him that their love was of the enduring sort. They had both avoided the infatuation syndrome.

Peter remembered well the wedding in Rio de Janeiro the following year. It was classically Catholic. The church was filled with dignitaries and many wealthy people, and just a small contingent from Europe, including Maria, excited by the prospect of being a grandmother at last.

Everything about Anna was 'classic' quality, she was trained in that at a very expensive finishing school, and it rubbed off gradually into the way Peter saw things and treated life.

Their honeymoon night was indeed classic to the nth degree. Her long white satin and lace trimmed nightdress, the silk pyjamas she'd selected for him, the music she chose to be played on the bedside cassette player, the lighting, the perfume, the way they made love and the crescendo at the absolutely correct moment, as if their joint respect was part of an orchestrated ballet.

Oh what a difference, Peter reflected, from when he was with Marcia.

He had said, "Thank you, that was beautiful."

She'd then cried in total agreement, until they both fell asleep for the first time in each other's arms, this time with greater trust, but leaving their bodies in a more common peasant-like condition, until they fought each other to be first in the shower in the morning.

Neither was surprised by Anna's announcement that she was pregnant.

So Peter became a father. Maria, a grandmother.

Their relationship was always smooth. Anna seriously encouraged his work ethic and graciously accepted the steps through which Peter excused himself from certain paternal duties, so he could put more work into his day and earn more, to improve the status to which even she had previously been accustomed.

"Look," he reasoned one night. "I love the time when we can bath the babies together, but maybe we might consider getting an au pair. Getting home that half hour later would really help me to get through the work I have to do."

"Of course," was her reply.

Anna gradually accepted the travel element of his job. She herself had gone back to work, leaving the au pairs they employed to fulfil her role at home so she could take a greater part in managing the ballet groups arriving and touring in the UK.

It was a perfect marriage, until some pig of a lorry driver executed God's plan for Anna, which decided, by dint of one of his wondrous but incomprehensible ways, that she was needed in his fold.

The phone rang. It was Jan Roberts.

"Look, Mr Martinez, we're just leaving my place. We're running ten minutes late. Mr Perry says it's no problem but perhaps you could be ready at the door in 20 minutes."

"Yes, fine, Jan. What's new when there's a young lady to get ready?"

They both laughed.

Peter rushed to his bedroom wardrobe and selected a change of suit, fresh shirt and tie, threw himself into the shower and had minutes to wait for Perry at the entrance to the apartment block.

As he waited, his thoughts returned to Anna being the reason for this 'date'.

Anna had taught Peter all the cultured things in life, like appreciating all types of music, ballet, art, even photography, which she had encouraged Peter to pursue as a hobby because he seemed to be able to imagine how a shot would print out.

And it was those 'Anna things' that he always seemed to associate with her, and the way she had introduced him to silence. Silence from having to receive or make conversation, he found so welcome. It created time for thought. Many of his best decisions had been made whilst a Bolshoi chorus had been performing. So maybe alongside Jan he might be able to tell if she appreciated the performance by way of understanding it, and perhaps that would have a different dimension in some way for her too if she knew he also could untangle complex situations.

She'd obviously learnt about ballet during her upbringing, like Petra, his daughter, had. At one time Peter had hoped Petra would become a world-renowned ballerina herself, but she'd developed an early knee problem, which put that prospect out of their lives.

The car arrived. Jan exuded quality perfume. The overture was just starting. They were perhaps a minute or two early.

When the first interval arrived, Peter said he had organised some champagne and canapés in the foyer bar.

"Let's get there before we get crushed." He grabbed Jan's hand and guided her through the milling but good-tempered throngs, who had similar ideas.

After the performance, Fred Perry sped them home. Jan lived north of Kensington High Street in Holland Park, in what looked to Peter like a pretty little mews house.

"Peter, thank you for a lovely evening. I shan't invite you in for a nightcap. We've an early start tomorrow. Jo had originally said you wanted shot of me in a morning, so I've overstayed my welcome already."

Jo annoyed him. Although she'd been with him a long time, there were things she often repeated which he would have preferred her not to. This was one of them.

"No, don't think that at all. You can have as long as it takes. I'm very dependent on you painting a picture that enables me to hang on to the job. Hopefully, we'll have my life behind us by early tomorrow and then deal with BCG… and what we'll call it to give it another 50-year lease of life."

"Oh, that sounds fun. Peter, I've had a lovely evening, in fact a delicious day. Thank you."

She respected the client/writer relationship and there was no way she'd want to break that with the soft goodnight brush of cheeks, which she would otherwise have liked.

Peter got out of the Bentley and went round to her side of the car. In the very short time he had allowed her to get out of her working clothes and into something more suitable for the ballet, she had presented herself admirably. He eased her out, appreciating that she'd gone for the safe option. She had elected for a little black dress with a tantalising square neck and side split to the fashionably short skirt.

He watched her put her key in the door and waited for the door to close, after she had sent him a little girlie wave.

"Home, sir, or the club?" Fred Perry enquired. He hoped it would be home; the overtime was very useful, but he needed sleep like anyone else. This new boss didn't seem to be bothered by it.

"I think a few hands at the club, Fred, please."

That meant the London Bridge Club, which served three purposes. Firstly it was the place to sharpen up on his game. He'd only been playing bridge for a couple of years, originally with Max, and although he had shown a natural aptitude, there was still a lot to be learnt. Secondly, he had met some pretty influential people at the club and mixing in the right circles was always fundamentally important. Finally, it saved him going back to his lonely apartment in Eaton Square.

The next morning, Jan breezed into Peter's office in a very sprightly manner after Jo had dutifully announced her. Again, it annoyed Peter that Jo had presumed too much familiarity by asking Jan if she had enjoyed the ballet. Jan didn't seem to mind, but Peter expected more discretion from his PA.

Something had altered in Jo's life, he thought. It had been showing recently in a number of ways. She seemed bored. Surely she wasn't pregnant or something like that? After all, she wasn't married and, as far as he knew, didn't have a regular boyfriend.

It was going to be a lovely spring day and obviously Jan had heard the forecast. She was wearing a short pink dress with an over jacket whose Liberty print lapels matched the short sleeves of the dress.

"That's a nice outfit," Peter said as she slipped the jacket off and laid it neatly on the arm of the sofa. Jan hardly seemed to have heard. She was in working mode.

"Armchairs again?" she said with a smile.

"Yes, fine with me or we could finish now and get a boat on the river."

"We've got work to do," she said, pretending to be stern. "So… according

135

to my notes, we left off where you'd signed up the government contract in Malaysia. Did that give you a taste for overseas development?"

Peter laughed. "You're not going to get cross with me, promise?"

She nodded. She was now beginning to know him and he was going to put her right on some detail or other, which was OK with her.

"Only you see, developing overseas is England to me. I'm from overseas to start with. So every land except Spain is a foreign one to me. But, in answer to your question, I don't believe shareholders should only have their funds tied up in one economy, one currency and one volatile business and domestic community."

"Are you pro-Europe and the promised single currency?"

"No. Europe has never ever been united. There's usually been a war of some sort being waged between European countries whose leaders are now saying, for their political aims, that all the past can be forgotten and we can all sit effectively as one parliament to see us through to the future."

"So what's had the most major effect on Europe to encourage your investment there?"

"Football."

"Football!" Jan repeated. "How?"

"Well, I learnt at an early age that 11 blokes in a football team are all individuals, and it takes a really good coach to bring them together as a single unit. But it is possible and eventually they'll all follow a regular enough pattern in order to gel. Add a few different nationalities into a team and that, with a little more difficulty, can also work. But take 11 different nationalities and I doubt you'd even get a total team to develop.

"It's because the culture, mentality, language and history of each nation is different. The only common denominator is that they all get paid, and then it would currently be in different currencies.

"That's what Europe is about and the prospects are, your team of 11 or so will superficially head out as a team and try to convince each other to use a common currency to bind them together. However, money is not culture.

"Now, where investment is concerned, and in my case it's an investment in bricks and mortar, it would be very dangerous to take our British prototype house and try to sell or let that in France or Germany... Holland... Italy... Scandinavia... they need their national image to be continued. It's called heritage.

"Some commercial developers have taken the concrete cladding ideas suitable to England, and to recoup the manufacturing plant set-up costs, have tried to build the same thing in the heart of Brussels, or Paris, even Milan. They've not been as successful as ourselves. We're bespoke builders. We use local architects and the materials they're used to working with.

"That's a long way round to answer your question, but it's the challenge of learning that development language which has taken me to Malaysia, the States, Europe, etc. So investing in Europe is approached no differently from dealing effectively with the USA or Asia some 6,000 to 7,000 miles away."

"That's very interesting," Jan said, with sincerity.

They both shared a professional awareness of a timetable and the need to move on, so they progressively got through Jan's agenda, with a few extra added value points. She quizzed him on relations with unions, equal rights and opportunities, forthcoming Health & Safety regulations, environmental protection, the age of the car, the place in society for the bike, increased air traffic… if, at the end of the interview, Peter was not convinced of Jan's effective research, she would have been surprised.

"Finally, Peter," she said, "you're about to become the Chief Executive of one of the top 100 UK companies in what to date has traditionally, through a number of generations, been a family-owned company. Do you see any major structural changes ahead… and will you take the opportunity, like the Murdochs of the world, to slot your family into place and oust the founder line of succession?"

"You're good at two-part questions. In principle, if anyone within the group is good at what they do, then there'll always be a place for them. The statistic that worries me is that currently, it would seem you don't get considered as Director material in the satellite companies until you've done at least 20 years' service. In that time, if the average length of service is about five years before people leave, and it does seem to be, I just wonder how many really good people we've been losing by not incentivising them into top management positions within that five-year timeframe. They can't all be plonkers. Some will have made their mark elsewhere within a few years of leaving us. I'd therefore like to look at that aspect. But if the existing family are good, then they'll be encouraged to stay."

"And if they're not good, will they be encouraged to leave?"

"Yes."

"At whatever level of seniority they currently function?"

"Yes."

"Then what about bringing your own family into those positions?"

"My son has a leaning towards the arts. He doesn't know the difference between one form of construction and another, and has no desire to, I believe. My daughter's too beautiful to be a builder. She'll do whatever she decides to do. So that's it.

"I'm inclined to forget I have a stepbrother. The son of my mother's husband. I'd make him something important if he wasn't important in his own right in what he's doing. He's a professional golfer and although he's not likely now to win The Open, he has the joy of doing what he loves. What's more, we jointly own a golf club we built behind Girasol, so he's probably made for life and he would be really, really disappointed to be dragged away from that into this mega-corporate structure."

"You keep coming back to Girasol. Is that your favourite success?"

"OK, I'll confess. Yes. To me, it has everything. Location, sun, a marina, golf course, small hotel and I have a home there. It was a home before I married Anna, so it doesn't miss her company and all her attendance to detail. There, the detail just happens. It forms itself and takes the mood of whoever's there. You must fly down for a weekend. When you've done the article, bring it down. We'll talk it through together."

"Peter, that's a lovely thought, but I would have hoped Gordon had made my style clear before throwing us together, like he has…"

"I'm sure he didn't mention anything special."

"Nobody gets to read the article. I network it out the way I've interpreted the discussions."

"Shit! That's not fair. Supposing you've written something down incorrectly?"

"I won't have done. Trust me, Peter. I'm good… and I'm fair."

"Do you mention in the article how you wouldn't let me in to your house last night?"

"Yes. You'll see that comes through. I'll probably write 'Peter Martinez is a shy, retiring workaholic who drops a young lady off and prefers to go on to play bridge'."

"How the hell do you know that?"

"Don't worry, I'll treat it with absolute discretion, but that's my job… knowing people."

"At least can we clear up the 'workaholic' connotation, in case that sticks?"

"By all means."

"I believe a workaholic is just like an alcoholic in every respect. They begin to hate the taste, wake up in the morning dreading the day ahead and really wish they could break the habit and give it up. Well, I actually don't feel like that about work. Yes, I could give it up. I could give it up now, I don't need it financially, but I do get a buzz out of the creativity. So could you avoid the 'workaholic' bit please?"

"I'll have to see," Jan teased. "What happens now is I write an article that represents the full interview. Someone like the Economist or Newsweek will take that and maybe a couple of specialist magazines worldwide might use it. I prepare a couple of trimmed versions for places like Malaysia, America and

European countries where you have a presence. There'll be something for the in-house magazine and then some general press releases for the UK papers to get their teeth into."

They elected to have a working lunch with smoked salmon sandwiches collected from the wine bar in the courtyard behind the offices, and eaten in near silence around the circular marble-topped table in his private office. Jo interrupted them and gave Peter a couple of messages. It seemed the head office in Manchester needed Peter's input on something major and Jo couldn't hold them off once they knew he was in a meeting at his more favoured London office. He would have to take a conference call at 3.30pm, so he and Jan were aiming to be finished by then.

In the event, they ran tight for time and their 'au revoirs' were hurried. It was sort of left that Peter would like to give Jan a call. She didn't volunteer a private number, but said that her number was on the card she had given him when they first started the interview. She was cool, he thought.

At 3.30pm, Peter had left the quieter, slower pace of the interview and was immersed in resolving an issue to do with a major construction project they had for the development of a complex through which to feed the supplies to North Sea oil rigs in Aberdeen.

In the end, despite Peter's fears, Jan Roberts had said there was no need to go over the purchase of Relko by BCG in any huge depth. She had already known BCG had got to hear of Relko, and their Non-Executive Directors saw the opportunity of not only buying that very successful business but also snapping up the captain at the helm, Peter, whom they saw as a means of breaking up the incestuous relationships within BCG, which were dragging it down. That, and Peter's view on the family leadership tests of quality, was subject to further conjecture.

Anyone listening in on Peter's input to the conference call would never have known he had not started out as a construction contract man, but more as a designer. His grasp of the rough and tumble of engineering and all the building disciplines seemed something special. What he said tended now to be accepted and the minor squabbles within BCG were receding.

He'd once joked with Gordon, in one of their sessions to discuss the revamp and branding of the conglomerate, that he wondered if the inner sanctum of BCG had its own special connotation, and that it really implied 'Bloody Can't Get on', which amused Gordon.

Maybe it really was true.

CHAPTER 13

Coco, for a girl of 28 years old, had a very responsible job in the Selangor Bank of Malaysia. Some of her female work colleagues talked behind her back, suggesting that she had only got her various promotions because of her extreme beauty, and that each successive boss had expected favours in return.

But Coco was not stupid, in fact the reverse. She knew what they expected, but no favours were ever promised, nor were any forthcoming. Coco was a girl who knew where she was going, following in the footsteps of her mother, showing the same drive and determination, and seeking to achieve what her mother might have done had circumstances been different.

Coco's mother had herself turned to banking in Ipoh within three or four months of Coco's birth. She'd been told her father had walked out on her mother a month after the birth; her mother always said that he was too young, at 19, to take the responsibility of parenthood.

But the real story emerged when Coco was 23 and her mother ruled that she was mature enough to know the truth. That was four years ago. Coco was constantly reminded of her mother's 'day of truth', as she had called it.

Today was apparently going to be another of those memory-jerkers. The headline in the business section of The Straits Times drew her eyes like a magnet. She almost needed not to have read the article. It contained news but no surprises.

The headline read:

NEW PRO-MALAYSIAN CHIEF EXECUTIVE OF BCG BOUND TO INVEST FURTHER IN NATIONAL ECONOMY
   by Jan Roberts.

Peter Martinez is at heart a kindly person who places great importance on the family unit, but stresses there is no room for sentiment in a family business. In a personal interview conducted just before taking up his new appointment, he revealed how, in his relative youth, he used the platform of a world conference on the protection of the environment to set every young Malaysian girl into a major panic by advising that they should give up using hair lacquer, get their fathers to re-insulate their homes to avoid the need for energy consuming air-conditioning, and to eat raw foods, all to protect the ozone layers and the future of the planet.

Since that original visit, Peter Martinez has been back to Malaysia a number of times looking for suitable developments, and hints at it being one country in the world where he finds his own sanity, and always hopes, even expects, to find that something special there.

He bases himself in his executive offices in London, to where he will transfer the group headquarters from Manchester and from which all the group housing, construction, commercial property and civil engineering activities will function. With Gensing behind him, Mr Martinez has just clinched a similar joint venture deal with the progressive Malaysian government. Malaysia, I feel, needs friends like this.

For further information on this exclusive interview, kindly contact Jan Roberts, AIMS PR Consultancy, Berkeley House, Berkeley Square, London.

The photograph was unmistakable. This one showed him to be 20-something years older, but then he was. Whether it was the quality of photo or printing, or just a likely fact, his hair had a few more tones of grey to it. Probably, Coco thought, from the extreme worry such a job as his would generate.

She'd never had anything but admiration for Peter since that memorable, life-changing day when her mother had sat her down and said she had two pieces of information to impart. On that day, Coco had matured with a special purpose.

Initially, she had fooled around, as she liked to do, trying to anticipate what her mother was going to tell her. "First, you're pregnant. Second, you're getting married again."

"No. Neither. It's not quite as happy as that. The first concerns you. Ben, your father, my husband through my arranged marriage, is not your father."

Coco's hand went to her mouth. "Shit! Mother! Then who the hell is?"

"Coco, I've told you before, that American language doesn't suit you. Your father is the most beautiful man on this planet. He was and he still is. We met when I was 18 and – I have to say God had something to do with it – I fell helplessly in love with him. In the most beautiful experience of my life, and it would be in anyone's, we made passionate love just for a short time. I was naïve at the time and I'm sure it was because your father was a gentleman he didn't use any protection. They say fertilising one egg on the right day at the right time of day is a miracle, and we achieved that. Which, in hindsight, bearing in mind the circumstances, was not at all surprising…"

"Mother, what circumstances?"

"It was my idea. I'd heard about a magic waterfall…"

"Mother, you're not going to tell me I was conceived in a waterfall, surely?"

"Well…" Honey started to giggle. "… Not exactly *in* it. Behind it. Anyway," Honey said, a little embarrassed and becoming flustered, "if ever that's the way you lose your virginity and with such a beautiful man, I hope your daughter or son will be pleased to hear about the circumstances."

Coco stood up, crossed to where Honey was sitting and leant over and kissed her. "Thank you, Mother… I've just been thinking, do you think that's why I'm such a good swimmer?"

"Coco!"

"What happened? Why didn't you keep in touch?"

"I really don't know. At one stage I thought he might have had a terrible accident and died. I really don't know. I didn't have his address, and anyway, I would never have contacted him. I should make it clear I was the one who rather pushed myself on him."

"Mother, you're too beautiful for any man to resist. Come on. It sounds very mutual."

"It was. There must be a very good reason why there was no contact. Anyway, I worked out I was pregnant and I panicked. I literally had no-one to tell. So I spoke to your grandmother and suggested it was time for me to get married. She and your grandfather had always talked about me having an arranged marriage with Ben. That all happened. He thought I got pregnant the first time we slept with each other on our wedding night, and was quite happy with that situation. I made out you were born prematurely and everything was fine. I think Ben was suspicious because he did, to be fair, wear protection and he asked one of the nurses if she thought you were premature… well, she gave her opinion… Ben believed her… and the rest is history."

"Mother, what's my father's name?

"Peter Martinez. Would you like to see him?"

"Oh, Mother, would I! Oh yes, please!"

Honey went to her sewing basket and took out a false bottom to it that she had built into the wickerware. She carefully lifted out a number of newspaper articles. Some were showing signs of age. The first was an article in the Penang Times reporting the conference and how Peter had set the tone by including the 'chaperones' in his presentation.

Coco looked at the photo. "Oh Mother, he's truly beautiful! Look at those lips."

"They're the lips of a very kind and loving father."

"What colour are his eyes?"

"Look in the mirror, darling, you have his eyes. You always have had and always will."

They spent a while sharing the other newspaper clippings.

"Why didn't you try and find him when he came to Malaysia? It may be he came looking for you really and that the business connection was all a front. If he was at the Gensing Highland complex, you could have driven there from Ipoh."

"I just didn't want to intrude on his life. Besides, I'm still technically married and I have a daughter."

"Mother, thank you for sharing that with me. I'll find him one day and bring him home to you. It's my duty."

"I said I had some other news."

"Oh yes. What's that?"

"I've been having pains in my chest… and I need to say this quickly… I don't think I'm going to be very good at this story. I thought I'd be sensible and go and have an x-ray… I've got a spot on the lung."

That was so much for Coco to take in on her 23rd birthday. She reassured Honey, told her that she would be alright. But Coco was wrong.

Honey passed away peacefully just two months later in a home run by nuns. Coco was there. Her mother pressed an almost finished bottle of Chanel perfume into her hand as she sank into her long sleep.

Coco was beside herself with grief for months. But time, as it usually does, became a healer and one day, without reason, she got up and said to herself, come what may, she'd now got a mission. One day she'd get the money to go to England, just to ask her father why he lost contact.

So she now had a current photograph and knew from the article that Peter was alive and well, and she had information in the UK about him. She also contacted the AIMS consultancy for the full version of the interview, which they kindly sent.

CHAPTER 14

Jo Smith was officious and always had been, but since tendering her resignation, she had become even more so. Peter had asked why she wanted to leave and Jo had simply said she felt she needed a change. What she really needed was some attention in her life and as she was unlikely to get that from Peter, she was off to pastures new.

Peter had given her attention but it was all of the business kind. He'd comment if she was wearing something new or had a new hairstyle, but where she was missing out was his obvious decision not to include her on his personal dating list. Peter had a lot of female 'friends', which was not too surprising for such a good-looking man, with widower – one might almost say bachelor – status and bags of money.

So her mind was made up. She might even travel for a while, but she was off, and today was Peter's first round of interviews to find her replacement. Ordinarily, over the years he had selected PAs who did not physically attract him. That would be the foundation for a purely working relationship.

The applicants arrived at 30-minute intervals. All had responded to Jo's advert in the Crème de la Crème section of *The Times*.

"You don't need your CV, dear," she almost shouted at one nervous applicant. "He's got all that stuff and your references."

Most of the time Jo was having a running dialogue with Amanda, the receptionist.

"Look at this one... smell her... she didn't get a suit like that on just a salary..." and then constantly, "Where's Miss Saigon then, do you think she's not going to show up?"

Coco Yim Lam had arrived in England on the previous Friday. She had sorted out her disrupted sleep pattern over the weekend and was now not feeling too bad. She had decided to go straight to Peter's office, which she discovered was in Duke of York Street, rather than ring for an appointment. At least face to face, anyone who fixed his diary would see that she was genuine. She planned to say that she knew all about his developments in Malaysia and was doing a thesis and wondered if he could give her some personal information.

If she walked boldly in and said, "I'd like to see my father," she knew there would be no chance of breaking down the family front door.

She had been to Peter Jones and spent some of her savings on a suit. The assistant had been most helpful and guided her into a smart yet with-it deep purple two-piece and a lilac silk blouse with a collar set above that of the jacket. She was advised to wear nearly black tights since the skirt was quite short, and high black court shoes. Certainly she felt good and the assistant said that she didn't know what the special event was, but whatever it was, she'd be an absolute stunner.

"Unless it's a funeral," she joked.

Coco's beautiful long Malaysian legs were like jelly as she turned into her targeted street from the Trafalgar Square end. Should she turn back and go home? She would at least find the building and if it looked too imposing, she would go sightseeing and come back another day.

She didn't know which number she was looking for but surely it would have a plaque. Sure enough, she was outside number ten and the cleaned brass plaque simply bore the letters BCG, engraved and in-filled in black. She could see into what she presumed to be the reception area. The focal point seemed to be a large brass chandelier. There was a young lady sitting behind a leather-topped reception desk and there appeared to be quite a lot of activity focused on two or three other young ladies. It looked friendly enough and, after all, she had travelled 6,000-odd miles to get there, so she'd just have to summon up enough courage to go in.

There was no bell, so she pushed on the heavy-panelled black glossy door and it swung open with ease. She stepped inside. The receptionist looked up from her telephone keypad.

"Good morning."

Coco had trouble saying the words she had practised so many times. As she was about to speak, she was overpowered.

"You're late." It was the over-officious Jo Smith who snapped at her. "Look, I'll still fit you in but you'll have to be last. There are two more before you. "

With that, Jo disappeared through a door leading out of the reception area.

Instinctively, Coco took her handbag from under her arm in readiness to put it onto her lap, anticipating she might be invited to take a seat.

Jo Smith seemed not to be a force with whom to argue, and she made Coco feel quite unwanted.

Why mention another two? she thought. She just did not understand.

Amanda got up from behind her work station and walked round the desk.

"Here. If you'd like to sit here," she said, pointing to one of the leather Chesterfields. It was a lot firmer than Coco had imagined it would be. "Can I get you a coffee or some water or juice?" Out of earshot from Jo Smith she whispered, "Don't let her worry you. She's having a bad day. She's a bit emotional, you see it's her job you're applying for and… well, I suppose it's understandable, she's been with Mr Martinez for ten years. So it's a bit of a wrench."

Coco's mouth was dry with a cocktail of tension and fear. "I'd love some water please."

Amanda re-appeared with a Stuart Crystal cut-glass tumbler. "Water with a slice," she said cheerfully. "Don't look so worried, he's a very nice man. He won't eat you."

Jo Smith came back with two crisp sheets of photocopy paper. "Sally Mae." Coco looked up. "Good, of course it must be you. There. One copy of your CV." And she handed the paper to Coco.

Coco sipped her water gratefully. She hurriedly read: *Sally Mae. Born Hong Kong of Chinese mother and British father…* The document went on to explain Sally Mae's attributes in fine detail.

Well, if a fake job interview got Coco a meeting with her father, then she had to grab any opportunity. After all, he would very likely freak out at the prospect of being confronted with a daughter he didn't know about if she was immediately straight about her real reason for wishing to see him. Besides, she doubted she would even have got past the venomous Miss Smith if she'd explained the true reason. Coco bet Jo could block almost anything.

A young lady came down the stairs, looking a bit strained.

"Did you have a coat?" Amanda asked.

"No. Thank you."

"How did it go?" Amanda asked.

"Let's put it this way, I doubt you'll ever see me here again. We didn't exactly gel."

"Oh well, you never know."

Jo Smith came back into reception and collected the other young lady who had been waiting ahead of Coco.

Amanda came across from her desk again. "Here, you might want to read this. It's the group house magazine."

"Thank you," Coco said. "You're very kind. How long have you been here?"

"Oh, five years. Four and a half of those were hell until Mr Martinez joined the group. Now this place hums. Before it was just a stopping off post for Mr

146

William in London on the way to his club, or Ascot, Lords or some other social engagement."

Coco hadn't looked at her watch but guessed 20 minutes had passed by the time the previous young lady returned on her way out.

Jo Smith made a rushed re-entrance.

"Come on, Miss Mae. We're running late now. You'll have to expect Mr Martinez to be fairly brief. He's got a stack of other appointments coming up."

Each tread on the deep pile Wilton staircase carpet they climbed seemed like a mountain to Coco. Her legs had almost given up on her. They always 'went' when she got tense or worried. She had straightened her skirt as she stood up.

At the top of the dog-leg flight of stairs, Jo Smith turned to the right, went through her own office and opened the right-hand leaf of a pair of doors and walked in.

"This is Sally Mae," she said, keeping her body between Peter's sight line to Coco. In a single sharp movement, simultaneous to Peter looking up and slowly lifting his eyes from Sally Mae's CV, which he had just speed read, as he did most documents these days, Jo did an about-turn and left briskly, exposing Coco completely to Peter's gaze.

He stood up slowly. Coco wouldn't have known but anyone who knew Peter well would probably have said that he had seen a ghost.

Honey! he gasped inwardly. Then he looked down at the CV with a degree of panic.

Coco smiled the next time he looked up. He left his chair and walked towards her, eyeing her slowly from the black court shoes to the shapely tights, the skirt, blouse, jacket, face, hair, then taking in the waft of Chanel No. 5. It was not the fragrance with which Marcia had overcome him, nor the stolen scent worn by Meribel and Tania. It was softer. It was Honey. Honey's body had made Chanel No.5 all her own, whereas the others had not.

He took Coco's hand and shook it.

Should she throw her arms around his neck and shriek, "Daddy! It's me!"?

He just looked at her, breathing in deeply all that he saw.

"I'm terribly sorry," he said, "I must appear very rude. You deserve an explanation. You're so very like somebody I knew years ago. On first impression you were her. I'm sorry. It was quite a shock."

"Please don't apologise. I have to say though – and you might want to throw me out of your office for saying so – any girl would recognise that's not the normal welcome to a candidate to be interviewed."

"Oh God, was I quite that obvious! But in hindsight it's all quite silly. The young lady I mistook you for would no longer be your age. I knew her a long time ago. But I do have to say, you could have been sisters."

"Sir! You're speaking historically... is my sister just part of something so long ago?"

"Hey – Sally, isn't it? – you're beginning to get inquisitive, like some journalist on a mission. But as you asked the question gently, in a way she would be asking the same question, and providing you promise not to take pity on the young lady in question and myself... it was a disaster."

"Disaster?" Coco was sad to hear such a word, knowing how her mother had felt. "Disaster?"

"Just quickly, because otherwise my dutiful PA will say our time is up together... she was in fact Malaysian, not from Hong Kong, and we were very close for a whirlwind period of time. I had to come back to the UK and I had one of her friend's addresses where I could write to her... you know, secretly, as it were... When I arrived back, I discovered I'd had my notebook, I think, stolen by some pick-pocket at Kuala Lumpur airport. I had no contact address. She didn't have one for me either, as I was due to move, and although I went back and searched the whole of Penang to find her, I couldn't. I've been back since. She just vanished.

"So there, you've got more out of me in five minutes than actually anyone else in the world in over 20 years. I have no idea how you've been able to do that and, by the way, it's a secret. I'd like you to treat it as such. I suppose I'll have to give you the job now, to make sure you do."

Peter was now relaxed and threw his head back with laughter.

"Thank you for sharing that with me," smiled Coco. "Of course, I will respect your confidence. May I just ask what was the name of my look-alike?"

"It was, well I hope it is, Honey Yim Lam."

"Could we sit down, sir, I can't feel my legs."

Peter motioned for her to move across into one of the armchairs. She turned quickly. The room started to spin and everything went black.

Afterwards they said she'd passed out for only 30 or 40 seconds. In that time, Jo had been summoned and Peter was leaning over Coco's outstretched body, holding her hand and patting the back of it, while Jo seemed to take some pleasure in loosening her blouse before Peter did.

Coco's eyes opened slowly. Peter asked if she was feeling alright.

"I'm sorry," she said. "How embarrassing! Did I pass out?"

"There," Peter said, with an arm around the back of her shoulders. He lifted her forward and encouraged her to drink cold water, which Jo had quickly procured from the water chiller in the outer office.

"Jo, can you give me a hand to get Miss Mae into the chair?"

If Jo had pulled this 'I need attention' stunt on her boss, he would have rung down to Amanda and a couple of the other girls and asked them to come and clear up the mess.

"Did you have breakfast?" he asked Coco.

Jo thought, *What bloody next?* Did she wash properly? Had she slept? Oh boy, if this one got the job, that would see Peter's rule of a lifetime go out of the window. She'd be surprised if they weren't shacked up on the sofa by close of play today, even.

She'd had croissant, Coco said.

"Jo, could you get a couple of sweet biscuits, I'll bet the girls have a stock of them downstairs."

Jo duly attended to her boss's instructions, before informing him, "Your 11.30 appointment's due any minute."

"Who's it with?"

"Bob Hare, the architect for Sheffield."

"When he comes, give him a coffee. Let him ogle Amanda for a while and then send him back to his office, find any excuse. He'll charge for his time anyway, so he won't lose out. What's after that?"

Jo went through the diary.

"Cancel everything until 3pm please."

"Cancel?"

"Yes, that's what I said."

"Very well!" Jo replied, obviously now very put-out. She exited, head held haughtily high.

"Are you OK now?" Peter asked Coco.

"I'll be OK, I'd say, in ten minutes or so."

"Do you want to go and sit somewhere cool?"

"No, not at all. What I really meant was after ten minutes of explanation. Could I just be allowed to talk, like you did?"

"You're a very lovely girl. I can't think of a greater punishment than to be able to sit here and just listen to your voice. I'm sure it's probably because you're both Oriental, but your voice, if I close my eyes, could be hers."

"It might help if you do close your eyes." She took a deep breath. "Are you listening? Could you please close your eyes?" He did as she asked.

"Honey Yim Lam knew there was some very good reason for you not having made contact."

Peter shot forward and opened his eyes. "Are you playing one of these aggravating party games where I start something off and then you add to it and in the end there's one big convoluted story?" he demanded.

"Please. Just close your eyes. You'll see. Anyway… she knew there would be a good reason because she loved you and trusted you." His eyes shot open again, but closed as she said hypnotically, "Please. But her circumstances changed dramatically. Her visit to a magic waterfall wasn't as magical as it should have been, in terms of outcome. She discovered, as quickly as one does, that she was pregnant. In her culture and at that time, to be pregnant with no husband would have been sufficient for the girl's father to encourage her to fall on the family sword.

"So she panicked and asked her parents to arrange a marriage, which they did. She made out she had conceived on the first night of the honeymoon. A month or so after the baby was born 'prematurely', her husband worked out, with a little help from the nursing staff, that he wasn't the father, and ran away, never to be seen again.

"Honey Yim Lam brought up the child and kept the secret about who'd been in the waterfall with her until the child was 23. Then she told me it was you."

Peter sat forward. "You said 'me'. *You! You* are really my daughter?"

"Yes I am. But I'm not here to be any trouble. Mother died four years ago."

Peter looked as though he had just had an arm severed. "Oh God. I'm so sorry."

"No, I'm sorry for the two of you. You weren't able to find each other. That was because my mother moved to Ipoh. You'll be pleased to hear she did really well and became assistant manager in the bank there, where I now work too."

Peter stood up. "Am I allowed to hold my beautiful daughter?"

Coco raised herself out of the chair. "Oh please, I'd love that. I've missed you so much for all these years."

Peter held her tightly as she sobbed into his chest. He was so powerful. So beautiful. The photos didn't do him justice. No wonder Honey had fallen in love with him. Coco had too.

The door opened and Jo strode in carrying a silver tray with a pot of coffee and a plate of biscuits. She nearly dropped the lot when she saw them linked in each other's arms.

Peter stood back. "Get your grubby little mind off what you're thinking. When I'm ready, I'll explain what this is all about," he said pointedly to Jo.

"No need, Peter. It's pretty obvious," she said, as she thumped the tray onto his coffee table.

"Jo, I'm taking exception to this mood you're in," he said very sternly. "I've said there's an explanation and I'll give you that when I'm ready."

"So do I presume Miss Mae gets my job?"

"No, you don't. Tell the agency I'll need a temp. I haven't interviewed the right one yet."

Jo looked surprised. "From when?" she said.

"Look, Jo, you've done two months of your three months' notice. Why don't we call it a day?"

"Fine with me. Let's say from the minute I walk through those doors," she hissed, pointing at the pair of panelled doors separating his office from hers.

"That seems a little petty. I would have thought in about a week."

"That's the first time you've been wrong about me. I mean now." And she stormed out.

"Look what I've done already," Coco said, with a worried expression.

"She's had that coming. Do you know something?" Peter said, emphatically.

"I do know some things."

"I don't know my daughter's name."

"It's Coco. Coco Yim Lam. Do you know why it's Coco?"

"No. But you're wearing Chanel perfume, aren't you?"

"Yes. Mother always did on special occasions."

"I gave her a bottle in Langkawi."

"Oh, that answers another question. When she died she pressed an almost empty Chanel bottle into my hands."

"Miss Chanel's name was Coco. You're named after one of the most beautiful things on the planet."

"Yim Lam means beauty too. I've inherited my mother's beauty. What shall I call you? Papa?"

"Just Peter."

"Is that alright? It's very grown up."

"Coco, we *are* very grown up."

"Peter, you're very busy. We've met. I'm going to write down my address in KL 20 times so that it can't be stolen or lost. We'll write often."

"Where are you staying in London?"

She started to fumble in her bag and produced the address of a hotel in Bayswater.

"Right, Fred Perry, my driver, will take you back to your hotel. Now these are paternal orders, which you have to obey. Fred will clear the hotel bill. You pack all your gear and he'll bring you to my apartment in Eaton Square. That's going to be home until we've sorted all these surprises out. OK?"

"Yes, Papa. Peter! Yes, I know… I just wanted to say it once." She leant forward and kissed his cheek, then walked to the door.

"Coco," he called out. She stopped and turned. "You are beautiful."

She kicked a foot in the air behind her, then waved like a little girl and made her exit – very much centre stage.

It did not take her many steps along the pavement outside Peter's offices towards the waiting car before her happiness forced her into a broad smile. She had found him. He was truly beautiful. They were able to communicate. More to the point, she was able to connect where her mother had been forced to fail.

CHAPTER 15

It seemed a long time since Peter had had cause to leave the office and go home, where Anna and the children had once been waiting for him.

Today, he expected Fred Perry to have moved Coco in to the apartment by five o'clock at the latest. Peter had phoned him and said to put her in the guest room. "… And by the way," he added, "don't go jumping to conclusions. Miss Lam is not a new girlfriend, so please keep your thoughts to yourself."

Fred had been with Peter for about ten years, as long as Jo had anyway. Generally, he could be trusted. He knew if he breached an employer's confidence in his line of work, he would never work again as a chauffeur.

There were times in that day when Peter felt 20 years older. The scene with Jo was all a bit unnecessary. He'd had words with William, whom he had effectively shunted sideways over them taking on a pipeline contract in the Sudan. William was impressed that there was a 35 per cent profit mark-up on the deal but Peter had reasoned that it was a scheme planned in a pretty volatile political climate, which might have to rely on payment via a bond anyway and they had nobody on board who had worked in Sudan, so they had no local knowledge.

Peter had cancelled his next day's appointments completely. Jo had gone.

"She just left, sir," Amanda explained. "As she went through reception I said to her 'I'll see you' and she turned on me and said 'I doubt that', and walked out."

Peter got a taxi from the office. As he put his key in the door, he knew immediately the apartment was alive again. He could smell her perfume already. The flat looked lived in. There were magazines spread over the coffee table.

Peter surveyed the sight with satisfaction. He walked through into the inner lobby, off which there were the two guest bedrooms, one of which was used as a study, then the guest's bathroom and the door into the master bedroom and its en suite bathroom. There was a separate cloakroom too.

The door of the guest's bathroom opened and, unaware that Peter had returned, Coco popped out with a crisp laundered Christie towel swathed round her body like a mini-sari. It left her shoulders bare, and showed a hint of cleavage and lots of leg. Seeing Peter, she stopped in her tracks. Her knees turned inwards in a gesture of embarrassment and she flung her arms up to provide added security.

"Oh, I'm sorry," she said, "I didn't know what time you'd be home. I was desperate for a shower. Another time I'll take my clothes into the bathroom."

"Don't be daft. I want you to treat the place like the home I never provided. Here, I won't say no to a welcome home hug." He held both his arms out. Without hesitation, she skipped across the lobby and tucked herself into his powerful hold. *Not again,* she thought. Her legs went like jelly, her thighs ached and there was a strange sensation in the pit of her stomach. She pressed her stomach into his for security and comfort. Confident in his arms, she slid her hands up round the back of his neck and hugged him hard.

"Here, I've got a surprise." She took him into his bedroom. There on the bed was a pair of Boss jeans she'd found in his wardrobe. A Ralph Lauren Polo shirt in a rich cream colour; a pair of Church's brown casual shoes, a pair of blue Burberry socks.

"I want to see you out of your smart suit and in clothes to relax in. I'm going to cook and we're going to talk all night."

Who was he to argue with a determined daughter?

She appeared in jeans and a T-shirt. They talked, ate dinner, talked some more, played music, watched the news on TV and eventually Peter announced that it was time for his little girl to go to bed. She'd had a busy, emotional day. More to the point, so had he.

"Tomorrow," he said, "we're going to get you some clothes. I've got places to take you where I want you to stun the world."

He'd listed all sorts of things she would need. He said he'd take her to Harrods and put her in the charge of one of their personal shopping consultants. He'd give them a list of places to cater for, clothes-wise.

He found it hard to get off to sleep. She was so like her mother. How fate had cheated them out of anything more than a three-day/three-hour relationship. Here was Honey's clone, in-situ, as indeed he had intended Honey herself to be. He eventually slept. He was calmer in his dreams than he'd been for many a year.

Coco had the same sleeping problems. If this man had walked into her life, a bachelor, she would have thought she had fallen in love for the first time, much as her mother had described her experience. But to be swept off her feet by her own father was incomprehensible.

She woke at five. The day was just dawning. She pinched herself to remind her where she was. She lay there for a while but, like a young child, she couldn't wait to go and see her father again. This second day would take her beyond the information phase, surely.

She went to the kitchen and worked out where all the traditional ingredients were for making the morning tea she had read about in a book she'd found in Malaysia about British habits.

She laid a tray. Prepared everything she thought was required. Put on a silk kimono and entered Peter's bedroom.

He stirred as she walked in. "Honey," he said, as he glimpsed her standing at the end of the bed holding out the tray. "I'm sorry. Coco. You're more like your mother today."

She poured out the tea. Put his cup at his side of the bed.

"Peter," she said, "when I was young, all the kids at school used to ask me if I enjoyed hopping into my parents' bed on Sundays like they did, and playing 'I spy' and things like that."

"What did you say?"

"I lied. I said I loved it."

"Did you go into your mother's bed?"

"Not really. Usually we'd wake and get up and go about doing what we had to do."

Peter threw back the cover, exposing the unoccupied side of his king-size bed.

"Come on then, daughter."

She felt a rush of excitement, which made the whole of her body tingle and the sinking feeling in the pit of her stomach returned.

Peter found the closeness of the following weeks more and more uncomfortable. Having Coco around was like having the companionship of the wife who was meant to be, but never was.

He was sure she was taking more out of the relationship than was natural for someone who had just found her blood father. But then, without her knowing it, she was putting a lot into Peter's life too. Consciously or subconsciously, she was flirting with him, and with such regularity that she was sure he must be totally aware of it. They dined out like lovers and were always pleased to see each other, even if only separated by the length of a day, which allowed her to learn about places and see things she could then talk about at length when they were together again.

He took her to Ascot and, under the strictest of pre-instructions on how to behave, introduced her to cricket at Lords, where at least 30 young men of the MCC almost broke their necks doing a double take. Her female beauty adorning the stands was a much rarer incident than the blokes witnessing a bowler's hat-trick at an important moment. Such attentions made Peter feel protective and were problematic.

Coco had a problem, too, with the reality of a recurring dream she'd had since Honey's death – that she was the reincarnation of the young girl whose love affair was not allowed to ripen and flourish as it should have done. Surely God was influencing the new-found lives of Coco and Peter in that direction. Any greater degree of affection between them would represent everything the Great Book decreed as being bad: man not sleeping with man, or woman with woman, father with daughter, mother with son or cousin with cousin.

But God was taking them to the same brink as he had taken Peter and her mother. Peter was again alone, as he had been in Malaysia, and needed the companionship Coco was giving so naturally. Coco was as strong in her resolve as her mother had been in switching the allocation of delegates and their respective chaperones. More and more, she was conscious of the need for her body to be fulfilled the way her mother's was, and indeed fuelled by the same lover.

The rhythm of the pattern of their life was disturbed one evening when Coco told Peter that she needed to register with a doctor. She'd been away from Malaysia for over a month now. Peter went into paternal mode.

"Are you alright?" he asked.

"Yes, of course. We girls just need to consult every now and again."

He didn't understand, but made out he did and suggested she register with his own GP, but to become a private patient. That was all done and Coco fixed her appointment. Her situation was simple and an everyday occurrence for Dr Bowen-Brown.

"Now what can I do for a beautiful young lady like you, my dear?" he offered.

"I'd like to go on the pill."

"And why not, my dear." Not an immediate warning that the development of that particular form of contraception was still relatively new and he was sure there were side effects yet to be discovered.

He checked her blood pressure, asked a few personal details and wrote out a prescription. He said he'd also check out her blood quality and filled a phial, with her hardly feeling the insertion of the needle.

That was plan 'A'.

Plan 'B' was evolved about two weeks later. Peter had taken her to see Madame Butterfly at Sadlers Wells. She had cried through a lot of it, relating Butterfly's waiting for Lieutenant Pinkerton to her mother's endless wait for Peter.

They got home. Peter had a nightcap seated in the very large lounge within the apartment. Coco went and showered and returned in her kimono, smelling lightly of Chanel. She curled up at Peter's feet, as she often did, but never in a daughterly manner. There was always a deep feeling of attachment far beyond a father/daughter relationship.

Ella Fitzgerald was playing in the background, 'A Foggy Day in London Town'.

"Peter. I've made a huge mistake."

"Darling, you could never make a huge mistake."

"I have. I lied to you."

"You could never lie to me."

"Well, I have."

"Over what?"

"The story I told you the day I turned up at the office."

"Oh! What mistake about the story?"

"Everything was true except for one important point."

"What was that?" Peter was now intrigued.

"You didn't leave my mother pregnant."

Peter was suddenly astounded. "Then what's the true version?"

"Mother did love you in every way and as deeply as I explained, and I think you knew anyway. But when you hadn't contacted her after four weeks or so, she gave in to Ben's pestering to yield to the arranged marriage and, as I said, they did get married. They did conceive, and little trouble me came along. But my mother couldn't forget the love she had for you on any longer and she told Ben about it… and indeed he left.

"When Mother was dying, I promised I would try and find you, and that if I found you shared the supposedly unrequited love she had for you, I would provide for you as she would have wished to do herself. From the full article by Jan Roberts, which the agency faxed out to the bank, I could see that Anna had passed away and it looked as though you might be alone. I saw the exercise as a mission to fulfil the promise I made to Mama. I had no idea I, too, would fall head over heels in love with you."

"Why are you telling me this now?"

"I need to show you the depth of my love for you… and I can't if you believe I'm your daughter, as we'd both be turned into stone."

"So why the daughter story?"

"I planned my introduction in a much different way, as you know, from the one forced on us both by Jo Smith, but I think we should both be thankful for her mistake, as it brought us together. When I saw how warm your welcome was, I could not bring myself to tell you I was the daughter of a previous girlfriend and a man you might have wanted to hate. You might have said 'So what?' and given me a few ringgits to go away. When I saw your deep love for my mother, I grabbed at the opportunity to be close to you too, and I dreamt up the daughter story as a way of achieving exactly that. Where that's gone wrong is that I love you more deeply now than would be possible between blood father and daughter."

There was a silence. Peter stared at her.

"You're cross, my darling Peter. I've screwed up. Kick me out tomorrow. I just didn't believe there was any chance of falling for you, at least the way mother did, although I'm sure she couldn't possibly have endured the same depth of feeling I have for you, otherwise she would have thrown her pride to the wind and come over and found you, as I have. I'm really sorry."

She got to her feet and leant over Peter's seated body, kissed him on the forehead and then allowed her soft cheek to slide down his. She stood up and turned away without saying more, walked slowly to the door into the lobby and into the guest's room.

It was a lot for Peter to take in. He took his time to finish his nightcap whilst analysing the situation.

The door to the guest room was ajar. It always had been while she'd been there. Coco had said she was afraid of the dark and could Peter leave the lobby light on.

"Are you asleep?" he enquired, silhouetted in the now open doorway.

Coco, he could see in the half-light, was lying on her side. She seemed to be sobbing. He approached the side of the bed she was facing away from. "So, my sweet one, if I'm not your father, then in what role do you see me?"

"Oh, as a really very good friend."

She didn't move. It was as though she had trouble facing Peter since her exposé.

"Then I want to give you this as a very good friend, but it would give me more pleasure if I still was your father."

He slowly lifted the duvet, exposing her naked back and the gift she had treated herself to from Harrods, satin knickers that covered her curvaceous buttocks. Peter lifted his hand chest-high and brought it down square on Coco's right buttock, in one meaningful solid smack. The sound resounded round the room. Coco, stung with pain, sat bolt upright, oblivious of the fact that, as Peter knew so well, she usually slept topless.

Her right hand was holding her bottom. "What's that for?" she said, choking back a tear of pain, not this time, as so often, one of emotion.

"You're a naughty little girl. Many a man would be screwing you by now,

158

using your great 'confession' as an excuse. However, my sweet, dear darling daughter, whom I do love, but with whom I would never be able to cement our relationship in the ultimate physical way, surely you expected me to be a little more inquisitive about your sudden arrival? I contacted my associates in the Malaysian government, actually while Fred Perry was moving you in, and they trawled through all the records they could lay their hands on. Your story, of course, checked out.

"Then it was down to the obvious question: had your mother and I conceived in the waterfall? Your eyes, my darling, are my eyes. Ben couldn't have produced those with his Chino/Malaysian eyes, that's for sure. It would take an expert to recognise it, but your skin colour has a hint of Mediterranean olive about it. Your mother's genes alone wouldn't have produced that and, I guess, Ben's would certainly not be olive.

"Then, when you saw the doctor of my choice, you gave him enough of a blood sample to allow for a DNA test. You *are* mine, damn it, and as much as I love you too, I'm not allowing that to be in a physical way.

"Finally, have you never wondered about the birthmark on your left elbow? In the morning I'll show you mine, if you haven't already noticed it. So, dear sweet darling daughter, you've been blown! But probably, and I'm not making a promise out of it, I love you all the more for a pretty amateurish attempt to get us both turned into stone."

Coco knelt higher and put both her arms round Peter's neck. "I need you so much. I'd do anything to have the love we've discovered for each other to be complete."

"Coco, if you don't put a top on, it's likely to happen. I am, after all, a man and, although I say it myself, a pretty virile one. You feel like you do at the moment. You've gone from effectively being an orphan to someone with a parent. That'll last you for life, or for my lifetime, at any rate. Don't do something you'd only come to regret – the time would come when remorse locks in and I think the love you feel now would be seen to have been abused, which is never a pretty word. There…" He held out his hand, having pulled back from her embrace, and stood up.

"Put your nightshirt on and I tell you what, you can sleep in my bed tonight, with me, like any caring father would allow with an over-emotional daughter. But we might put a bolster roll between us."

"Oh!" she said, like a disappointed child.

Morning dawned. Peter had got up at his usual time and made tea and taken it into his room. Coco was always awake from the first lifting of her eyelids.

"I can have you for grievous bodily harm," she said, rolling onto her tummy and exposing one buttock cheek to show a small circular black bruise, and the clear definition of four fingers. "It really hurt, you know," she added, as scolded children always say when they get round to talking about any punishment once it has been administered.

Peter kissed the palm of his open hand and tapped the bruised area of her buttock. "It was meant to hurt. Your lies hurt me more."

"Peter, I'll never lie to you again, you're too clever."

"That was a pact I had with Honey too."

"Peter, I've grown up overnight. I've been thinking, if I hang around you any longer you're going to have to tell everybody about your misspent youth and how you're now lumbered with a love child. Max will see that as some sort of hurt to Anna, with her not knowing about your past. Your son and daughter might not think too highly about having a Malaysian half-sister. BCG might say they should have known.

"As for your mother, she might feel cheated that you didn't tell her and it's far too complicated a story to keep having to tell, however true it may be. I ought to go back to Malaysia. We could promise to write. I could try especially hard to find someone to marry and produce grandchildren for you to love. You might be able to come and see the projects you have in Asia, and if I continue to do well at the bank, I could fly out to wherever you are and have the odd family weekend together."

"I don't like the idea," Peter said, with a touch of melancholy in his voice.

"We'll talk about it tonight."

There was no 'tonight'. As soon as Peter put his key in the door when he returned home, he knew the apartment had reverted into a morgue. The happiness had gone, the youth, the loving attentiveness, all had vanished.

That was confirmed when he saw the envelope propped up on the coffee table. He cried as he slit the seal. He could smell Coco as he opened it.

Darling Peter (Papa).

Everything I have ever told you (apart from one attempt at cunning) is true. Everything I said this morning makes supreme unpalatable sense.

I've left before I cause you any more trouble.

I've also left 20 copies of where I'll be – desperately waiting to hear from you.

You're crying. I know you are. Please don't. I've learnt that what joy you gave to Mama is not mine to expect or demand. What was original to you both cannot be replicated and it was intrusive of me to attempt to steal Honey's only treasure.

The bruise is very painful. I'll forgive you though. It was administered out of love.

Now stop crying, Papa. I will see you soon. I'm missing you already.

It was signed:

Your doting daughter, with all my love, Coco. XXX

CHAPTER 16

Peter's first call, once he'd pulled himself together, was to Marcia.

"How are you fixed?" he said, which was the usual way of seeing if she could get up to see him.

"Peter Martinez, you're a really lucky bloke. I can be sitting at home with a full diary and a list of suitors as long as your arm, not feeling in the slightest inclined towards sexual activity. You ring, I hear your voice, and I go randy as hell and drop everything, make some lame excuses to others and come running. Do you mean tonight?"

"Whenever. You know how it is. How I love to see you."

"It's 6.30 now. I'll see you about 8.30. Do you think I'd best plan to stop over?"

"If you'd like to."

"Well, my darling Peter, you'd better be up to it! I'll pack my pyjamas then."

"I love your jokes!"

"See you then."

Marcia had gone through a very 'off' stage when Peter married Anna. Not that she would have married him, despite then being widowed. She rang when she heard about the accident and since then had reverted to her usual bouncy, sexual self. She'd eventually got around to confessing why Peter had been her 'first'.

"Quite frankly, all the men before you made their expectancy or availability too obvious. Besides, I really fancied you," she had explained.

The following day, Peter rang Coco. She was home. They had a sensible chat and Peter promised to find a business reason to check on the development in Kuala Lumpur within a couple of months.

"Don't you dare not to," had been Coco's final command before they ended the 30-minute call.

On the following Friday, Peter realised he had nothing in his diary for the weekend. In recent weeks he and Coco had just let things happen, nothing planned, and they'd finished up with some memorable moments.

He now reverted to his fundamental need if he was returning, as he was, from a short break without 100 per cent commitment to work.

He needed an unattractive PA. PA-less, he rang his travel organiser. "Can you fly me to Spain?" he enquired. "Barcelona or Gerona will do."

He managed to get an evening flight on the Friday. He'd be pleased to see his mother with José and Marco and Virginia. He could visit Michelle and Miguel and their family of two boys and a girl. Apart from that, perhaps a game of golf, but generally he would chill out. His kids were both OK. He'd checked out with phone calls. Having been at boarding school and away either with Maria in Spain or his parents-in-law in Argentina, they were not particularly clinging. When they were together, they got on like houses on fire, and were closer. Apart, it took a lot of communicating to keep them in touch.

Maria was delighted to see Peter, as she always was. She barraged him with question after question, as she never failed to do. He always spent the first night home with his mother and then went up to his place at Girasol for the rest of the stay. He'd got used to the exercise up there. Golf was on the agenda, and he expected to get a thrashing from José Jnr, his stepbrother and now good friend. He had also got accustomed to walking in the hills, which reminded him so often of his morning outings with Paco.

José Jnr, who had now in fact generally managed to drop the José Jnr tag, putted out on 17th to win the 1000 pesetas he and Peter always staked, and which Peter rarely won.

Peter looked up to the hills. "They look beautiful at this time of the year, don't they? The green's a young and vibrant sign of early summer. The woods will be cool and shady again."

"That reminds me," José said, "there are an occasional few unwanted visitors up there. They apparently come to poach boar. The locals say they're gypsy types from down south who stop over on their drug-running trips from Africa into France."

In some perverse way, that reminded Peter of Tania. The time-bomb Tania. She'd held out the ultimate ultimatum to Marco after her thorough beating up, which Peter had heard about all those years ago as he left for London. The men who did it were caught by the police and sentenced for grievous bodily harm, possessing drugs and a number of other offences, and had been put away for life. That freed Tania from the family influence, which Peter had experienced to his detriment.

It appeared that Tania's cousins blamed Marco for stimulating the jealousy that led to the beating. So Tania had laid down her law that she wanted some form of security from Marco – a more important role, maybe leading to a career.

When Marco took the franchise on the hotel at Girasol, he offered Tania the housekeeping role, then she rose to under-manager and now, by all accounts, she was the manager. Maybe Peter would go there for a meal that Saturday and see if, and how much, she had changed.

He had a beer and a sandwich at the clubhouse and made his way back to the house he had held back in the development for himself. It was, of course, in the best and quietest location. Anna had always found it boring, with nothing to do. Peter, in his busy life, always found it a bonus if there was nothing to do.

This Saturday afternoon, 'nothing to do' gave him the opportunity to have a siesta. He'd lost a night's sleep the night Coco shared his bed. He registered how lucky he and Honey had been, despite their share of misfortune, to have produced such beauty. The thought of what joy was in store for some young man who would spend a real night with Coco kept Peter from sleeping himself.

Then he had, admittedly by his own invitation and as much for his pleasure as hers, had Marcia flying around with him all night. She was still remarkably fit and very good indeed in bed.

So his snooze on a lounger in the patio garden of his home was very rewarding. God, how he loved the faces of the sunflowers looking down on him.

He woke refreshed and, as it was still a warm late afternoon, he decided to set out on a walk and climbed the track into the hills. Birds flew in panic from one tree to another. Young rabbits raced around, using up their day's allocation of energy. The odd doe raised its head to enquire who was walking in its territory and then continued feeding on the fresh young leaves and sprigs of grass that managed to grow in the sunless wood.

Peter sensed a rustling up ahead. It would be a boar. He walked into a clearing. Suddenly the bushes parted unnaturally on the far side of the glade. Two young men stepped out briskly. They both had balaclavas on their heads, with silk scarves covering their noses and mouths and tied firmly at the back of their heads. They were both wearing flak jackets and green camouflage trousers. One was carrying a shotgun and the other a baseball bat and a canvas bag slung over his shoulder. They were bandits.

"Párese todavía. Ponga las manos en el aire."

Peter froze. He had a sick feeling in his stomach. The two young men walked towards him. *Christ,* he thought, *those bloody black eyes! I thought I would have forgotten them by now. Bloody Tania gypsies.* In going through those thought processes, he hadn't obeyed their command.

"Párese todavía. Ponga las manos en el aire. Haga como te es dicho y te no obtendrá las herida."

Sure, he'd do as he was told. So he stood still and put his hands in the air. He knew what it was like to be hurt by these bastards. The taller of the two came close and looked Peter square in the face. It seemed he knew it, but could not recollect from where.

"¿Tiene una cartera?"

Peter thought quickly as to whether he'd got anything too valuable in his wallet. *Shit!* he thought. *Coco's address.* But then he remembered, thank God, he'd got 19 more. He reached for his wallet, and as he did he caught the glimpse of a dull, deep blue form moving quickly and silently between two clumps of bushes, roughly in the direct sight line between himself and the bandits. He took his wallet out of his inside pocket and threw it to the ground.

"Lo recoge!" the lead gypsy shouted.

Peter did as he was told and picked it up. He could see blue uniforms about 50 metres away. *Guardia Civilia,* he thought. *Without a doubt. Thank God for that.*

This time he handed the wallet to the more forward and commanding of the assailants, who opened the wallet and counted out 30,000 pesetas. He looked pleased about that. He then rummaged in the mainly old bills and visiting cards and brought Peter's passport out in his free hand. Thumbing it open, he looked hard at the picture and related it back to Peter's face. He then flicked the pages and came to the personal information. Date of birth, name, etc.

The bandit focused on the name. "Martinez. Ah! Pedro Martinez. Toda la familia Martinez debe estar en el nombre de Tania Henriques, deberias morir."

Peter had cause to be concerned. The black eyes said it all. If he was a Tania cousin he might well have known that Tania was fooling with one of the Martinez family, and had now had the best part of 20 years in prison for that to fester into unparalleled hate.

Why this weekend? Why on this walk? Suddenly Peter remembered Toni and his mouth went dry. That's it, they were Toni's eyes behind the scarf.

The bandido raised the double-barrelled shotgun in careful aim at Peter's head.

"Nosotros lo tenemos rodeo, deje caer sus fusiles," came sudden firm instructions through a loud hailer. "Es la Policia. Deje caer, sus fusiles y no serías dolido."

The bandido seemed to freeze with a sudden determined deafness. Peter thought, *You mad bastard. You don't want to be hurt, do as you're told. Drop your gun. For Christ's sake, drop your gun.*

Toni – if it was him, and Peter was now sure that it was – rather than dropping his gun as instructed, started to turn, with his shotgun forced into his shoulder, towards the direction of the loud hailer. Interpreting Toni's disobedience as defiance, and compelled by a defence mechanism, the police marksmen reacted. There were three loud explosive cracks from their rifles. Toni was hit and his whole body twisted. His huge inner strength kept him upright until he lost all control as his knees began to buckle.

Peter was momentarily relieved. This was no killing of a young boar by a protective father intent on feeding his family. This was the removal of a dangerous psychopath and those shots might well have saved Peter's life.

The impact of the police bullets which riddled his body caused the bandit's scarf to come free and Peter saw the twisted, thinner, now older face of Toni, who had caused him so much pain during that previous beating.

There was a loud, deep explosion and Peter saw a red flash a few metres in front of him. The gypsy's trigger finger had been engaged when he was hit, and one of the barrels of his sawn down shotgun had been activated. His reflexes caused him to tense and as the support of his knees finally gave way, he fell towards the ground.

In those few seconds before, in which he had been made aware of a red flash, Peter experienced pain of a far deeper degree than he had ever suffered before. He felt instinctively towards his right shoulder where he felt the agony. There was another flash as a shot from the second barrel exploded. As the bullet hit his right knee, his legs would no longer carry his weight and he had no resistance to the supernatural force that caused him to fall to his left. The impact as he hit the ground forced him to submit to all the pain, and he lost consciousness.

The police were on the scene. They felt Toni's jugular. There was no pulse.

"El esta muerto," the principal officer announced.

Toni was dead.

They leant over Peter. "El es dolido malo."

He was hurt badly. That was an understatement. Police radios crackled while officers shouted panic instructions. There was suddenly an unearthly noise from above, which became louder. A helicopter appeared above the glade and made a perilous descent into the clearing, its revolving blades almost touching the surrounding trees.

As soon as the craft landed, a side door burst open and a paramedic team leapt into frantic but controlled action. They used a sign language as one tackled Peter's shoulder, which was gushing blood, while the other cut away his trouser leg and applied a tourniquet to his left thigh. An oxygen mask was clamped over his nose and mouth.

Peter's subconscious went into a colourful slide show. First a flash of an image of his mother, then Anna in her wedding gown, followed by his father with a shotgun carefully carried on his shoulder. Then slides of deep red and mauve patterns, which cleared to show Coco looking down at him... then there was a field of sunflowers, gold and bronze with deep brown centres.

Peter's motionless body was strapped onto a stretcher and loaded into the side door of the helicopter.

The helicopter's arrival at Palafrugell Hospital was expected. There had been two-way messages between the paramedics and the consultant surgeon, who was escorted by a couple of police motorcycle outriders to speed him onto duty.

A trolley was waiting on the lawn behind the hospital and Peter was rushed with care across to it and into the hospital like some late delivery of post that had to make the overnight van.

The surgeons operated for five hours. Stemming the blood from the shoulder was their first concern. Peter was on a full transfusion and was under heavy anaesthetic.

The anaesthetist advised the senior surgeon that he thought if the anaesthetic were to be stopped, Peter would by now be conscious.

"Good. That's one thing going for him."

One nurse was trying her best to be the professional she had been brought up to be. Working as part of the team to keep Peter alive, choking back her tears, Gina waited until it seemed consultants, nurses and orderlies had done what they could and then asked to be relieved from the theatre, on account of knowing the patient.

She was immediately pounced upon by the lone patient intake clerk on duty, who pumped her for information. Peter had no form of ID on him, as Toni had died with Peter's wallet tucked into his ammunition belt, and that fact had not been realised by the shell-shocked police. Gina was giving such information as she had.

"Maria, his mother, runs the Playa Hotel."

"Right, get the Playa…"

Marcia would know everything, Gina thought… but she was in England. The overseas operator was put to work. Immediately the admin staff were manning the external lines.

They found Maria in the hotel. Immediately she'd heard the news, she was on her way. They said they would be trying to contact Marcia in England on the number Gina had remembered.

Peter was kept in intensive care.

The senior consultant, a Mr Benito Alvor, was at the door of the hospital when Maria arrived. The look of fear in her face set her aside from any other late middle-aged women visiting patients. He knew who she was and the mission she was on.

"Mrs Martinez?" he asked sombrely.

This was no time to explain she'd changed her name by marriage. "Yes, it is."

"Your son has had a rough time."

"Oh dear," she said, going weak at the knees.

"He's OK."

"Oh, thank God for that!"

"Yes, I actually think you ought to do that. Your son clearly has a protecting influence on his life."

"Is there permanent damage?"

"His right shoulder took a pounding. He seems a physical sort of man. With determined physiotherapy, he'll get 90 per cent use. His right knee is shot to bits. It may be that in a week or two we'll go back and have a look at it and consider a knee replacement. Nowadays that's quite successful. He's conscious and can remember what happened. He was delirious for a while. He had an urge for honey and cocoa, which is strange for a chap close to death at the time."

"Thank you, Doctor," Maria said with relief, inadvertently lowering him from his Mr Consultant status. "Thank you for mending him so far."

The consultant said, "It's our job. We're not always much good on the psychological side of things, though. As you're his mother, when he asks whether he can play sport again, you'll have to let him down lightly."

"I'll do that, with reservation," she said sadly, wiping a tear from her cheek, as she immediately remembered Paco, Pedro and herself in Rosas.

Was the Sardana a sport? she wondered. The consultant was clearly of Catalan stock. He would know the answer she needed.

"But what if he asks if he'll dance the Sardana again?"

"Why the Sardana?" Benito Alvor enquired.

"It's special."

"Then yes, I'd say he will. But I doubt he'll tango."

CHAPTER 17

Jan Roberts had come to the biggest conclusion in her life in the communications business: that you were there to be contacted, availability was a 24-hour requirement. A mobile for the privileged few was good where signals were in place, but being at home was not only for recharging her own batteries but those in the phone as well.

She seemed often to have been caught out when either in the loo or bathroom, so had bought one of the new Philips 'walk around the apartment' landline set-ups. She now had extensions by her bedside, in the lounge/open diner/kitchen area, one in the loo and the fourth surreptitiously placed behind the large glass jar she had adapted as a holder for cotton wool balls.

It was Sunday night and she had driven back into town after having lunch with her parents in Reigate. It was a sort of courtesy family day, and her sister and brother-in-law had been invited too. She was sure her mother always arranged such days to bring Jan into contact with her two nieces and nephew in the hope that it might make her broody and bring her out of her bachelor life. She seemed to be getting more deeply involved in the quicksands of her career after she had left Richard, and the local paper, for the hierarchy of PR and the development of her individual style of interview.

Her mother had been hopeful that her younger daughter, when she was with Richard, would follow in the footsteps of the elder sibling and produce a few more grandchildren for the clan.

OK, Jan had accepted that Richard was never going to be the greatest breadwinner, but their relationship was homely. At least in those days, when they spoke on the phone, her mother knew exactly where Jan was when she was speaking to her. She would either be propped up in the comfort of the corner chair or curled up on the adjoining sofa. Back then, there was just the one phone and its umbilical cord of communication could only be stretched about six.

Nowadays, her mother felt the need to say at the beginning of every call, "So where are you, darling?" That riled Jan because it made no difference which bloody part of the flat she was in. She still said how nice it was to hear from her mother, still asked how her father was, and had to pretend to be interested in how her sister and family were doing.

The phone rang and although the ring tone was soft, it still made her jump. Maybe it was guilt or embarrassment that the caller might be able to see that she was nude, in the bath and shaving her legs with a slightly over-used BIC, which she kept forgetting to replenish.

She glanced quickly at the seashell-clad clock she had bought back from some junk tourist shop in St Johns in Antigua. It looked alright on the tiled shelf, not as naff as she thought it might. It was an unusual instinctive purchase because Jan normally displayed great taste and style in her acquisitions for the home.

10.35pm. It wouldn't be her mother. And Jan was all out of a regular boyfriend at the moment, so it wouldn't be him wanting to off-load some problem before he got his good night's sleep, leaving her struggling to get off while she continued to think the conversational problem through. She dried her hands.

"Hello."

"Hi, Jan?" It was a male voice.

"You didn't ask if Jan was in please."

"Well listen, if it's not Jan either I've got the wrong number or you've got a lesbian lover in tow, and she's got to the phone first. Aren't you pleased to hear from me?"

"A qualified yes if you've got me lined up for some interview with a juicy millionaire on some nice warm beach, oh and with an unlimited expense allowance, but otherwise no. Do you know it's 20 to 11 and also that I've done with lovers of any persuasion at the moment, but you can bet on them having a husky male voice if they come back into fashion."

"I think I knew it was late. Did I wake you?"

"Look, Martin, I'm in the bath…"

"In the bath?"

"Yes, in the bath… and if you really want to ruin your night's sleep, I've got no clothes on, as one doesn't in the bath, I'm wet and bubbly and I'm doing my legs."

"Christ! You're right. I won't bloody sleep… might not even ever sleep again… but by sheer coincidence, it is about a millionaire close to a pleasantly warm beach."

Jan sat up straight. "Will I need a pen?"

"Of course you bloody will. It's an interview."

"No, darling, I mean how complicated is this call going to be? Do I need to drip dry out of the bath and make some notes?"

"No. Just lie back, as I can imagine you are anyway. You remember the pieces you did on Peter Martinez?"

Jan positively squirmed. She blushed. The name always raised the hairs on her body. She'd just got rid of the ones on her legs. She'd thought about Peter a lot since the two days on which they had met.

On balance, she had concluded, he was probably the most charming interviewee she had encountered. He had let her down lightly when she'd asked why there wasn't a Mrs Martinez, when he had explained that it was because she had died. He'd shown her a cultured side by taking her to the ballet and then not pushing himself on her for a nightcap, or more. She just overall liked him, which was a bonus in her vocation.

"Of course I remember Peter, and the articles. You said they were some of my best work. But what about Peter?"

"Have you not seen the ten o'clock news?"

"Yes, I haven't seen the news. For Christ's sake, what's this very late call all about?"

"Well, Peter Martinez has been shot."

Jan's body went limp, her stomach sank. Strangely, she felt she wanted to cry.

"Shot? Shot dead?"

"No. Not dead, apparently, but you know what it's like in Spain. We can't find out much from the hospital."

Jan stiffened into her professional self. Martin was her agent and hadn't let her down yet in helping her earn more, year on year, and enhancing her profile, which, if anything, was more important.

"So Martin, darling, at this late hour and having ruined my weekend by giving me some half-news, what have you got in mind?"

"Well, obviously, BCG will be devastated, almost in turmoil if control can't be put back into the hands of Mr William and the family. I thought I ought to contact the Chairman and suggest that here's a story they could actually capitalise upon… you know, Chief Executive shot. Board support his welfare and recovery. How it happened. How it's going to be overcome… you know… launch a mega PR exercise out of it."

"Have you put it to them yet?"

"No."

"Well, why waste my time then? I can't see I've a role to play… the result of your call is that the bloody water's now cold… and what was to be my most pleasurable event of the weekend is in tatters."

"Sounds like a call for help. I'll be right over to warm you up."

"Martin Kemp, my love. Get lost. Get to the point. What's my involvement?"

171

"If I speak to BCG, they'll insist on you doing the job. I need to know your availability to get out there to cover the position."

"I've got Monday, Tuesday booked on the Shell Chief Executive's interview for 'Time' and the Dutch press. Wednesday, Thursday would be earliest."

"Fine, darling. I'll work on that."

"Martin?"

"Yes," he answered to a plea tone in her voice.

"Could you ring me first thing and tell me how Peter is? He's too lovely to die."

"If you say so, Jan. Leave it to Uncle Martin to ensure there's enough life in him to go under your pen for a second time."

"Thank you. Oh, and I suppose I have to thank you for the call."

"Not at all, darling. Now are you sure you don't want me to come over?"

"Yes, certain. Speak in the morning."

"Have a good night."

"You too."

Jan pressed the end call button and replaced the phone to its cradle. Her hands were showing signs of exposure to the rapidly cooling bath water. She hadn't realised quite how cold she was. She splashed water over her upper body to flush off the dried soapy foam and gently raised herself up out of the bath. She reached for a towel and in one throw, as if a matador's cape, it was around her shoulders and upper body, soaking up the surplus water.

She began to dry herself. She felt warmer already. As she rubbed the towel upwards on the left leg, she realised that, comparatively, it was rough. *Shit!* she thought. She had only shaved the right leg when the phone rang. She'd have to finish the job in the shower in the morning.

Reaching into the warmth of the bathroom airing cupboard, she selected some pyjamas, the Liberty ones her sister had bought her a couple of Christmases ago. She put on her towelling robe, reached in to the bath to pull out the plug and left, leaving the water gurgling into its waste.

A quick glance in the mirror said she was now tired. Playing with the kids had been fun but energetic. The phone call had drained her more than she might have expected.

She took milk from the fridge and put a filled mug into the microwave. In the 30 seconds it took to heat up she located the remote control for the TV, which she could see across the breakfast bar in the lounge. Melvyn Bragg was deep in explanation on a subject Jan was not inclined to wish to understand.

The sounder on the microwave indicated 'time's up'. She took out the mug and, still with remote in hand, walked over to the TV. She flicked through channels until she found a current news bulletin and sat comfortably on the floor like a young child allowed the treat of watching an extra ration of cartoons.

The newsreader went through the usual cocktail of Sunday light politics and a traffic story concerning an abandoned van on a motorway in Kent, which the police had treated as a suspect vehicle until a young French couple appeared from across the adjoining fields to explain that they had both had a call of nature. There was a hint that their call of nature was not one that could be accomplished standing behind a tree or squatting under a bush. *Good for them,* Jan thought, *but what a waste of public money.*

The newsreader's face turned serious as he began the next story. "A Spanish-born British businessman has been shot by bandits in the hills of northern Spain close to Palafrugell. It is believed the bandits were part of a drug-running syndicate and it appears Peter Martinez, CEO of the BCG Group, stumbled across them in a clearing. Spanish police were at the scene and had the gang under surveillance. Reports say there was some sort of shoot-out in which Mr Martinez, who originates from that part of the world, was severely injured and was flown to Palafrugell Hospital by helicopter. It is understood the injured executive is in a stable condition after surgery..."

Without knowing she had done it, Jan had switched the TV off but was still sitting hunched in front of the dead set. She hadn't realised tears were slowly rolling down both cheeks absolutely in tandem, dropping with equal velocity onto her white robe. As her emotions flooded out, her shoulders shuddered in unison with the heaving of her stomach. Fortunately she'd drunk her milk and was holding the empty mug to her chest. She felt sick to her stomach.

What was more, she felt sick in her chest too. Then in her throat, which led to her experiencing that sucking downwards feeling when the back of the tongue is pulled towards the oesophagus. She lifted herself deftly from the floor and ran to the toilet. She fell to her knees and retched into the pan.

She emptied her body of all her mother's much-planned gastronomic treats, then went to the adjacent bathroom and cleaned her teeth. This time the mirror showed her as being ashen. Her bed in the adjoining room was welcoming and she climbed in and slid under the duvet.

"Oh God, please be kind to Peter Martinez. He's a kind man himself and doesn't deserve this. Please tell me he'll be alright. Please." She drifted into sleep.

Martin didn't ring till about ten the next morning. He reached Jan on her mobile just as she arrived at Shell's riverside headquarters.

"What's the news?" she instinctively shouted down the phone, to overcome the ambient noise of the passing traffic.

"Well, babe, it looks as though you'll be in Spain by the end of the week..."

She interrupted forcefully. "You hard bastard! Not that bloody news. How's Peter?"

"Oh sorry, old love. He seems to be OK. BCG are in touch and he came through a pretty nasty operation, by all accounts, but he's quite conscious and apparently had a conversation with the office earlier this morning, presumably to sort out the panic of running a business from a hospital bed. Peter Martinez's spokesman says the Chairman thinks you coming on the scene is a great idea… just the person, he said… but he's concerned about expenditure. It wasn't budgeted for."

"You're a cynic, Martin. Of course it wasn't budgeted for. I doubt if Peter had budgeted for it in his life either. Anyway, I'm very pleased about Peter's recovery and I look forward to seeing him for myself later in the week."

As she said that, she was ashamed instantly at the thought of her one unshaven leg. She was sure the CEO of Shell wouldn't notice, but why was the prospect of seeing Peter a reminder to her? She'd get on to Interflora if she got a break during the day and send some flowers. She was sure 'Peter Martinez, Palafrugell Hospital, Palafrugell, Spain' would find him.

Jan got through the rest of the day just about satisfactorily. She felt she hadn't gelled with the guy at Shell. He was very full of himself and the gift he was to mankind, ecology and global warming. She had to get out of her mind that his principal product of oil was now no gift to mankind, as important as it had become as a raw material. It was responsible for producing the fumes that were progressively polluting the atmosphere, causing deaths in their wake. The oil prospectors were tearing up seabeds and landscapes to extract their black syrup of gold and had been one of the greatest causes of the climate spiralling out of control.

So how could the PR team, who had briefed him on what he should be preaching, expect her, in turn, to pass that message on to the world? She might for once now have to bite her tongue. She'd have to be advised. Shell, after all, weren't paying her, Time magazine and others were.

Jan went back to the office to write up the first day basics of the interview. As she left at about 8.30pm, she realised she'd hardly eaten all day. Her stomach still felt a bit sore. This was when she wished she could call a boyfriend and suggest they meet for a snack and a chat to take her away from the pressures of the day. She'd ring Martin. No, on second thoughts she'd get a light Chinese takeaway from Beijing Garden just round the corner from her mews house.

When she got home, her first priority was to transfer the contents of the foil into microwave containers. She didn't want to waste that. As she prepared her food, she caught a glimpse of the LED display of the answerphone. There was that ever-threatening numeric 'one' showing. Should she play the message back before eating, or after? She was a sucker. She'd always give way to her natural inquisitiveness. She couldn't not know.

"Hi." She recognised her agent's voice. "Before you scream at me, your millionaire man's fine. Apparently one of his knees has been shot to bits and he took a slug in his shoulder. But the prognosis, according to a conversation between his mother, no less, and the BCG PR team, is that he'll walk OK, though there's some strange overtone that he won't dance much. I didn't know he was into dancing but you might be able to understand the importance of that.

"He's resting in Palafrugell Hospital but BCG want him transferred either to Barcelona or flown back to the UK to be treated. There's no decision yet, obviously. The other bit of news is I've got you a booking on BA to Barcelona, Thursday 08:00… business class… it's all expenses paid. Naughty girl, your mobile's off."

So it was, she realised.

CHAPTER 18

Fortunately, when Marcia was contacted by the Spanish police, the news of Peter's shooting was not a huge shock to her. In any case, the police were able to reassure her that after a night of nursing, he was out of danger.

She had been on the terrace when the call came, literally looking into the distance and not being able to get Peter out of her mind. That was not an unusual experience.

Marcia realised she had remained standing during the entire call. She was brought back to reality by the strange bleeping sound down the line, letting her know the phone had been left off the hook, and was still connected to the previous incoming call.

The terrace and accompanying lifestyle was the result of Marcia's invite to the King George and Queen Elizabeth Diamond Stakes meeting at Ascot by some new neighbours. She'd not kept up with Bob's horses and had sold them on, with the help of the turf accountant John Jones. Bob's various insurance policies, and her widow's pension, and the income from the shares in the company, dividends, etc, brought her in a very good income by most people's standards. She seemed to be able to spend most of it, however, which worried her.

She had a good social life. Better, of course, when Peter was on her agenda. They'd known each other a long time now; she never counted it up but she knew it was over 30 years. If Peter had been destined to be the second husband in her life, she would have relished the opportunity. She often wondered about that and whether, in fact, they now had anything in common other than keeping their respective bodies in trim, and a mutual enjoyment of each other's sexual attributes. Their age difference was of no consequence.

Still, she was not on Peter's agenda for permanency, so there was no point in postulating.

When Marcia was invited into a new environment, therefore, she was bound to invest a little in the presentation of the goods she had to offer. She certainly had no intention of heading into old age without a permanent companion. It wasn't totally realistic to say she only indulged herself when entering new company. It was her habit normally. But new introductions set fresh horizons, so on those occasions she went to special trouble on her personal marketing front.

She had what she called 'lucky days'. Some mornings she woke positively brimming with adrenalin. That was the sign of a day that would bring good fortune. They usually did. She never knew exactly what caused the feeling as soon as she opened her eyes. It was not necessarily that it was a bright sunny morning with birds tweeting, or that she she'd find a Premium Bond win tucked under the door. They just turned out to be happy days.

The Ascot Day was going to be a lucky one.

Marcia showered and washed her hair. It set wonderfully with just the lightest hint of assistance from her hair-drier. She'd got no bloating to cope with and fitted smoothly into her white linen skirt; likewise her blue jacket with its white piping. The high, matching blue stilettos fitted as though they had been made for her, but then at that price, she thought, they should have been anyway. She'd had just fruit for breakfast and had gone light on the champagne plied at the neighbours' house, where a dozen or so guests had met up to accept the offer of a lift in a couple of people carriers they had hired in with drivers for the occasion.

It seemed strange that she categorised some people as being nouveau riche because she, of all people, was exactly that. Somehow or other Bob had brought style out in her and even she could sense it. She utilised it to the full, but was just as much at ease talking to a jockey or stable lad as she was the knights of the realm she met, who seemed to hang around racehorses and the courses where they performed.

Marcia knew that two or three glasses of Moet would give her a headache but put a bottle of Roederer or Krug in front of her, and she would drink through the night and show the pleasure by giggling when taken to bed.

The Grants had been most welcoming, conscious that she wouldn't know anyone else there. The introductions were of the nature of, "You must meet…", "Now George Henning will make you laugh all day." "Speak to Mel about her dear little grand-daughter… she's a terrible two."

Marcia, at heart, regretted not having had children. Her marriage to Bob had not included a family on the agenda. A slip-up with Peter might have touched his conscience and that would have been a different matter. Wouldn't they both have indulged a son athletically? He'd have been Olympic material, without a doubt, and might even have faced the dilemma of seeking a place in either the British or Spanish teams in the 1992 games.

Strangely, though, Marcia thought Peter had not over-indulged his actual children. He appeared to have left them to form their own life patterns and from what Peter said, that had worked. More so perhaps after Anna's death, their relative independence and instant allegiances to grandparents stopped them from being too demanding on their father's time and allowed him to build his ever more successful career.

As she left the Grants', there was nobody Marcia had met in the large through lounge who made her rush to the people carrier and jockey them into the adjoining seat. OK, every male head had turned as she entered the room, and if it was socially acceptable, all the wives would have loved to kick their husbands in the balls to remind them that they were there to be kicked by wives, rather than to conjure up erotic thoughts of unattached ladies in blue.

So, Marcia resolved, she'd enjoy the day and accept that her lucky feeling about finding a further male companion to add to her list might not come to fruition. Her luck might manifest itself in the form of the bookmakers paying her out a lot of money when the horses John Jones told her to bet on came home.

Marcia always rang Bob's faithful bookmaker and asked his advice on any day's outing to enjoy the sport of kings. She didn't follow her husband's habit of a lifetime by having a bet most days. She loved the thrill of winning, too much to have to learn the disappointment of losing.

They got away from Dulwich by about 11.45am, although the aim had been 11.30am, to grab the first race at 1.30pm. The journey was fine. At least there was laughter stimulated through Moet from those who didn't already have a headache.

They were dropped by the entrance to the main stand and everyone followed George Henning, who appeared to know the way up to the box. He insisted on making himself look an absolute prat by holding an unfurled Barclays Bank umbrella above his head and shouting, "Onward men and upward." Most of the party apparently found it screechingly funny. Marcia wished she wasn't with them. She knew the way anyway without needing to be part of the Charge of the Bank Brigade. She giggled inwardly at her own joke, recalling how Bob had taught her to hate bank charges.

They had a runner laid on to take the bets, an ex-mathematics teacher who could explain to the novices the nuances of bets to win, each-way placings, accumulators and all the other attractions to strip them of their hard-earned income or ill-gotten gains.

Marcia had her own programme firmly written down. She must have used up the time of the runner for at least five minutes while the others in the box waited anxiously to get on to the first race. Her target of the day was a rolled up bet on all six races which, if they all came home, would keep her in tights and new stilettos for quite a few years to come.

William Forrester had a debenture through Amalgamated Electrics on the adjoining box. His guests were the usual boring bunch of fuddy-duddies his co-executives thought were worth treating to a day out. They never used to invite the wives as well, on account of the fact that, by experience, they rarely had an interest in thoroughbred racing and William, anyway, loathed trying to talk to women about their kids' education, how hard their other halves were working and the like. He had needed to escape into the air. It was a fine warm day with no threat of a shower until well into the night.

He panned the enclosures around the course, wondering how so many people could be off work on a weekday. Perhaps, he mused, they were all part of the 7000-strong workforce Amalgamated Electrics employed, who knew that the boss and most of the executives weren't going to be around to check up on who was at work and who was skiving. The turf looked firm and very green. William scanned the view slowly and determinedly through his binoculars. Not many people wore morning dress nowadays and the women were decidedly dressed down, not that that did any harm to some of the younger bodies.

The box on his left was noisy and obviously, to his practised eyes and ears, the occupants had been drinking since breakfast. He quickly glanced through the 20 or so gathered on the enclosed patio to see if he knew any of them. The problem with his neighbours' debenture holder was that they did not support every meeting and let the facility out to 'friends'. They were not always aficionados of the sport.

The noisy throng seemed to part reverently to make a pathway clearing for their leader or some dignitary or other. William really wasn't that interested and so started to assess the far more dignified box to his right. Well, at least there he knew some of his contemporaries, mainly bankers and professional parasites. He waved politely with the back of his hand at some of the faces he knew, and they nonchalantly returned the insincere compliment.

So it was another day at the races… *Shit!* Suddenly, no! It wasn't. A filly had appeared on the front rails of the terrace of the rowdy box to his left. Her head was topped with groomed short blonde hair. Not tarty and flowing, in the style adopted by most who naturally or artificially sponsored that colour hair, he thought. She looked tall and was certainly slim. The colour of her tailored jacket was what he saw as Masonic leather blue, a few shades lighter than the Santorini blue he so loved on that Greek island. The jacket lapels were neatly set off by white piping. The white pencil skirt, with its discreet overlap split, obviously covered a lovely backside, firmly supported, he imagined, by lengthy legs that tapered in an intriguing disappearing act into what he was sure must be blue leather stilettos. *Turn around… for God's sake,* he thought.

Her eyes were glued as if looking out into the distance on the Derby Day printed canvas his grandmother had once had hanging on the wall of her treasured Pimlico flat. William often wondered who had inherited that canvas when she died. It was so big and faded that he expected his proud mother threw it in as part of the deal with the 'Honest and established house and flat clearance' chap she had turned to, to save her the bother and embarrassment of having to dispose of his grandmother's junk.

"Sorry to disturb your thoughts, Bill, but Gunter Hauser of Deutsche Bank needs buttering up. You know they're close to signing the Hamburg Turbine finance deal. He says he needs advice on which horse will win and perhaps you can guide him. We blokes haven't got a clue."

William had had to accept the natural nickname given to him at school, which then stuck with his close associates and friends. He reluctantly moved away from studying the female human form, to perform the more serious support role he so often had to play in the development of his group's business.

Patron Saint was his final selection for the banker. The TV set in the box showed the horses being ridden to the stalls. "Excuse me," he said politely as he extricated himself from the German, "I like to watch from the rails. By all means join me and see if my prediction's right."

William had stepped outside back on to the terrace, and immediately looked towards where Marcia had been standing when he had been so inconveniently dragged away. She was there now, looking towards the starting post, through binoculars that Bob had bought her, with diamonds set into the bridge between the two sights. You either need to know what you're looking for as a racing enthusiast, or you don't. Her stance told him she did. As much as William had tried to teach his wife, she was always out of place at the racetrack. That didn't need to count in her busy life anyway. She was an eminent paediatrician and hated being dragged from her consulting rooms and NHS commitments.

"William," as his previous wife (who always called him by his given name) used to say, "I can add nothing to the lives of those who want to lose their money in such foolish pursuits, putting their faith and trust in, first a horse, ridden by a jockey, trained by a person used to playing hunches, and owned by either someone with too much money or who has little respect for what they do with their money anyway."

He missed such profound speeches now and bitterly regretted that, despite all the young lives she had saved, or helped to create, nobody could protect hers when it was discovered she had advanced cancer, which she should have been able to screen herself but hadn't.

Fortunately, William always comforted himself with the knowledge that she'd suffered relatively little pain and it was all over, much to the shock and horror of everyone who knew her, or depended on her, in just three weeks. He missed a female companion but did not want a relationship to compromise his position as the revered, squeaky-clean head of a major PLC, in line, so his closer business associates encouraged him to believe, for a knighthood.

He ambled down to the rail which, as he reached it, made him realise the object of his distraction was not quite as tall as he had imagined, as she was standing on the second step up from the balustrade. He'd got his positioning wrong, to the extent that she had a better view of him than he of her, but he worked out that with some casual glimpsing to his left, he would be able to see her face and whether she was a bat out of hell with a bloody good body, great dress sense, and a husband who gave her an unlimited allowance.

A cheer went up from the crowds on the terraces as the large screen showed the 'off'. The commentary conveyed over the public Tannoy system led everybody to believe that each of the dozen charging horses was well positioned to win.

Patron Saint looked there, or thereabouts, as they came into close view around the right-hand turn. The purple and green colours were distinctive.

"Go on, Saint!" he heard distinctly from a keen female voice to his left. As he was distracted by that, he turned, looking up slightly at Marcia's fine bone structure and tasteful makeup. She was no bat. She was a beauty.

Marcia, meanwhile, was oblivious to his glances. "Go on, my Saint... go on, my Saint!" Her body was writhing as though she herself was in the saddle and kicking into the last two furlongs. Sure, he wanted to see his bet cross the line first. He knew her face and simple commentary of encouragement would tell him. Her vision of the closing pack was becoming something of a blur. It was close. The purple and green was hidden by a couple of horses on the stand side, which must have been in contention.

"Patron Saint!" she heard herself scream.

As if in reply, suddenly one head and neck clearly emerged and then, with 300 yards to go, the purple and green of the jockey's shirt could be seen ahead of the other colours.

"Come on, Saint! Come on, Saint! Bloody come on, Saint!" she screamed.

She was totally breathless. Her heart was pounding. She clenched her teeth and closed her eyes, raising her face to the sky. She heard a voice to her right say, "So which one were you on?"

Strange, she thought. It seemed the question *was* directed to her.

"Did you have the winner after all that screaming?" It was directed to her.

Marcia opened her eyes and tried to focus down the sound beam along which the questions had travelled. She found this open face looking up towards her. Fifty-something, she thought. Lovely head of cultured grey hair worn respectably long onto the ears. Contact lenses, she supposed, and groomed in his morning grey with an unusual pink tie. The face was smiling.

"Sorry, is the question to me?"

"Both were," he said precisely, but with a deepening grin.

"I'm not saying," she said, "in case you're the bookmaker and you do a runner."

"Who'd do a runner away from you?" He meant it, but also in jest. She might not have understood that. "I mean that as a compliment," he said, and moved towards the timber rails dividing the boxes from each other. He held his hand into her air space, indicating that she should take it.

"I'm William Forrester, Bill Forrester to friends and those who share my winning intentions, and I'm pleased for you that you won."

Marcia reflected that he had a lovely open smile, and did take his hand without giving her involuntary reaction a further thought.

"Look, I don't normally talk to strangers over a dividing fence, but I'm Marcia Hunt. Did you have a bet?"

"Yes."

"Oh dear. Are you going to say my choice beat yours?"

"No."

"I don't follow…"

"You were shouting for both of us. I had Patron Saint too."

She liked his openness, so took him into her confidence. "I'm on a roll up into the second race."

"What on?"

"Princess Royal."

"That's OK."

"What do you mean by that?"

"It'll win."

"Really!"

"Yes. I think so, anyway."

"… And the third race?"

"Now that would be really saying, wouldn't it? I'll tell you after the next race."

Marcia studied his face and deep-set, sharp clear eyes. He was looking after himself, or being very well looked after. He was either married or queer. Not queer, surely. Probably married. They all were. All the seemingly pleasant ones were spoken for, or queer.

"Look, I got a little excited. You'll have to excuse me. I need to go to the ladies'."

"You go. You worked hard to bring the Saint home. Go and check out your winnings too."

"We've got a runner. I don't have to. Besides, by the end of this lucky day, I'll need Securicor to protect me. I really must go. Nature calls."

Bill Forrester was very impressed. But she'd be married, of course. Surely she couldn't be available, and it was one of his precepts not to get tangled up in somebody else's matrimonial arrangement. Still, she was light fun.

"Who's the lady?" John Thompson, Chief Executive of the Cables Division, asked.

"Never you mind. Let's just say we have the same taste in horses."

As Marcia left the box to go to the end of the open corridor, which she knew led to the ladies' loo, she had a quick glance at the card adjacent to the entrance door of the adjoining box. She made a mental note of 'William Forrester – Amalgamated Electrics', and hurried on to spend her penny.

She returned to find the waitresses were passing round canapés. Food would be useful, she thought, so accepted a small piece of toast with a floral design in smoked salmon, in the middle of which was a little arrangement of caviar. She'd be careful not to spill it on her jacket.

George Henning was suddenly at her side. "How did you get on?"

"Well, I backed Patron Saint."

"Well done. What about the second race?"

"I'll tell you after," she found herself saying. "George, isn't it?"

"Yes, that's right."

Hell, he thought, *she remembered my name, I might just be in here.*

"Are you in business?" Marcia asked.

"Well, not strictly. Why?"

"I wondered who Amalgamated Electrics are."

"Oh, I'd say everybody knows that. They're a huge international conglomerate that's resulted from some smooth mergers and takeovers orchestrated by their new Chairman, I think he is anyway, a bloke called Bill Forrester. Why the interest?"

"Oh nothing really. I just saw their name on a box and I didn't know who they are."

Marcia suddenly realised she had done a most unusual thing. She usually listened intently to her first introduction to somebody she had not met before. Her habit was to repeat the name to herself three times and then give it an association with somebody else. In the excitement of the moment, she had not done that with her distinguished new neighbour. She repeated to herself now: "Bill Forrester… tree…" *Was* that what he'd said his name was? Not that it really mattered. She liked him without knowing his CV.

She sipped a small glass of Chablis and noticed from the TV screen that the horses were again on their way to the start. For fear of repetition, she stayed on the top step of the private terrace and did her shouting and encouragement from there. Next-door neighbour was in the position he had taken up last time. From a distance, he cut a solitary figure. Obviously a creature of habit, to be standing back there where they had first met.

Marcia willed the Princess Royal to the line, noticing little emotion from Bill Forrester. She didn't like to see him alone so she walked slowly down the shallow steps. As she reached his shoulder level, yet divided by the fence, she was the first to speak.

"Well, there you go. We told each other, didn't we?"

"Oh, hello. Yes, we certainly did. But then it was bound to win. The next is more difficult."

"I don't see that… William… or did you say it was Bill?"

"Bill's fine. Yes, I did. So who do you fancy?"

"It's a bit late really. As I said, I've got an accumulator going."

"Well, you have to say."

She listed her few choices. He looked surprised.

"It's Marcia, isn't it? I don't know where you get your advice from, Marcia, or it might just be a lucky pen, but out of the four I'd have money on two of yours for certain. I'd have a difficulty with one and I'd totally disagree with another."

"Totally disagree." She repeated his words and reflected again. If he was the dynamic go-getter she believed him to be, maybe she should listen when he seemed so certain she had one loser.

"How can you be so sure? Which race?"

"The last."

"The last. That's going to be a nightmare. If I've won five in an accumulation, I'd be devastated. How can you be so certain?"

"Here, look at the programme."

She looked at the page he had opened and read the write-up on her horse. Fourth at Sandown and faded. Fourth in a Derby trial. It had really little form. What had John Jones done to her?

"That's OK. You can't win all the time," said William. "But you didn't look carefully."

She felt humbled. "What have I missed that's likely to lose me the fortune I thought I was heading for?"

"The owner, Marcia."

She looked again. "Oh my God, William Forrester! That's you, isn't it?"

"Well, yes, and I know that horse. He hasn't got a cat in hell's chance of finishing above four. In terms of being able to count, he learnt to do that backwards, starting at ten. He got to four and stopped learning. He doesn't know the meaning of third, second never enters his vocabulary and as for first… forget it. I'm terribly sorry but your pin got stuck in the wrong animal."

"Look, it's difficult. I'm a guest of some new neighbours… so I'm enjoying their hospitability… but would it be possible for me to have a word with your horse?"

William roared with laughter. "Why the hell did I have to meet you… let alone meet you today? Have a word? To what extent?"

"Could I just whisper in his ear?"

"OK. But I'm a conditional sort of bloke. I'll take you down to the parade ring before the race but it's subject to you telling me what you're going to say and, if you work a miracle and he does win, you'll receive the winner's prize on my behalf."

"It's no to the first part, though I will tell you after… but if I'm to accept the prize then I'd like to speak to the jockey too."

"Now the last bit makes sense. OK, that's all a deal."

"Can I ask one more question?"

"Yes, OK, crazy woman. What is this going to be?"

"What about Mrs Forrester? Won't she mind about all this?"

He suddenly looked as though he'd aged ten years.

"I'm a widower. Mrs Forrester, unfortunately, can't mind any more." He pondered a little further. "And what will Mr Hunt say when he sees your picture in *Hello*, or wherever, because the press are bound to snap your presence up?"

Marcia was already braced for his counter-question. She was half-prepared. "It's just possible Mr Hunt will be getting cross with both of us from where he is, alongside Mrs Forrester. I'm a widow. Bob died… oh, over ten years ago."

"I'm sorry."

"I'm sorry for you too. I know how it feels."

"Look, I'll have to make my excuses to my guests. The race is at 4pm. Could we meet outside the box immediately after the fifth race? I'll take you into the enclosure and you can whisper in Amber's ear." The horse was called 'Always Amber', William explained, on account of it never quite knowing whether to stop or go.

Marcia could hardly contain herself. Her third, then fourth and fifth bets had all come home. She didn't know how much, but she knew that the win on the last race would be huge money. Close to, William had even greater presence, she thought. Likewise, she was more natural not at a distance, although William had initially put down her good skin to an expensive make-up consultant.

She felt young and elated as he held out an old-fashioned arm for her to take.

"Should we? I imagine you're quite well known in these circles. Won't people talk?"

"It is bound to be all complimentary. Most will think you're the wife of the owner of a company I'm about to pounce upon and I'm stitching you up into the bargain. Besides, it's a bit soft going in the paddock and I don't want you breaking an ankle on my behalf."

The horse towered above her but William took the bridle and firmly pulled its head within reach of Marcia. She put one arm over its neck and pulled its head close to her ready pursed lips. She whispered in its ear. The horse did not rear or jerk as it might have done. It turned and nudged her gently with its nose and then was led off in a controlled way by the young stable girl. Compared to the four-legged part of this important duo, Marcia was a lot taller than the jockey, decked out in, apparently, Forrester's colours of black polka dots on a not dissimilar blue to the jacket Marcia was wearing.

William introduced them and waited to hear what Marcia had to say. She turned to him and said, "William, I did mean a private word."

He looked uncomfortable but walked three paces away while Marcia turned her back on him and spoke quickly and precisely to the jockey.

"That's it then, William. The horse will win."

William looked gobsmacked.

"Look, Marcia, you must promise me. This is all great fun but I think you ought to know, if you don't already know, you're about to be a very disappointed young lady."

"I'm not saying I wouldn't like to win the money… I would. But more than anything I want you to have faith in that horse. It *will* win and then you'll have at least to re-name it."

They agreed not to watch the race within sight of each other.

William Forrester positively ran to the adjoining box borrowed by Marcia's hosts for the day. He burst in and pushed his way through a few of the other guests, who appeared to have lost interest in the racing and were intent on mixing the remains of a number of opened bottles of champagne, white and red wine and brandy before their school buses took them home. He set eyes on Marcia, who was looking distinctly shocked. She looked relieved to see him and stood ten shallow steps down, looking up with tears running down her cheeks but arms wide open to welcome him.

"Well done!" he shouted.

She choked back her tears. "As I said, I'm so pleased for Amber."

"You don't know how pleased I am for him, and you too. What was your stake?"

"£10."

"Hell, Marcia, you've just won about £135,000."

"I think I knew," she said, "as long as our man doesn't do a runner."

"He won't. He's OK and he's betting with the Tote anyway. Don't lose the ticket. Come on, you've got to come and pick up some dreadful cut glass or something, I suppose. You'll need to blot your eyes. I'll wait outside the ladies' for you." She was quick and they rushed together into the winners' enclosure. Marcia kissed Amber's nose and whispered again in his ear.

William was intrigued.

Marcia then shook the excited and somewhat bewildered jockey's hand and engaged him in brief but apparently serious conversation. The announcement was made and William, in his 'proper mode', extended a gracious hand, indicating that the lady would collect what was indeed a pretty naff but very expensive cut-glass vase, which Marcia could hardly hold because it was so heavy.

There was a clamouring to, "Look here, please, Madam… smile please…." as indeed the racing fraternity press sensed there was a new lady on the block, well worthy of photographing.

A number of obvious acquaintances came and congratulated him: one of the McAlpine family, lords of the race circuit, knights of the realm and other Mafia characters in brown trilby hats were all pleased for him, in their shallow ways.

The proud owner ushered Marcia away from the throngs. "Look, I've taken a liberty."

"What's that?" she said, still excited by the events.

"I've said to your neighbours we've known each other for years and have been out of touch and that I'll see you home… and I've pinned the runner down and I'm proposing to come to the Tote with you to see fair play."

"Bill, I *have* known you for years."

"… And the other thing is, what did you say to the horse and the jockey?"

"You don't want to know."

"I do. That was the deal. If you can produce miracles, I need to know how."

"OK. I said to one of them I'd give them a bonus of £20,000 if they won and to the other that I'd kiss him on the willie… and I'm not going to tell you which was which."

William looked shocked. But he lifted at least 15 or 20 years off his face through the release of a huge laugh, which veered on the uncontrollable.

"So you think you can shock me in that way, do you? Well, so what, is what

I say. One's gay and the other's de-gendered, so I'm left with the real prize."

"What's that?"

"A quiet dinner and a catch-up on the lost years."

The courtship that developed was reminiscent of the whirlwind romance with Bob. William Forrester had been quite precise about his intentions towards Marcia after only three weeks.

"Look," he'd said. "We're a couple of mature people having great fun. My intentions are totally honourable. I'd say if I was honest with myself that I'm in love with you. But another part of me says that it could be a serious infatuation, so we ought to sort that out. What if we jet away for a weekend with the declared intention of sharing a bed, to see if sleeping together works out, and whether the wildly passionate potential is built to last."

"How do we decide?"

"We don't, we just see what happens."

"It's conditional."

"Oh no! Please, it's always conditional. What rules this time?"

"I buy the champagne."

"OK. Providing you whisper in my ear."

"I'm not promising you money, you'll need to know that."

"I'd expect that, and I'm not a horse either."

Marcia laughed, and wagged her finger in a negative way. "You're wrong!" she shrieked.

They shared homes about three or four nights each week and their relationship was both loving and, on some occasions, as wild and as passionate as she had ever known.

Poor old Bob, she thought in one of her moments of reflection. *And he was satisfied by just watching me undress. Thank God for Peter releasing me from being scared of my own emotions.*

Strangely, Peter had been on her mind that fated Sunday. She'd woken up feeling apprehensive. She had no idea why. They were having Sunday lunch with some close friends of William's in Henley, and then back to Esher overnight before William flew to New York for Amalgamated's US conference.

"It'll be three days," he'd explained. "It'll give you a chance to catch up with your friends. You really mustn't lose touch. I'll phone you every morning and evening, that's if I can get the time difference right. You have your bath."

This pre-supposed they'd indulge that night, as was habitual if William was off on a trip.

Marcia had her bath, then let William know she was chilling down in bed waiting for him. She flicked on the TV. Sunday evenings were generally rubbish, but TV was a habit. She skipped channels and found the BBC news in full flood.

She half-watched as she also flicked through the pages of a *Hello* magazine. She found herself half-listening. "A Spanish-born British entrepreneur has been shot by drug-runners on the Costa Brava…" She heard Costa Brava and casually glanced up to look more intently at the map being shown on the screen. She saw the word 'Girasol' and her stomach heaved.

"… The circumstances as to how he came to be in secluded woods behind his villa are not yet known. Local police had the bandits under surveillance and it would appear Peter Martinez was perhaps a victim of circumstance, in the wrong place at the wrong time. Latest reports are that the injured man has had a life-saving operation in Palafrugell Hospital but is stable in intensive care. All three bandits were shot dead by the police.

"In the forthcoming meetings between the prime ministers of the UK, France…"

Marcia hit the abort button and sat bolt upright.

"Costa Brava… Girasol… Peter Martinez…" The words echoed in her now spinning head. The reminder of Bob in Palafrugell Hospital drained all the blood from her body.

William appeared in one of his silk dressing gowns. Marcia looked like death.

"You alright?" he asked anxiously.

"I've just had a shock. Somebody I know has been shot in Spain."

"Shot in Spain. How did that come about?"

"Apparently by some bandits in the hills."

"Have I heard you mention… I'm sorry, is it a male or a female friend?"

"I don't know. He was equally a friend and business associate of Bob's, Peter Martinez. Male."

"Is that a name I'd know?"

"Maybe. He's a property man. He's just taking over as Chief Executive at BCG."

"Do you know, that rings a bell. I don't think I've met him but I've either read about him or somebody's talked about him. In fact, I know they did a Jan Roberts exposé in one of the financial magazines, I'd say in the last couple of weeks."

Marcia thought to herself *…and he saved Bob's life…and indirectly over the years, mine too.*

It didn't seem appropriate to mention that thought while William believed himself currently to be the be all and end all of relationship providers.

"Can I get you something to comfort you? Milk and brandy, just hot milk?"

"No, I'm fine. Just totally shocked and, I have to say, worried."

She suddenly had a brainwave. "William, I'm going to fly out. I can comfort his mother, she's lovely. She also saw Bob through his heart attack. In the morning, I'll get the first plane out."

"OK, darling. Do leave me a number, though, I'd like to speak to her. I can find out how you're getting on, too."

"May we go straight to sleep, William?"

"Of course."

They did. She didn't. She relived every second of her time together with Peter, from the memory of their first meeting on a run to each of those times when they'd rung each other and explained how one needed the other. She eventually cried herself to sleep.

CHAPTER 19

It had always been just as well that Marguerite appeared not to have inherited a single gene from her father's side. She was a pedigree clone of her mother. There was not a freckle or birthmark that might have identified her with the father who sired her. Tania couldn't believe her good fortune. Even at her first glance of Marguerite, at under a minute old, she knew instinctively that was the case. It was not unusual among gypsy stock for that to happen.

The door burst open into the kitchen where Tania was helping with the preparation of the evening menu. Tania shot round, intending to say, if it was Marguerite, as expected, that she really shouldn't run into a kitchen area. She would be likely to knock the tray out of the hands of even the most experienced waiter/waitress and cause the hotel a great financial loss in the process. But, before she could postulate, Marguerite continued without taking breath.

"Shooting!" she screamed. "Shooting in the woods... Peter... Peter Martinez..."

Tania knew the Romany tone all too well. It was panic. But then whenever she heard the name Peter Martinez, her stomach still churned and her pulse picked up a beat or two. However, she resolved never to show her alarm outwardly.

"Shooting," she said, "what sort of shooting?" She dreaded the reply. "Peter Martinez... was he doing the shooting?"

"No, Mother. Shooting. Shooting at each other. Mr Martinez is probably dead."

Now that did upset Tania's rhythm. She called her daughter over to stand directly in front of her. She steadied both her shoulders and then, in one deft swipe of her open right hand, she smacked Marguerite deftly on her left cheek.

"Now pull yourself together," she advised. "Start slowly at the beginning and tell me what you think has happened."

As she said that, distant sirens could be heard. It was indistinguishable as to whether they were police, ambulances or even the fire tenders who occasionally raced to the odd tourists' chip pan fire, or the more serious risks brought about by forest ones.

"They're saying Peter Martinez met up with some drug-runners, presumably to trade, and they fell out and the bandits shot him. There's militia all over the place. Up in trees, blocking the roads… it was out there," she said, pointing up into the hills.

Even allowing for the extreme interpretations of a 20-year-old, Tania rated the situation as sounding pretty bad. But then it seemed it always was whenever she stepped in or out of Peter's life.

Their last proposed assignation on the night before he left for England seemed to incur the wrath of the Gods. Toni had jumped to all the wrong conclusions and because he felt Tania was playing an advanced game of chess, with him as a passive pawn, he lost his temper completely. He had as near as damn it killed her with the beating and when the police found her, after a tip-off, dumped by the roadside, they took her into hospital, and into custody too. She was guarded by two special women police officers flown up from Seville, where they were used to tribal fall-outs among the Romanies. They counselled her through her recuperation, particularly when she was in moments of enormous pain.

The first exposé was when she screamed in anger when pushed as to, "Who did this, who did this dreadful deed to you, who'd want to hurt you so much, who hates you this way…?" It was like a dripping tap inflicting torture. "… Tell us and we'll remove him from your life… no more pain from him… no more hurt… a new free life with the accent on love… who's the bastard? Tell us and we'll give you morphine…"

They stretched her to the limit. She wasn't breaking.

"Try the 'be kind' syndrome," one whispered to the other.

"OK, darling. We'll get you morphine this time but next time we need the name first."

They knew from experience this would have been an intra-family war of some kind or other.

Often with those being questioned in this fashion, as the pain subsided and they came out of stress, there was a hint of the hate experienced. The police were practised at jumping on the slightest clue.

As Tania's eyes closed, she uttered the word, "Bastados."

"Who?" the senior officer asked gently.

"Toni."

The officers looked at each other. One put her thumb up to gesticulate a chink in Tania's tough outer skin.

"Toni and who else – the bastards?"

The word 'cousins' was breathed out as she dropped into a deep, morphine-induced sleep.

"We'll get the rest from her sister," one said to the other.

When Beth arrived, the police ladies went into officious mode.

"We now know who beat your sister up."

"Good," Beth said, somewhat brazenly, as she doubtless knew at least the likelihood.

"Now if we take you into our confidence and tell you, if you know where we'll find the culprits you'll have to tell us. If you know the gang, or person, and you don't tell us where to find them, then you'd be guilty of harbouring information that would lead to an arrest and you'll go to prison. Now do you understand?"

Beth would at that stage have agreed to anything to save her sister from further punishment, and certainly from being sent to prison herself, and worked out that if the cousins were inside she wouldn't face the beatings and sexual abuse that had befallen her elder sister.

"So," the senior officer explained, "we need to locate Toni and the cousins. Do you understand?"

"Yes."

"So where are they?"

She started to cry.

"Where are they?" The second officer asking had a certain menace about it.

Beth thought apparently long and hard. "In the hills behind Estartit, a village known as Santa Maria de Quevo."

The officer took a mobile transmitter out of her briefcase. She dialled into a connection and went into rapid and detailed conversation.

At three that morning, Toni and the two cousins were arrested and the rest, for the next 20-odd years, had been history. After the trial, at which Tania was the chief prosecution witness, she discovered she was pregnant. The father might have been Marco and, although unlikely, she felt that was what she'd tell him privately, but telling him clearly that it was as much her fault as his, and that she would not burden him. That way she hoped she'd secure her financial future. It could just as likely have been one of the waiters at the Playa, with whom she had got very drunk at the fiesta and, freed from the intense eyes of Toni and the cousins, she had actually enjoyed sex for the first time.

Then again, in her gypsy fantasy mind, it could have been God implanting her with the seeds from her Pedro. Yes, she was happy to bear Peter's child and not to submit to the syringe of the elder stateswoman in the tribe who had rid generations of unwanted children.

Marco was flattered when he was accused, and pleaded like a small boy for her not to let it be known to Virginia, who would have probably slit Tania's throat, not for indulging with her husband but for being more capable of bearing fruit from his seeds than she had been.

"I'll need to move you both away from the Playa," Marco said. She would only go under duress, she insisted.

"So how can I overcome that?" Marco continued to plead.

"By sending me somewhere where I can work to provide for my child, not as a chambermaid but where I can use my brain."

Girasol sprang to mind. They were going to open a small hotel there which she could quite well cope with. More to the point, he could go up there to check things out on a regular basis and watch his child develop. Maybe even to enjoy Tania's favours from time to time.

That seemed one of his better ideas. All that had come to pass. There she now was, hearing news of Peter.

Toni had been released early on account of good behaviour. That, too, was conditional on an order that he should make no attempt to find Tania. Breach of that, and making any actual contact, would see him sent back to prison for the rest of his life. Toni seemed to understand the futility of breaking the order. He was bright and even still controlled the brains of the cousins. So it was through them, and the development of a contact he had made in prison for the supply of modern social drugs, that he was able to locate Tania, in exchange for a basic supply of weed to keep them happy, and probably through them give her the last rites in Romany style for having co-operated with the police.

It had taken them 18 months of following trails of covered tracks to find Tania's workplace. His obsession with her had not waned while he was in prison. Hate, in that he knew she had shopped him, was a part of that. Need for her body to be under his submission was an equal part. Toni had stuck to his pledge and made no actual contact, but he now knew where she was. From the hills above Girasol he was quite content to watch Tania through binoculars he'd stolen on an earlier escapade.

The girl was clearly her daughter. She was a replica of Tania. He worked out that she was likely to be his daughter, conceived under force but as of a family right. The judges hadn't, of course, said he couldn't see his own daughter but he'd bide his time in the hills.

The sirens had gone through a spell of increasing decibels and then came to a total silence. Tania didn't actually know that they were vehicles into which the various bandit body corpses were to be loaded, while others were to bring gendarmerie to the spot to collect conclusive evidence of the battle.

When Tania said she ran the Girasol Playa, she actually did. She'd developed as much as Maria, who was still one of her role models. She could now speak good conversational English. Marco had bought her a Linguaphone outfit on one of Marguerite's birthdays. "I want a daughter of mine to speak good English," he had ruled. It was surprising to Tania that he had never wanted the child's parenthood to be authenticated. She had read it was a relatively easy process nowadays, what with DNA checks. However, if Marco was happy to accept the position and pick up the financial burdens that went with it, why should she be concerned?

Peter had shown no problem with the arrangement. Tania had matured save that she still always enjoyed showing off her other attributes whenever Peter called into the subsidiary hotel, as he usually did the three or four times a year he visited. She'd do some special cooking on the nights he was dining there. They'd got on better again after Anna's death. He seemed shy about having a wife and staying in his small villa, knowing Tania was just down the road, and still as obviously available to him as ever.

He had never taken her up on her offer, which in part hurt her but on the other hand gave her pleasure in knowing that such a great man had respect for her. She had had the odd short affair in the decades after moving on to Girasol but she still inwardly longed for some more intimate moments alone with Peter, like they'd had when he first shared his vision of Girasol with her, or when they'd danced the Sardana together the night Toni took his first revenge on him.

On this particular fated Saturday, Tania asked Marguerite to look after the hotel reception while she went to see what news there was of Peter. She feared the bandits would in some way be Toni-related. She'd been driving along the road at the foot of the hills just two weeks earlier when she saw three men run from one side of the road to the other, one of them carrying a large box. It seemed a sort of hallucination at the time, but she momentarily thought the one leading the other two had a certain run like Toni had. It was a distinctive rounding of the shoulders, she thought, which fogged the memory bank. But she concluded it was purely an illusion and put it out of her mind.

Now the prospect of Peter having been shot within his own territory, as it were, and by bandits, had sent her mind racing. In heading out to confront the issue, she had no thought for her own safety, only for her Peter's wellbeing.

There was a car park at the foot of the hills where weekend ramblers left their cars. There weren't many there now, it was getting towards dusk, but the place was swarming with ambulances and police cars and vehicles of other kinds. There were police dotted all around.

Suddenly there was a noise from above she could not recognise. It was loud and sort of throbbed, a pulsating, pumping sound associated with a heavy mechanical overtone. All at once it became very windy and Tania presumed it was a helicopter. Then the great noisy beast was above her and disappearing, apparently, into the hillside. It was in fact flying into the clearing.

Police radios seemed to be crackling all around her. She knew some of the local police. In fact, she'd had a light-hearted fling with one of the sergeants, though he did not appear to be on duty. The controller on this assignment was a middle-aged military figure in his dark navy blue uniform and more braid than all of the others. Tania made her way across and introduced herself once she sensed that there was a lull in his radio communication.

"I'm Tania…" she began, extending a strong hand towards him. He looked a little surprised as to why a total stranger should introduce herself at a time like this. He was about to question her presence when she continued to speak, in control of the situation.

"I'm the manageress of the Girasol Playa, the hotel just over there. If I can be of any assistance or put rooms at your disposal, please let me know. Tell me how many officers are here and I'll send out coffee and food if needed."

Captain Fernandes relaxed a little and took her hand into his. "That's thoughtful," he said. "It might be useful as we'll lose light soon."

The background noise of an engine ticking over suddenly burst forth into a roar as the repetitious *thud, thud, thud* of the helicopter reversed into uplift mode. The turbulence spun around their heads and Tania's neatly coiffured hair was blown out of place.

The captain's radio was alive again. He had an intense conversation. "OK. OK. Yes, yes go. We'll take the risk… no, that's the most important thing. Get him there. What do the medics say?"

Tania felt she could have written the script. They were talking about a passenger in the helicopter. The need for such a means of transport told her it was an emergency. It was a rescue effort. Definitely, she thought, it was to rush somebody to hospital, otherwise a corpse would be taken away at a speed more reflective of respect.

Instinctively, something told her Peter was the passenger.

She crossed herself to her Father, the Son and the Holy Spirit and lifted her neat gold crucifix, kissing it gently. She whispered, "Dear God. Please save my Peter."

She had a vision of him strapped into a stretcher. "They wouldn't be so concerned about bandits," she told herself. "Oh God, what if it was a question of saving Peter or Toni? Who would God save?"

The captain temporarily closed down the radio. "Well, wish him the best of luck," he said, pointing upwards.

"Who are you referring to?" Tania asked tentatively.

"The British man. He's been shot by gypsies."

"Is he alive?"

"Yes. So it seems."

"Do you know what the paramedics have said?"

"Look, Tania. Most of this is top secret, you know. Why are you so interested?"

"I've been told the man is Peter Martinez and if it is, he was responsible for all this development." She illustrated with a proud sweep of her hand. "His mother and father-in-law own the hotel I manage."

"Oh, I'm sorry. I hadn't realised you had a personal concern for the injured man. Look, I shouldn't say this because the press will be all over the place soon, that's for sure – this is, after all, an important tourist area and if it's spread far and wide that there are bandits in the hills, it could seriously affect everybody, especially your hotel. But the medics say they have the situation under control. It seems part of his shoulder has been shot away and a knee's badly damaged. They're giving him blood... it looks stable... but it'll take 20 vital minutes to get him to Palafrugell and there they'll be rushing around alerting the emergency teams. Keep your fingers crossed, dear."

"Are the bandits local?"

"Now, enough is enough. I really can't say."

"Are they all alive?"

"No. They all appeared to be resisting arrest and – this is not for the press, you understand – but they're all dead."

"Thank you for that," Tania said. "Thank you, officer. Remember, if I can help, I'm just down the road there."

Tania turned and walked back to the hotel. She'd set everything up through Marguerite for the evening in case it was practical for her to drive herself to Palafrugell. Marco or Maria or even Peter himself might need her.

CHAPTER 20

Gina had been due a day off. She'd been in great demand now that she'd had UK experience in theatre nursing, which was all very good to help subsidise her husband's banking salary and to provide for the needs of her two teenage daughters. She and her husband thought having his mother staying with them permanently after his father's death was going to be an absolute pain. As it turned out, it was a godsend because her mother-in-law was an automatic au pair and was able to deal with the children's needs when Gina's agency found her work.

So now it was more a case of avoiding bookings every now and again so that she could catch up on overdue housework, and have just a little time for herself. They'd even talked of slipping out for a family meal that Saturday night.

It was approaching five when the phone rang. Gina called out to Marina, her elder daughter, to answer it.

"Mum, I can't, I'm drying my hair."

So Gina let it ring, hoping it would be one of those usual calls for one of her daughters anyway. But it soon became clear that the caller was not going to go away.

Damn it, she thought, *it's going to be the hospital.* She always found it hard to say no when her special nursing capabilities were needed. That's why she wanted her daughter to answer. They had a standard routine, which broadly was that one of her daughters would explain that Gina was out and therefore not available.

"Hello," Gina said as she finally answered the phone, still hoping she'd got an option of making out she was not Gina, the nurse, but a daughter. However, the caller recognised her voice. It was Sñr Benito Alvor. He never normally made calls. Of all the surgeons who attended the hospital, he was her favourite. They were about the same age and she found him rather dishy, particularly during their silent exchanges where only their eyes did the talking, which was essential when their masks covered their mouths and they would otherwise mumble instructions.

Together they had saved many lives. The first occasion that had brought them into the same team was when they were confronted by a young mother who was clearly, for some reason, not going to deliver her baby by normal means and was set up for a caesarean. The paediatric surgeon hadn't been available and Sñr Alvor and Gina were called in to deal with the situation. It transpired the labour was camouflaging an appendicitis, and the battle was on to save both lives. In the event, as a result of outstanding teamwork, all turned out well for both mother and child.

Benito Alvor had been first in the scrub up area and had had time to remove his own mask as Gina entered through the double swing doors using her backside to open them, as one did. She was crying. Benito removed her mask and picked up a handful of wipes to dry her cheeks and mop the perspiration from her brow, showing the same calm talents he practised so well in theatre.

"Here," he said and, reacting to his instinct that this important member of the team was severely under stress, he leant forward and pressed his cheek against hers. Slowly he enveloped her in his strong masculine arms. In a way, that was tender and respectful. Most of all it was intended to be supportive in a professional way.

"You were terrific," he announced.

"No. *You* were," she countered.

He laughed. "We both were," he agreed.

"We both *are*," she replied.

Their exchange of mutual admiration had not been face to face. Her temple area comfortably nestled into the crook of his neck. Neither could see the expression in the other's eyes, as they did under operating conditions. They held each other in silence.

Then they laughed and, on impulse, he sealed the moment with a gentle, affectionate brush of the back of his hand on her cheek. But he'd aroused her in a way she would have difficulty in forgetting. If he'd lowered her to the floor, there and then, she would have given herself to him. She later excused herself for that thought on the basis that she was over-emotional after helping to save two important lives. She had been exhausted, but she could not forget those few minutes.

They had worked together subsequently. Both were a little reserved.

His voice on the other end of the phone sounded young and in control.

"Hi! Sorry to bother you…" She knew it would be an emergency call so he couldn't really mean that from a professional standpoint.

"Hi," she said in response, "don't worry. You haven't bothered me yet. But I'm sure you're going to. First, though, how are you?"

"Great. Well, I was until I got a call."

"Is that where I come in?"

"Yes. I'm afraid so."

"What's the problem?"

"Well, the paramedics say they're putting this guy into a helicopter. By all accounts he's been seriously wounded by shotgun shots to a shoulder and into one knee and is in poor shape. He's lost a lot of blood. It might be a lower leg amputation and who knows what damage there is around the arm and neck."

"How long have I got?"

"Let's put it this way, Gina. He's got as long as it takes us to get him under anaesthetic and I doubt much longer."

"I can be there in 15 minutes."

"You're a star. This seems a big one. I'll see you there."

He then said in fun, "How will I recognise you?"

"I'll still have my gardening gloves on."

"Great… then I'll bring the fork and trowel."

Gina shouted up to her elder daughter. "Tell Dad I've had to go to the hospital… big emergency. I'll see everybody when I get back. Tell Dad sorry about the family dinner."

When her husband had got the message, he was not surprised. He was initially put out when life had started to revolve around her job and the unsocial hours, but they needed her contribution to the income so he accepted it.

As it happened, Gina was in the scrub-up room marginally before Benito. There was the not uncommon noise of a helicopter approaching. Palafrugell Hospital was small but the only Accident and Emergency receiving unit along the coast and, as the roads were still not good, air transport was the norm.

The routine was not regular. Patients in dire need of emergency treatment were treated with no questions asked if necessary. Forms were filled in after any operative procedures. On occasions, when a patient's life was lost, temporarily nobody would know the identity. That sometimes helped Gina, as she then didn't need to think about the pain dependent relatives would have to live through when they eventually found out.

Gina was setting out the equipment that she knew from experience Sñr Alvor would need. She had never let him down yet. A voice announced over an internal link loudspeaker between A&E reception and the theatre.

"Patient being trolleyed to theatre." Theatre was on the second floor.

Benito Alvor arrived. He muttered, "Got delayed," and stripped off his shirt, exposing a well-fitting T-shirt. He turned to Gina, as a second nurse fastened his gown from behind. "Thanks for being here," he said before he lifted his mask to cover his mouth. She followed suit and covered the lips he rarely saw

200

in their working environment, but longed to touch. She smiled calmly at him through her eyes.

On the other side of the doors, the injured party had arrived. There had been no time for a pre-theatre assessment. Benito was going to probe and operate all at once. Nobody in any profession likes to have to do that. How would the defence counsel, in a murder case, cope if they hadn't had the benefit of interviewing the accused beforehand? The patient was only semi-conscious anyway, so a needle in the back of his hand would make no difference to him. The anaesthetist wouldn't be counting up to ten for him.

Gina followed Benito into the theatre. They both went to the centre of the operating table. Sñr Alvor held out his right hand and, like a practised runner in the second leg of an Olympic relay, Gina placed exactly the right scalpel into it. He deftly cut away the remains of the patient's shirt while the two assistant nurses stifled chuckles as they slid the remains of the pair of trousers from his body.

The paramedics' emergency tourniquets had done their job. The blood pressure readings and pulses in the feet did not indicate any clotting. Benito surveyed the now bare body on the slab. There was no time for the courtesy of a gown. This was emergency surgery. He understood the relative amateurism shown by the assistant nurses, who were clearly giggling at the sight of this patient's private bits and pieces. Gina couldn't help but think how well endowed he was as she laid a muslin cover across his stomach and on to his thighs. That seemed to highlight the bloody mess the poor chap was in.

Benito was probing the wounded shoulder, which gaped open as the paramedics' temporary dressings were removed. A five-minute assessment encouraged him to nod his head to Gina. She felt slightly more relieved.

Then the practised consultant examined the right knee. *God,* he thought, *that's a mess.* He had less than ten minutes in which to decide whether to amputate or not.

Gina passed him the tools of his trade almost as part of a mind-reading process. After each delivery, she looked up into the consultant's expressive eyes for an indication of his prognosis.

Eventually there was a sign from the master himself. He shrugged his shoulders and held both gloved blood-covered hands in the 'I really don't know' position. He muttered, "50-50," which brought a lump into Gina's throat. How would this patient react to coming round, if he did survive, after the trauma of a few hours of body re-building, to find part of his leg missing?

Benito indicated he wanted to view the damage from her side of the table. He'd done that during previous operations and she knew instinctively that he would move in an anti-clockwise direction as that way he would not bump into the anaesthetist at the head of the table, who always seemed to be the principal stabilising influence during any operation. So Gina moved anti-clockwise too, but necessarily passing behind the anaesthetist. As she reached the equipment monitoring blood, heart, oxygen, she casually looked down at the patient's head. In fact, until then it had simply been an unidentifiable body in distress.

It was strong, which would help him through the trauma to come. It was a handsome face, line-free under the influence of the anaesthetic. She continued round the head of the table. Suddenly, as if hitting a brick wall, she stopped. She turned back to re-assess the features. She winced. Her stomach heaved. Her memory flashed back to a shared journey, all those years ago, nursing Bob Hunt back to England. Then the prospect of being forced to share a bed with this man as one of Bob's joke suggestions. Not that at the time she ever saw that as anything other than a potential pleasurable experience, but she was young and shy then. However, it had not come to pass. She'd only met him since a couple of times. But this was, without a doubt, Peter Martinez.

This time she let out a loud gasp, which clearly unsettled Sñr Alvor, the usually cool, calm expert surgeon. His eyes seemingly glared at her from his new position. He needed to get on.

Gina needed to summon up all the professionalism she had ever learnt. She must not show her anguish. She hurried back into position and the exchanges of delicate probes and instruments continued. Unusually, Sñr Alvor spoke loudly for the entire team to hear.

First, he addressed the anaesthetist. "Can you give me three or four hours?" Everybody seemed stunned. That was a long operating time for Palafrugell. A few calculations later, the answer came back in the affirmative.

"Right." The air was tense, but Sñr Alvor sensed there was more to Gina's gasp than was at that moment apparent. "This is not going to be easy and we could operate for two hours or so and then have to abort and amputate, but I intend to try and save the leg. The shoulder's routinely OK, just time-consuming… and we'll do that last. Anyone who skipped having a pee before theatre had better be very good at holding back from hereon in. Let's try and make this guy comfortable, OK. Here we go."

It was, in fact four-and-a-quarter hours of micro surgery, removing pieces of shot from all sorts of crevices in the knee, and likewise in the shoulder. Blood-carrying body conduits all needed some fine attention from scalpel and current stitching techniques. They worked flat out as a team. The young nurses matured under the seriousness of the occasion.

Eventually Benito Alvor pronounced, "Gentleman," – addressing the anaesthetist – "and ladies, thank you profusely for your assistance. We've not just saved a leg. I couldn't say earlier, but the shot in the chest, which I didn't expect to encounter, would have been life-threatening if we hadn't had the good fortune to locate it. I'd say we cleaned everything up. Twenty-four hours will tell us if that's right."

An intensive care nurse was in the outer lobby, waiting to monitor Peter through those next vital hours. The two theatre nurses were obviously on a mission to scrub up and get off to meet their dates at the Saturday disco. The anaesthetist, too, was clearly on a promise. The consultant and principal nursing attendant were soon left alone.

Almost no sooner than the doors out into the lobby had shut, Gina made sure she spoke first.

"Please don't say a word… I need to explain."

"No, you don't. I know what happened."

"How can you?"

"I just know you well… or at least I think I do… the patient is an old boyfriend, isn't he?"

Gina laughed. "Close, but not in the way you think. He's little more than an acquaintance of, oh, some 20 years ago." She knew it was in fact over 30 years, but that would have told Sñr Alvor she could be in her late 40s. She wanted to be perceived as a younger woman than that. "He certainly wasn't a boyfriend in your sense of the word… but yes, I had an enormous shock… Can I ask you a question?"

"Ask. But I don't promise to answer it."

"If you'd worked out he was some sort of friend, did it alter your judgment on the amputation question?"

"Pass. My medical ethics wouldn't allow that to affect my judgment. You know that, surely," he said with a smile. "Look, this is hardly the place to carry on this conversation. I'm not going to suggest tonight, I'm absolutely exhausted and I have no doubt, friend of everybody as you are, that what you're going to do now is to ring your husband and tell him what's happened and that you're going to sit with your friend and see him through the next few hours.

"But maybe, on another less stressful occasion, we could have a coffee or a drink together and you can explain all the circumstances… I have an inkling it's bound to be a long story. Oh, and besides, the guy's mother is apparently anxiously waiting to see me, of course."

"You're right again. Yes, I will call home and yes, I would like to sit with him. Peter – that's his name, Peter Martinez – is going to have a pretty hard 24 hours, but he'll make it, I'm sure – he comes from tough Catalan stock."

"As for the coffee or a drink, I'd really love to. You call the shots. You've got a family too and neither of us wants to get the washerwomen of the Costa Brava wagging their tongues in our direction."

Gina stepped forward. Suddenly, Benito Alvor looked exposed. Just like a spaniel puppy. He must have been exhausted, the concentration through the earlier four or five hours was enormous.

"So there's the deal," she concluded.

Their eyes were glued to each other's. Neither of them voluntarily moved. There was some magnetic force slowly pulling them together. Their eyes, as though a principal tenor and soprano directed by some philharmonic conductor, changed focus onto each other's lips as the positive electric forces generated between them closed one gentle mouth onto the other. There was no further physical contact, just a male looking down slightly into an open female face, neither believing themselves to have been a party to what had just happened.

A tear ran down Gina's cheek. Benito pulled away.

"Is that a tear of sorrow?"

"No! It's one of happiness."

He took her hand and squeezed it.

"If we can work out a complex operation together... then I'm sure we'll work this one out too."

"I do hope so. But nobody gets hurt, please," Gina almost pleaded.

"Suppose it's only us?"

"Oh! That's fine," she resolved, now beginning to capitalise on the closeness that had developed between them, although neither had been prepared for that.

"Go and see our patient. I'll speak to his mother... Mrs Martinez, is it?"

"No. I don't think so. She remarried, I think."

"Well, I'm sure I'll work out a name. Take care. I'll ring you, if I may."

"Sure!" Then, as if as an afterthought: "Oh! Be careful, even my mother can't tell the difference between my daughters' voices and mine on the phone."

"I'll be careful."

CHAPTER 21

Marco and Virginia were never likely to be out of Maria's life. After all, they were effectively her closest family after Peter, and although she and José were very close and, again, always likely to be, Marco had so often been her rock – never, of course, replacing Paco but providing a family link to what should have been.

Tania had taken an enormous gamble by ringing Marco when she returned to the Girasol Playa after obtaining most of the low-down on Peter's accident from the police at the scene. Marco's immediate instinct when he answered the phone was to chastise her for phoning. She'd only done it once before and fortunately then Virginia had been taking a nap. On this occasion, she wasn't. She was pruning some roses in the little garden they'd kept for themselves as a sanctuary away from the ever-changing series of guests who seemed to think that their package deal gave them rights over the management's property as well as the hotel. They'd had the fence erected once they found a German couple on their lilos who, when challenged about not respecting the 'private' sign, explained that it looked as though it was the coolest spot they could find.

"That is precisely why it's ours," Virginia screeched, to no effect. They obviously didn't want to understand. As a nation, they soon understood the purpose of the Berlin wall, Marco had said sardonically.

So they built what came to be called the Playa wall, and put a sign up in Spanish, German, French and English indicating it was private property reserved for the management inside the fortress.

It seemed to have had the desired effect.

Marco recognised Tania's voice immediately. "I've told you not to ring me here!"

"I couldn't help it."

"Then you'll have to be taught how to overcome it."

"Marco," (she was now allowed to call him that since he had been familiar enough with her to sire her child), "it's Peter!"

"What about Peter?"

"He's been shot!"

"Shot!" Marco repeated. "Spurt it out, tell me quickly what's happened."

She was as quick as she could be amidst her tears, which were partially in fear for Peter, knowing how seriously the police had said he was injured, and equally because she so often cried when she thought about him. She had been beside herself after the first time she'd slept with José Jnr, once she worked out that he was Peter's stepbrother. It seemed inevitable, as José Jnr went to the Girasol Hotel every single day of the week for a lunch proudly served up by Tania, that sooner or later the animal in them would bring their needs together on the right day, or wrong one, whichever one's perspective was on the subject.

It had been a cooler day, on which everybody seemed to have more energy. José had arrived in the dining room of the hotel, where a table was reserved daily for hotel management and friends.

Food supply reps made it their favourite midday call, principally because Tania acted as a magnet. She'd still got the nicest legs on either of the Costas and she'd not lost a centimetre of her figure since having the baby. In fact (and she was the only one to know it), she had gone up a bra size and had changed for comfort from a 'B' cup to a 'C' cup, which gave her a deeper cleavage, like she had seen advertised in the smart magazines the guests from around Europe brought with them. It was never long before the market stallholders' suppliers caught on with fashion and at Rosas market on a Saturday morning, the choice was plentiful. Reds, pinks, blues, greens or yellows, flesh colour, white and, always her favourite, black.

José Jnr was aroused anyway because he'd had a one-to-one lesson on the golf course with a nubile 18-year-old English girl who felt she had to learn golf to keep the attention of her boyfriend, who seemed intent to think, drink and sleep the game, which he thought he had begun to master, thereby showing her even less attention. To teach, José had to be a scratch golfer, and had to maintain that handicap well after passing out from the Academy. That didn't stop him from thinking how his pupil crushed her boobs as she began the swing, and surely she would need to learn no more from him to retain the boyfriend's rapt attention. It certainly captured José's, especially when her excitement at hitting a wonder shot, a specially successful one for a beginner, showed behind her Adidas sports shirt.

Tania's rear was the salient feature of the empty dining room, exposed as she bent to get some glasses out of the dresser unit. It was too much for José to ignore. He slapped her bottom playfully.

The shock, and a pretence of offence at anyone taking liberties with her backside, made her turn sharply. The surprise that it was José, the otherwise Mr Cool, Mr Proper and sometimes Mr Shy in her life, gave her a sudden stimulation, causing her to drop a glass.

"Shit," he said, "I'm sorry. I didn't mean to make you drop the glass."

"Then what did you mean to make me drop?" she said, in her most mischievous and challenging gypsy way.

José was speechless. Tania put the other glass she was holding on top of the dresser and strutted towards him. She placed her right hand around the firm muscular left buttock she'd always noticed was over-developed compared with the right one, presumably after many years of swinging his right-hander's golf clubs.

"Now, how would you like it if I did that to you?" she said, gently rubbing her open-palmed hand in a clockwise circular movement round the cheek of his bottom.

Oh shit! he thought, as his trousers bulged.

She'd noticed. She giggled. "You've just answered the question. It seems you'd like it quite a lot. Here, come with me. I want you to say sorry. I expect you've bruised me."

She held out her hands, which he dutifully took into his. She pulled him behind her through the rear door of the dining room, which led to the back service stairs. There weren't any staff around as they were all having lunch in the staff mess in the kitchen. Tania pulled on a leather thong she wore around her neck, which, instead of carrying a modern wooden crucifix, had the master room key, the cellar one and a couple of other essential security keys that were naturally suspended into her cleavage for safe keeping.

She took the master key into her spare hand and slipped it into the keyhole of room number 17. She always knew in intimate detail which rooms were occupied and those waiting arrivals. Seventeen was down for a French couple coming to do some serious walking, they had explained.

Tania went into the room first, gently pulling José with her. She leant against the door and slid her right hand partially behind her to lock the door.

José was now staring at her semi-reclining body.

"So… let's see if you bruised me," she said, in a tantalising and hurt tone.

Her hands went straight to the zip on her black mini-skirt, allowing it to fall to the floor immediately. She strutted past him and towards the bed and as she did so, she let her right hand brush his right thigh. Before he could react, she had lifted her light cotton top over her head, and that too finished in a heap on the floor. Her mid-high heels gave the impression of very much longer legs than in fact they were.

Now she hooked a thumb from each hand into the sides of her black lace knickers, which she then slid down over her thighs, then rolled onto her tummy with her bottom uppermost. She looked over her right shoulder towards José.

"Tell me the truth. Am I bruised for life?"

José was actually surprised. He had slapped her harder than intended. He could see quite distinctly the outline of his four fingers as red elongated strips of inflamed skin.

"Ouch! I am sorry. Not scarred for life but enough for me to say sorry."

He stepped forward without turning her body and threaded each arm under her armpits, cupping both her breasts in his firm hands. Her hands dropped to her sides and felt behind her for the buckle of his belt. Then each fly button was agonisingly slowly undone, allowing his trousers to join her top on the floor.

Sliding out of his clutch, Tania turned, putting both her arms around the back of his neck. She arched her back, causing the top of her body to weigh more than the lower half and then leant fully backwards. He would not have been able to hold back the impetus of that force as she fell heavily towards the bed, taking him with her. Together they shuffled into the inevitable position in which their lusts were to be satisfied.

They screwed. Well, it couldn't realistically be termed lovemaking. It was all too frenetic for that. José was not to know that Tania closed her eyes and imagined he was Peter. But he, too, cheated. He conjured up feelings of this not being Tania writhing below him, but his young student golfer with the fair skin.

They allowed time to giggle about her confessing, "I can tell you now, you didn't hurt me," which was countered by him saying, "Actually, I did like you fumbling with my backside."

"Thank you," she said, "you're great."

"As they say, it takes two to tango."

"Now that's nice," said Tania. "I'm not going to promise it's going to be an everyday hors d'oeuvre but it'll be your turn next to drag me into bed. That was my go. You rotter, you made me so cross I had to do it," she added, amidst one of her most natural laughs. "Hey, we'd best go and eat. I'll go down. You go out of the front hotel door and come into the dining room as you usually do."

He was OK with that.

It was later that afternoon that the thought had passed through her mind. She'd screwed José Jnr, Peter's stepbrother. Now she knew the Bible said something about indulging in the flesh of a brother. The roots of her own Romany family didn't naturally allow her a faith in God, but since she had built an effective new life at Girasol, she'd shown an interest in Catholicism, probably because, had she chosen to adopt a religion, that would have been the most likely faith to follow for someone from a gypsy background.

"Father," she had said at confession on the following Friday morning Mass, "is it a sin to sleep with your husband's brother?"

"Well, yes, of course, dear. It's a sin to sleep with anyone other than your husband. But if you did, a brother or cousin would be a cardinal sin."

"What's the penalty if I confess to that?"

"I'd say ten Hail Marys."

"Suppose it was a stepbrother."

The priest laughed. "Tania, my daughter, you make me laugh. It's still ten."

"I'd hoped it would be five."

As incorrect as it was, her sin was a laughing point between them.

Then she whispered, "… And supposing the man isn't my husband anyway… it's got to be a freebie, surely."

She nevertheless gave herself her own self-judgment. It had been wrong to sleep with Peter's stepbrother… but, on the other hand, as Peter was not around, and had never reacted to her invitations, at least it was another member of the family.

Marco was being clear and precise, trying to get through Tania's emotional disturbance. "So the last you know is Peter is being flown to Palafrugell by helicopter. OK, thanks for ringing, Tania. Forgive my outburst. I'll make it up to you."

Virginia came in from their garden. "Did I hear the phone?"

"Yes. There's a problem. Peter's been shot."

"What? Where?"

"Apparently in the shoulder and the knee."

"Marco! At times like this you don't show any intelligence. Where… where was Peter, or more importantly, where is he now?"

"He was walking in the hills above Girasol and somehow or other he got mixed up with some bandits. There was a shoot-out and he was injured. He's being flown to Palafrugell Hospital by helicopter as we talk."

"Who told you all this?"

"The staff at Girasol Playa."

Probably that Tania, Virginia thought. She could never understand why Maria agreed with Marco that she should run that place. Still, to be fair, Marco didn't seem to need to keep going up there to check on things, as he'd forecast would be the case.

"You must find Maria," Virginia suggested.

"Yes, I hope they're not out on the boat. I'd say she'll be in the office checking out the dinner menus. We've got a fairly big Thomsons' intake today. I'll hurry across."

Marco rushed in to the reception lobby. Sñr Martin was there, which bode ill because rarely now were Maria and Sñr Martin on duty at the same time.

"Have you seen Maria?" Marco asked.

"She's slipped down to the village to get some bits and pieces she said we need."

Blast it, Marco thought. Tania had implied time was of the essence to Peter being OK. He would hurry down to the village to see if she was around. It was Saturday early evening. *The church,* he thought. *I bet she's gone to church.*

Marco, Maria and churches somehow seemed synonymous. First he looked in the graveyard where Paco was buried. There was a posy of fresh flowers, so she had been recently. He now knew how to open the heavy, 200-year-old door without waking all the church mice or disturbing those in prayer.

Maria had had one of her 'uncertain feelings' as soon as she awoke that morning. She knew her body so well now. It had been put through so many traumas. She was, after all, now approaching 60. She never felt it, and her husband José didn't feel his age either, so this common sense of youthfulness was good for them. José was talking about retiring in five years' time. He'd forecast he could help out around the hotel, perhaps set up an overnight shoe-cleaning service, he had joked. More seriously, he could do sea trips for the paying guests.

Maria was in the third pew back. She knew and feared that some ill fate was about to strike. It already had. Marco knew it was the right thing to disturb her. He should really have brought the car, then they could have gone straight to the hospital. He hadn't, so they would just have to hurry up the hill, through the back entrance to the hotel and into his car in the car park.

He walked softly but loud enough for his footsteps to be heard by Maria. He stopped at the end of the pew.

Sensing somebody's presence, Maria looked along the empty spaces leading to the aisle. She made out Marco's form. He didn't have to beckon her over. She raised herself from her kneeling position.

Was it going to be her husband, José, one of the grandchildren…? Not Peter. Maybe she'd taken an essential key with her, inadvertently bringing the hotel to a temporary standstill. She bobbed reverently to the altar and all its various meaningful religious artefacts. She moved sideways to where Marco was standing, looked into his face for a clue as to why he was there.

Then she heard the words that were to ricochet around her head for days. "Peter's had an accident."

Her knees went weak. She had a feeling of déjà vu. Paco had had an accident. Was he saying Peter was dead? Before she could ask, Marco showed the experience he had now gained in life to deliver the answer to her unsubmitted question.

"He's OK." That seemed all she needed to hear.

Her life was then shattered by one of Marco's precise 'but's. "But he's in a serious condition. We really must hurry."

During their half-walking, half-running climb up the hill, Marco told her what he knew. There was suddenly the thumping, drumming, whining noise of an approaching helicopter. They felt the turbulence and watched anxiously to see whether it was on a flight path to or away from the hospital.

"They've dropped him. He's in safe hands," Marco announced confidently, as he realised the helicopter was on an outward course. He had been holding her hand throughout their hurried journey. Now he squeezed it lightly. She felt comforted but her heart was pumping.

"Where's José?" Marco asked.

"He's visiting his mother."

"I'll let him know. We're going straight to the hospital. Is it best I attend to letting essential people know or stay with you at the hospital?"

"I'll stay alone. I won't be alone, you know what I mean."

"What about Virginia coming with you?"

Maria forced a smile. "I'm best alone. Paco will be there… but don't tell José, he gets funny about such stupidities."

"Why?" Marco interjected. "Paco wouldn't let you down at a time like this. But I won't say."

They sped at breakneck speed to the hospital. Overall, it took 25 minutes from the church to get to A&E reception. Maria announced to the duty staff nurse who she was. The nurse looked as though it didn't mean a thing to her. She'd said, for simplicity, that she was Maria Martinez, thinking it would help to identify the relationship.

"I'm sorry," the nurse said, realising that Maria was in a state of anguish. "Can you tell me a little more?"

"I'm told my son has been shot and he's been brought here by helicopter." The tears welled up in her eyes.

"Oh God!" the nurse said, putting her hand to her mouth. "Of course, only you see the patient wasn't identified on arrival. He wasn't carrying any identity. Let me get the duty doctor to see you. It will be a few minutes. Can I get you some water?"

"Yes please. You're very kind."

The doctor appeared some ten anxious minutes later. He shook Maria's hand and said for her to come into the office. As he did, two police officers arrived. The doctor hesitated.

"Look, let me tell you what we know, but the officers might be able to tell us more about the circumstances. I've seen your son. What's his name?"

"Peter. Peter Martinez."

He made a note. "I'll have to ask you more in a minute. It appears he's been shot by a shotgun, which means the pellets have spread beyond the point of impact of an ordinary bullet. I have to tell you he was badly wounded in the shoulder and knee. He was rushed into emergency surgery in the hands of one of the finest remedial surgeons in the country, Sñr Benito Alvor. They're operating now.

"The good news is, take my word for it, that a message has come out of the theatre that they might be operating for more than four hours. I can tell that's good news because it means Sñr Alvor will be working at his intricate best. I would have thought myself, looking quickly at the wound, that an amputation was a probability… that would, regrettably, have meant a lot less time in surgery.

"So we'll all have to be very brave and sit it out. Now, why don't I call the officers in? If you can take it, it'll be a way of you hearing at first hand what happened. Now, how do you feel about that?"

Maria's head was spinning. Without a lot of thought, she elected to stay. The officers were very good with her and spared her from some of the more gruesome details. The senior officer explained it might just have been that Peter was in the wrong place at the wrong time but had to ask certain questions.

"Is your son a drug-user, Mrs Martinez?"

"Good God, no. Well… no, I'm sure he isn't but he's been away from home now for 20-odd years. Habits could change. But no, I'd be very certain he's not."

"So it wouldn't seem he was there by appointment. I'd say he was just very unlucky. You see, we'd had this gang under surveillance. They were fairly recently released from prison. They'd received life sentences for beating up one of their Romany family, a young girl, about 20 years ago. They were under restraining orders not to see her on their discharge. But we think there was some sort of gypsy vendetta to be settled. They were a bad lot. Why we asked about Peter and drugs is that they were drug-running from Africa up into southern Europe."

"You say 'were this and were that' – where are they now?"

"In the morgue. They're all dead. The one we think shot Peter was almost dead when he shot him. As he fell to the ground, the gun went off and, unfortunately, your son was in the line of fire."

Although some of explanations were a blur, Maria focused on the last part of the story, and the description that the bandits had been to prison for the offence against a young woman. She had memories of Tania's beatings and wondered whether it was the same feud. But that hardly mattered for the moment. Peter, and others, were fighting for his life.

A message came out of the theatre that they were optimistic about the leg, and were now looking at the shoulder; then, an hour or so later, that the operation was over and Peter was in intensive care. She could expect to see the consultant. It all seemed to take an age.

When Maria had had her chat with Benito Alvor she was relieved by the words of this important man who had entered her life. He seemed a nice, kind man of educated Catalan stock, not another import from other parts of Europe to complement the needs of tourism.

So it didn't matter if Peter couldn't Sardana again or, at worst, would definitely not tango. At least he could watch, she thought somewhat philosophically; but knowing her son, as she did, and the genes inherited from Paco, she did not doubt he would make a very big effort.

Alvor's parting words to Maria were, "We're going to let you see your son in a short while. We're not going to encourage you to stay with him. He's got to be brought out of shock slowly and calmly. There's a Florence Nightingale of a nurse in our team who played a very major role in the successful operation."

He was pensive for a few split seconds after he had said that. What an inspiration she was to him. She made him perform to his upper limit, almost encouraged him to show off all the skills he had. By comparison, he'd get home and his wife would show little interest in how his day had been, why he'd had to rush off on a Saturday night. She'd probably just pitch in as to how inconvenient it was that they had had to cancel a dinner engagement, or just generally change their plans because of his job.

"Can't you get a locum?" she had said on one occasion. She'd missed out on understanding her husband's considerable skills.

Benito Alvor re-focussed on the patient's mother.

"The nurse in question, Gina Faro, knows your son from way back, apparently. She says she wants to bring him out of the anaesthetic. He couldn't, in my view, be in better hands. She'll probably come and meet you and you'll go and see him together, and then I suggest you go home. Ring during the night whenever you want to."

Maria got a glimpse of José standing outside the entrance doors leading to the accident unit. "There's my husband," she said proudly. "Thank you, Sñr Alvor for all that you've done, and your kindness."

Benito Alvor left.

José came in. "I've left you to yourself. I've been watching you through the windows – hospitals don't have curtains and an orderly has been keeping me posted. In fact, Tania's in the car park too. She's concerned and confused about what happened. She apparently rang Marco and felt she had to be within a close distance to pray for Peter's wellbeing."

"That's kind of her," Maria said. "I think he's going to be fine," she added, as if to comfort José and reassure herself.

"Mrs Martinez? I'm Gina, Gina Faro, we met just once early one morning. I was the nurse who drove back to the UK with Mr and Mrs Hunt and Peter. He's OK. He's tough but he's been in the hands of a genius. Would you like to see your son?"

"Oh yes, of course. But I've been told not to stay. I gather you'll have an important part to play in his immediate convalescence."

"Well, I don't know about that, but I expect I'll hold Peter's hand on your behalf. But then once he's on the recovery road, the family will come into its own. You'll have a very big part to play."

CHAPTER 22

By the Monday, Palafrugell had become a virtual circus town. The press were stimulated by the anti-gypsy factor and it seemed everybody who had ever known the Martinez family had surfaced from under their respective damp stones and were lining up either to send their regards to Peter for a speedy recovery, or to his mother to pass the messages on.

Sunday had been a tense day, but with a satisfactory outcome. Maria hadn't slept, or so it seemed once she'd got home on the previous night and had taken the option of phoning every two hours. Each time Gina sent a personal message back.

"He's resting calmly."

"He's moving his good arm and leg."

"He's semi-conscious."

"We've helped the pain."

"He's looking around."

"He's hearing what I say."

When Maria called at eight on the Sunday morning the news was, "He's speaking but a bit delirious."

Maria was there by ten. It would have been sooner if there hadn't been calls generated by the local news media. Most followed the theme that somebody seemed to have released.

"… Local man…"

"… Boy made good…"

"… Went to UK at 19…"

"… Multi-millionaire businessman…"

"… Designer of Girasol, award-winning resort complex…"

"… Was he out for a normal innocent walk?"

"… Encountered bandits under surveillance for suspected drug-running…"

"… Allegedly got caught up in strong crossfire…"

"… Knocked on death's door…"

"… Life saved by micro-surgeon, Señor Benito Alvor and longstanding friend of the victim, star nurse Gina Faro…"

"… Peter Martinez now stable…"

"… Mother and uncle, owners of the four-star hotels the Playa in Calella de Palafrugell and the Playa Girasol, relieved but not prepared to comment…"

"… BCG, of which Martinez is new whizz-kid Chief Executive, also not prepared to comment. Press office advised there will be a statement at the end of the week…"

Maria wouldn't have expected so many mutual acquaintances to listen to the Sunday morning bulletins. The news hadn't hit the papers.

Maria had rung Sñr Martin at about nine when it was obvious the phone wasn't going to stop ringing or the telex and fax halt their respective churnings out of messages. On the way to the hospital, she made a mental list of who she must contact, as soon as she had seen Peter's condition for herself. Alex, his son, and Petra, his daughter. She supposed Marcia Hunt and definitely his old friend, Michelle. Peter had told his mother all about Honey and Coco just the previous Thursday evening over the sort of one-to-one dinner they were used to sharing together on any of Peter's first nights 'home'. It was always an extension of that initial bonding that had developed those years before, which had its roots firmly planted in those early days after Paco's death back in Rosas, all those many years ago.

They'd always have a special relationship. She was his special lady. He was her second special man. That she felt guilty about because in terms of pure love and affection, she owed so much to José. But the pecking order would always be Paco, Peter, José and then Marco. On the occasions when she considered the importance of the other man in her life close to the lead quartet, it was Carlos, librarian extraordinaire, who had so encouraged the changes in her life.

She knew Sñr Martin would anchor the situation at the hotel. He was an experienced diplomat and understood when Maria had said, "The hotel is not prepared to make any comment for at least 24 hours."

She parked at the hospital in the same car park she had used on her visits to Bob Hunt, when he was recovering from his massive heart attack. That gave her spirit. They'd pulled him round. Peter, pray God, would be alright too.

There were more visitors, she thought, for a Sunday morning than normal. Usually families had their Sunday lunch and then, sometimes begrudgingly, would go in the afternoon to sit at the bedsides of ailing grandmothers and grandfathers, uncles and aunts, friends, for whom they summoned up light conversation.

"Mrs Martinez?"

"Yes," Maria replied to the total stranger, somewhat in surprise that he knew her name.

"How do you view the prospect…" As he said that, there were two large flashes that made her wince and close her eyes which, in turn, made the inside of her head momentarily change from black to light luminous blue.

"… For your son's recovery?"

Another of the strangers followed that more outrageously.

"Do you think Peter was at a meeting that backfired? How well did he know the bandits?"

Maria ran into the hospital, followed closely by two further flashes from the cameraman in pursuit.

The nurse at reception stood up and gesticulated by open arms that she could shelter Maria from the onslaught.

"Here," she said, "they've been waiting since dawn. We've been trying to ring you to warn you but the phone's been busy."

"How do they know all about it?" Maria said, in some natural distress.

"We never know. It's annoying what information will be given out for money. Sometimes we think information on patients is fed out by the paramedics who bring them in, maybe a hospital porter or one of the young nurses they ply with drink at discos, asking if they've had a busy day. It's the news-hungry paparazzi, I'm afraid. Another time, can I suggest you park in the staff car park? It's under-used, there are usually spaces, and you can come in through that door there," she said, pointing to a secondary entrance. "Tell your daughter-in-law to do the same when she arrives."

Maria looked quizzically. "Daughter-in-law?"

"I'd presumed there's a Mrs Martinez Jnr."

"Oh there…" Maria was about to say, "There was, but she died," but stopped in her tracks for fear of seeing a headline 'Widower Millionaire makes steady recovery…' etc.

"Oh there," she said, acknowledging the potential entrance. "That's kind of you. Thank you. Can I go up to see my son now?"

"Well, actually Sñr Alvor is visiting him at the moment."

"On a Sunday morning?"

"Oh, Sundays, Mondays, the day doesn't seem to make a difference to him. He must have a very understanding wife. He apparently telephoned as many times as you did last night. He was getting technical feedback from a distance. Blood pressure, temperature, pulse. He and Gina are a real duo. They'll get anybody back to normal if there's a chance. Let me ring through to the care unit. I'll see if you can go up."

She dialled an extension and spoke to one of the monitoring nurses outside Peter's actual room. She in turn must have asked the question at a more senior level.

"Sñr Alvor says to go up. He'll have a word with you."

Maria's heart missed a beat. "Bad news?" she asked herself. No, he'd be fine. God had told her so.

She climbed the two flights of stairs and turned left, as directed. There was a nurse sitting behind a desk, alongside a capless uniformed police officer. Maria was surprised to see the police presence.

"Oh, I didn't know there would be police here."

The officer stepped forward. "I hope you don't mind, but do you have some form of identity with you?"

"Of course," Maria responded, hoping she had her driver's licence with her. She normally carried it. But today, she was not the most collected. She fumbled in her bottomless bag. "Yes, here," she said with relief.

He checked out the details and the photograph was obviously of her, but at least a decade old.

"Fine, Mrs Martinez. You're also known as Mrs Romanez, is that right?"

"Yes, that's my current married name. Martinez was my former married name, which I still use in business."

The officer checked some notes. "Yes, that's right."

"I'm sorry to be inquisitive, but why the security?"

"Well, your son needs to be questioned as soon as we get the OK. Just to establish the connection he had with the bandits. Then we also need to know if he can pass on any more information about who they were. We are, after all, only just finding out more about the identity of your son."

Maria chilled at the realisation of the seriousness of it all.

"The other thing is, as you'll discover, your son is quite newsworthy at the moment. There's quite an anti-Romany camp around, largely due to the fact that the Europeans who have now settled here are scared silly that their homes will be requisitioned by a gypsy family. If they do that, even if you're the owner on paper, you'd still have to move. It would take heaven and earth to get them evicted as they have special rights of possession, albeit temporary. In that time, they've been known to strip out the copper and other metal and take it down the road to sell. So an attack on a locally bred man by gypsies is quite newsworthy."

"Tell me about it," Maria agreed. "I had quite a battle to get in, question after question from the press."

"Can I give you some advice?"

"Please."

"Announce to the press that you'll have a daily press briefing. Even line up the medics alongside you. The police will co-operate too. Then let it be known you'll cancel them altogether if you get hounded between press announcements. At least then you'll get some peace, as they'd rather have some information than none."

"That sounds a good idea," Maria said, as she noticed Sñr Alvor coming out of the fortress they were all defending.

Maria held out her hand. "Sñr Alvor, I'm pleased to see you again. I know Peter is getting wonderful attention."

"Well, at least he's reacting well to it too. Pop over to the chairs there and I'll update you on his progress."

They moved to the other side of the reception area, where they'd have more privacy. Benito Alvor broke the ice.

"I'm not too worried now. Well, a lot less worried anyway. Peter's come through 14 or 15 critical hours after the operation. This evening I'll be a lot more confident. Let me explain. His body has not only suffered a huge mechanical intrusion, gunshot, he's in total shock too, plus the effects of an operation and post-operative trauma. He lost a lot of blood and had effectively two complete transfusions. But blood pressure is now good. Can you tell me, as we don't have any previous medical history, what sort of pulse does he normally have?"

"I think low, possibly very low because one of the masters at school advised him to take up long-distance running on account of an advantageously slow pulse."

"Now that's useful news, because we've been a bit concerned about his low pulse. We've got the temperature steady. If that flipped up, then we'd probably have an idea that we'd missed an area of shot in his body. That would manifest itself by poisoning his system. He's on intravenous antibiotics to prevent that. But I'd say at this stage the signs look good. The body reacts very quickly to a foreign presence.

"Come in and see your son. There's a large team at work. One more won't make a difference."

CHAPTER 23

There weren't many times in Peter's life that he hadn't had direct control over it. Now his brain seemed to be working, but it was reading a long dream rather than a reality replay.

First, he remembered being a child again, playing with the kaleidoscope his parents had bought for him. Then he was aware of diffused daylight and the presence of a guardian angel, when in fact his mother was holding his hand. Although he wanted to get up and go to school, he had weights on his body and was tied down, like in the picture of Gulliver he had in a book as a kid, with all the little folk from Lilliput who now had him under their control.

He knew he was in pain. He didn't know what was causing it but when he focused on it, he could see blinding blue lights on full beam hitting the corner of his eyeballs. There were noises in his head too. Fire crackers at the end of a fiesta signifying it was time to go home, yet he knew he was too tired to walk.

The pain faded and he slept. He awoke, and this time he could focus on the friendly face of a girl. She had a pale face and wore white, but not as a bride or a novice in a convent. She was there to help free him from the little people's guy ropes. She spoke words he could hear but not understand. He was getting better. Why did he need to be better? Why did she keep telling him that?

However, her constant asking him if he was feeling better was working. He *was* better. He felt movement in his one leg. He sensed movement in both, but he thought only one actually moved. He felt control over his arms. One was too heavily tied to the ground for him to move it alone. The girl was there to help him. He felt sleepy.

His mother was then patting his hand and talking to him.

"Oh Mother!" he said.

That made Maria happy. It made the young girl happy too. Peter could move his head. The girl had cut it free of its restrictions.

"Oh Mother!" he said again.

"Yes, dear. Don't speak. Don't try and speak. We're getting you better."

"Fiesta!" he said.

"What about fiesta, Peter?"

He didn't know, but he would work it out, he was sure.

He was sleepy. His mother kissed him on the forehead and sent him to sleep. At the three o'clock issue of drugs, they'd been ordered to cut down the sedatives. He woke unknowingly at about five.

Yes, pain woke him but it was not now over all of his body. He could feel both his hands. He knew he was moving his fingers. One arm he could move. The other was still tied down. He could feel both feet and each set of toes. Again, one leg he could move. The other was still padlocked to the bed.

Yes. He was in bed. It was a white room with shafts of light. He could look around the room now. It hurt, but if he lifted his head he could see the door he wanted to walk through. He turned his head to the right. The girl with the pale face wasn't there. This one had black hair.

"Name," came into his head. "Name," passed through his lips.

Unbeknown to Peter, she wrote frantically.

Moved both sets of fingers and lifted arm voluntarily.

Saw beneath the sheet both sets of toes moving.

He moved good leg.

Seemed alert and was looking around the room.

Turned to me and said, "Name," and answered for himself, "Maria." He repeated, "Maria."

I said, "How are you, Peter?" Did not answer. Asked again. He frowned.

He mentioned, "Pedro." I asked, "Why Pedro?" No answer.

Slept for rest of hour. When he woke, he went through some body motions. Hands first, then feet. Looked around room and turned to me. Said, "Maria."

I said, "Very good, Peter. Very, very good."

He smiled and said, "Yes, Peter," and then said, "Pedro."

He then said, "Mother." I said, "She'll be here soon."

He said, "Fiesta," and screwed his face up in a sort of pain.

Closed eyes, went to sleep. BP. 140/85. Pulse 38. Temperature 37 degrees. Skin colour pale.

Peter seemed confused by the number of people surrounding his bed at the eight o'clock viewing. Gina held his hand.

The pleasant man said to him. "Do you know what happened, Peter?"

He shook his head negatively.

"I want you to squeeze Gina's hand."

Peter looked at Gina, and squeezed her hand. She took his other hand. The one lucky still to be attached to his shoulder. "And again," he said.

"Pressure, Gina?" Alvor asked.

"Yes. Good."

221

"Excellent."

The consultant lifted the lower part of the sheet.

"If you can feel your toes, Peter, I'd like you to waggle them. No, both together."

Peter obeyed.

"Oh, excellent, Peter."

Benito Alvor turned to his entourage of student medics and said, "Fully co-ordinated. Brain, muscle, control functions, all very encouraging."

He then focused on Peter again. "Peter, can you see your mother?"

Peter lifted his head slightly and lifted what was to be termed as his good arm, then pointed his index finger towards Maria, who was sitting observing the examinations discreetly across the room.

A tear rolled down Maria's cheek. She could not restrain herself. "Oh, Pedro, darling!"

Peter's head lifted from the pillow at hearing the word Pedro. The nurse with the shrouds of black hair suddenly said, "He said that this afternoon. He didn't react to Peter. He did to the word Pedro."

Maria said would the consultant like her to explain.

"Please, but in simple terms."

"He was born Pedro and later called Peter."

"Thank you. Now Peter, do you remember, as a little boy, you were Pedro. Who are you now?"

There was silence.

Then, "Peter," came the reply. "Peter Martinez," was the finesse.

Benito Alvor turned to everybody, then addressed his comments to his patient.

"Peter Martinez, you are making excellent progress. What we're going to do is to sit you out of the bed for a few minutes, with a lot of help, and then we'll find you a different room. OK?"

Peter nodded. OK.

Benito Alvor addressed his entourage again. "Now what do you think? Here's a strong man, I'd guess going on 200lbs, with a short-term disability. He's going to feel a bit woozy when he sits up. That will be the combination of change in blood pressure and the after-effects of almost five hours of anaesthetic. So how do we get him out of bed?"

"We concentrate on getting all his weight and leverage onto his left side," offered one of the young medics.

"OK. So then he'll fall over. He's got to be balanced onto his left leg with the right side stabilised by an equal force."

Another student piped up keenly, "Then it's the stronger two in attendance on his left side and, say, two female nurses taking his right shoulder and the other his right thigh."

"The thigh situation is good but touch his shoulder and he'll justifiably go through the roof. It's the right rib cage you concentrate on with the right thigh. OK, you sort that out. Get him into the chair and I'll have another look at him. If that's OK, we'll take the catheter out and remove the urine bag. Anything to get this man more comfortable."

Benito smiled at Gina, who had come in specially to see how Peter was doing.

"You're in charge, Gina, OK? I'm going to update Mrs Martinez."

Maria had been watching intently, full of gratitude for the care and attention Peter was being given.

"Let's step outside, shall we? You don't want to be here when the crowd drop your son on the floor, do you?" he announced with an impish smile.

"They won't do that," Maria countered in their defence, but showing a grimace, just in case they might.

Outside in the lobby, the police officer pounced.

"Doctor, can we have words with him yet?"

Sñr Alvor showed his annoyance. "Look, I reiterate my first prognosis that the patient won't be thinking straight until the morning at the earliest. You really must just wait. I'll say as soon as he's ready. I know the job you have to do. On the drug front, you're wasting your time. Mr Martinez is not a user. His blood and urine tested negative to drug intrusion."

Maria looked shocked. She instinctively intervened to come to her son's defence. "What's more, I can confirm he's very anti the habit. He's saved people himself from the addiction. When you get to interview him, I wouldn't go down that route if I were you. He'd go wild."

Benito Alvor took Maria's elbow and led her across to the corner by the window in the outer reception lobby. They sat down, knees almost touching so that their conversation remained private.

"Well, I hope you gathered it's all good news this far. It's really going very well. I think it must be that your son has a very strong constitution."

"He gets that from his father, I'd say. He was tough."

"You say was. Is he not alive?"

"He died nearly 40 years ago."

"It may help just to know how he died in case there's a hereditary gene problem that might come through while Peter's at his most vulnerable."

"Unlikely. You're not to know, of course, but he was drowned at sea in a fishing accident."

"Oh, I am sorry," Alvor said sincerely. "Anyway, as you saw, there's no apparent problem with his brain communicating with the extremities. He hasn't, of course, yet realised what's been damaged. He'll start to know when he's sitting out of bed. That's another reason for getting him up.

"So yes, I'd say I'm pretty happy 24 hours on. That's a critical milestone in this sort of case. Relax a little. I don't want him burdened with visitors too much yet. We've got to nurse his head through the trauma, it will be bound to suffer for a few days.

"I gather you want to give a statement to the press to get them away from your front door, as it were. I'll see Peter in the morning and then either give you a statement to make or join you in making it. I think it's a good idea to take them along with you. Otherwise, they'll start climbing in through windows to get their own photos and make up their own stories, as they do. Why don't we say 11 in the morning? Here at the hospital. There's quite a good local authority press agency we can look into. Yes, that's the idea. We'll do that."

"It's good with me too." Maria made a mental note to let the police officer know, if he didn't already, and she would fix an appointment with the police before that and get Tania along to allay her fears.

Gina came out of the double doors that led into the intensive care unit.

"Well, your boy's up and ready to be seen by his most important visitor." She then addressed Sñr Alvor. "Sir, he's worked out he's got a problem with his shoulder and leg. He doesn't seem to be worried by it because he can control his hand and foot. In the morning, we can begin to explain, I'd think."

"I'd agree," Sñr Alvor replied, acknowledging her confidence. He held the door open for Maria to go in first. There was a nurse on each side of Peter, but he was sitting fairly well upright. He smiled as he saw his mother.

"Oh, there's a smart boy then," she said approvingly. They'd combed his hair for him.

Peter lifted his left hand and pointed to his heavily strapped and bandaged right shoulder, then dropped the same hand level with his knees and pointed to his right knee.

"Fell over!" he said, almost knowledgeably.

A third nurse appeared with an electric razor and proceeded to remove what was nearly two days' facial hair growth. She left and reappeared with a bowl of water, a towel and a bar of hospital soap.

Sñr Alvor advised, "They'll make him feel more comfortable and then move him to his own room. The police are saying either they want to be in the room with him or they want a nurse to be there, on oath to report anything that he says. They're still hell bent on knowing whether Peter was an active part of the bandit gang. If not, why he was there?"

"I think you'll find it was all innocent," said Maria. "He was doing what he loved to do at Girasol and was just out for a walk and got dragged into something by chance. We'll see. He'll remember, I'm sure."

Peter's only cover for his naked body was still the cotton sheet. Things became more organised when they found an operating gown without sleeves, which they put onto him before removing the sheet.

Benito Alvor announced, "That's been a good 15 minutes, which is enough for a first outing. I'd suggest he goes straight onto the trolley. You can then remove the catheter. Keep the drip going overnight. He won't eat until tomorrow. Then get him to his new home." He patted Peter's good hand. "You alright, old son?"

Peter nodded, then creased his brow into a series of furrows. He was clearly still in shock but not bothered, apparently, by the situation. Sñr Alvor hoped it was the expert attention he was getting.

Peter put his hand up to his head. "Tired," he announced.

"Wait to close your eyes until you're tucked up in bed," the consultant suggested. He turned to Gina and asked if she would advise the police that he was being moved, which she did.

Maria saw Peter into bed. She then kissed his forehead and said she wasn't leaving and would be back after he'd had a sleep. He seemed calm and accepted that situation, and was asleep by the time she got to the door of the new room and turned to wave him good night. She noticed the outer ward clock said 9 o'clock.

"We predict he's not going to be an easy patient," Gina said.

"I'll be in touch during the day and plan to see him in the evening about eight. If he's steady then we'll have him sitting out of bed again for 15 minutes or so, to help his circulation. Monday morning's inspection is going to be the relax point. So, it looks steady, but keep your fingers crossed," Benito Alvor said confidently.

"Thank you, Sñr Alvor. And thank you for all that you did. Peter will be very grateful, I know."

"I think he is already. He's saying apparently only one nurse can get to attend to his body, and that's Gina, who saved 50 per cent of his life, at least. Go in now and see him. We want to keep him calm."

Maria and Benito shook hands. She held back from raising herself on to tiptoes and pecking his cheek in thanks and admiration.

She returned to the louvre-shuttered room, which was naturally cool. Peter seemed still to be asleep. She sat on the chair which the attending nurse vacated, telling Maria, "I'll give you six or seven minutes."

Maria picked up his hand and held it in hers. His head looked strong but she could see numerous dressings showing through beneath the light cotton gown. There were wires going to various parts of his body and a thin tube supplying nutrients into a vein. He was still linked to a urine bag below the metal under-rail of the steel bed. That was due to be taken out, she understood.

He opened his eyes and began to pull his hand away from hers. She covered it with both her hands, holding it securely. He slowly turned his head towards her. She stood up to allow the muted light to illuminate her face.

"Mother," he said.

"Peter! Don't try and move."

"Mother, please don't start lecturing me."

She laughed. "Oh Pedro, mi chiquito," and leant down and kissed his forehead. They were silent for the next couple of minutes.

"I got hurt," he said. "Lots of blood."

Maria comforted him. "That's over, darling. You're OK now."

"Am I?" he asked.

"Yes. If you relax and do what they say. You're fine. The surgeon has just confirmed that."

He lay silent again. His head moved, enabling him to look up at the ceiling. He turned his face again to Maria. His lips moved slowly. "Tania. Cousins," he said.

"Yes, we know. Don't worry any more. I promise you faithfully."

"Really. Oh good."

His eyelids closed and his head fell further sideways.

The nurse returned. "Mrs Martinez, time's up, I'm afraid. He'll sleep now."

"How long for?"

"Probably four hours. That's how long the sedative will last."

"Can I come back during the night?"

"Of course, you could stay if you want but he doesn't need crowding. Will his wife be arriving?"

"No."

"Are you likely to be the only visitor then?"

"Yes, I'd imagine so. His daughters are abroad. One in South America, the other in Malaysia."

"Which one's Tania?"

"Why?"

"That's the only name he's mentioned."

"Oh, that's funny. That's my middle name he sometimes uses when I'm angry with him," Maria lied.

"Oh, that's another part of the circle put together, I'll make a note and tell the police. They need to know what things he focuses on, what names he seems to be attached to."

"What for?"

"Oh, they're experienced in such things, they piece together jigsaws."

Maria leant down and kissed Peter on the forehead. She whispered. "See you later, duermes bien."

She took her leave and walked slowly down the stairs.

'La Capilla' said the sign, accompanied by an arrow going to the left. Maria turned left and then stopped. Instinctively she turned through 180 degrees.

The chapel door was wide open. The flowers were fresh and the candles showed that they had been lit at various times, not at one organised mass. She bobbed to the altar and crossed herself, walking on tiptoe to the second row of pews. She never, for some reason, went to the front row. She thought perhaps that that position indicated you were chief mourner, as with Paco's service, or a bride. It did not seem right for it to be just anybody's prerogative.

When she got back to the reception area, the same nurse was on duty as with her arrival. Now there were three or four bouquets newly arrived on a table. *On a Sunday,* Maria thought.

The nurse looked up and, seeing Maria, said, "Your son's going to bring this hospital to a standstill if he goes on like this," pointing at the flowers and then the now five or six members of the press standing around like a small pack of waiting meerkats, turning their heads as any car door slammed or there was an exit out of the hospital.

Now they pounced, asking, "You seeing the Martinez man?" or, "Have you visited the Martinez man?"

Maria asked why.

"Well, all these flowers are for him, and it's only Sunday evening."

Maria walked across. One bouquet was from Marco and Virginia. Another just said 'Speedy recovery'. The third looked homemade and personally tied together. One bore a card with the single name 'Tania' in personalised writing. The other was from José's son, José Jnr and his wife.

Maria took the card saying 'Tania' out of the bunch and palmed it without the nurse seeing. She bet the police would go through those. She really felt that for the time being, she wanted to keep Tania out of the equation. She'd talk to her and maybe suggest they then jointly went to the police. She felt sure Tania would be an innocent party to everything.

Maria turned back to the reception nurse. "If you like, I'll take these up to my son's room."

"No, not at all. The porter will take them. He'll get some vases too."

"You sure?"

"Yes, certain. Are you going back home?"

"Yes."

"Is it far?"

"No. No distance." Maria was not going to get drawn. She'd be as unidentifiable as possible.

The nurse pointed outside. "There's a number of paparazzi now. Why don't you go out through the gardens? That way, you'll approach your car from the other side and avoid any questioning."

"Are you sure?"

"Yes, and do come into the staff parking when you visit." She seemed harmless and co-operative. But it was better to be certain.

Maria reached her car without further interrogation. She had reversed into the bay and was therefore facing outwards once she got into the car. She put the key into the ignition and was about to start it when she noticed a female behind the wheel of a small Peugeot in one of the opposite bays. She thought she recognised the outline. Yes, she had. It was Tania. Tania the bad penny. Tania the supportive. Tania the loyal.

Maria threw a friendly wave. Tania returned it. Maria removed the keys from the ignition and opened the driver's door to get out. Tania followed suit. They met in no man's land. Maria held out her arms to invite a friendly hug and embrace. Not that she normally did that to employees, but it seemed appropriate.

"I saw your flowers. They were pretty," Maria said, breaking the ice.

Tania went straight to the point. "I haven't been able to find out how Mr Peter is. Is he going to be alright? The police in Girasol said he was badly shot up."

"He's fine," Maria said comfortingly. "He's on a comfortable critical list until this evening and from then on, I hope it's onwards and upwards."

"Mrs Martinez, I've always been honest to you. You know that."

"Yes, of course, Tania."

"Can I take you into my confidence?"

"Yes, of course."

She started to sob. Maria put her arms around her again.

"Here, spill it out. It will be better."

"Oh, I do hope so. I'm so scared."

"Why?"

"Well, I think it's my fault that Peter was shot."

"Why do you say that?"

Tania told her own version of how she had split on Toni and the cousins and how she thought they were close to considering a vendetta to teach her a final lesson.

Maria had listened intently. "It's not really your fault, Tania. Fate has a lot to do with these things. Look, I'm happy to help you. We'll go to the police and get the air cleared. As long as you didn't encourage them to come to the area, you've got no reason to be concerned."

Maria hesitated. "Tania, tell me, are you in a confessional frame of mind?"

"Why, Mrs Martinez? I've told you the whole story."

"There's another one I thought you might want to clear your conscience on."

"Oh. I don't think there is anything else. What do you think it is?"

"It's about Marco's child."

Tania positively bristled. That was her business, not his sister-in-law's. "I don't want to talk about my daughter," she replied brusquely.

"Tania, I do."

"You can't make me." Tania was now acting out the performance of a child not wanting to be made to do something by its overpowering parent.

"Tania. You've always been the first to try to look after Mr Peter's best interests. He's my son, so I appreciate that. In return, I want to try to look after your daughter's best interests.

"I'll explain anyway. You know, and I know, Marco is not the blood father to your child. He says he is but, bearing in mind there was medical evidence years ago to show he and Virginia couldn't produce a child, it's unlikely that the ageing process will have reversed that position. Marco has said he's the father to fulfil a dream, and it's convenient for you to have his name or, I'm inclined to say, any name, on Marguerite's birth certificate.

"Now if it were as simple as that, I'd leave well alone. But it's not. As it is, if Marco were to die, and he will, as we all do, one day, Marguerite could claim Marco's estate, or at least if Virginia were to die too. Now that would mean, at the least, that Marguerite could become my senior partner in the hotel."

Tania's jaw dropped. "But she wouldn't do that. I wouldn't let her do that."

"You might not, but I bet her husband would."

Tania was speechless.

"Now if that were to happen, I would challenge that and I've available DNA evidence from Marco to prove he's not the father. As and when that's proved publically, as it will be, or could be, then Marguerite would revert to being fatherless. In short, a bastard love child of somebody other than Marco. Our family interests will be satisfied. Yours will not."

"Would you do that?"

"I'd rather not."

"So how can I help the matter?"

"By signing a disclaimer agreement, which can be filed with me until it passes to Peter. The quid pro quo would be that we would acknowledge Marco's birth certificate support, and Marguerite would have her honour, and yours, protected for all time. Think about it. She couldn't be married in the Catholic religion if she had… well, let's say, an incomplete certificate."

Tania said, "And what about the current problem with me probably being the reason for another of Peter's accidents?"

"Another?"

"Oh, that's a matter for Peter and me. But I do seem to bring him a lot of harm."

"Well, I'd come along to the police with you and help you explain. They'd understand the position better if an older woman was there to help."

"Maria… may I, Mrs Martinez?"

"When it's the two of us alone together, yes, call me Maria."

"Maria, I don't want Marguerite to inherit anything she's not entitled to. I do want her to have a named father. So, yes, I agree. You get a solicitor to draw up a document and I'll sign it. Does Marco know about your plan?"

"Yes."

"Does he agree?"

"Yes."

"Why? He seems so keen on owning Marguerite."

"He is. But if Virginia found out, she'd divorce him and take 50 per cent of everything he's got, and have her freedom. So Marco doesn't want that."

"Maria. I've always thought of you as being the shrewd one, the power behind the Martinez throne."

"Thank you, Tania. Now I need to get home and I suggest you go too. You won't get to see Peter for a couple of days anyway. I'll phone you early in the morning and we'll see the police tomorrow."

They naturally took a step each towards one another. They brushed cheeks and both let out a comforting *mwa*.

They drove off their different ways. Maria felt drained. She was worried still about Peter but relieved that she had forced the opportunity to sort out the family's potential inheritance problems.

As she walked from her parked car towards the hotel reception, a man in light brown trousers with a safari-type matching shirt stepped out in front of her.

"May I say how sorry UK media group are about your son's accident. Can you tell our readers how he is, and what happened?"

Maria was furious. This was her own home yet even here she was being invaded by a dubious character, no doubt intent on reversing any story she told him anyway.

"Look," she said, "this is private property, I'm a private person and I'm nursing very private anxious moments. Just go away."

She learnt a few days later how that had inspired one of the UK newspaper headlines: 'MOTHER IN BANDIT SHOOTOUT SAYS SHE'S AT BREAKING POINT.'

Maria pushed the man aside.

Back in the hotel, she had never seen Sñr Martin quite so stressed out before. He saw her crossing the foyer towards the office. Marco was hovering behind him. As she approached, she could see Sñr Martin was busy making notes and talking in German. Marco looked relieved to see her.

"It's really good to see you. First, how's Peter?" Marco enquired.

She explained as fully and as quickly as she could. Then: "I sense an air of panic here," she said with concern.

"You'd be amazed how many people have picked up the news bulletins. The phone hasn't stopped. I've been here helping Sñr Martin most of the morning. The good news is, we've gone fully booked and guess what?"

"What?"

"Well, when I realised the first booking was for a news team of six people from the UK, BBC News, with all expenses paid, I doubled the usual price."

"Marco, that's dreadful! But good thinking! From what I've seen today, they deserve it. The media are everywhere. The police suggest we give a regular daily press conference. But not until after today, when we'll know more about how Peter is."

Sñr Martin came off the phone. "Wow, Maria! What is Peter these days? Some sort of film star or football player? That's a list of people who I don't think are even acquainted with him who have called," he said, handing her a sheet of paper. "And those are names I know and those, I'm sure, are genuine people and organisations who do seem to know him."

Maria cast her eyes down to the list of names known.

Meribel.

Michelle.

Jaimé's wife.

José Jnr.

Carlos.

Miguel, Michelle's husband, calling a second time for Michelle... blokes from school, builders, his local travel agent... so the list went on.

"That's, of course, just at the local level. What happens if it does become international news?" she said. "Can I get a line out?"

"Yes, go into the back office," Marco directed.

"Only I must ring Alex and Petra and probably Max, oh, and one other in Malaysia." She had recently discovered Peter would want that.

"Who's in Malaysia?" Marco pried. Maria touched his nose with her forefinger. "Never you mind."

Husband José had seen her car come back.

"How's Peter?"

They all meant so well. She now understood why, when a member of the British Royal Family was ill, they apparently posted a report at regular intervals on the railings outside Buckingham Palace. She reported Peter's condition, said she was going to make three calls and then they would have a sandwich together. She'd go back to the hospital at 2pm and then probably again at 8pm, when she would hopefully see Benito Alvor for an update.

Maria found Peter a few degrees brighter when she saw him at two and stayed for 30 minutes. Using the staff car park was better and, thank God, the same police officer was on duty so she was let in this time with a nod.

At eight that evening when she arrived, there were half a dozen medics already by Peter's bed. She could see through the glass panel set in the door leading into the intensive care unit.

Sñr Alvor was the only one in shirt sleeves. The others, male and female, wore white coats. She thought she recognised Gina.

"Is everything alright?" she asked the nurse outside the door.

"Yes. Don't be put off if it looks a bit officious. If Peter gets the clearance, he'll be out of intensive and into a ward with less wires and equipment."

"Oh God!" Maria said, putting her hand to her mouth. "I hadn't thought about that. Do you mean a ward with other people?"

"Yes. Normally. But Sñr Alvor, and the police anyway, have stipulated he has to have a private room, which can be barricaded. That son of yours is a news item. He'll make a fortune with his first 'this is actually what happened' interview."

"I bet he doesn't," Maria countered.

"Why?"

"Knowing Peter, he probably won't ever tell anybody. Maybe a jury or a coroner's court. Anyway, how's he seemed since I was here in the afternoon?"

"Good. I'd say, and I've seen a few cases. He'll be moved by 10pm."

CHAPTER 24

It seemed that for the imminent future, Peter was to be like some great radio transmitter of worldwide news.

Coco had cried and cried and cried when Maria had broken the news to her. She listened intently to every word. How Maria had said that it was on Peter's agenda to take Coco to Spain to meet his family, but how she had run away back home before it had been possible. Maria explained that Peter had only told her on the previous Thursday about her third grandchild, and said how inappropriate it seemed that their first point of contact was with news that he was dangerously ill.

Coco's tears were stimulated as much by the fact that her grandmother was so prepared to accept her into the family and even include her on the telephone list of those to be informed about Peter's shooting and his subsequent progress. Her beautiful father should not have been shot. Nobody could hate him that much. Coco hadn't fully realised that it could just have been an accident. Nobody yet seemed to know what had really happened.

Then she blamed herself. If she hadn't returned home, they would still be in his beautiful home in London. She would be waiting for him to return from his hard day's toil at the office. She should have taken him back to Malaysia with her. For her mother's sake. To protect him from such a fate.

Maria had been adamant that Coco shouldn't make any arrangements to fly over yet. Her advice was that her granddaughter should wait a couple of days to see how things worked out.

In London, Marcia Hunt and Jan Roberts both had their reasons for not getting to sleep. Back in Spain, Tania and Gina had theirs.

Bill Forrester, the new man in Marcia's life, had been very understanding and compassionate when she'd told him what she had seen on the news, and how it affected her. He had suggested they make love to take her mind off the news and to make her feel good before she went to sleep.

But his rather boring approach to lovemaking had, in fact had the reverse effect and all she could focus on was how, if Peter could have walked into the room at that moment, all he would have needed to do was lightly kiss her breasts and place his magnetic hand on the flat of her stomach, and she would have been completed. Indeed, whenever Marcia thought about Peter, especially when she was in bed, she was automatically aroused.

The prospect of seeing Peter incapacitated was, to her, heartbreaking enough. To think he was in the same intensive care unit as Bob had been was just too much for her. Her thoughts churned over and over through that night. She even got close to prayer in her otherwise agnostic mind. She wished for God to mend Peter's body sufficiently for them to enjoy each other's company one more time. She later realised she meant… *at least.*

Jan was churning over in her mind whether she was being sent out too early. It wouldn't do the company too much good if her review of the situation led them to start thinking about a claim on their Keyman Insurance cover, and an instruction to a tribe of headhunters to find a replacement the Chief Executive. It wouldn't, she further thought, do her much good if Peter was severely damaged.

She had only got to know him over two days and, she realised, it had been unusual for her to have accepted his invitation of hospitality into the evening. It was, she supposed, that he was a nice man, no doubt commercially brutal at times otherwise he would not have got to where he now was; but he was kind and had that graduateship in the development of a dynamic personality which one only gets from studying on the street, as opposed to the campus.

Strange, she also thought, he had mentioned Girasol, his place in Spain, and had said she must go out there sometime. How very strange if this was indeed that calling. She presumed BCG would pave the way for her to have time to do her job. They'd get prime access to him. Little did she know she would be fighting the press, police, other well-meaning friends, and family too. It was what she referred to, when speaking to her mother, as being her 'quieter time' anyway, so she would ask for an open return ticket. She was quietly looking forward to a change of environment and slightly slower pace for a while. Maybe she would get out there on Thursday.

The impact of the previous 30-odd hours was just sinking in for Tania. How the hell she hadn't worked things through more clearly before, she suddenly just did not know. Her body began to tremble. It usually curled up quite easily in bed, particularly as her lifestyle and lack of permanent attachment meant she enjoyed her bed to herself. Marguerite no longer came through in the night for maternal comfort; that must have stopped six or seven years ago, such was the secure feeling Tania had been able to instil in her since taking up her new life at Girasol.

Yet now Tania was lying awake, overcome by fear.

If the news of Peter's 'accident' was spreading across the news channels, the police would soon have to release the identities of the bandits to complete the story.

'The family', the tightly-knit community of Romany wanderers, would certainly know who Toni and the cousins were. They knew very well why they had been put away all those years ago and Tania had received word that even from within the security of the courtroom, and the prison, Toni had been able to issue a family edict that Tania should be 'taught a lesson' for giving the evidence that had put them behind bars.

Her beating was well deserved in the first place. She was Toni's property and that special chattel should not have been allowed to be messed with by another party, especially outside the family. Toni and the cousins never knew exactly who it had been. Their theory that it was Peter was totally destroyed when it was discovered he was on his way through France to England. Except, of course, with their usual clumsy inaccuracies, they had interpreted the date incorrectly. The police at the time of the trial had confirmed to Tania that it would not be unusual for there to be a vendetta pledge, even in the modern era in which they lived. That encouraged her to vanish from Calella and move, with an effective change of identity, to Girasol.

Tania's mouth was now dry with fear. Had Toni tracked her down, or was it just coincidence they were hiding in the hills, almost within sight of her hanging out the washing, had they been so inclined to break the restraining order? Now word would be released that the cousins had been shot dead by the police. Would there be a link that she again was the catalyst? After all, that's what she had told Maria.

Oh, what a day. Supposing the family were to find her? The vendetta would follow the principle of an eye for an eye and a tooth for a tooth. Death. Death for her would mean orphanhood for Marguerite and no birthright, as Tania was about to sign that away. All that, and Peter close to death's door.

Maybe the police could help her when she went to see them with Maria. Maria would help. Maria, she was sure, was a friend. She was safe until the names of the bandits were released. She was safe anyway in the knowledge that the Girasol hotel was brimming with police.

That reminded her of what she'd heard in the bar just hours earlier. That the bandits had no form of identity. Perhaps they never would have and the family would not get to hear who they were. But then there would be fingerprints, surely. They'd get to know. Names would have to be released.

"Oh God," Tania whispered. "Oh God, bless my Peter and first and foremost help him to recovery. Then, if you have time, only if you have time of course," she confided, in the usual chatty way in which she prayed to God, "please help me. For Marguerite's sake, save me from my roots. Please teach the family to grow up and give up on pointless traditions. Eyes for eyes and teeth for teeth won't solve anything."

She sobbed as she expressed her fears to her God. She must have sobbed herself to sleep, eventually.

Gina had gone through the motions of expressing her love for her husband. She was desperately tired and it helped to be philosophical, knowing that as long as she acted out her marital vows, she would get away with keeping her new emotions to herself, without questions. During their lovemaking, she now admitted to herself, she had been thinking about Benito. Would he, at this very moment, be pretending to satisfy his wife too? Well, if he was, so what? She sensed it meant very little. Gina wondered if Benito Alvor had had the same initial effect on his wife as he was suddenly having on her. She had been swept off her feet.

Even so, he had been the one to talk of a bond, a bond from which no one other than themselves would get hurt. That seemed, at least to her, to be equitable.

Supposing the positions were reversed and it were her husband who had established a similar relationship with some super-efficient bank cashier? Would Gina understand that relationship, as she thought she was beginning to read her own? It didn't matter, she told herself. It was hypothetical. She lay there wondering if Benito Alvor would remember saying they'd meet to talk things through. She knew he would, or at least prayed he might. How would she find an excuse for that? Supposing they were seen. Then people would get hurt. It would have to be a very private encounter. He was very intelligent. He'd work something out.

In the meantime, Gina knew that what had finally brought them together was, in fact, the young man whom she had always felt she knew well, now older and with some sort of superstar status she did not quite understand. She had obviously missed out on seeing Peter's career develop from being the hired hand, part-time chauffeur and physical trainer to the dreadful Marcia Hunt to the high-flying position he now clearly held.

He would pull through, of that she was confident. She bet he'd be walking, in a manner of speaking, within days. She had seen patients with determination before. They walked their way through a variety of pain thresholds. Then she

236

had seen the reverse. The ones who were precious with themselves, and winced their way through every twinge. Peter would not waver towards that category.

"Can't you sleep?" Her husband's voice broke into her thoughts.

"I'm just a bit strung up. I'm OK. Saturday was possibly one of the more taxing ops I've been through." She thought: *in more ways than one.* "Go to sleep. You've got to run the bank tomorrow. Got to be bright for that." She always made out her husband didn't just work for the bank but was so important in his contributions that he actually ran it.

She turned towards him and kissed him on the forehead. Now if that was Benito, he'd know how to lull her to sleep. What had got into her? She was thinking as she would expect her daughters to react over a new boyfriend. Had the work and the intensity affected her mind?

CHAPTER 25

At just before seven on the Monday morning, Maria awoke to find José at the side of the bed, battling with a cup filled with tea in its saucer.

She opened first one eye, then the other. "Hey! Room service, eh!"

José joked, "Well, you've been up and down all night. I was going to let you sleep in but I know you've got a lot to do. So I thought I'd help you to do it gradually. Incidentally, I've brought you your robe. There's been a posse of press outside all night and I'm sure they'd love a photo of you slipping across into the bathroom. 'Carefree mother bares all to get her son out of the headlines', the lead story would be likely to read."

"José, darling. You're still the loveliest man on this planet."

"Not lovelier than Peter!"

"Oh, come on, jealous! That's different. He's lovely in a way that can only be between mother or father and son or daughter. You know what I mean. You're just really lovely as my man."

She sat up and drank her tea. "I don't care what time it is in South America, England or Malaysia. I really must let the grandchildren know how things are."

Petra was asleep as it was the middle of the night in South America, but once awakened, she was pleased to hear her father's progress. Coco was up and working, and both anxious and delighted to get the update.

Alex swore he'd been awake but wasn't too convincing about it. He was nevertheless pleased to hear the update and was planning to fly down.

José warned Maria that the list of people who had called was getting even longer. The whole international media-following public were aware of what had happened and those who recognised the name Peter Martinez had looked up their Filofax Christmas presents of the previous year and traced the centre of operations to the Playa.

Maria said that after she had showered she'd check with Marco how he was coping, then shoot off to the hospital and, from there, fix up with the police to see Tania and then confront the press at about 11. *What a busy schedule,* she thought.

When Maria was allowed in to see Peter once the team had finished with him, he was actually sitting up in bed and having a bowl of cereal and a cup of coffee for breakfast. He wasn't perhaps quite as quick as he would usually have been but, unprompted, he greeted his mother with a determined, "Hello, Mother."

"How are you, darling?" she said emphatically. He didn't have to think for too long.

"OK. Yes, OK. Still a bit confused. I know I've damaged this shoulder," indicating his right one, "and this leg. They still hurt me. But nobody will tell me what happened. Will you?"

"Yes. But when you've had some more breakfast and a bit more rest. I'm sure the doctors will tell you when you're ready."

"Tell them I'm ready," he responded in his more normal, determined way.

"Listen. You mustn't sit here fretting about anything other than getting better."

"Mother, tell me something. When the door opens, I can see a man in uniform reflected in the mirror. Is he police?"

She just did not know how much she was expected to tell him. Once he got a few degrees better, he'd turn this place inside out, she knew that.

"I'll find out for you. There's a nurse there, certainly, to stop you being disturbed."

"Why won't they open the shutters?"

"The sun might hurt your eyes." (And she was sorely tempted to add: because some bastard interfering member of the paparazzi would take the photograph they all wanted for their 'Millionaire caught up in crossfire' or the 'Was he meant to be there?' story. But couldn't.) "Darling, be patient. I promise as soon as they say you're ready, all will be explained."

"OK, then. I'll believe you. Many wouldn't."

She realised that had been one of his favourite expressions as a child, whenever he'd had to take her word for something. At least she was now hearing that again. Twenty-four hours before, she'd had her doubts about ever hearing it again.

Sñr Alvor appeared at Peter's bedside. "I can see you're progressing, without asking."

Peter smiled. "I'm sorry," he said with a long pause. "I really don't know who you are. I know the face. But I don't know who you are, let alone know your name."

Alvor held out his left hand tactfully. Peter looked confused but shook it with his own left hand.

"I don't usually use this hand, do I?"

"I really don't know," Benito Alvor responded honestly, "but you'll have difficulty for a while using the other one."

Peter looked at the damaged arm, a bit perplexed.

"I'm the surgeon who put you in all this plaster and bandages."

"Oh… I see."

"Peter, I need you to be patient. You're a very intelligent man. Can I ask you, do you still feel confused?"

"A little… I think," Peter said honestly.

"I need to test you. If I say New York is in America, what would you say?"

Peter frowned. "I'd say it is."

"Good! If I said Paris is in France, would that be OK?"

"Yes, because it is."

"Good. How about if I told you, you've broken your leg. What would you say?"

"I'd ask how I did it."

"… And if I said to you, do you know how you damaged your arm and leg, what would you say?"

"Other than you told me I'd broken my leg?"

"Yes."

"Then I'd say I wouldn't have a clue."

"If I said what's the last thing you remember before this conversation and seeing your mother yesterday, what would you say?"

"I can remember a dream, but I don't know what it was about. Oh, I can remember sunflowers." Each time something else came into his mind, he pre-empted his responses with a sharp, shocked, "Oh!"

"… And anything else?" Alvor pursued his questioning.

"Oh, and walking."

Benito Alvor left Peter's memory to unfurl without assistance.

"Oh, a fiesta. Oh, and blue light."

"Peter, have a break. I'll be back in a few minutes – I promise not with more questions from me."

Sñr Alvor stepped outside. He suggested the officer join him in the sister's office along the corridor.

"I've just checked out the patient but I regret to say he's not ready to talk to you."

"Look, Doctor…"

Alvor interrupted. "I'm not a doctor. I'm a specialist, and I'm exceedingly knowledgeable in cases like this. Twenty-four hours too early and you run the danger of implanting ideas into the patient's empty memory bank, which are then there for good. That eventually makes him a very unreliable witness, if he's needed."

"My office has told me I must get to speak to the patient."

"I frankly don't care what they say. The man is in my care and if I say no, it's no. But I realise you have a job to do. I tell you what, I'm happy for you to come in and listen to me talking to him, but that's conditional."

"On what?"

"You wearing a white coat and making out you're a medic."

"I'll phone the office."

The office had agreed. Maria was tipped off as to what was going to happen and insisted on being present, in her son's interests. Sñr Alvor repeated his previous line of questioning and, not surprisingly, Peter's brain and memory had not moved on. The consultant and his makeshift colleague took their leave, returning the patient to a one-to-one with his mother. Peter seemed tired. He closed his eyes, then surprisingly he spoke.

"Mother."

"Yes, dear."

"Am I alright?"

"Perfectly, darling. Your body has had a bit of a shock. But apart from that, you're perfectly OK."

"You would tell me, wouldn't you?"

"Yes, of course, but there's nothing to tell at the moment."

"Good! I'll sleep, I think. Will you come later?"

"Yes. To force some food into you."

"Oh, Mother. Leave me be." He'd hardly finished the sentence before his eyes were closed and he was asleep.

Maria stood up and kissed him on the forehead. She said a courteous, "Adiós," to the officer and headed down the stairs. It was the same staircase as led to the intensive care unit. *Gosh,* she thought, *was that only yesterday?*

She looked at her watch. Tania was going to the hospital at 11 and they had arranged to see the police in a mobile police unit that had been set up in the grounds. When Maria arrived, she realised the unit was in full view of the press, whose hunger was growing for a story ahead of the official release. So she'd asked the officer on duty outside Peter's room to get it relocated to the police station just 400 metres from the hospital itself.

Maria got to the foot of the stairs and, without hesitating, turned to the right and into the chapel. God was receptive, she thought. She thanked him for the progress thus far and in return, He assured her He would take her through the press briefing alongside the police and Alvor.

As she left, she said to herself, "Now to deal with Tania." She hadn't thought quite how to play it, but then she didn't fully understand Tania's great concerns. They'd have to see.

There were just two officers: one was male and they appeared to have seconded a female officer to the interview to deal with Maria's request. Maria had indicated it might assist the police in their enquiries.

The male officer, who was obviously of senior rank, introduced himself as Superintendent Santé, and said he was going to put the police position to the press at 11.

"And this is my colleague, Sergeant Pulao, who will conduct this interview."

Sergeant Pulao was quite small-framed. Hardly big enough, or strong enough, to get through the rigorous trauma she must have had to get through to become a senior in the job.

"Ladies," she began, "how can we help? What do you wish to tell us?"

Tania looked petrified. Maria led the conversation. "Can I presume that you know I am the mother of the injured man in the hospital?"

"Yes, Mrs Martinez. We know that."

"Can I ask a pertinent question, which is fundamental to what we're here to say?"

"You certainly may ask, but you'll understand we're not here to provide answers. We may not elect to reply. You'll have to trust that position," the officer responded.

"Then I will. Are you able to identify my son's assailants?"

The senior officer shuffled uncomfortably. "Why do you ask?" he said, to the annoyance of his female colleague.

"Well, if you do know who they are, then we have nothing to say."

"And if we don't?"

"Then we think this young lady may be able to help you identify them."

"I think you should accept the trust my colleague mentioned. Anyway, why not presume we don't know?" he said.

"Then we'll have to." Maria turned to Tania. "Do you want to talk or shall I continue?"

"Oh please, Mrs Martinez. You go on."

"Tania has worked for my hotel for about 25 years. She's a trusted friend of the family. You'll tell, though, from her complexion that she's not of our stock. She's got Romany roots.

"About 20 years ago, she went home from working at the hotel. Even now I don't know the circumstances, and they're private to her, so I would ask you to respect that fact. When she returned to her home village, she apparently encountered someone who alleged he was her husband, or, in gypsy terms, was entitled to be. They had an argument, which I understand was about whether she'd had an affair with somebody at the hotel. She denied it but, so the history books will show, her boyfriend didn't believe her. She was severely beaten up as a punishment, without any hint of a Romany fair trial.

"Tania will tell you, because it's a matter of court record on oath, that the young man, who she didn't feel the same way about, tortured her to tell him the truth. Two cousins were also involved. The judge called them psychopaths of the most dangerous order, probably influenced by drugs. They were found guilty and imprisoned for life. Since then, the probation and welfare services have kept in touch with Tania to help her through her recovery.

"As employers, we haven't had anything to do with that, we've left her to her own privacy. But since her evidence was the principal reason for the three convictions, the police at the time suggested it might pay to change her address. Obviously, all this is said in confidentiality, but it's the point of us being here. Tania was advised a month or so ago, she now informs us, that Toni Cortés and his cousins had been released from prison and…"

"Let me hold you there," Superintendent Santé interrupted. "You said Toni Cortés." He turned to Tania. "What was the name under which he was convicted?"

"Oh, I see." Tania started speaking for the first time. "Of course, we all knew him by his mother's name. When he was convicted, it was under his father's one. It would have been Herez. Toni Herez. That's how I shall refer to him as the police record."

"Police work is about jigsaws a lot of the time," said the superintendent. "Shall I carry on your story for you? Toni Herez was indeed released about the time you mentioned. In the police bulletin, there were two things mentioned. One was that there was a restraining order against them approaching two girls. From what you say, you were one of them. Who would the other be?"

"My younger sister, Beth. But she's not in this part of the world. She moved right away."

"I can't tell you, I'm afraid, what the second matter was but tell me, has Toni Herez been in touch with you?"

"No."

Maria interrupted. "Tania, you must tell the police everything."

"Well, I was driving along the main road a few days ago and my heart turned over because I thought I'd seen them crossing the road. But I wasn't sure."

"Why do you not want to tell us about this, miss?"

"Well, two reasons really. I was told by the probation officer I'm in touch with to tell the police if I got any sightings of them, and I didn't, so I thought I'd be in trouble."

"Why didn't you?"

"I wasn't sure, and they scare me and I thought if I reported the sightings they might find out it was me again who shopped them and… well, the family have great rules on loyalty. Beating a woman up is frowned on by Romanies, they'd get no support from others in the family for the original attack. But messing with someone's freedom is a real no-no, and if they'd been arrested for trying to make contact with me and maybe sent back to prison, the next generations would hunt me down and punish me again. It's the laws of the tribe. Now I've got my daughter and we've had a life of peace for 20-odd years. It was too much to risk. I thought they'd have matured and seen I have no interest in them, and have quietly moved on."

The male officer had clearly taken over completely. He now turned to Maria.

"Thank you for bringing Tania along. To be fair, I can say you have helped us. We don't at this moment have the evidence that will tell us who the bandits are. We have their fingerprints but as the international bureau, where prints of more than five years old are kept, has been closed over the weekend, we won't get our positive identity until late this afternoon. We'd presumed that these gentlemen would have records but had no way to tie them in with Toni Herez."

Santé turned to Tania. "I have to say, if you had come forward when you first thought you'd seen them, none of this might have happened."

"But I could have been punished."

"Well, that's true… still, there is another avenue we need to go down. I think I ought to caution you both that the next series of questions must be on the record. Sergeant Pulao, I need you to take formal notes. It's about your son, Mrs Martinez. Did he know this Toni?"

"Good God, no."

Tania's hand went up to her mouth. Santé noticed her involuntary movement.

"Are you sure, Mrs Martinez?"

"Yes, absolutely."

"Tania, you seem to think they were acquainted."

She crossed herself. "Oh God, why are you doing this to me?"

"Tell us the truth and God will look after you the way He always does. Tell me, do you think Peter Martinez and Toni Herez are acquainted?"

"Oh, Maria, I'm so sorry. I have to tell the truth. In a manner of speaking, they did know one another. One night Toni and the cousins beat Peter up. He always said to me he could never forget their faces."

It was Maria's turn to look aghast. "Tania, he would have told me. If they'd beaten him up, it surely would have shown."

"It did. It was when he walked into the tree."

Maria's hands covered her face. Exposing herself from behind her temporary shield of shock and shame, she said, "But that was so convincing. Are you sure? Well, I suppose you must be. Oh, now it's my turn to ask questions of God."

"Ladies, I'm prepared to continue this discussion together but I must warn you, it may lead to you being dealt with individually."

Maria's mood changed. "Dealt with, officer? What exactly do you imply by that? You will remember, and I must ask your colleague to make a note, that it was I, we, who asked to see you to help you with your enquiries. Your tone is leading me to feel under suspicion."

"You're an intelligent lady, Mrs Martinez. You must see the difference in the situation now that we know your son has been shot and seriously wounded not by bandits he didn't know, but by bandits he did know. Tania, do you know why your cousins beat Peter Martinez up?"

"Not really."

"Did, or does, to your knowledge, Peter Martinez take drugs?"

Maria stood up. "Look, this is getting silly. I'd like to call my lawyer."

"Why is it getting silly, Mrs Martinez? Supposing the gypsies had supplied your son with drugs as a student. If he had reneged on a payment, then unfortunately users do get beaten up. There's a further background to our current enquiries. The secondary reason why we're so keen to interview your son is to find out his version of what happened. Now Tania, what do you know about their relationship? Your cousins and Mr Martinez."

"It was nothing like you'd suspect. Firstly, I'm absolutely sure Peter Martinez does not indulge in drugs, and never has. Secondly, I doubt Mr Peter had ever spoken to Toni. What caused him to get beaten up was twofold, or so I understand. The first reason was due to Toni's insatiable jealousy. Peter asked me to dance a Sardana with him, in public, at a fiesta. We knew each other from the hotel. Mrs Martinez will tell you I had a soft spot for him when I was a young chambermaid and he represented everything I admired, so kind and generous, the handsome son of the owner.

"More importantly, on that day, there'd been an enormous fracas at the hotel. Mr Peter had walked into the staff changing room to get something from his girlfriend's locker and he caught my sister and myself changing, and I thought I could capitalise on the situation and blackmail him into a relationship he had no desire whatsoever to have. At the fiesta, Toni asked Beth, my younger sister, who Peter was. She had been plied with sangria and was tight and said he was the one who got caught peeping at us in the hotel staff room. Toni went into a blind rage, waited for Peter by his car, and seriously beat him up. I, of course, suffered punishment too."

The door opened and a young officer walked in with a note. He handed it at first to Sergeant Pulao, who passed it over to her superior. Santé looked at it and then at his watch.

"We're meant to be on our way to the press conference you called, Mrs Martinez."

"Oh hell, I'd forgotten all about that. Tell me, Superintendent, where is all this leading to now?"

Santé looked at Sergeant Pulao. She indicated she was in agreement with his unspoken thoughts.

"Look," he said. "I'll level with you both. We suspect it was coincidence that these three bandits were close to Tania's home. We didn't know who they were but the underworld led us to believe they were drug-runners. Word had it that they were due to have an assignation with 'Mr Big', a drug baron we've wanted to know about for some while. He's a man who uses convicts, or people who can't make an honest living, to distribute his filthy wares for him. We believed, in fact, to be honest, subject to all our further enquiries, we still, I suppose, have to believe, that 'Mr Big' is your son, Peter Martinez."

Maria stood up again very slowly. "Look, I can see some circumstantial evidence that might make you believe that but I know it's absolutely unfounded… but I accept you'll have to get to that point by yourselves.

"Surely we've got to get the media circus off our backs. On the one hand, so that my family can have a normal existence through Peter's all-important convalescence. Then, from your point of view, to flush out your drug baron, if he hasn't already flown.

"Why don't we go to the press briefing? Say what each party had intended to say. Undertake to keep them informed and ask for privacy until your enquiries are through. I'm sure Tania and myself would accept any sensible restrictions you put upon us."

Quite where Maria had got this ability from, none of the witnessing trio could fathom. She had suddenly run circles around a senior police officer intending his inquiry to go only in the one direction, and knocked him off course. Santé looked again for agreement from his junior officer. She read his apparent thoughts. In fact, she'd probably agree to anything the more confident Maria had suggested.

"OK, Mrs Martinez. I wish to have a signed confidentiality agreement that you'll work with the police in this matter and not divulge any of this discussion elsewhere. Furthermore, there shall be an officer present at all your attendances with your son in hospital. You, Tania, will have a friend staying with you for a while, morning, noon and night. It will be a female officer, armed and with radio contact with a base. Nobody is to know the true identity. Failure to comply and we'll have to put you into a safe house to protect you. We hope you'll be some bait for the next generation of cousins to come out from under their stones to seek vengeance for the loss of their brothers."

Both Tania and Maria, for their different reasons, agreed.

The press conference was now 30 minutes late. "May I formally introduce myself. I'm Superintendent Santé of the Gerona Police Regional HQ."

Benito Alvor was comfortable in the student lecture theatre they had recently added to the hospital's facilities. Maria wasn't. Neither was Tania, placed with a temporary friend in the audience seating looking towards the four chairs on the rostrum. Santé was trained for such occasions. He had insisted Alvor should stick to medical evidence, Maria to the personal issues and that the police should lead any answers to questions from the now hungry press.

The fourth chair on the rostrum was taken by the local authority press officer, who opened the proceedings. He commenced, remaining seated as the international TV cameras rolled and cameras flashed.

"Ladies and gentlemen. Firstly, may I welcome those of you who are not representing the local press to Palafrugell. Normally, as I'd like the press to report, we are merely a backwater on the way to tourism in the area. We have no sea or sand but, as Benito Alvor, one of our eminent hospital consultants will tell you, we have a superbly equipped hospital, now extended to keep pace with the requirements of the additional hundreds of thousands of visitors the area now attracts each year. We also, of course, have a modern internationally influenced police force for our changing environment.

"May I apologise for keeping you all waiting an extra 30 minutes for the first official announcement to be made regarding circumstances about which you are currently jumping to your own conclusions. The format of this briefing will be concise and to the point. We will invite questions, of course, but because of the nature of these events, which are still unfolding, we may wish simply not to make comments.

"I would further say this briefing has been stimulated by Mrs Maria Martinez, whose son is still lying in this hospital recovering from what is believed to be an unfortunate encounter with bandits intruding into our hillside. Ladies and gentlemen. Chief Superintendent Santé will give you a synopsis of events."

Yes, Santé confessed, his officers had been tracking three bandits. Yes, they'd been on the point of an arrest. Yes, the bandits did resist and were armed, and finally, yes, Peter Martinez was injured in the crossfire.

Alvor immediately sensed that would not be good enough for these hardened pros of the press corps. Even he could see the leading questions were bound to be, "What was Peter doing there anyway?"

Sñr Benito Alvor was introduced next. He gave a clinical review, beginning with the part played by the paramedics, the helicopter crew, his supporting team. He was able to report that the damage suffered was life-threatening, not caused by a single gunshot but by cartridges from a hunting device that had caused the complications of spread shot damage inside the right shoulder and close to the patient's heart and right knee, which entailed micro-surgery. In terms of the patient's current condition, he was off the danger list. Stable. Talking, and taking light food.

For Maria's part, she could not praise enough the medical attention her son had received. She understood the paramedics had had a major role in saving her son's life. She was optimistic and prayed to God for his safe recovery, but asked that the media representatives give them all space in which to convalesce.

Some reporters were taking statements down in shorthand or, who could tell at a distance, speedwriting or T-line; the more IT-influenced had sensitive audio cassette recorders to pick up every word, which they could then distort.

The local authority press liaison man invited questions. Hands shot up like a class of schoolkids who had all just remembered to do their homework.

A local newspaper correspondent, known to the local authority liaison man, was the first to be invited to put his questions. If the story was good, he'd shoot it down the line to Madrid and Seville if their papers weren't represented.

"Can you tell us more about the hospitalised man?"

The PR man for the local authority gesticulated with a raised open hand. "Who better to do that than his mother?"

A voice from the third row piped up, "Why not the police?"

That put the panel into some disarray. The PR man said, "I think his mother."

The voice this time came from the same man, who was now standing. "Surely we need to hear the police version."

"Shall we ask the first questioner who he thinks would be the most appropriate?"

"For my purpose, Mrs Martinez. I'm just seeking background for my readers."

Maria started. "Well, he was born in Rosas and educated here in Palafrugell. He studied architecture in London and designed and developed Girasol Resort. He's been living in London for over 30 years but loves, or should I say, did love to come back home."

"Why do you think he might not like to do that in the future? Will he want to avoid the police?" came the voice from the gentleman who was promoting the case for the police to answer.

Maria looked perplexed. The PR acting chairman asked if the local man had the information he wanted.

"Not quite," he replied. "Various of my colleagues allege Peter Martinez is a very rich man. Would you subscribe to that?"

"He's rich in family support and in the way Sñr Benito Alvor and his team cared for him."

"Madam, you'll have to appreciate none of this glib stuff is going to sell newspapers. Can we try and get the truth out of this story, then we can meet our editor's deadlines." This came from a now agitated British man in the third row.

"Would you identify yourself, sir?"

"Yes. Grant Tovey, UKM, United Kingdom Media, the UK's biggest tabloid company." There was a hint of laughter in response from his fellow journalists, who obviously did not agree with the rating.

"OK, Mr Tovey. What's your question?"

"I have a number of questions. Are drugs associated with this story? Could the police, rather than the mother, answer please?"

"We're still in the early days of our investigations," Superintendent Santé volunteered.

"So are drugs on the agenda for inquiry?"

"All angles are being investigated."

There was suddenly more attention being given to the note-taking.

"The official hand-out refers to the bandits as being unnamed. Can the police name them?"

"We'd rather not answer that question," was the official police response.

"Can you confirm that the police shot three bandits?"

"Yes."

"And did they also shoot Peter Martinez?"

"No."

"Did Mr Martinez know the bandits?"

Santé thought that if only Tania hadn't been to see them, he could have answered the question and moved on. How did he answer this one now?

"Lines of enquiry will pursue that."

"Is that a yes?"

"No. It's not."

"Then is it a no?"

"It's a factual statement that the circumstances of the bandits and Mr Martinez's meeting is fundamental to our inquiry."

"Can I ask, on behalf of our readers, if drugs were on the agenda, was Mr Martinez in fact part of a trading network? He's very rich, apparently. Do the police suspect that Mr Martinez is the drug baron we've heard has been operating here for a while?"

"We have no comment."

"OK, no one's being very helpful. Let's ask the mother to comment. Can you say whether phone calls to South America and Malaysia are the norm in your household?"

Officer Santé turned and looked hard at Maria. He seemed shocked and as eager to hear that answer as all the vultures on their perches on the opposite side of the table.

Maria was now angry. Her privacy was being invaded.

"Would the gentleman from the British press tell me if it's his company's usual habit to tap into private phone calls?"

"So you're saying you *did* make those calls? So are they routine?"

"No! I am *not* saying I made those calls. Whether I did or didn't is of no consequence. I'm asking if, for you to have made that suggestion, you've been tapping our calls?"

"With all respect, Mrs Martinez, the calls are of consequence. A mother is likely to come to the assistance of her only son in times of need. My imagination just leads me to ask whether calls have been made to renowned drug-trading centres in the world and if they might have been made on your son's behalf."

The officer and all those in the room were stunned by the exchange.

"Sir," Maria said, "your imagination is not only flawed, it portrays the mind of a person wanting to be mischievous for the sake of one banner headline, and to then move on to upset some new innocent's life. I see it as no business of yours whatsoever but, for the public record, yes, I did phone South America – not once, but twice. Not to cancel a delivery of drugs, but first to inform my grand-daughter of her father's accident, and then to tell her about his progress and put her mind at ease. Likewise, I phoned another relative who's currently in Malaysia with the same messages. If your information was complete, you'd know I also phoned my grandson in London, who's due now to be flying out to see his father.

"On the topic of my son being wealthy, I'd guess he probably is. He's made all his money out of property-related matters and I'm quite sure the UK tax authorities can supply you with his tax returns.

"For my part, I don't wish to say any more, so please excuse me. I'm due to visit my son to check on his improvement."

"Doctor, when would you expect the patient to be able to tell us his version of what happened?"

"Maybe at the weekend."

The aggressor in the third row came back for more. "Will the police confirm they've mounted a police guard on the patient?" Santé thought again, as he had been trained to do. "There is a police presence in the hospital."

"Is that because the patient is under suspicion, or even under arrest, or just for his own welfare as a result of having fallen foul of a Romany family?"

"The police do not wish to comment."

The PR man felt he was now somehow a wiser expert than before.

"Ladies and gentleman, we set 15 minutes for this conference. It has now overrun by ten. I therefore duly close this first exchange of information. We'll meet again on, say, Friday. In the meantime, we would ask you to respect the family's wish for privacy."

Third Row Man was certainly not going to go away. He called out, "Can the ladies and gentleman of the press rely on the police PR machine informing us regularly, say daily, of new information?"

Santé always needed press support; besides, he liked his wife and her friends telling him they'd seen him on TV or read his comments and how very interesting his job was.

"Yes, as normal," he replied.

The PR man said, with some relief, "OK. We'll call that a day. Thank you."

CHAPTER 26

It was one o'clock by the time Maria's negotiations with Santé as to the way the officers would accompany her on her visits to Peter were concluded. They would be plain clothes officers and, from the beginning, they would explain they were police, there for their joint protection.

Sñr Alvor thought that by that evening, Peter might be able to be told how he had been shot, providing there were two officers present – one to ensure nobody would try to influence Peter's story, the other to note precisely what he did say.

Maria entered the room. Peter was sitting out of bed with a table lowered a comfortable height in front of him. There was one large empty plate with a knife and fork correctly parked on its rim, signifying that Peter had finished his meal. He'd had chicken and rice and told his mother he had enjoyed it. No, he hadn't had a bowel movement but on the positive side, he had stood by the side of the bed supported in a frame, which Maria thought more suited to a geriatric ward than for the use of a youngish man. *Still,* she thought, *if it supports him then it doesn't matter what it looks like. It's progress.*

Peter was very much more alert. He leant forward as though wishing to confide in Maria. She was suitably responsive but cautious, on account of the presence of the female officer she'd asked to have on her first accompanied visit.

"Who's your friend?" Peter whispered.

She had to keep faith with her pledge to Santé, so included the officer in the dialogue.

"Peter's asking who you are. Is it alright with you if I tell him? He's more likely to relax if he knows."

The officer agreed.

"You had an accident, which is likely to be explained to you later today, if you're up to it. The police want to see me properly looked after, so they have me accompanied almost everywhere I go. So this is Elspeth. Elspeth, you know of my son, Peter."

Elspeth smiled, almost flirting with this strong, upright, rather handsome inmate.

Peter held out his left hand. "Sorry, the other one doesn't work too well. Hi."

He actually had no real news. He didn't mention the fiesta and seemed pretty well back to normal.

"I'm pleased they're going to tell me what happened because I don't think I can remember. They say maybe one word and it'll possibly all come back to me. I hope so, anyway."

An hour or so earlier, Mr William had been sitting at the top of the boardroom table at head office. He'd had a call the night before when the head of PR had somewhat accidentally switched on to the UK evening news bulletin.

He was known as Mr William because his father's name was William too, but he had always been addressed by his surname. So when William Junior came into the business, and before he demanded rank, he was addressed by his Christian name alone. As he had climbed into his seat of power, he had demanded to go up a notch and be known as Mr William.

Mr William was like one of his own labradors with a bone once he got hold of a topic he could start whingeing about. He had whinged all his life, really. All the way through public school. Then, at the insult of the junior position his father had put him into in the family business, which led on to his criticisms about the way his father chaired the company. Along the way, he moaned about racehorses and the way they performed, and likewise the ineptitudes of his first and second wives, whom people thought had both left him because he was such a shit.

The bone he just could not put down these days bore the name of Peter Martinez. Not that Mr William dared mention it publicly, but he'd convinced himself that he had never trusted the Spanish since the Armada. That was just his excuse for still being annoyed that the three all-powerful Non-Executive Directors had persuaded him, with the force of the requirements of the institutional shareholders behind them, to move away from the dual role he had commandeered for the previous decade as Chairman and Chief Executive. The Board doubted he would actually have nodded through the appointment of any of the shortlisted heads on the hunting block if he was not certain he would still retain the power he had inherited when his father was ousted by his coup, for exactly the same titled position, ten years earlier. He'd bought him off with a life presidency. Which, of course, in the event meant nothing.

So, at any opportunity, Mr William tried to steer his colleagues against the new incumbent, despite the fact that Peter's presence and influence to date had been, in William's terms, the coincidental reason for the shares having moved upwards by 28 per cent. Peter's press conferences and the private 'chat' sessions he had organised with selected pension fund and banking investors had really gone down very well, but tended to disturb any support there was for the Chairman's hand on the reins.

So when the news of Peter's reportedly very serious accident broke, Mr William's personal secretary had phoned the 11 available members of the Board to break the news, some that night and the others early in the morning so that, as a Board, they could consider their position. The second piece of information she passed on was that the Chairman had called an emergency Board meeting for the following day.

William presumed the Board would go along with his idea that he should revert immediately to the role of Chairman and acting Chief Executive until, at least, they could assess Peter's capabilities – assuming he'd pull through at all. He'd thought it a good idea to get Jan Roberts out there when Peter would not be at his best. Her unflinching and consistent honesty in her interviews would no doubt confirm that Peter's future ability to control the BCG empire was, at best, in doubt.

All this news was just too good for Mr William, thus far. He thought he would take control from the start of the meeting. Three Non-Execs were able to attend. Apologies were noted by the company secretary for three absent Executive Directors, who all had, quite naturally, other plans. They were at the sharp end of their divisions running the business.

William opened the meeting with its single agenda point. Peter Martinez. "I suppose we ought to deal with apologies."

The company secretary, Brian Jones, who ate so voraciously out of the Chairman's hand that it would even have been obscene at feeding time at the zoo, listed the three execs who couldn't make it.

Sir Richard 'Dick' Richards, who so often appeared to take a lead role for the Non-Execs, now had the delicate task of supporting the Chairman for old times' sake, and the recently appointed Chief Executive for future times' sake. The latter was his long-term preferred option, as he could see the day when William's lack of contribution and real helmsmanship would be rumbled and the group would go the fashionable route that others had taken by appointing a figurehead Chairman. William would, he felt sure, be reverting to his long-winded calls to his stable girls to obtain their views as to whether their charges were on or off form (his only daytime mental exercise), and then he'd be off to the bridge club or casino at sunset.

"Chairman," Sir Richard led from the middle of the table, "I presume we are at a formal but unscheduled Board meeting."

The Chairman looked to his Company Secretary.

"Yes, it is. It's been called under the emergency powers vested in the chair," Brian Jones ruled, with a slight plum in his mouth.

"Good. I just thought we all ought to know that."

William's shoulders relaxed into their more normal stoop, then tensed just as quickly as Sir Richard carried on.

"Only I notice there's no apology from Peter. I assume he was invited?"

William looked across the table to Brian Jones. "Well, was he, Brian?"

"I have no idea, Chairman. Your personal secretary called the meeting. I was only informed about it when I got in at 8.35 this morning," he said, making the point, as company secretaries and accountants so often do, that he was in, as always, early.

"Anyway," William reasoned, "the chap was in no condition to be asked and the point of the meeting is that, for all we know, he might by now be dead, and we could be in the position of not having a Chief Executive."

Dick Richards now had the bone. "I think you're missing the point. As a member who's going to be the subject of formal discussion, I think he normally has to have been invited. Usually, a gentleman knows when his attendance isn't desired and he takes appropriate action by not turning up, but still apologises for the record."

"Oh, balls! I just don't agree."

"Chairman." This time Sir Cyril Smith decided to speak. "Why don't we revert the meeting to an informal one? After all, it would be helpful for us to know Peter's health status anyway. If that's going to be stated informally, it wouldn't need to be officially recorded.

"As much as anything, I've got the shareholders in mind. Make no mistake, they and their advisors couldn't have missed the news bulletins. If they know we're sitting here talking about 'what if Peter can't continue for whatever reason' in panic, because of Peter's success thus far, they'll probably start a wave of selling. Surely we don't want that?"

"Oh sod it," William reacted grumpily. "That's fine with me. We can be more outspoken that way. I'll tell you why I'm concerned. There's the risk, in any event, that Peter will either not pull through, or at best do so with some form of permanent mental or physical disability. I've had pieced together the facts that, for a time after the incident, Peter was short of blood, which bodes ill for the brain. His shoulder took a short-range shot from a shotgun. You've all seen what happens to a pheasant or a grouse, so you can imagine he could lose an arm, or the use of it. Then he's had his knee shot to bits, apparently…"

"Chairman." It was Sir Richard again. "I've seen the news and read Sunday's papers, which hardly covered the event, and then this morning's versions, which don't seem to be reporting in as much depth as you are now. How are we able to assess the position on the basis you're outlining?"

William smiled inwardly. *There you are,* he thought. *I'm jumps ahead of all of you, and by the way, it's not what you know, it's who you know, and how you use them.* Outwardly he'd need to be more factual.

"Well, in confidence, on Sunday morning my good friend, Lord Rothman, phoned me to offer condolences on Peter's reported demise. Being head of UK Media, he gets all sorts of preview reports before they hit the presses. He offered the group help in the form of one of his employees, a fiery investigative reporter named Grant Tovey. Of course, you know Rothman is a BCG shareholder and he was saying that, reading between the lines, all was not what it seemed. There've been rumours that Peter was part of the bandit set-up that tangled with the police. Allegedly, and of course we all know it couldn't be true, the local thinking is that Peter might have been the one sponsoring some drug-running."

Sir Richard interjected. "Look, William old man, it's just as well this is an informal meeting. We really shouldn't be hearing words like this. 'Allegedly', etc is for the gutter press Lord Rothman owns. They're not papers I like to read or am in the habit of reading…"

William interrupted. "Look, I'm telling the Board in confidence what a very good, dependable friend of mine told me. That I see as my duty as Chairman. Let me also tell you what I've arranged. This chap, Grant Tovey, will ferret around over in Spain and keep me directly informed, alongside Rothman, as to the state of play. He's probably currently at the first press briefing and I'd expect an on-the-scene update within a couple of hours. After all, the Board should take notice of the fact that there's been no effort yet by any member of Peter's family even to give us a thought."

Sir Richard bristled. "William, you're being unfair. The poor bloke was shot to bits on Saturday and underwent major surgery and was out of the world as we know it until well into yesterday. That much I can pick up on the news and in the quality newspapers. It's not as though the poor bloke has had a moment to open his eyes and, in a last gasp, mutter 'please let the Board know… phone…' before passing away. It's now Monday and our switchboards are open. Do we know if there've been any answerphone messages, any attempts for anyone to update us?

"I personally think this is all very sad. There's no hint that anyone round this table has a thought for how Peter is and what help he may need. Furthermore,

I'm uncomfortable about making any judgments on the reliance of what a chap called Grant... what was it?... has to report. Why should we?"

William could see the impetus falling away from his lead. "Because, Sir Richard, I've agreed to share the expense of Mr Tovey in Spain with UK Media."

"What! That's cheap! We, a respected public company, employing the services of the gutter press to protect our shareholding. I move that what we need is an immediate press release to say we're shattered by the news of what's happened to our appointed Chief Executive, but that the Board is reserving judgement on the situation until representatives have assessed the position. You said Jan Roberts is going out – she can be our on-the-spot reporter. In the meantime, we're confident that Peter's strength of character and physical fitness will hold him in good stead. We might also express our concern for members of his family at this difficult time."

"Hear, hear," came a response from Sir Cyril, then the other Non-Execs in turn.

Suddenly, the Board was in almost total unison. William was the odd one out. Not for the first time in his life, he felt outdone.

"Alright, gentlemen. I agree. Brian, see that wording gets to the press office. Tell Tim to get it out by the usual 4pm deadline. Then we make the evening news if anybody finds it appropriate, then the morning papers. I'll keep you privately informed of what Grant Tovey reports."

"I wouldn't bother," Sir Richard mumbled.

CHAPTER 27

Just before 7pm, Sñr Alvor, Superintendent Santé, a recording officer and, despite Santé's objection, Maria, were gathered together in Alvor's office to discuss the way Peter would be informed of the details of the shooting. Alvor explained there were medical ways in which to stimulate the brain's re-awakening, and Santé would have to go along with that. The superintendent reluctantly agreed.

Benito Alvor entered Peter's room within earshot of Santé.

"How's your day been?" he enquired.

"Good," came the answer. "My bowels worked and the pain's not so intense." Peter frowned. "Not like me to miss a visit. Was it last Saturday? I didn't remember that, even. What's today?"

"Monday."

"Gosh, that's two days I've missed out on."

"That's good, Peter. I think this might be quite easy for you. Do you remember Saturday?"

"I think I do."

"You went to Girasol."

"Yes, that's right. Sunflowers. Oh, that's right, I sat in the garden with the sunflowers."

"Do you remember anything else?" Alvor's questioning was gentle. He was not a trained psychiatrist but had plenty of experience in remedial treatment.

"No. Nothing," Peter said blankly.

"Were you in a sun chair?"

"Yes."

"Was it a warm afternoon?"

"After golf it cooled down."

"After golf?"

"Yes. I played golf."

"Do you know who with?"

"No. I don't."

"Did you win?"

"No." He paused for moment, then something seemed to click. "José Jnr always wins. He's good."

Alvor would have to coax out of him who José was.

"So it was a warm afternoon after golf?"

"Yes. I felt sleepy."

"Did you drop off to sleep?"

Peter hesitated. "I dreamt, I think."

"Do you remember the dream?"

"Walking. I went walking."

"By yourself?"

"Yes."

"Do you always walk by yourself?"

"Yes. Quite often."

"Wouldn't José walk with you?"

"No. Too dangerous."

"Too dangerous. Who said it was?"

"José Jnr."

"Why?"

"I don't remember."

"This dream. Were you just walking alone in this dream?"

"No. No. I think on my walk, there was a fiesta."

"At a place you know?"

"No, on the walk. In the trees."

"A big fiesta?"

"No. Bad people at the fiesta."

"Dangerous people?"

"Yes."

"How did you know they were dangerous?"

"José told me they were dangerous."

"Peter. That's enough of my silly questions. We'll have another chat another time."

Peter looked quizzically at Benito. "Aren't you going to tell me what I've got wrong with me?"

"Yes. After you've had a rest. I'll pop back about ten. I don't want to excite you too much. Your mother and the officer will stay with you."

Peter looked at the young policeman on duty with his mother. "Why does he need to stay? Just mother will be nice."

"It's like your friend José said. It could be dangerous."

"José is my brother."

"Really. Is he?" Benito Alvor had never heard of him having a brother before.

Alvor turned to the policeman and indicated: was it OK to ask more questions about the brother? The officer nodded. Santé was out of Peter's sight but listening intently.

"Brother. Brother José. I didn't know you had a brother?"

"He's my stepbrother."

"Stepbrother?"

Peter was tiring. He turned to Maria and said, "You explain."

Maria looked to get sanction from Santé to do the explaining for Peter. She got the nod. When she turned back, Peter had his eyes closed. He was drifting into a shallow sleep. Alvor indicated that Maria should continue.

"José is the son of my second husband, so yes, he's Peter's stepbrother. He and Peter own the golf course at Girasol. It's one of Peter's loves, to play golf on the course he helped to build and design."

Peter opened one eye, just said the single word, "Yes," and then was asleep. Sñr Alvor beckoned to Maria and Santé to come over into the doorway.

"I'll guess," he said confidently, "that as Peter has in his mind that the walk was in a dream, he may just dream the actual circumstances and act out what happened, and could wake up and repeat it. It could be jumbled the first time round. Then, if I tell him how he was wounded, it might just all come back to him. Not as clear as a TV documentary, but the bones of the history will be there. Of course, that's a guess. Everyone's different."

"Would you object to us taping the repeat bit?" Santé said.

"Well, we would be basically OK with that but I'd rather do it on our equipment and then it's part of Peter's medical record. To be honest, it's a long shot, but the risk is he could just dream that he's a drugs baron and wake up announcing that fact. That, to my mind, would not be constructive clinical evidence and I think Peter ought to have the option on that piece of tape. Remember, he's not under any form of police caution."

"You're a clever chap, Doc! To be fair, I can see you could be right. I'll have to go along with it as a matter of police protocol. OK. The awakening will be confidential, if we rule it needs to be. Is that OK with you both?" He included Maria.

They both agreed.

How she too would have given anything to close her eyes alongside Peter. She was exhausted. The brush with the press had done her no good. The prognosis put forward by Santé had really knocked the stuffing out of her.

She fell into a nap and Peter's stirring brought her to. Benito Alvor touched her arm, sensing Peter was disturbed and probably in a dream.

Santé had also nodded off. He had done so with his clipboard, complete with bulldog clip, laid across his knees, the police-issue metallic cased Philips detailing machine finely balanced on its surface. One knee had fallen away from supporting the clipboard as he slumbered. The dictating machine slid across the board and fell heavily on to the hard surface of the hospital terrazzo. The noise on impact echoed around the silent room, followed by the heavy thud of the clipboard and its metallic clip not far behind its mechanical companion.

They all jumped.

Had Peter not been restricted by his heavily weighted shoulder dressings, he would have shot into an upright sitting position.

"Gun!" he shouted. Alvor had had the presence of mind to switch on the tape automatically as he picked up the dictating machine and as soon as the explosive impact had happened. Maybe he'd been in time. Who'd know until he played it back?

Peter's eyes were wide open. He was dazed. He turned to Maria and said, "Silly. No, it wasn't. I was at a fiesta. Fire crackers."

Alvor let his presence be seen by the patient. "Fiesta?" he questioned.

"Yes."

"Where?"

"On my walk in my dream."

"Lots of people, Peter, with fire crackers?"

"No. I don't know why not. People happy and shouting. In uniforms."

Then his complexion went ashen. He screwed his eyes up as his face aged ten years.

"Oh God," he said, as if in pain. "Those eyes again. Not those eyes again. They always hurt."

"Whose eyes, Peter? In your dream?"

"Tania's."

"Tania's? Hasn't Tania got beautiful eyes? Tania's a pretty friend."

Still with his eyes shut, Peter laughed. "Not Tania's eyes. Tania's friend's eyes."

"What friend of Tania?"

"Don't know. José Jnr said dangerous."

Superintendent Santé, now wide awake, was on the edge of his seat. They all stayed silent for a while. Peter was again the first to speak. He was close to tears.

"Mother, help. Help me… please."

"I'm here, dear," she reassured him.

"Mother, the walk is not a dream. It's not a dream, is it?"

She looked at Santé to seek permission to answer. He nodded.

"No, darling. It's not a dream."

Then Santé's deep voice, to which he hoped he had attached a modicum of compassion, spoke firmly.

"No, Peter, it's not a dream. It's how you got hurt. Can you tell us what happened?"

Peter pondered the question. His eyes were still shut.

"I did play golf. I did lose. I did go for a walk. José Jnr had said there was talk of danger in my hills. They *are* my hills. He said bandits. Dangerous bandits. Not in my hills, I said. There's no danger. Then I saw those eyes. Tania's friend's eyes. Black ones. Dangerous ones. They wanted my money. OK, they could have my money. There were gunshots, not firecrackers at a fiesta. They pointed guns at me. Then they fired. The shots sounded not too near. Then there were two blue flashes. Loud, like when you kill a boar, like with father. They hurt."

He tried to sit up. "Mother, Doctor. What happened? Tell me I'm alive."

Maria said, "Of course you're alive. What's more, your own brain has told you what happened."

Santé suggested they have a break. Maybe Peter could do with a hot drink or some soup. He'd clearly gone through another ordeal. Offered the options, Peter asked if he could be washed. He felt unclean. Then could he have some chicken broth? Sñr Alvor suggested Maria and the two officers should have some coffee or juice and that they should go outside to have it.

"See you in 30 minutes," he said to Peter. "Well done. You've done really well. You're a good patient to have."

For some reason, although he had jerked up some pain in his brain, Peter felt good. His brain seemed to have cleared. He suddenly thought about Coco in London, then Marcia, the insatiable Marcia Hunt, and being home with Marco and Virginia and Maria and José senior, as he nicknamed him. He was comfortable with life.

Thirty minutes later, it had been agreed that it was now Superintendent Santé's uninterrupted turn. The evidence being sought would be after a formal warning. He might need to be forceful. Alvor recommended to Maria that they had no option but to agree. As a concession, Santé did agree that Maria would explain the importance of the resumed line of investigation.

"Peter. This is Superintendent Santé. He needs to question you. He also needs to tell you that what you say may be used in evidence. Do you know what that means?"

Peter laughed. "Have I been caught speeding, then?"

"No. You must be serious. Do you know what that means?"

"Oh yes, Mother, of course I do. It might be written down and used in court."

"Yes, it's going to be recorded and then you can hear what's been said tomorrow, and it'll be typed and you'll be able to sign it."

"Fine," Peter confirmed. "Can I still write then?"

Alvor reassured him.

Santé recapped. "Is it a fact you took a walk? Was it planned? Did you intend to meet anybody? When you met some men... do you recollect how many... ?"

"Three," was a good answer to give.

"Did you know any of them?"

"No," was not the answer Santé had been hoping for. But Peter remained insistent.

"Are you saying did I recognise any of them? Then the answer is yes... they were family friends of Tania... an old friend of mine."

"How did you know them?" Santé continued. Peter said that he'd seen them at a fiesta and because they thought he'd made a pass at their girl, they had beaten him up... yes it had hurt...yes, there was evidence because he'd been to Palafrugell Hospital and had his face treated.

"That's this hospital?" Santé said.

Peter looked surprised. "Maybe. Nobody's told me which hospital I'm in."

Did Peter understand about drugs? Yes, he did. Did Peter have a view on drugs? Yes, he had. Could he express that view? Yes, he hated drugs. Did he have friends who took drugs? No, not that he knew of.

"But I bought treatment for a friend who was on drugs once."

"Do you have connections in South America?"

"I married a girl from South America. Sadly, she died. My daughter used to visit quite often to keep up with her grandparents. Now she lives there."

"What about the Far East?"

Peter answered. All this apparently pointless questioning was nevertheless stimulating his memory back into gear.

"Do you have a bank account in Spain?"

"Yes. I think it's very modest though."

Benito Alvor held his right hand up as if to say, "The patient has had enough."

"Finally, do you think you could identify your assailants?"

Peter thought that one through. "Only if they had their eyes open."

"Fine, Mr Martinez. Thank you for co-operating. Perhaps I could call back in the morning."

"Sure! I'm not planning anything special."

Alvor, sensing the interview was over, he felt with some relief, countered what Peter had said. "Yes you are, sir. I need to look at the 48 stitches I put into your body, and then I want to see you move your knee. So get a good

263

sleep. I'll leave you now in the good hands of the night staff. I'd recommend a sedative," he said to the duty sister who'd come in once the junior officer had left, "he's just come out of hibernation."

Maria said she would leave too. She bent over and kissed Peter's forehead fondly, and whispered, "Well done." She turned to the sister. "Dile lavate bien." She left.

Peter felt relaxed. He wasn't sure why the police were so interested, but so what. He knew he needed sleep. Tomorrow, he felt he would understand all.

CHAPTER 28

Tuesday morning, and Peter woke up feeling refreshed for the first time in a while. Maybe he had been on the other mornings but didn't know about it. He wanted to get moving on.

The sister seemed an obliging sort of 28-year-old. Perhaps 30, but not to be asked the question. He did have one burning request for her, though. He was lost without a phone. He had a very heavy mobile device in England, which was often more nuisance than it was worth on account of the coverage being totally dependent on spasmodically located masts, so he didn't travel with it.

"Sister. Am I in private treatment?"

"I really don't know. Sñr Alvor just took over your case and we all accommodated it, largely, I think, on account of you needing the police protection. Why do you ask?"

"I wondered if you had a walk around plug-in ward phone I could use. I've got four calls I'd like to make."

"Well, I'll see. But we'll have to clear it with the police if I can get it. Do you have any money for the calls?"

"No, I don't suppose I have. My credit's good, though."

"I'll see what I can do."

She left him and went straight out to the duty police officer.

"As predicted, Mr Martinez has asked if there's a phone he can use. Would that be OK?"

"Give me five minutes and I'll tell you."

The officer pressed buttons on his crackly walkie-talkie. He checked whether they had the phone tap in place. Superintendent Santé had predicted if he was the principal of a drug running syndicate, he would at least try and contact his network to ensure the drugs, which hadn't been passed over, or the money in exchange, which had not been found by the squad of police left combing the hills, were still intact. It was apparently a big money operation.

The officer told the sister she had clearance to provide the phone.

"Did I have any clothes when I came in?" asked Peter, when she returned. "I usually carry a diary with essential numbers in it."

"I haven't seen anything."

"I'll ring my mother. She'll have all the numbers I'll need."

He knew the hotel number off by heart. An exhausted Sñr Martin answered the phone with a very dull, "Buenos dias, Hotel Playa."

"Cheer up, Sñr Martin. It makes the hotel sound drab."

"¿Quien es?"

"Peter. Peter Martinez."

"Good God, Mr Peter! You're the last person I expected would call. The whole world, literally, is calling to ask how you are. *You* can't be ringing to find out, because you obviously know."

"That's actually why I'm ringing. I'm actually dead."

There was silence. Sñr Martin was not best known for his sense of humour. He wasn't even sure he had heard correctly.

"Who can I put you on to?"

"If I was dead, I'd suggest the national press. It would be a hell of a story and I wouldn't want to miss out on the exclusive deal."

"Mr Peter, it's no time to joke. We've all been very worried about you. You don't want me to tell everybody who rings to enquire that you're out of your head, do you?"

"No. I'm sorry. Who's been ringing?"

"Mr Peter, literally everybody I could think of. Your children, a lady called Marcia Hunt, the Admiral, Miss Michelle, your English friend Max, Miss Meribel... I'd lose count but there are lists here... and of course, all the press. You're big news."

"Go on," Peter replied.

"So is it your mother to whom you'd like me to connect you?"

"Please, Sñr Martin. Oh, by the way, I don't mind who you tell I'm dead, but keep the news from Marcia Hunt, I'd like to surprise her."

"She has called, as I said, sir. I'll connect you with your mother now."

"Peter!" his mother's stern voice shouted down the phone. "What do you think you're playing at? You shouldn't be on the phone. You still have to rest."

"Oh come on, I want to tell a few people I'm not dead..."

"Peter. I don't appreciate Max's sense of humour. He's been a bad influence on you. Now listen. Tell me why you've called and then get back to rest..." As she said that, Marco entered the back office and indicated he'd like to speak to her.

"Peter, you'll have to hold for a second. Yes, Marco?"

"Sñr Martin says it's Peter. Is that true?"

"Yes."

"Can I have a word?"

"OK, but don't be long. He's meant to be convalescing."

"Hi Peter. It's Marco. How are you doing?"

"Fine," Peter replied, "I've hardly got a right shoulder and I'm told my knee's shot to bits, but my privates are OK and I guess they still work so, all in all, it's good."

"Well I'm glad you've still got your sense of humour. You'll need that when the press get hold of you. By the way, do you know a lady called Jan Roberts?"

"Why, yes!"

"Well, you'd best get ready for her. She's arriving on Thursday and the press corps, who're already here, are very put out that she'll get to interview you before they do. Word is she's being sent by your company."

"Where's she staying?"

"Here, at the Playa."

"Marco, do me a favour. Give her the best. The first floor the Hunts used to have."

"That's taken by a journalist anyway."

"Then chuck him out. You'll find Jan special."

"Your mother wants you back," Marco said with an air of panic.

"Yup! Fine. Look after yourself."

Marco was actually overjoyed. That was Peter. Powerful, persuasive, personable Peter. But putting Peter's requirements into action with a tough newspaper reporter who had got used to that room would not, he sensed, be that easy.

"Now I'm going to stop this call very soon," Maria said curtly.

Peter explained he wanted the numbers of the head office, Alex and Petra and Coco.

"What on earth are you going to do?"

"Mother, come on. Use your imagination! I'm going to phone them. They've been worried about me, I don't doubt. Look, I've just realised I can't write the numbers down. I'll see you later. I'll get my secretary to write them down for me."

He beckoned to the sister, who had been listening to most of his end of the conversation. She obeyed his powerful persuasion and came and stood at his bedside. He passed her the phone from his left hand, and then let that same hand lower itself to be level with her bottom, against which he let it stray with two playful little pats. She swivelled her hips away with a death-threatening glance, but continued in the task set.

She bade her farewells to Maria and then put the phone down firmly, before swinging round to look at Peter, still apparently furious. Before she could speak, he put his left hand up to his forehead.

"Sister," he said meekly, "I don't feel well, I feel out of control. I just don't know what I'm doing."

"Well, a bed-bath, a water bottle and a bedpan will soon put that right. Oh! And when you've been a good boy and performed the three tasks, I'll break your good arm to remind you I don't appreciate patients patting my bottom."

Peter pressed his hand more firmly against his forehead. "Did I really do that? God forgive me. Oh, I'm so sorry."

Finally, she could not hold back a huge smile. He was destined to need a lot of nursing, she thought, but not on account of a stray friendly, and as she had noticed, very masculine hand.

She got him all four numbers in the order in which he gave them to her.

Petra in South America was thrilled to hear from her father. It was one of the more relaxing calls. She did all the questioning and he hardly got a word in edgeways. She finished the call as her mother would have done. "Daddy, I'm so, so pleased you're OK. Nothing must ever hurt the most wonderful man in the world."

The call with Alex was far more masculine. Had he seen the wounds? How many stitches? "Forty-eight! Shit! Dad, you were really hurt, weren't you? Listen, I was planning to fly out."

"You don't need to do that. I'm fine. I'll be back in the UK in a week or so. We'll meet up then. If you come out here, we won't get a lot of time together. I expect they'll have me into physio in a day or so. Yes, of course I'll take care. You too."

Coco was next. How could he know it was two in the morning? But Coco said she couldn't sleep anyway because she was worrying about him and praying for him. She cried virtually through the whole call as she said she thought it was all her fault. If she hadn't have left him, she would still be there looking after him and he wouldn't have gone to the silly hills filled with bandits. If she was there, she sobbed, she would be able to tend his wounds. She'd been thinking anyway she might give up banking and become a nurse. Were the nurses being kind to him? Did he really hurt? Did they arrest the men who attacked him? Obviously no one had told her they'd been killed but there would have been no need anyway.

He eventually had to say that the sister was pressing him to get off the phone. He promised to ring Coco at the weekend, and to get his time clock right. But, on her insistence, he could ring day or night.

As far as the call to Mr William was concerned, it was a duty call. Peter must have been feeling bright because he rehearsed the sister into pretending to be his real stand-in secretary. She got all the way through to William and only then handed the phone to Peter.

At first the receptionist had asked in an officious way who wanted to speak to Mr William. "Oh!" she said with total surprise. "I'll connect you to his secretary."

The secretary had said it couldn't be Peter Martinez and that it must be the press. Pam, the old retainer/receptionist from the first generation of the company, said she was sure it was him coming on the line. Certainly she could tell it was a call from abroad.

"Oh, put them through," Vera, Mr William's secretary, eventually said, though with reluctance. She then developed a pitched battle with the sister, denying it could possibly be Mr Martinez because the reports were he was terribly injured.

"He *has* been injured badly," said the sister in her best English, "but I assure you it *is* Mr Martinez. Now he's getting agitated and would like to be connected."

Vera had been protecting and covering for William for at least a decade. She rang through to his office.

"It's Peter Martinez."

"It can't be."

"I'm sure it is."

"I'm telling you my information is he's virtually under arrest and in any event, struggling with everything: thinking, breathing, the lot… oh, good God, put whoever is on through."

"Good morning, William. It's Peter, Peter Martinez. How are you?"

William heard it as a voice from the dead. "Peter, I'm fine. More to the point," he added begrudgingly, "how are you?"

"I'm OK. What do you know?"

"Well, we know you appear to have been shot. We don't really know the circumstances as to whether it was some Spanish vendetta from the past…" He had such a habit of aggravating Peter.

"Actually, although I wouldn't want too many to know it, I made a pass at this local lady and her husband didn't like it. Out in these backward parts, such things are still settled by pistols at dawn. The guy was aiming at my balls, hence I was shot in one shoulder and a knee.

"Look, enough about that. I gather no one's been in touch with the company, so I'm checking in. The consultant is restricting me at the moment but I'd say that at the weekend I'll have set up some sort of communication network and we'll get back to business as usual."

William hesitated. "Are you up to a chat, old boy?" he eventually suggested.

"Yes, of course. But I might get interrupted by the medics."

"Look, it's a bit tricky, old chap. Well… to be perfectly blunt, the Board is worried about your welfare."

"Tell them not to worry."

"That's all very well but we don't want the shareholders to react. At the moment, it's only Tuesday. The newspapers are full of your story and Cazenoves have already been asking us for our plans to steady the Stock Exchange."

"Tell them all not to be so bloody silly. My input's only likely to be affected by a week or so. Tell them to pretend I'm on holiday which, in fact, is the truth. I did only plan to come out for the weekend but I've now got to stay over. Put a press release out saying we had a lengthy business call this morning and they should all then turn their attention to some really bad news."

"Look, old chap. It's a bit more delicate than that. The papers are saying you're under some sort of hospital arrest."

"Tell them 'balls'."

"Peter, you're not being helpful. Can you confirm there's an officer at your door?"

"Well, yes. But he's there to protect me from some threat that might come from family and friends of the bandits I somehow got tangled up with. By the way, I was joking about the local bloke's wife."

"Peter. You'll have to level with me. Of course, I'll understand if you say you can't, but I need to ask you directly. Were you in league with the bandits?"

Peter saw this as a ridiculous waste of time but obviously William had been fed some story or other, which he seemed to believe. He'd best take his Chairman's questions seriously.

"No, William. Categorically not."

The papers are hinting that you may be the Mr Big behind a drug-running ring out of Spain into the rest of Europe."

"Do you believe that's possible, William?"

"It's not whether I believe it's possible or not. My role is to protect shareholders' interests and while there's a whiff of that story about, we're exposed."

"Go on, you amaze me. I thought at least you would be able to quash such suggestions."

"Well, I could if… well frankly, it was one of the other members of the Board. I know their histories, their schools, backgrounds, life-long friends who can vouch for them. In your case, you'll have to make allowances for it not being automatic that I can dispel the odd rumour or two."

"Well, if that's the case, William, you'll have to continue digging up the shit until you find one of my old school mates who's sufficiently in bed with some of yours to vouch for me. In the meantime, I'm happy for those who're able to recognise talent to continue to have faith in me, and in my morality vis-à-vis drug-peddling or the like. I've got a flat in London where there could now be four girls co-habiting, who knows, if the caretaker thinks I'm dead. Tell your friends in the press to check out whether I'm running it as a brothel."

"Peter, old boy, you're taking all this very strangely."

"Oh yes, so strangely that I'm too bloody cross to continue this conversation. I'll call you when the communications network is established."

The sister heard him slam the phone down.

"I'm going to take your blood pressure, Mr Martinez."

"It'll be high, I warn you. So bloody high you won't believe it." After a pause: "What was it?"

"Well, I'm amazed. It's 150/85, which is fine."

"Then ring my last caller and tell him to tell the bloody Stock Exchange that the word should be 'buy'."

"Now you're cross. You must keep calm."

"Can you get me one more number?"

"I don't think you ought to."

"Come on, sister… this next call will get you the biggest bunch of flowers you've ever had, let alone ever seen outside a church. The number is 0044 to get you into the UK, then 1 778 1414. Ask, if you would, for Max. Say it's Peter."

In the temporary mobile building in the hospital grounds, two officers wearing headsets looked across to each other as though on the brink of an amazing discovery. One gave the other a thumbs-up sign as they both edged forward in their seats to listen intently. Both had been picked for this duty on account of their good English. They were interested in Peter's side of the story.

"Max. Hi, it's Peter. I'm great. No, really… I'm fine. Yes, shot to bits but I've still got my balls, so nothing's the end of the world. Listen, I need a favour."

"What's that, you crazy Spaniard?"

"When's your stockbroker's account date?"

"July 31st."

"How long's that?"

"Say six weeks."

"Right, can you buy £250k shares in each of the names of Alex and Petra's trusts and an additional £500k in the name of Coco Yim Lam."

"Sorry, old sport. Shares in what?"

"BCG, you idiot!"

"Oh, I see. OK, no questions asked."

"Thanks, but make a note of the price. Instruct to buy at 260p."

"Aren't they 380-400?"

"Not any more. I'll cut you in on ten per cent of the gain."

"You that confident?"

"Too bloody true! Cheers, Max. You're a mate. Love you."

This time, Peter put the phone down and laughed.

"Take it again now, sister," he said in a challenging tone, referring to his blood pressure. "It's peaking. About to go through the roof." Shit, he felt tired and he'd not even got out of bed.

As quickly as Peter had picked up the phone to Max, so William kept his receiver in his hand, flashing his secretary's extension a number of times, much to her annoyance. There really were days when she could see the truth in what some said about her boss behind his back.

"Yes, Mr William?"

"Will you check on Sir Richard Richards' availability and arrange that we speak in 30 minutes or so."

"Yes, sir."

"If you don't let me know to the contrary, I'll presume that's OK and tailor my other calls around that, OK?"

"Yes, sir."

He pressed the cradle bar to kill that call and then released it, which provided him with an external private line that he knew could not be tapped by the switchboard operators in his office. The phone rang for a while. It usually did. She was probably busy doing what she was paid to do.

"Hello," came a Devonian accent.

"Hello," he said in the best imitation he could do of her native dialogue.

She knew who it was instantly. He never seemed to be sure it was her, and always sought re-assurance.

"Is that little Jilly?"

"Yes, Chairman. It is." He always insisted she keep rank between them.

"The little Jilly who's not so little up top and wears tight t-shirts just to turn the Chairman on?"

She giggled profusely. "If you say so, Chairman, but it's not intentional."

"... And the boss supposes it's not intentional that you wear certain underclothes..."

She giggled again. "Nothing, sir, is intentional with me. Sir, I always try to tell you that."

Now this girl was different, he'd always thought. She could look after horses like nobody's business. She loved the animals and indulged them with deep attention. If they won, she always curled up and slept in the straw alongside them in their box. If they lost, she'd offer them condolences and encouragement for the next outing.

Where the boss was concerned, he needed no trainer to get him to peak. He was like butter in her fingers. She always made sure he became too excited too soon to be able to actually screw her, but he talked about doing that all the time when they were alone. He'd arranged for her to have her own caravan at the stables and it was there that they finished up with regularity after he'd visited his animal possessions.

"The Chairman thought of coming down for a visit this afternoon."

"Jilly would be pleased to see him, as would the horses."

"I thought about three."

"Three times, sir?" she said encouragingly.

"No, you naughty girl, 3pm."

"Oh," she said in what he imagined was disappointment, suspecting she put her forefinger into her mouth as she said it.

"Oi'll have to get my skates on then to finish the boys early," she said in her best Devonian.

"Y're sure will," he imitated. "Oh, seriously what did Nostra Dame canter like this morning?"

"She did fine."

"Will she win?"

"Won't be easy to beat over eight furlongs."

"Then I'll put a fiver of your little bonus on her nose for you. You mustn't be a naughty girl and bet on her yourself."

"Oh, thank ye, kind sir."

Then he sent his parting shot, although how he'd had the gumption to invent it, who would know.

"OK, then. See you later, stable-girl," whereupon she replied, "Oh Chairman, you really know how to get a girl in a whirl."

As it happened, his timing was perfect on that occasion, as Vera came in just as the call ended. She often did that because she could tell from the tone of William's voice, which she could hear through the pair of panelled doors separating his baronial suite from her small but efficient cell, that he was making a prat of himself with somebody.

"Sir Richard isn't available for much longer in his office," she said.

"Alright, alright Vera, I couldn't have freed myself much sooner. OK, get him on the phone."

She returned to her own office and got Sir Richard on the line before putting Mr William through.

"Richard, old boy. How are we?" The fact was there was some ice left over from the Board meeting that needed to be broken.

"Fine," came back the response. "Now what can I do for you? Right busy timetable today, you know. Being pressed to move on." His conversations were often like a number of bullet points, denoting a man in a real hurry.

"Won't keep you. Just an update." William tried to follow the style. "Actually made contact with Peter. He was pretending to be OK. Not too severely damaged. Brain's gone a bit. Tried to get me to believe he'd had pistols at dawn over some female he'd made a pass at but her old man found out. Brain clearly not so good.

"Richard, Peter thinks the City will just think he's on holiday and it won't have an effect on share price. However, importantly, I said we just didn't know whether there was any truth in the drugs scandal. He just would not deny it. Just wanted to keep you informed. On a lighter topic, tell Lady Sarah to put the housekeeping on Nostra Dame in the 3.45 at Kempton. My girls say she's looking very good."

"Thanks, William, for all that news. I'd stick to my guns that Peter is OK. I like and trust the chap. Let's take a rain check when we hear from Jan Roberts. Say about Friday. We might get some good news for the Sunday papers. Oh, I'll tell Lady Sarah about your tip. Cheers, William."

"Cheers, Sir Richard."

It hadn't quite gone the way he wanted it to, William thought. So lunch, then the stables and after, just see what develops, he decided.

Sir Richard based himself, in the main, in his executive office at Goodes Bank in the City. He'd been Chairman there for the last seven years and was much respected. Chaps from English public schools, who are 6 foot 3½ inches tall and got a double blue at rugby and cricket at Cambridge, do tend to be much respected wherever they turn up. His other Directorships kept him as busy as he had ever been, except for his stint in Hong Kong in the 80s. Perhaps it was there that had most opened up his abilities as a respectable go-between, from which he got himself high on the popularity list of fashionable Non-Executive Directors.

He had the services of a pleasantly motivated temporary South African secretary.

"Debbie, can you get me Jan Roberts on the phone. Most likely her mobile."

"Yes, sir," she said politely.

She did eventually track Jan down, who explained she was tied up for about 15 minutes. Could she ring them back? Sir Richard was given that option but declined so that he could make some more calls himself rather than having to keep his lines free for her return call.

He dialled the bank's brokers on autodial. He had a direct routing to Charles Davis, who reputedly had one of the best noses in the market.

"Hi, Charles. Can you glance at the screen and tell me what BCG are doing?"

"I don't have to look, Sir Richard, I've got it on permanent view. There's a lot of selling. Apparently Peter Martinez, the Chief Exec..." He stopped in his tracks. "I'm sorry, of course you'd know. Well, his current indisposition is being held against the company at the moment. They're at 302p and being propped. They've got a clear sell tag on them."

"What's the buzz? Why are they being marked down just because one executive gets hurt on a holiday?" Sir Richard enquired.

"There's a fear he's very badly hurt and in the short-term, William McArthur will claw back the Chief Executive helm."

"Well, I don't need to tell you, when he got moved over the shares were 200. I can't see that level happening but they're certainly on the slippery down path. Could you let me know by three what the position is? But you can't expect me to say I'd not expect it to be good news."

"OK! Cheers, Charles. Game of golf some day. I'll need a few bob off you if this continues."

That was Sir Richard's quiet effective style. Everybody's friend, and a real macho at heart. He made a couple of unrelated calls and then got reminded by Debbie that he was due to make the call to Jan Roberts. He and Jan got on well. He was responsible for a lot of her work. He seemed to be on everybody's network of 'who-or-what-do-you-know' for any single event. Jan was his number one interviewer/professional journalist. Not just because of her classic slim legs, but for her professional, honest and open style... and, what was more, her ability to dig deep. It was her in-depth exposé of Peter just weeks earlier that had moved the share price 50p in 48 hours, against the hype that had preceded William being 'moved over'.

"Hi, Jan."

"Hello, Sir Richard," she said, with respect.

"Now what's this I hear, old love, that you've got yourself a trip to Spain on the excuse of helping to tuck Peter Martinez up for a couple of nights in hospital?"

She laughed. "I don't actually think it's like that, Sir Richard. Yes, I've been given a brief, but I have to say, and I would only say this to you as a friend, it seems to be getting a bit cloak and daggerish."

"What do you mean by that, Jan?"

"Well, it's difficult to explain really. I think it's because, as you know, I hate being directed on how to deal with a subject, and that's really what I'm getting. Not through the normal channels, you know, BCG's PR or my agent, but William McArthur's been on to me directly three times now."

"What's he been saying?"

"Oh, this and that," she said cautiously.

"Do you want to tell me about it?"

"Not really, but are you saying will I tell you about it? Then that's different, there are means of charming it out of me."

"OK then, Jan. Will you tell me about it? But shall I lay some cards on the table which might help?"

"Please." Jan was beginning to wilt to his charming and always open, honest ways. She always bet he wasn't like this at home. He'd be just like any other demanding husband, no doubt, bearing in mind his stature. His wife would doubtless be a little woman. Still, here she was talking to somebody who certainly got her a lot of work, indirectly…

"For purely personal reasons, Mr William's after Peter's head. Now I'm very fond of Peter and I got the impression that you liked the chap, because that came through in your various articles. I'll say more when you've told me something about any pressure William's been putting you under."

"Well, the first call, I think I'm right in saying, was to say it's not as superficial as it looks." Jan was smart. If she thought she was right in reading a situation, then she usually was. "The second was to say would I touch base with a friend of William's who's out there for UKM, a chap called Grant Tovey. Now ordinarily, I'd have difficulty having a spritzer in the same pub as Mr 'Bad Reputation' Tovey. He's gutter tabloid stuff and is renowned for 'inventing' stories and then burying the apologies in small print in an edition that nobody gets to read. I doubt if he can afford libel insurance cover.

"Then, just this morning I got another call, which got worse really. The Chairman said would I be prepared to work jointly on the subject with Mr Tovey."

"What did you say?"

"I said perhaps it might be better to cancel the brief and not go. I said I'd meet with Mr Tovey, and of course any other journalists as, for some reason, the place is apparently crawling with press and agency colleagues anyway, because I found it hard to get a hotel."

"What did Mr William say to that?"

"Well, he backed off a bit and said the Board wants me to do the interview. But then I'm not sure, from what I've read, that the poor chap's interviewable anyway."

"Jan. Stick with it, old love. Stay over the weekend and see how things develop. I need you on this one, not to be rolled in the gutter with Mr Tovey, who I remember raking up a load of muck in Hong Kong when I was out there. I think the hospital have done their battle to save Peter's life successfully. We've got ours to come, to protect his business one. William's got an agenda to use this to move Peter away. If you follow the BCG share price, you'll see that's not the way the City reads it, or indeed wants it. Thanks for our little tête-à-tête. Save the boy's life for me and I'll love you forever."

Naughty old conniving flirt, she thought. "I'll do what I can."

It was at three that afternoon that Sir Richard got his confirmation of that forecast. Charles Davis phoned to say the price had hit 250p but there was some support showing and there was a buyer.

An hour later Sir Richard rang a racing mate who would know about such matters. "Who won the 3.45 at Kempton?" he asked.

"Sir Richard. It's unlike you to show an interest. What did you put all the bank's money on?"

"Never you mind. What won?"

He had never heard the name of the winner before.

"And second?"

Again, never heard of it.

"Third?"

That didn't ring a bell either.

"OK. What about Nostra Dame?"

"Oh, I really don't know. She just didn't show."

CHAPTER 29

Superintendent Santé was still very much in the loop but had now moved north to Girasol itself. He had gone early that morning. The night before, he had been pretty convinced that Peter had had nothing to do with the drug-running. It was looking more certain that it was just a case of him being on his home patch, walking in woods he knew backwards, but at the wrong time. There was still some doubt in his mind as to whether the girl was implicated, either voluntarily or under threat. It was just all too coincidental for his liking that what they had heard was going to be a big drug handover was due to be carried out just half a mile or so away from an establishment run by a girl from whom the three deceased gypsies were restricted from any form of contact.

She was in it somehow, he felt sure.

He called his five senior officers at the scene to an evening meeting, but not in the hotel where they all seemed to be staying as they couldn't get back to their bases in Barcelona each night.

They each reported on their own disciplines. The officer in charge of combing the bushes for drugs or money reported none had yet been found. The officer who briefed the national network of police, through which they had selected trained officers for what they termed their 'little men' squad, chaps who looked inconsequential and infiltrated without being noticed or bringing attention to themselves, had some news. The officer linked with Interpol as well. He reported that a large container of 'coke' had come across from North Africa and worked its way up through the outskirts of Barcelona. Commonly the package got broken down as parts of the syndicate bought their street supplies.

South of the French border, they now knew, had been chosen as the place where there was going to be a deal that would send money back into the pockets of those who had started the chain way back in Tunisia. From there, they would shoot the drugs into the affluent markets of the South of France. The port and seas around Marseilles were now virtually blockaded by Interpol drug squads and infiltrators into the gangs, so the Spanish route market price had doubled in just this summer period and had not been similarly closed down.

Santé had put a fourth officer in charge of a stake on the Girasol Playa and whoever might be staying there. By 'borrowing' the government records, which still required passport numbers to be entered alongside guests' names, they were looking for regular visitors on a short stay. They were pretty certain they need only follow up Spanish nationals, or perhaps anyone with a North African connection.

The fifth officer, Officer Perez, was female and controlled the 24-hour watch on Tania. She described the now three nights of shifts as being particularly boring due to their regularity, and said she first got the feeling that there was something false in the repetitiveness of Tania's days. The daughter, too, didn't venture far and didn't seem to do things a 20-year-old might be expected to do. There were no boys on the scene for her, and no male suitors pestering Tania. In fact, there were few regular callers at all. One was a chap called Marco, one of the joint owners of the hotel, who rang daily, though their conversations stuck to business. Anyway, no sign of him arriving yet.

"Maria Martinez rings and makes innocent conversation, mostly about Peter's progress and her and Tania's 'deal'. "I think it's harmless," Officer Perez stated. "They mention how the hotel's doing. Tania reports the police presence, but not in any sinister way. She just thinks it's good for business.

"But there's one strange call. The phone rings and there's nobody there… well, that is, nobody speaks, and then it cuts off. Within a couple of minutes the same thing's repeated but the second time, if Tania took the first call with a businesslike 'Bon dias, Hotel Girasol Playa', the second time she goes silent and doesn't say a word. We've watched her take these calls. She doesn't seem fazed by them but huffs a little. Maybe they're heavy breathing calls from an admirer. We'd guess she's had a few in her time – that's admirers, not just calls. We've got a tap on the line permanently but the durations are too quick for us to pick up. Do you think I ought to get one of our team to get a bit relaxed with her to see what beans she spills out of the can?"

Santé thought for a moment. "No, I think I'll have a chat with her. See if I can frighten her into telling me the facts in her life. I'll fix that for early evening."

Tania was behind reception. Her 'minder' was sitting reading in the foyer. Santé was turning over some papers at the little corner table, certainly well within her sight. The hotel phone rang.

"Buenas noches, Hotel Girasol Playa." No more was said. She replaced the receiver.

Santé got up from his chair, and crossed to the desk.

"Do you get many of those?" he enquired.

"Many of what?" Tania said confidently.

"Ghost calls."

"I don't know what you mean."

"Calls received when nobody speaks."

"Oh, somebody spoke there."

"So what did they say?"

"They apologised and said, once they heard the words 'Girasol Playa', 'Sorry, wrong number' and put the phone down straightaway."

"Wouldn't you consider saying 'that's alright', or something?"

"There wasn't time. They'd gone."

"I've got a sort of intuition going in me," Santé announced. "I've the feeling that phone is about to ring and the same thing will happen again. What happens if you speak next time it rings?"

"I don't know what you mean. I will speak. I'll answer the call the same way. Good evening, Hotel Girasol Playa."

"Well, I'd just like to hear when that happens. Mind if I stand here?"

Tania looked uncomfortable. "Look, you're making me feel as though this is no longer my home. If I feel like answering a call, I will. If I don't, then I'm not going to be pushed into something I don't want to do as part of your whim."

"I'd like you to answer the next call that comes in, come what may. Alternatively, my officer there will answer the phone for you. She's a great impersonator. The caller will believe it's you. Remember, miss, we're here in the midst of an attempted murder inquiry, we believe there may be drug-running and, by your own admission, you're afraid your cousins' family will come and put you down for grassing on the three bandits all those years ago. We're here to catch up with either the guy with the purse strings or the supplier of the raw commodity."

Tania looked on edge. That's what he had to do. He had to rattle her. His hunch was that there was more to the Girasol connection than was apparent. He was sure that would come to fruition.

The phone rang. Tania was hesitant to answer. She let it ring at least seven times.

"Answer it. It may be a booking. Your bosses wouldn't want you to miss that."

"I'm not having you tell me how to run my own hotel."

Santé looked to his officer and flicked his fingers. She was across to the desk in a flash.

"Answer it," he said, indicating that the officer should do exactly that.

She pushed Tania to one side and lifted the handset.

"Buenas noches, Hotel Girasol Playa," she said in an exact imitation of Tania's voice and Romany dialect.

The caller spoke. "Is it you?"

Officer Mendes said, "Si." No more needed to be said.

The voice was on the older side of 50, maybe even 60.

"Can we speak?"

"Si."

"Little sister sends her love."

The officer had to think on her feet. "Is she OK?" seemed an appropriate thing to say.

Tania was inclined to lean across and kill the call but it looked as though Santé had seen that coming, and dared not let it happen. His arm was poised to restrain her. She couldn't hear the other end of the conversation, of course.

"That's up to you as to how she is. Can I get across?"

The officer took a chance, knowing that with any luck, the tap would be on the call any time now. They needed about a minute.

"Just hold on a few seconds, somebody here…"

She covered the mouthpiece, while the vital seconds were wasted. Then: "When?" she asked.

"The usual."

"Si. OK."

The phone went dead. Tania looked embarrassed.

Santé said, "I think we need to talk." As he said that, the phone rang again. "Don't answer that," he indicated to both Tania and the officer. It rang ten times, then stopped.

"Who can cover reception?" he asked.

"My daughter."

"She'll have to do as she's told."

"She always does."

He turned to Officer Mendes. "Don't let this young lady out of your sight. I need to check that call."

He went outside to the front of the hotel and punched in the extension number on his walkie-talkie, which would connect to the officers in charge of the phone tap.

"Santé," he announced.

"Sir," came the reply.

"Did you get it?"

"Yes."

"Where?"

"As far as we can tell, at the border of La Jonquera."

"A land-line?"

"Well, yes. It has to be."

"How far is that by-road, would you say?"

"A good hour. Maybe 90 minutes."

"Great job, chaps. You might just have got us a lead. Keep listening."

It was at times like this that Santé wished he could just have one cigarette and put the packet down, or throw it away, once the craving had died away. He couldn't. One puff even and he'd be back to 40 a day, and the wrath of his wife into the bargain.

He got back onto the walkie-talkie, this time to the central control unit on site.

"Is there another female officer on duty apart from Officer Mendes? Fine, send her as she is. As long as she can deal with transcript she'll do fine. How many officers do we have on duty?"

The answer came back, "Eight."

Santé thought. He'd need at least eight to surround the hotel. He'd need two at the top of the road turn-off from the through highway linking La Jonquera to Barcelona, a couple more halfway down and a couple spare. Who could know who was likely to turn up, but they'd best prepare for a change of shift at midnight.

He issued his instructions with an oral stamp of 'top priority'.

Santé went back into the hotel. Marguerite was now at reception and Tania was with Officer Mendes, looking as white as a sheet.

Santé said, "Where can we talk?" Tania suggested the back office.

The newly seconded woman police officer had arrived, looking a little flustered and in civvy uniform. She didn't know Santé but had heard about his reputation.

"So let's adjourn to the back office, ladies," he said, with a degree of charm.

Tania expected him to attack from the word go. He didn't.

"Tania, I'm worried about you. But before we talk about that, have you heard about Peter Martinez's progress."

"Yes. I've had calls from Maria. Thank God he's on the mend."

"He's given us a lot of detail about his assailants."

Tania remained silent.

"Tell me, how difficult was it being brought up as a gypsy?"

"It was fine."

"Who had the greater influence on you, your mother or father?"

She cringed when she remembered the games she had to engage in when her mother was out working. "About equal," she answered.

"And now?"

"What do you mean?"

"Well now. Who has the greater influence on you?"

That was an uncanny question to ask. "Well, not my mother," she eventually said.

"Why's that?"

"She's dead."

"I'm sorry about that. So's mine. I know what it's like missing her chats with me. You too?"

"Not really. I was away from home most of the time working in Miss Maria's hotel."

"Then tell me about your father's influence."

"Look, Superintendent, this is all very friendly, you delving into my family tree. You've effectively got me under house arrest. What's this all about?"

"Well Tania, it's about two things. One, whether you can help the police further in their enquiries as to why three men would be prepared to kill Peter Martinez. Secondly, whether you are in fact obstructing the police in their duty."

"I'm certainly not obstructing the police. You've probably got your own views as to why my cousins would be prepared to kill. You're the experts, I'm not, but what I do know is they weren't far short of killing me."

"Where's your sister?"

Tania went cold. She didn't answer.

Santé was using the information his colleague had passed on from the phone call. They said the caller was somewhat menacing about how little sister was, and indicated Tania could in some way control her destiny.

"Now it's at this point that I can tell you if you don't co-operate, then you'll have to understand how much trouble you'll be in. I want two things from you. Both of those are about information. If I get that information, then you'll get an easier time, I've no doubt."

For Tania to have an easier time, just for once, was certainly a thought to relish.

"What two things are you on about this time, Superintendent?"

"Let's start again. What influence did your father have on you?"

"The sort of influence any man would have who forced you into incest."

"I'm sorry about that."

God, he needed a cigarette. He had never realised his previous dependency when interrogating. This was again a time he missed them. His walkie-talkie crackled.

"You'd best take this call outside, Super!"

Santé asked if the girls could go and rustle up some coffee. He needed to step outside for a few minutes. They agreed.

The female officers had not worked together before, and the new arrival had certainly not been seconded to Santé previously.

"They say he's OK," the newcomer pronounced as they waited for the kettle to boil. "They say he's very fair, when that's justified, but mean as hell if he doesn't get what he wants."

Tania didn't join the conversation. She didn't want to make friends. She had no doubt about Santé's capabilities. Not once had he diverted his attention to her cleavage, suitably exposed to attract the eye of any one of the male officers who were providing the attention she was nowadays so short of.

"We've got a fix," Santé's caller was telling him. "The call came from a motel on the hill road leading up to La Jonquera border. Mostly it's frequented by lorry drivers hauling up from Gibraltar. They don't have phones in rooms. There's a pay phone that takes a card. The girl at reception remembers a man making some calls in the last 15 minutes or so. He's a chap who she says is staying either with his young girlfriend or even a daughter. He's a Romany type with jet-black hair and sideburns. Apparently he gets very agitated if they can't get the news channel on the room TV. He went berserk a few days ago when the aerial reception went down. The local boys picked up all this information exceedingly quickly. By sheer luck, they had a patrol watching for untaxed drivers doing the north run out of Africa, and on instruction went to see the girl at reception. They just missed him going out, apparently, she said alone. He didn't say where he was going. He's not talkative."

"Where do they think the girl is?" Santé asked.

"Well, possibly still in the room. But there aren't any lights on."

"Could they get into the room, do you think?"

"I've got them on the radio. Do you want me to ask?"

"Yes please. Maybe they could rent a key against the show of a police identity card. They'll be armed, won't they?"

"Yes, of course, I'll ask about a key. Should we tell them what they're looking for?"

"No, just say we're worried for the safety of a girl, and to go easy on her if she's there."

"OK, but why the question of going easy on her? Supposing she's got a shooter? Do they still go easy on her?"

"No. Any signs of being under attack, they're to be fully protective towards themselves, and their wives and families. I'll hold on the line. I want a running commentary on what they find."

"Roger," came back the answer.

Marguerite appeared in the doorway, closely shadowed by Officer Mendes. "Superintendent, my mother says your coffee's getting cold."

"Thanks, Marguerite," Santé said sincerely.

284

She turned to go inside.

"Hey, Marguerite!" She stepped forward.

"Oh, that's OK," he indicated for the officer to back away. "Officer, Marguerite and I will be alright without the police all around us for a few minutes."

"I thought you *were* police," Marguerite said innocently.

"Well, yes… I suppose I am. I'm certainly part of the police, but not quite as brutal as them. Then, you see, they don't issue me with a gun. Do you enjoy it here, Marguerite?" Santé was laying on his charm offensive.

"Yes, of course, it's my only home."

"Has your mother taken you to the family down south?"

"No. She's separated from them really."

"Do they come here?"

"My aunt used to, but then mother said that had to stop."

"… And your grandfather… he comes and goes, presumably?"

"You know him then?"

"Not personally, but I know of him. It must be nice for you to get back to your roots, though. He's been here more often recently, I understand?"

"Usually when he wants shelter or a few pesetas to help clear a debt. Mama usually finds him a job to do as an excuse."

"Can he turn his hand to most things? Painting, I suppose, gardening?"

"Yes, he dug out the patch behind the dining-room, oh, about a month ago, and laid the new decking."

"Do you think your mother's cousins could have been looking for him, over one of his debts or something like that?"

"Look, Superintendent, you've had me talking out here, just chit-chatting away for far too long. I'm meant to be doing reception." She turned to go in and then stopped. "Superintendent. Don't ask Mama about her father and the cousins. She really doesn't want that right now with my father's nephew in such trouble as well."

"Your father's nephew?" Santé hurriedly took a chance at putting two and two together. "Do you mean Peter Martinez?"

"Yes, you knew that, didn't you?"

"Well, I'd never actually worked it out before."

His radio crackled. It was base control just up the road in the car park at Girasol.

"Superintendent. Mission up at La Jonquera accomplished. No harm done. Didn't even have to break the door down. This bloke is a bit of a sadist, by all accounts. He'd left his girlfriend tied by hands and feet to the bedsteads. Poor kid's pretty badly treated, apparently. Seems he's a bit heavy handed on the sexual treatment. She's drugged up and got her mouth taped over. Wait till they get their hands on him. I wouldn't want to be in his shoes. Both the officers have got daughters."

"Was she able to talk?"

"Hardly. They've called an ambulance and a couple of female officers. There's a hospital just south of there."

"Tell the officers well done. Alert all officers in Girasol. I want them wide awake, guns primed but on hold-back. Suspect is about 60 years old. Did they say what car he was driving up at Jonquera? The motel should know. When you know that, circulate all officers and let the car come to the hotel if that's where he's heading. We want this chap alive. I think Miss Tania will see to that for us."

Santé turned back to re-enter the hotel. He passed one of the eight officers seconded to surround the building, then stopped and tapped his hand against the outer right-hand pocket of his jacket. Feeling nothing inside it, he said to the young officer, "Suppose you don't happen to have a cigarette?"

"Don't use them, sir," came an athletic reply.

Tania said the coffee was cold. It was.

Santé looked at his watch. Quickly he realised they were short of time.

"Your sister's fine. She's in police custody and on her way to the hospital. Your father hasn't been treating her very well. No time to go into the detail. We're presuming he's on his way here. That's what we understand by the coded telephone calls. Which way will he come in?"

She looked shocked. "You're bluffing. You couldn't know all that. I'm not falling for it."

"Then we're right back to where we were. If you decide to take up option one to help the police, you'll be OK. That's you, Marguerite and no doubt your sister Beth, isn't it, can come out in the open and you can fulfil the role of mother and father for Beth. By all accounts, she's going to need some convalescing.

"The second route, I'll remind you again, is to work against the police. You can try to obstruct us. All we want to achieve is to take your father alive and interview him. We believe he's in possession of a quantity of drugs, which he'd planned to sell on to your cousins. As it happens, they didn't appear to have any money and we believe they were going to hijack your father and steal the gear. He's doubtless not a stupid man and wouldn't have had the drugs on his person had he met with them last Saturday. Peter Martinez got in the way of all that and your father needs to get back here to pick up the drugs, and we'd guess make for the hills into France so he can ply the goods himself along the beaches there. We've done our bit..." He stopped mid-flow as headlights lit up the hotel drive, then continued in a determined tone, "We've done our bit, we've saved your sister's life, and indirectly your father's."

"He'll come in through the staff entrance," Tania said hurriedly, pointing towards the side of the foyer.

"Let him in. Be natural. Say you'll make him a coffee and show him in here."

He pressed the key to his two-way radio. "Suspect parking at the hotel. Allow to enter staff entrance. Surround hotel and give close cover to window behind reception... light on... shutters open... view one... female officer... and manageress... all not armed... repeat, not armed... shoot, if indicated, to wound suspect if possible... buena suerte." *Good luck.*

He heard Marguerite greet her grandfather loudly. "Papa! Oh good, you're back." She stepped forward to kiss him, which Santé could see through the crack between the door and the frame. Tania was ushering her father into the office as instructed. Santé had taken up position in the manager's chair with his back to the window.

Tania's father followed his daughter into the room. Instantly he realised he had entered a trap. His hand went as fast as a 60-year-old could react into the inside of his light summer anorak. Unbeknown to Santé, his young unarmed female colleague was trained in martial art combat. Her skirt went up around her hips in a flash and a long Mediterranean leg, which would have turned heads on any beach, was flashed in the air at speed. It hit the father on the point of his elbow, making him lose hold of what transpired to be a pistol. The glass in the window behind Santé smashed and the extended arms of two young police officers were thrown between the pieces of jagged glass.

"Deje caer su arma. Ponga sus manos en el aire."

Slowly, Tania's father did as he was told. He had already dropped his gun because of the instant pain rendered by the officer's kick-punch to his elbow. He put his hands above his head. As he did so, he turned to Tania and shouted that she was the daughter of a bitch, and spat at her face from a range of about a metre and a half, or so. A tear rolled down Tania's face.

"Dearest Father, I had nothing to do with this. The police knew everything. But now you'll be saved from the gypsy cousins. You'll be looked after and fed in jail, probably for the rest of your life, and your warped, evil mind of an incestuous vampire will harm others no more." Tania sobbed her way through a truly compassionate resumé of her innermost feelings, knowing what, in truth, was best for both her father and sister, in each different way.

Santé needed to remain in control. There were now two armed officers waiting outside the open door. The two covering the broken window were still in their positions to shoot Tania's father should he make the slightest wrong move. Santé directed the officers in the doorway to come in and handcuff this bad influence in Tania's life. He suggested the female officer take a break and congratulated her on her swift thinking and agility.

"By the way," he said, "it's one of the prettiest limbs yet to save my, or come to that, any life. Right, gentlemen, take the man into custody. Accompany him to a car and sit either side of him."

They did as instructed. The officers at the window were ordered to stand down.

It was now a one-to-one situation with Tania.

"You OK?" Santé asked.

"As OK as I'll ever be. It's not every day you lure your father into a trap that will effectively close him down for life."

"I don't have to tell you he's a bad lot, do I?"

"No, I know him. What about Beth? Is she OK?"

"I'll check for you. I suppose you don't have a cigarette machine, do you?"

"Actually we do. What do you smoke?"

"I don't. I've given up. But just one would be a treat."

"I tell you what, I think Marguerite has the odd smoke on the side. Why don't I just get one from her?"

She came back into the reception area carrying a single cigarette with a box of matches. She handed the cigarette to Santé. He looked longingly at it for a few seconds, then crumpled it firmly in the palm of his right hand.

"I've got more willpower than that," he said with a wry smile as he threw the tobacco remains into an empty umbrella-stand, which he had momentarily taken to be a waste bin. Then, turning to Tania: "Thanks for your eventual co-operation."

Tania laughed for the first time in quite a few days. Santé realised what he'd done with the unwanted cigarette, and apologised.

"That's OK," Tania said, "the cleaner will deal with it."

That was an expression of her pride. She *was* the cleaner but she needed to display a managerial role to try to cover the fact that deep down, she was from distrustful Romany stock, as her father's roots had clearly displayed.

"You were greatly co-operative in the end, you know."

"There was no point in not being. Where does that place me now? Am I still out of favour, or getting back in?"

"Let's see if you were in time to save your sister suffering too much permanent damage. I'll contact the boys at the hospital. Maybe I could use your phone."

"By all means. I do so hope she's OK."

The news was encouraging. They had put Beth under sedation for the night.

The preliminary diagnosis was that she had been severely sexually abused and it would appear she had not voluntarily taken drugs. They thought they had been administered in drink or food. She had no tell-tale needle marks.

"They recommend no visitors for 24 hours. They've put her on penicillin to kill any germs she's had fed into her. I'd say your father needs a medical too. Physically and mentally. Anyway, your sister's going to be OK. Now… about where you are with us. Tell me truthfully, did you know he was into drugs?"

"He always has been. It's a Romany thing."

"No. I mean dealing."

"He doesn't deal."

"It appears he does now."

"Surely to deal, you need money."

"You'd think so."

"He's never had that."

"Well, we'll have to investigate that. We've reason to believe he's kept a consignment of cocaine here."

"Here?"

"Yes. At the hotel. He knew this would be a safe haven which he could get in and out of under cover of seeing you and Marguerite. Do you know, she's actually very fond of him. She told us all about that, she's a typical sheltered 20-year-old who'd tell you anything. She let on that Maria Martinez's brother-in-law is her father."

"Oh! Twenty-year-olds are dreamers, you know."

"Is that not true then?"

"Totally false, but you're not to shatter her illusion please."

"Fine, so let's see if I can structure some sort of respectable exit for you from this whole sordid business. The world and press don't know of your connection with the cousins. I don't see there's a need for that. How can we get you extricated from your father's implication?"

"I don't know. I'd say you pull the strings."

"I'd pull them if we had assistance in finding the drugs."

"Well, I didn't even know they existed, so I can't really help."

"Where was your father working around the hotel?"

"Behind the restaurant."

"What did he do?"

"He built a decked area and a garden store."

"Is the store finished?"

"I'd say so."

"Do you have a torch?"

"Yes, in the lobby. One thing we're not short of here are power cuts."

"Why don't we look in the store?"

"Sure. OK with me."

It didn't take Santé long to discover there was a false timber floor in the small outhouse. Below it were four parcels, each about the size of four cigar boxes piled together. They were sealed in waxed paper and strong duct tape. He lifted one out of its compartment.

"Huh!" he grunted. "Four like this would have a street value of 80 million pesetas if it's treated."

"But that would need to have been bought and my father would never have access to money to fund that."

"He had the equivalent to money in his inside pocket. Did you know he carried a gun?"

"Good God, no! It's not a gypsy custom. A knife, yes. But guns were not part of basic equipment."

"Well at this stage, I'd best pass all this across to the drug squad. I seem to remember some bulletin, oh, possibly up to a year ago that talked of some shoot-out in the south. That was some sort of war over drugs, they thought, but I don't know if it got resolved. We'll see. Enough's enough. Your torch is going to run down if we're out here much longer."

He cranked his walkie-talkie into action and called for his troops to come out to the deck behind the restaurant. He oversaw the four parcels carefully handled into a police van guarded over by a black mongrel labrador, whose tail was likely to fall off if he wagged it any longer, or with more excitement. It understood drugs.

CHAPTER 30

Maria had settled into a pattern for her visits to Peter. She got there about 11, by which time he'd had his early morning medical attention and some physio, and had received and made the odd phone call. She knew Sñr Alvor was due to see him that morning. He had indicated he would review the case with his team and she was eager to get that diagnosis.

She, too, had had a busy morning. Superintendent Santé had phoned her to say he would like to see her as soon as possible, with a view to bringing the Friday press conference forward. Maria had said she would see him by all means but as for being any more co-operative with the press, she doubted that would be on the cards.

She also needed to get from Peter exactly what Jan Roberts's role was to be. The mention of her name in the hotel bar had caused quite some consternation with the other members of the media, so Maria needed to know a little more about the magic spell this young lady would be casting on the scene

Today she felt happy, even lucky, and she was early anyway, so she reversed her routine and went to the chapel first. She thanked God for starting her off with a happy day and prayed for Peter's continuing recovery. She wished God to show her appreciation to husband José and Sñr Alvor. Little did Benito Alvor know how God would react to this request in his direction.

She bobbed, crossed herself reverently and skipped up the stairs to the second floor. The officer on duty bade her good morning and the duty nurse said, "Oh dear," and looked at her watch. "They're still with Mr Martinez. It's been about 45 minutes. I'm afraid I can't let you go in. Do you mind waiting?"

"Of course not. How are you, anyway?"

"Good, thank you. One of the kids is home with a cold but fortunately my mother's on hand, so it's no big problem."

They exchanged small talk. "Look, I'm sure you're busy. If you have a magazine, I'll sit here and wait out of the way."

The nurse found a copy of Spanish Cosmopolitan and Maria caught up with what the buzz was in magazine language. It was then a bit like the school bell going at the end of an allocated period. There was shuffling from the other side of the private room door as the medical conference concluded.

A couple of the underlings were released first, obviously with assigned tasks. Maria now knew the faces quite well, although she had no names to link with any of them. She could see Gina, though, hovering in the background. Sñr Alvor was in deep conversation with a person Maria had not seen before. She was a tall, upright woman in her mid-30s, with light brown hair and a tanned complexion. She didn't look Spanish to Maria. Gina was the first to break rank and go across to Maria.

"Gosh, what a change in circumstances since Saturday," she said chirpily.

"Is everything OK?" Maria asked.

"Well, it's not up to me to say, but it all seems good. Obviously there's a long way to go. Peter's wounds were pretty grim. But he's making good progress. Sñr Alvor will tell you, I'm sure." Gina seemed elated. "I gate-crashed the viewing. We were operating early this morning and I asked if I could have a peep at Peter."

Sñr Alvor appeared. "Hello, Señora Martinez. You look good."

"I'm feeling good. What's the news?"

"The shoulder I can deal with, that's pretty routine for me. The knee is what they call a different kettle of fish. It's probably the most complicated joint in the body. I've called in the assistance of this young lady, Fraulein Smitt, who's an orthopaedic consultant from Germany, specialising in knees. She's on the way to being the tops. Anyway, she's prodded it around and twisted it and turned it under a stethoscope to assess how it's grating and grinding. She's fairly happy but is recommending we get Peter into a specialist physio unit they're developing in Barcelona. It's designed for sports injuries principally, footballers and snow ski ones. She thinks Peter would benefit from that, so we might talk about a transfer in four or five days' time."

"You won't take him away from me, surely?"

"If it's for his good, then the answer has to be yes. Anyway, you could get down there in a couple of hours so you could see him maybe twice a week, and besides you could do some shopping."

"Now, that's a good idea. Can I ask an impertinent question?"

"Try me."

"How long do you think before he can return to England?"

"Ordinarily, I'd say four weeks. In Peter's case, because of the 'Peter' factor, perhaps three. However, if he has his way, and with the assistance of a wheelchair and nursing at the other end, I wouldn't rule out two weeks, once he's had, say, ten days of treatment in Barcelona. But why the hurry?"

"Oh, because of the 'Peter' factor, and because there'll be pressure from his company for him to be helping them make all the right decisions before long. I think they'll flounder without him. We sometimes even do, in our own little way. He's an inspirational leader and consultant."

The door had been shut once the whole team had left. Suddenly, it was thrown open as if hit by a tornado or a tsunami.

"Like fuck I need to go to some quack unit in Barcelona! Would someone be so kind as to get me a taxi. I'm off to the airport."

They all turned in amazement. The fraulein was speechless. Gina was shocked. The police officer looked panicky and the duty nurse moved across as though to bar any exit through the outer door.

Maria reacted swiftly. "Well, my son," she pronounced. "First, you'll have to shuffle through a barricade of journalists, and the photographers and film crews will get what they've been waiting for to plaster over the front page of their newspapers. 'Tycoon in a hurry… forgets to put his trousers and underpants on'."

Peter stopped in his tracks. He looked down to find that his bed robe, which tied at the back, had been lifted up during the consultant's inspection and had got itself stuck to the top of the dressing high up on his right thigh, revealing a very masculine Peter Martinez in the raw.

"Shit! Now who's responsible for seeing I'm dressing properly?" Whenever he felt exposed in any way, Peter sought out anybody he felt should have been advising, or looking after him.

"You are," his mother said abruptly. "Now be your age and behave. I'll come back and see you when you're human. Out of this spoilt brat paddy."

Peter reacted like a scalded spaniel. He turned with tail between his bare legs and hobbled with the aid of a walking frame back into his kennel. Maria thanked Benito Alvor and Fraulein Smitt for all their interest and headed through the guarded door to avoid further confrontation and breaking down when on a one-to-one basis with Peter, as she would have done, as part of the apology she owed him for treating him like a small boy. But it had been essential.

She remembered her earlier call of the day and wondered what Santé wanted. He wasn't letting up on the importance he either placed on protecting Peter's life or keeping him under surveillance in the hope of tying him in with what appeared to her to be that horrible reporter's plot. Gina was waiting in the corridor to walk down the stairs with her mentor, Manuel Alvor. "I haven't had the chance to say thank you for nominating me to go to the conference. I'm sure there are others on the staff far more deserving than me."

He smiled and tweaked her left cheek between his gentle surgeon's thumb and forefinger.

"I thought it would get us out of this environment. We're always behind masks, and tensed up with the rigours of the job when we see each other. It'll be quite a relaxed occasion." Thank God he hadn't said 'affair', which was on the tip of his tongue. "You'll be allowed to doze off during the first day's proceedings so that you're ready to dance the night away after the dinner… God, how stupid of me, I haven't said can you make it? Can you make it?"

"Yes, of course."

"Thank goodness for that. I would have been devastated if you couldn't… so there you are… I got to the point of you being able to dance the night away, and that was it really."

"I usually follow everything you say, I don't quite get the dozing off bit."

"Oh, that. Well, I don't get away with a couple of days off, it seems, ever. I've got to do a paper on current trends in emergency surgery… an hour should do that. As you'll know everything I talk about, you're excused… that's when you can sit at the back and doze off. Would you like to drive down from here? If we left about ten, we'd be in Barcelona by, say, midday, comfortably. I don't know if they put a programme in with the letter but there's a casual lunch and then a formal session between 3 and 6pm. The first night's dinner is a pretty formal affair." *(Shit, he'd used the word but she didn't flinch… that was lucky).* "The second day gets busy and the evening has almost got back to being like those old medical balls… a lot of fun and joking. Then it's home the next morning. Tell your husband I'll look after you."

She looked steadily at him, remembering it was only four nights before that their barriers had been dropped. Masks off, just for those few seconds.

"Do I need to reciprocate those sentiments back to your wife?"

"No. No. Not at all."

"So you just behaved like a stupid spoilt boy who didn't want to go back to boarding school. What got into you?" Maria was castigating Peter for his outburst. "You, my dear Peter, are nowhere near getting on a plane just yet."

"Come on, Mother. I've always had to move on. Or had a target of moving on anyway. I've got a business to run. I see BCG as a hugely interesting opportunity… but I understand what you mean. So anyway, now I know the plan I can weigh up the options."

Maria passed on what Manuel Alvor had outlined and repeated his predictions on moving forward, asking Peter to be reasonable for everybody's sake.

"Well, OK, perhaps a week in Barcelona. I'll do double physio sessions if need be, so that would effectively be two weeks, four days more than they want me for. Max has enquired for me, and St Thomas's in London has a specialist knee unit too. They're, on balance, years ahead in the replacement therapy business. So don't worry, old luv, if I did get on a plane, with my trousers on, I'd have something in mind the other end."

"Peter darling, I have no doubt you would have. You always do. Now listen, there's something else I need to know."

"Now Mother, they say I need rest. A lot of sleep during the day. When you talk of your 'something else', I know it's going to get heavy. So I'm going to have a nap. Ask me next time."

"It can't wait till next time. Tomorrow's another day. Tell me, who's this Jan Roberts?"

"Come on, Mother, I'm sure I've mentioned her before. She's the company's preferred PR/profile maker. She did the piece on me I sent across from London. Why the interest?"

"For a couple of reasons. Firstly, you've let it be known that she ought to have the 'Marcia Hunt suite', which has led to enormous problems because on Monday, Marcia phoned to say she'd seen the news of your 'accident' and felt she had to come across."

"Oh shit, Mother! Not Marcia here as well as the paparazzi circus."

"I said to leave it and see how you were and I would level with her as to whether dropping everything and flying out would be worthwhile. The way it was for health and police security reasons, she might have come all that way and not been able to see you, which, let's face it, is the point in her coming. So by Tuesday, when Jan Roberts seemed to take over as flavour of the month, I put Marcia off. She says to send her love and to say she was always confident of your recovery because she'll know when your time is up. Which I think is a grim thing to say. But that's Marcia all over." That did bring a knowing smile to Peter's face.

"On the Jan front," continued Maria, "the media people are saying that's their lot, they might just as well go home. She'll get the exclusive. How's she do that?"

"She's good, for a start, and what she says will be respected by the world of big finance. What would you say if I warned you she could make me £1 million overnight on share price movement?"

"Wow! Then she is important."

"The other thing is, she's lovely. Very kind and absolutely straight. But don't let that get to you, there's still only one girl in the world for me."

"Who's that at the moment? You haven't told me."

"Mother, you're an old soak for compliments. You know it's you. You're my one love through thick and thin."

Maria was speechless. She didn't think she'd ever heard him say that before. *Maybe,* thought Maria, *this Jan woman is something special, and he's feeling guilty.*

Jan wasn't sure what to pack. It was a working assignment but being at the side of a hospital bed was not going to be too formal. But then, her agent had picked up the fact there was a press conference on Friday. She'd need a suit for that. Perhaps not trousers. One of her short skirts.

So basically that was settled. Her wardrobe was always kept up to date and she hardly got behind on her washing and ironing. The Filipino who came in four times a week was a dab hand on an ironing board.

She'd had no more instructions from Sir Richard, but then that was to be expected. He'd said what he needed to say quite directly and succinctly. He was trained in the art of precise instruction. She would have expected to hear from William again, but perhaps she had made her professional position a bit too clear and frightened him off. He, of course, wouldn't go away. He'd just try and get at her a different way.

Her flight was the first one out on the Thursday from Heathrow to Gerona. She'd pick up a taxi from there. She'd got confirmation about the room at the Playa. Once there, she had no doubt she'd get to her target.

Marcia, meanwhile, was quietly put out. She bet that if Peter had been making his own visiting arrangements, he would have got her a slot. It also meant that she didn't have much on the agenda while her new man was in the States, and a visit to Palafrugell would have filled the time a bit. Goodness knows why there was so much interest in Peter being in the centre of a bandit heist. She knew only too well that he was often in the middle of trouble. It had become part of his cavalier entrepreneurial nature, she thought, encouraged by Max, whom she really didn't like because he always made fun of her.

She'd go out later in the year and maybe take in a week of light tanning and relaxation before taking her husband-to-be's side at the Ascot meeting. By then, that set would have their shining tans topped up in advance of the serious skin bashing in Greece, and then home waiting to get out to the sunny climes of Dubai in their November/December guaranteed sun. She didn't fit in well with the female cliques on the horse-racing circuit and always wanted to put them right when they exclaimed that life was such a bore when, if they did but know it, any outsider would have judged from their copper skin tone and sun-battered, leathery flesh, that it really looked as though life, to them, was one long beach.

Tania had slept for the first time, so it seemed, in quite a while. That is in technical terms, she'd had her eyes closed from midnight through to six, when she'd really had enough and just had to get up. Once again in that hard life of hers, she'd had a lot to take in, in a short space of time.

Santé, to her surprise, had been alright and by all accounts he would stick to what he said and keep her out of the picture. She and her father need not be connected in any way. Even the most thorough snooper would miss the association if the story released was about the trap set, and did not reveal that anyone else was implicated.

She'd filled Marguerite in on the situation. Her daughter was quite satisfied to keep quiet and listen to her mother's version of the story. She realised she had fed the police with vital information about her grandfather's relatively regular recent visits. How was she to know? She had not been exposed to the guile of many men. Her mother tended to cocoon her from such company. Inwardly, Marguerite thought she'd miss the police presence. She enjoyed the attention she got from the young officers. Maybe they'd come back at weekends, as they had promised, once they were off the case. She'd like that, she thought, as Girasol was not exactly the epicentre of Club Med living.

"Peter, once I've finished putting your behaviour right and knocked your damaged brain into some sense in connection with your treatment in Barcelona, Santé wants to see me."

"Oh, what's that for? He's been to see me again, I meant to tell you."

"Why didn't you?"

"I don't know, it didn't seem important."

"Come on, Peter, what was the subject?"

"In a nutshell, I think he had the sweats for Tania."

"Peter, what's got into you? He's a respectable married man."

"Aren't we all? She's a young lady men tend to get the sweats over."

"Do you, Peter?"

"No. But that's not to say I didn't as a much younger man."

"Good. I'm pleased to hear that. I think you've done quite well to resist. I've admired you for that. She's always been pretty invitational to you."

"Yes but then, fortunately, so have others."

"So, what did Santé want?"

"Background info. Brothers, mother, father, those wretched cousins. Was she leading an honest life? Could she still be beholden to the family? Owe them a debt? What about her sister? Why did they go their separate ways?"

"What did you tell him?"

"I said my mind was cloudy. Every time Tania came into it, so did the piercing eyes of the cousins and the blue flashes of the explosive detonations from their shotguns."

"Is that true?"

"Too true. That's an absolute fact."

"Poor Peter."

"Poor Santé."

"Why?"

"He said I was no help to him at all."

"You know I've told you about the press conference."

"Yes."

"Well, there's another planned for Friday. Santé's second point was to ask me if I would bring that forward to today some time."

"Mother, please don't do that."

"That was my inclination. Why help him? He hasn't been a great help to us, thinking you're somehow implicated as Mr Big."

"Mother, leave it as planned for Friday."

"I'm inclined to that anyway. But why are you so adamant?"

"It's the Jan Roberts factor."

"What's that?"

"Oh, have her around. Plant the right questions and maybe answers too with her. You'd be amazed how that can change the tone of what's reported."

"Too true. Don't remind me. That's certainly what Grant Tovey did last time."

"Forget him, Mother. He belongs in the gutter."

Peter's brain and memory seemed to be back in gear.

CHAPTER 31

Gina picked up her car from the staff car park. She could not believe how her heart was still racing. If it were her daughters acting like this, she'd put them into a cold shower and tell them to calm down, and that they weren't going out on a one-to-one basis with the particular young man who had aroused them. However, she could not disguise the fact that she was excited. Marcel used to give her such moments when they first met. That was once she had got over the introduction by one of their mutual friends.

"I'd like you to meet Gina," the potential matchmaker had said. "And Gina, this is Marcelino."

Marcelino, Gina had thought at first. *What a very strange name, it must have crept forward from a past generation.*

"Please," he had said, "it's Marcel or Marc. My mother and father must have been in a time warp when I was born."

So, it was 'Marcel' generally, and when they were in a more intimate mood, it was 'Marc'.

While Gina, and definitely Marc in those instances, were putting together their planned family of two, they'd enjoyed the procreation process. But after they'd accomplished their objective, albeit that Marc had not obtained the son he so wanted, it seemed to Gina that he had little interest in sex for sex's sake or, even more to the point, through which to express their love for each other. To be fair (and she tried to be objective about most things), once they had their two daughters, the financial demands became greater on her husband. She couldn't nurse, as she had when they were first married, and for a short spell had to be available to look after the children.

So the only way for Marcel to get more take-home pay was to seek promotion. Each uplift brought, it seemed, a disproportionately higher stress factor. Gina tried to comfort him. "It's banking, darling. It's just about moving money around as people want their money moved around. In my profession, you're moving people around on operating tables who don't want to be there in the first place. But, in our case, one bad move by a team player and we can at worst have a death on our hands and at best a hard fight to keep them alive. Now there's real stress.

"The worst that can happen to you, it seems, is to lose somebody's cash, and you've surely got all those reserves just set aside for that day."

But he said it wasn't that simple. So he would have to learn to cope with the flak.

They didn't see eye to eye on those comparisons, and bed was for occasional sex, as the kids demanded more from their resources as they grew older. So, compared with the excitement of any successful operation, or encounter with Benito, their lives together had become dull.

Gina's perception was that Benito Alvor was the exact opposite of Marcel. Calm, hungry for more experience, better techniques, a high success rate and probably a break from the rigours of work, which equally applied to the demands put upon him by a materialistic wife who generally got what she wanted. Whether she satisfied Benito proportionately was not in Gina's knowledge. All the pointers looked as though she didn't.

Dangerously, Gina was thinking she and Benito needed each other's affection to replace the dying embers of their respective marriages. She hoped, on the one hand, that might be the case anyway, but feared it on the other.

Gina had just about got back into her normal sleep pattern some four days later when she received a call from the hospital. Sñr Alvor had specifically requested that she should assist him in an upcoming operation the following day.

That put paid to her sleep that night, and brought her mid-week hair-wash morning a day early. She was bound to say yes, she was available.

She hoped it would not show but inwardly she felt she had blushed when she came face to face with Benito in the preparation room. What was worse was that three of the scrub-up basins were in use and only the one next to Alvor was available. She took a deep breath for self-control, and occupied that empty one. They spoke reflection to reflection through the mirror.

"Hi!"

He sounded years younger when he spoke casually.

"You OK? You up for it? Looking for some repeat stress? Oh… and thank you for accepting yet another task in theatre with me."

The rapid fire questions threw her a little.

"Oh no problem. My pleasure. My honour to be chosen again."

"How short is your memory?"

"Sorry?"

"Had you forgotten I'd suggested we should have a chat?"

Gina hesitated. She knew she shouldn't be too quick in her reply. In fact she waited for the theatre orderly on his left hand side to move away before she answered. Coincidentally, the nurse on her right vacated the basin too.

"Of course not."

"Are you still on for that?"

"… Yes. I think I'd be pleased to." Why… why had she said that? But she had.

"I'd hoped you'd say you were. Can you manage after the op? We just have the one to deal with, emergencies excepted. Maybe lunch somewhere?"

"I'd love that."

"Let's get the work done. Do you come by car?"

"Yes."

"OK. We'll scrub up after and casually walk out to the car park together. Perhaps you could then follow me. There's a place 15 minutes' drive away. I've not been there myself but it looks nice from the outside and it's a bit out of the way."

"That's all fine," she affirmed, trying to mask the fact her heart was racing. *How stupid,* she told herself.

The op went well.

Following Alvor in the car worked.

The place was nice inside.

Chatting was easy and light. He guided her choice through an avocado and into a crab salad. He chose some moules, which he confessed would be a treat and then fillet of dorada, which he assured her was good for him.

They shared a half bottle of Marquis de Montcalm, as they were both driving, and anyway he didn't want to be accused of undue influence over her to the point of her not having her wits about her.

Once the order had been taken, he said he had a serious agenda which, if she didn't mind, he'd like to get over and done with.

That was fine with her.

Suddenly he somewhat blurted out the fact that, despite his level of maturity, he couldn't get her out of his mind since the aftermath of the operation on the mother and child.

"It's as simple as that," he said. "I'm married. I suppose I get the 50 per cent share satisfaction from that in most terms, but I've been left with a total longing to be with you. I expect there are many songs written on the theme but I can't get you out of my mind."

She plucked up courage. "Are you trying to tell me that you want to seduce me?"

"Good God, no. Well… to be honest… not an unequivocal no but that doesn't seem to be my motivation. I'd like to hold you… look I don't want you to think I'm some sort of mid-life crisis freak. I just found our few moments alone together ones which I… well… like an 18-year-old, they just keep haunting me, in a way."

"Then I'll level with you."

"OK. I'm rehearsed for this. You do think I'm some strange man with this useless chat-up line."

"Not at all. You see… I feel exactly the same. There's a difference."

"Oh dear!"

"You see, if you were building up to asking me to sleep with you, I'd hope to be a little coy, bearing in mind I've only had… well, that sort of experience with my husband. But my stomach churns, and I can't explain or stop that, and inwardly I'm longing to reach that level of completeness with you. So there. We're probably a bit stuck with those facts."

Benito thought on.

"I'm not experienced myself. What's the form? A hotel, the back of a car, an empty bed in the private wing of the hospital?"

"No. Let's share the bill, but put another bottle of wine on it. I'll drive off, you follow me this time and there's that new motel on the Gerona Road where I'd guess they're perfectly experienced at putting a couple of amateurs at ease and accommodating their hugely wanting each other."

The young manager there was just that. Neither of them noticed the allocated room, other than that it was very new, exceptionally clean and provided them with the wherewithal to cope silently and unobtrusively with their three hours of mutual discovery.

Conversation was limited as actions spoke volumes. Words of reality came first from him. They were simple.

"Oh my God!" he suddenly said from behind an unlined face, looking like someone who had shed ten or 20 years in an hour or two.

"Oh my God, too!" said Gina later, gazing at a body rejuvenated beyond her own recognition in the mirror, when she eventually tidied herself up in the small en suite bathroom.

Some few days later there was an envelope waiting in her locker. It contained an invitation to attend an upcoming Medical Consultants' seminar weekend in her formal capacity as a lead Theatre Sister in A & E.

The nomination for her to go to the conference was a compliment in two ways. In the one sense, he couldn't have got the Institution to send an invite to a ward orderly or one of the cleaners. The selection would have to be sustainable. Secondly, if his intentions were not strictly honourable, she took it to be a compliment in itself. She felt sure there would be plenty of aspiring female consultants who would be sufficiently attracted to him, and not least his seniority by way of experience, to use the excuse of one too many glasses of wine to slip across the hotel corridor into his room, to confess the next morning "Silly me… let's forget about it… these things happen at conferences…"

However, here he was, apparently through the appearance of the third-party invitation, taking his own wine to the party. It was all perversely flattering to a 40-something-year-old suffering boredom, from which she was beginning to extricate herself with the fulfilment of her now successful career.

She'd heard there was a boutique in San Feliu, where she might invest in some conference attire, something youthful. She'd tell Marcel the hospital gave her a special allowance to represent them at the conference.

Peter was genuinely tired after the morning's prodding and probing, and then his mother's visit. He'd always been kept on his toes by Maria, which in his current state took it out of him quite considerably. Maria recognised that she was not holding his attention any longer, so suggested she might leave. He patted the back of her hand. "Tactful as ever, Mother. Yes, I reckon I could just have a morning nap."

"Peter, can I ask you a question?"

Oh no, he thought, *another cross examination.*

"If you have to, Mother."

"Well, it's about this 'mother' bit. In a lot of modern parental relationships, the sons and daughters refer to their parents by their Christian names. Would you feel more relaxed, more modern, calling me Maria? After all, you call José, José and Marco, Marco, even Virginia, Virginia. What do you think?"

Peter looked aghast. "Good God no, Mother. Not at all. Now do let me close my eyes and you go and discuss some of your silly ideas with Sñr Santé."

Jan had gone straight from Gerona airport to the Playa. Peter had invited his mother to read his incoming mail as a diversionary tactic before it got to him. That saved him the barrage of questions: How was he feeling? Would he promise to do as the medics told him? Would he please not hurry back to work? Why hadn't he found himself a new wife to settle down with… surely he was over Anna's death by now?

Maria had truly liked Anna, and her two grandchildren she loved dearly and cherished their visits; but she'd love her boy to be cared for by some suitable young lady, although the practical side of her said, as Peter approached middle age, he might not now have the allure to attract a younger woman.

She'd feared for some years after Bob Hunt's death that Peter would move in with Marcia. They were, after all, good friends. "Good God, Mother!" Peter had exclaimed in his very loud officious voice, when she'd put this to him. "Life with Marcia, lovely as she is, and fond of her as I am, would be a living hell."

So that was that, Maria had resolved. She would still hope he'd find someone to care for him, to get him away from those weeks where he seemingly worked all day and night, or didn't go to bed till dawn after satisfying his obsession for bridge 'at the club'.

Jan's letter had seemed friendly and genuinely caring, which had prompted Maria to ask a bit more about her again.

"This Jan, Peter?"

"Oh, here we go. I shouldn't have left her letter in the pile. She's exactly the girl you'll try to marry me off to. She's a lesbian nun I've done some charity fund-raising with."

Maria looked aghast. "Are you pulling my leg, you naughty boy? Nuns wouldn't wear the perfume she uses – I smelled it on the notepaper. You're having me on. You'll get reported to the priest, one of these days. So why is she such a successful PR guru?"

"She's an unusual PR consultant who, without baring her teeth, could get you dispatched to the wolves and never heard of again, hypothetically speaking. She does personality profiles and if she thinks it justified, she can cement your career forever."

"So how has she performed for you?"

"Actually, very fairly. She did my first profile. In a sense it helped, in another it didn't."

"How did it help?"

"Well, I'm still CEO, and the City of London hasn't exactly crucified me for what I'm doing."

"And in another sense?" Maria asked, still probing.

"Oh, Mother! Questions, questions, questions, you tire me out. Another day. Please." He was just in no mood to explain that Jan had released the details of their interview in a worldwide sense and it had been reprinted in Malaysia. It was that article Coco had read, which pointed her to Peter's actual existence and her appearance in his office. To break the news of a third grandchild for his mother at this time was just not within his agenda.

"OK, dear. But I'll not forget to keep asking you."

"I know you won't, dearest Mother."

"So this Jan says she's coming out to see you. Should I really put her into the hotel?"

"Now that's not just a kind idea. It's a good one. By the way, she's as straight as a pétanque alley. I'd guess you'll like her."

"Am I meant to be checking her over as a prospective… ?"

Peter interrupted, close to exploding again. "Mother! One question too many. Leave me to rest. At times, you're still a fisherman's wife."

"… And, young man, without offence to José, I'm proud of it."

She stood up and kissed his forehead. "See you tomorrow, darling."

She's incorrigible, he thought.

Maria's car knew the road so well between Palafrugell and the Playa. Not just from the library but now from her hospital trips. Visits to Bob were always worrying, and those to Peter had been too, until he'd begun his recovery. She was not now too worried. If he'd be sensible about some constructive rehab, she'd be more relaxed. All this 'I have to get back to the UK' was doing her no good nor, if he did just that, would it help him. Peter had always had a few too many unreliable phases in his intriguing life. Not to rebuild his body would indeed be one of those.

Autumn at the Playa was not proving to be the disappointment Marco and Maria had feared, so it took a little juggling to fit Jan Roberts in. Maria pulled through the 'Peter's bright idea' entrance columns onto the cobbled drive up to the front lobby of the hotel. She parked in her 'Reservado' bay and walked lightly and quickly towards the now automatic people-sensored sliding doors. As she did so, she was confronted by an unknown female guest leaving from the reverse direction.

Maria stepped to one side, ushering her through. It was always a difficult moment because she had to make a quick assessment as to how to greet an unknown in his or her native tongue. Usually clothes were a great help. The Germans wore better casual wear than the Brits. The French sometimes looked as though they were dressed for a smart lunch but more often were not. They were renowned for their mismatching of pick and mix tops, skirts and accessories.

This young lady had a smart white trouser suit with black stitching around the lapels of the jacket and down the outside side seam of the trousers. Maria sensed she was wearing smart black high sandals. The top of the three jacket buttons was designed at just the right height to give a glimpse of cleavage to a discerning eye. She had blonde neat hair in a style that said she would always be able to get up in the morning, rise, shower, dress and get off to whatever work she did in minimum time. English bordering on German, Maria thought.

"Good day," Maria greeted her, followed swiftly by, "Tag!" just in case she'd got it wrong.

"Good afternoon," came the friendly response. English.

"I'm Maria Martinez, a Director here. I'm sorry I haven't had the pleasure of making your acquaintance," she said, holding out a hand of welcome.

"Oh! Mrs Martinez. I'm Jan Roberts, an acquaintance of your son Peter."

Now that, Maria worked out, was typically loaded. The intro was firm and bold, suggesting the statement was made so as to ensure her name would not be forgotten. Men would melt, Maria postulated. Then the young lady had made her role in Peter's life quite clear. 'Acquaintance' certainly did not give the connotation that they were sleeping together, and there had been no tone of possessiveness in her voice. Then she'd been very specific about Maria's 'son' when, for all Jan presumably knew, Maria might have had several. It displayed a very journalistic 'who', 'what' and 'with whom' precision, with which Maria was now familiar.

Maria cemented the greeting by extending her left arm over Jan's shoulder and pulling her close to her still honed though ageing body. Jan found that comfortable. At least one of the Martinez family was able to show their emotions. Peter's barriers had been well up when they'd met. True, he was warm. Yes, there were always warm greetings, but never a hint that she might be able to get behind the controlled glinting eyes, or beyond the surface charm that oozed from his naturally broad, deep smile. To know what he was feeling, apart from assessing how you looked, what you were wearing, how he was going to control you and just how much he was going to allow you to discover of what lay behind his professional mask – that would be a major feat.

So the Martinez barrier that Maria had broken down was most welcome. Jan instantly liked her; Maria had a reciprocal feeling, without knowing what Jan was thinking or, in truth, really understanding why she was here.

Jan stepped back. "Actually, I was on my way to see Peter."

This might be quite serious, Maria thought. She couldn't have landed at Gerona much before midday. Thirty to 45 minutes to clear customs and reclaim her baggage. Half an hour journey to the hotel, check-in with Sñr Martin, which was never quick, then a shower, perhaps. Change of clothes, undoubtedly. She'd almost certainly not stopped for lunch and was in a hurry to see Peter. *She's serious,* Maria thought.

"Have you had lunch?" Maria asked.

"No. I had some plastic on the plane."

"Listen, you can't see Peter on an empty stomach. Let me get you a sandwich and a nice glass of Vina Sol to set you up for your visit."

Jan thought all this was a bit of a nuisance. She actually felt she couldn't wait to see Peter. She'd pinched herself once or twice since she had heard that first news breaking on TV that Peter had been shot by bandits. She knew she liked him after those first meetings. Immediately she saw an early photo of who was to be her latest interviewee, she'd had more than a professional interest in this one. At least all that explained why she was looking forward to the new brief stimulated by Mr William.

"Why?" she'd asked herself. He's got a reputation as a bit of a hard pig. He used people as stepping stones and he fired from the hip with a pen to bring many a competitor to their doom, or a senior in the chain of command to an early retirement. But there was something there… the ballet was a giveaway. Not many men Jan had known actually understood the emotions expressed through hand gesticulations, and the bowing and lifting of a female head.

And she could not remove from her mind the way he had let her off the hook when she'd dropped what could have been the clanger of a lifetime about why he hadn't ever married. Widowed, she'd so often thought afterwards. That must have been cruel for him to have to explain, by way of defence, to her stupid, irrelevant interrogation. It made no difference whatsoever to his ability to steer a new path for BCG whether he had a devoted little woman to go home to in the evenings, or whether he relied on a bottle of champagne and his obvious wealth to attract female companionship at the Gargoyle or Blue Elephant.

Then, when she had written to him about the accident after being asked to do a piece on him to release to the press, she was surprised by his reply, obviously written for him, perhaps by an adoring nurse. (*But who would blame her for that? Jan thought.*)

He'd replied, *"Bugger writing about the fact of cheating death again. Come over and cheer me up. Tell Mr William he'll have to pick up the flight cost and with your personal savings, could you bring me some nougat from Fortnum's. I'm interviewing particularly slowly, forecast you'll need at least two weeks, then I'll have time to show you the sunflowers. Seriously, please come over. I'd enjoy seeing you. Cheers, Peter."*

No more than that. Not a hint of just one 'x'. But it seemed a genuine invite. Enough, she thought, to make any girl's heart flutter, not just hers, surely?

Jan got back to the offer of a sandwich and a glass of wine. Before she could decline, Maria interjected.

"I left Peter, oh, about an hour ago, I suppose. He was actually a bit grumpy. He won't admit it but he still gets quite a lot of pain. So I'd suggest give it another hour or so. I'll ring through and say you're on your way and I bet he'll pull himself together. Come on, Jan. May I call you Jan? Oh, by the way, it's Maria. Drop the Martinez bit. I feel we'll get to know each other on a girl-to-girl basis."

Jan gave in. "You're very kind. I'd actually love a sandwich. I'd also like him not to be grumpy."

The next hour was like that old-fashioned British TV series called 'Twenty Questions'. A panel would ask up to 20 questions as they tried to guess what a particular chosen subject was. In Maria and Jan's case, they overstepped the mark by the number of questions. Jan rattled off poser after poser as to what had happened to Peter, how the police enquiries had gone and who these Romany gypsies were who offered such threats.

Maria was equally voracious in her questioning. "Where did you meet?" "Where has he taken you?" "Have you been to bed with him yet?" "Are you divorced?" "Do you have children?" "Are your parents alive…?" Well, not quite as blatantly obvious as that. In fact, the picture Jan was able to paint appeared to be that she and Peter had only met through business. That encounter lasted two days and produced a serious article profile about Peter, which he had sent to Maria to read. So that proved they had talked a lot about business. Jan voluntarily described the night between their two days and how Peter had gone off to play bridge, which only led to one conclusion in Maria's mind. They actually hardly knew each other in social terms but they seemed to have a high regard for each other. This all seemed unlike Peter, her son, to her.

The hour whizzed by and both women laughed a lot and warmed even more to each other by the minute, admittedly the Vina Sol having been an ice-breaker. It was 3.30pm when Jan asked if Maria thought Peter would be rested by now.

"Yes, if you leave now, you'll arrive just about the time he has his English pot of tea. At about four. How are you getting there? Would you like to borrow my car?"

No. Jan had changed her mind about a taxi and hired a car from the airport. Maria said she thought she would have taken a taxi from the airport and how brave Jan was to be driving around in a strange car in a foreign country. Jan said she was used to it and explained how she actually quite liked the challenge and the independence it created. She did check with Maria on the instructions she'd already had as to how to get to the hospital.

It seemed natural as they both got up from the terrace table, almost simultaneously, for them to give each other a token handshake and a brush of left with right cheek.

"It's been nice touching base with you, as I think you say. Now I've met the young lady Peter intends to get himself back into trousers for," Maria confided.

"Trousers? Can he wear trousers yet over the dressings?"

"Well, I doubt it," Maria informed her, in a way that suggested she knew she was bound to be right.

"So what happens if he can't get into them?"

"Fireworks, I'd say. Do you know how determined that son of mine is?"

"Yes, I think I do. Perhaps I'll put the visit off until tomorrow!"

They both laughed, knowing that to be a most unlikely proposition.

"Hey ho, then. Off I go. This could be the end of a good business relationship."

"Good luck," were Maria's seriously intended parting words. Then, with a look of concern, she added: "Jan, could I have just 15 minutes more with you?" She paused, as if unsure what to say. "There haven't been many males in my life apart from Peter, of course, and close family, and in that I include both my husbands. But there's one particular friend. His name is Carlos Sanchez. I've known him years and worked with him in both the local library and in his life when he was mayor for three years. That was a record mayoral term for any one person.

"He's one of the kindest people in the world. So kind he has very little money, having supported charities all his life. He and I have a combined dream. Spain is built very much on the basis of very rich people being able to provide for themselves almost anything they need, or want. Nowadays, a big boat is available to them but when it comes to illness, even they are dependent on the hospital where Peter himself is now being repaired.

"That sometimes doesn't suit the middle and upper strata of society. The rich can fly off with their ailments to Switzerland or the UK and have private medical treatment. But Peter wouldn't have survived that journey, according to the consultant who operated to save his life.

"But because of Peter's lifestyle, and a man called Bob Hunt, a friend to us all who was taken ill while staying at the hotel, there's a local need for a private hospital. In time it could be self-supporting through insurance-led private healthcare, which is an area my husband is currently investigating for his company. Likewise, tourists would come with insurance cover, and the odd child could be accommodated who needed instant treatment in more conducive surroundings than the only ones currently available, alongside locals with TB and other diseases.

"Carlos has inherited a piece of land locally, which he believes could accommodate a suitable building with car park and other facilities. He's got together with some close friends and had estimates prepared, showing costs of about 100 million pesetas – that's £5 million sterling, I'm told.

"Carlos was a great help to Peter in establishing Girasol, and it was our joint intention to put it to Peter to see if this BCG of his, yours, could help fund the idea. But we're missing the one principal ingredient: a medical man to administer the project. I hope when you meet Sñr Alvor, you'll find him commercially aware, and a life-saver too. He could be our man, if approached in the right way."

Part of Jan's vocation was to just let the person in conversation with her do the talking.

"So where do I come in?"

"Well… because of Peter's accident, let's just say he hasn't been very receptive to any business proposition. While you were talking earlier, you seemed to be saying BCG could devaluate by a fortune if it's seen that Peter is off the pulse, as I think he once called it. The story could be 'Injured CEO discovers huge commercial opportunity in the need for private medicine to supplement excellent Spanish facilities that saved his life. BCG considering backing local benefactor who is prepared to put land at the disposal of a special project.' Oh, I know that sounds so clumsy, but… oh, Jan! You would know completely how to put it."

"But how can I help?"

"Do two things, and do them in your way. Talk Peter into going to Barcelona. That would so please Sñr Alvor. Approach Benito Alvor about his potential support for such a project. And… maybe a third thing. This one is dreadful! I'm shy about it."

"Go on. I can't be shocked any more beyond the trust you seem happy to put in me. Go on, Maria… what is it?"

"Marry Peter."

Jan roared with laughter.

"Dear Maria! That sort of deal only nowadays still happens in India by arrangement! I'll speak to Benito Alvor and I'll tell Peter he's going to Barcelona and do the investment, because it would be exactly what BCG needs. But as for marrying him, accepting your proposal on his behalf just can't be on the agenda."

"Listen, Jan. You must fly. Let's say we'll keep that option open, but definitely see if you can have a quiet word with dear Sñr Alvor."

Jan arrived at the ground floor reception.

"Sñr Martinez, please."

The duty nurse pointed upwards. Jan gesticulated: one floor up or two? Two fingers, came the reply. Jan took the staircase. She passed through a first floor reception area and proceeded up to the further gleaming, rubber-clad flight of treads and risers to the upper floor.

310

She presumed she'd report to a nurse and would check whether Peter was ready to receive a guest. She hoped she would then be announced, just to break the uncertain ice she was now about to skate upon. After all, she had only seen Peter for two days in her life. Admittedly it was for two whole, long days and she did find out about most of his history in that time. She could have dated a male friend for six months and still not, she felt, have known him properly in that period of time.

Would they shake hands? She'd leave that up to him. As they had left each other on the second day of their acquaintanceship, they had finally touched cheeks in the now prevalent professional fashion and she had stolen a *mwa* through pursed lips. What did *mwa* even mean? Was it meant to be a murmur of satisfaction, or did it perhaps derive from one of the parties demanding 'more', and in midst of that excited moment cocking the words up.

Jan alighted on the top landing and entered through the double swing doors into the reception area, which was a replica of the first floor. Except there was apparently nobody around. Then she heard voices. She didn't understand the words but she got the gist. The male shouts from within were saying, "Pull, you silly girls. Pull. You'll never get the fucking trousers on pussying around. Oh, for God's sake!"

Without knowing a word of Spanish, Jan was sure that was it, without a doubt. That was Peter's distinctive voice alright, booming from the second open door along the whole corridor. Jan smiled to herself. *I bet he wouldn't be making all that fuss if they were taking his trousers off for a bit of therapeutic playtime. It's ironic, really.*

She walked quietly to where the fuss was coming from and could see through the gap between the heel of the door and the frame, three nurses in varying stages of disarray. Two had their hands firmly magnetised to the trouser waistband, while the third was trying to ease the knee part of the trouser leg over the thick dressing. Jan hadn't got a clue about such things but if she'd been a gambler, she would not have rated the odds of getting the slim cut pants up over Peter's damaged knee.

Suddenly, the expletives reached a new peak.

"Fucking useless!" Peter shouted in his second native tongue. Then: "Scissors!" he yelled. "Tijeras!"

One of the nurses hurried out of the room, seeming not to notice Jan's presence. What the hell did he want the scissors for? Surely he wasn't going to remove the dressing? The nurse returned with a stainless steel tray bearing in fact three different-sized scissors. She obviously didn't have a clue either.

Maria would have wanted Jan to do what she herself would have done, had she been there, and to stop Peter causing himself untold harm by removing the dressing, just to get his trousers on for her visit. So she decided to take the bull by its horns, as they do in Spain. She held her arm out to stop the flight of the dutiful nurse with the choices of cutting appliances, then took the medium-sized pair off the tray.

Jan put a forefinger up to the lips she had overhauled with pink lipstick in the car park, using the car's rear view mirror. The nurse seemed to understand and reacted with a hint of relief. Jan entered the white painted room with louvred blinds keeping out the autumn sunlight.

"If anything's going to get cut off, sir, I'm going to be doing it."

"Give them bloody here… !" Peter shouted, then quickly followed with, "Jan!"

"Mr Martinez, sir, that's no way to greet a lady."

"Greet a lady, be damned! I'm trying to get myself smartened up exactly for that purpose."

"No, I didn't mean that."

"Oh, here we go. Bloody journalist comes in and starts talking riddles."

"Peter. It's your pants. That's no way to greet a lady."

Peter looked down at the dishevelled trousers, half on and half off, during which exercise his boxer shorts had burst open, exposing, at least Jan thought that to be the case after a quick glimpse, quite an amount of masculinity.

Peter looked up in mixed horror and humour. "Listen, baby, that's how I greet all my female visitors these days. It's a compliment. Hey, come here," he said behind a broad smile, extending his hand and inviting her to hold it. "Look, you nurses, take a break. I feel this young lady will have the talent to sort me out. Allez, allez, rapido, rapido."

They scurried out with more than a hint of relief.

Peter's hand was big and strong and if Jan had not let her body be dragged towards him, she felt her whole arm would have been ripped out of its socket. She found herself sitting side-saddle on the bed and then completely overpowered by his free arm enveloping her shoulders and pulling her close to his chest. She had never been this close to his face… or, in fact, the beautiful lips that always framed each word, each smile and every quiver as he made a point. The impetus was still entwining them together and had she not turned her face away slightly, they were sure to have been locked into a passionate embrace. Their cheeks touched, maybe only for ten or 20 seconds, but long enough for Jan to find this welcome pleasurable.

She pulled back. "Now… what do you want me to cut off with these scissors? Give me flak and I can tidy you up for life."

"Don't do that. Please. Precisely what I had in mind was to cut the trouser legs down just above the knee, turn them into shorts, if you like, then I think they'll pull up over the waist and pass over the dressing."

"You know, I really thought you were going to cut the dressing off."

"Listen, young lady, I may have lost lots lying here, but I've still got all my marbles to survive this lot, and cutting the dressing off wouldn't be the most progressive thing to do. Listen, chuck that sheet over, would you," he said, beckoning to a sheet neatly folded after its use through the previous night.

He threw it over his waist and thighs, patting the mattress, where he was inviting Jan to plant her backside on the edge of the bed alongside him. She dutifully obeyed his command.

"Now. Let's start again. How was the journey? Is the hotel OK? How did you get to the hospital? How's work been? How long can you stay out here…?" The barrage of questions ricocheted out as staccato shots to force out valuable information.

"Hey," she said, as soon as Peter paused for breath. "I'm here to see you, and to get your news, find out what they have in mind for you by way of recuperation. I'll need a message for the Board and your parasites in the City…"

"Tell me how long you're here for and I'll answer part of the cross-examination."

"Five days!"

Peter's head dropped visibly. "That's cheating," he said, as though the bad news had just sunk in.

"Why's that?"

"You walk back into my life and introduce me back to sweet smelling perfume, as opposed to Dettol and antiseptic. By the way, what is it?"

"Missoni."

"It's very nice… and I don't want to be personal, but you know me. I speak as I feel… and you've walked in here like a refreshing flower neutrally colour-clad to blend with the nurses in their white and bringing me the rare gift of a hint of cleavage – something that's been off the treatment list, it seems, forever. So, thank you. But is all that really to last just five days?"

Jan felt herself blush. "Look, I don't know what tablets you're on but you need to take them with more water." Secretly, though, as she said that, by way of a diversionary tactic, she smiled inwardly… her concentration on femininity had worked on the patient, she thought.

"Let's get your trousers cut down, then you'll look half-decent for those five days."

"Do you have an agenda?"

"What, with the scissors?"

"OK, I see. You're here to sharpen my wits up a bit, are you? God, you're right. I've vegetated."

"You still blossom as a very lovely vegetable, I assure you," Jan said meaningfully. "So... agenda. Well, to be serious, Mr William and BCG PR want a fax as soon as possible. We need to get it a bit upbeat. I'll work on that for you. We also need to tell the City not to write you off. I don't think I'll have to work on that. You'll never be written off," she said, delivered with a friendly pat on what she remembered, hopefully, was his good thigh. "Then there's the rehab."

"That's when I'm back in England."

"Your mother and I think not. It's got to be gradual. It's got to be prescribed by the guys who did the operation, too."

"How have you and my mother been getting that joint storyline together?"

Jan stretched her right hand out and flicked Peter's nose a couple of times, indicating he was not to be nosy.

"Come on. How?"

"We had a sandwich and a glass of chilled white wine before I came here today."

"Oh my God! I've been stitched up."

Jan cut the legs off the trousers.

"Are you going to help me put them on?" Peter said boyishly.

"Not bloody likely! You seemed to be having a special rapport with the nurses here. They're trained with chaps like you. Besides, I've got some scheming to do. I don't want just to send a medical bulletin back to the UK."

"What have you got in mind?"

Jan lifted her finger and patted his nose again. They both realised they were staring hard at each other. She retracted the extremity and lowered it to his lips. She leant forward and brushed them with that same finger. "Now you're going to be a good boy. Aren't you!"

"Undo that top button and I'll let you know."

"Clearly you're feeling a lot better! Peter, I'm so pleased to see you."

"Me you too," Peter replied. "Now that's not vegetable garbage, is it?"

"No. I take it as a compliment, as I intended towards you, too," she smiled. "I'll see you in an hour. Don't give the nurses too much of a hard time."

The combination of Maria's advice with Jan's was, at least in principle, a dual force to be reckoned with. Jan had explained that part of her reason for being in Palafrugell was to send home news of Peter's recovery. Somehow, too, she needed to let it be known that the vultures amassing in the BCG empire were going to have their predatory beaks well and truly blunted. How, she did not quite yet know, but if there was an angle to be exploited, Jan was the girl for the challenge.

Maria had phoned the hospital immediately Jan left. She still had the open option to speak to Sñr Alvor whenever she needed. She was in luck and he rang her back within ten minutes.

Maria asked, "Could you see one of Peter's colleagues at, say 4.30? I think she'll get him to go to Barcelona."

Jan's meeting at 4.30pm with Peter's orthopaedic consultant was to see if any newsworthy ideas could be set in motion to be remitted to London.

"Thank you for seeing me at such short notice," Jan explained to Benito Alvor, after introducing herself. "I'm a business associate of Peter Martinez, here to explore an idea he has."

"That associate of yours is a truly tough man and any idea from his brain is bound to be intriguing. Intrigue me, Miss Roberts, please do."

"First, I need some background about the hospital set up here. I understand the service is fundamentally government-run. I gather that's the case, as Mr Martinez was frustrated that he couldn't convert to a private customer but is here as part of the NHS arrangements with its European partners."

"Yes, that's basically the case," Sñr Alvor responded.

"So if one wanted to avoid the obvious state health service wait, where would a patient go with private money?"

"Maybe, if he or she was a matador or famous football player, to Madrid. There is a facility there. It's very expensive and your average Spaniard, or tourist even with insurance, would not be able to afford it. So if not Madrid, it's likely to be London where you are years ahead of the world, apart from the USA, in such service provision."

"So why not Palafrugell?"

Benito laughed. "Sorry, I thought you would understand. The government would need to provide the facility and most ministers have probably not even heard of Palafrugell and, that apart, the Catalan area would be a taboo one for such an investment. You've got ETA up in the hills not so far away from here and Madrid would not want to do anything to strengthen the north-east area."

"Supposing there was private money prepared to be invested in Palafrugell?"

"This time I don't understand."

"Building a hotel costs approximately £10,000 sterling per room." Jan knew that from a previous review she had done. "That's a precast concrete system of prefabricated buildings, such as is patented in the UK and Germany. Let's say a hospital would cost twice that, as the room equipment goes far beyond the mini-bar and a couple of wardrobes and an en suite shower. Let's consider operating facilities in terms of the cost within construction of the fabric, and x-ray, scanning facilities, physio and rehab units which might add 100 per cent at an overall, say, £4 million.

"I apologise, incidentally, that this is all in sterling but if, for argument's sake, you convert at 200 pesetas to the pound, you're talking mega sums. Throw another £1 million in for good measure and you're at £5 million, 1 billion pesetas. It would not be impossible to raise that sort of money from the UK on, say, a ten-year equity participating loan. I could give you the breakdown but you would find that would produce a cost of £6 per room per hour, which is much easier to see in peseta terms as being 1,200. It's not much money for a room for each hour. Some motels are three times that just for courting couples to use!"

Did she know about, or at least guess at, his trips to motels through her own previous relationships? he thought. No, that couldn't be possible. But she was right in her arithmetic. What a convincing young lady.

"… And Miss Roberts, I suppose you are next going to say that you and Peter Martinez have that money to invest."

"Yes."

Sñr Alvor looked shocked. "Yes?"

"Yes, that's right. Mr Martinez is CEO of one of the UK's top 100 companies. On a bad day, they invest that sort of money by the hour."

"Are you really serious? Am I hearing this correctly? So why are you discussing this with me, a mere orthopaedic surgeon who's not a particularly good businessman?"

"We can have as much financial muscle as you like but we would only invest if we knew the facilities would be managed to the highest order by medical experts. Mrs Martinez was very impressed by how you managed the presence of the police and the world's press around the hospital when Peter was first admitted. She feels you have organisational talents yet to be exploited. Say you're at least interested in the principle behind the package, and Peter and his other colleagues will start to put something more formal together."

"Can I be blunt?"

"Please feel free."

"I don't understand what's in it for Mr Martinez's organisation. He doesn't run a charity, that's quite clear."

"That's easy. A BCG consortium would charge around ten per cent interest on the £5 million. They'd take a probable 25-30 per cent equity stake and their International Construction division would expect to be awarded the design and build contract, at competitive rates, you understand."

Jan felt that her whole body beneath the cool white slightly pin-stripped exterior was oozing sweat. If this went on much longer, she'd be the first patient in the vascular wing of the planned private hospital. She was sure her pulse rate had doubled.

"OK. I'm convinced," Benito announced, after some thought. "I'd like to take it on a bit further."

"I'll report back to Peter and fix up another meeting. Oh, by the way, could I broach another part of the preliminary agenda?"

Alvor's heart sank a little. Was she going to be like some sort of cheap hooker who got her client all hyped up and then slipped out the bombshell, like more money?

"Mention it to me. Please do," he replied unenthusiastically.

"Maria Martinez and I would like you to try to convince Peter to stay on having treatment in Spain. Once he gets back to London, his life won't be his own. Any treatment will be put off for his preference to keep working on ideas, and so we're afraid for his long-term health."

"Is that it?"

"Yes, of course."

"OK. I know how to do that. I'll transfer him to the rehab unit in Barcelona."

"Is that difficult to achieve?"

"No, not difficult to achieve. But I do not believe it will be easy to get Peter Martinez to go there too willingly. I've already seen in him what some would say is determination. I call it stubborn. Is that the right word in English?"

"For Peter, yes, absolutely right."

"Was Peter a sportsman, do you know?"

"Yes. I'm sure he was. Probably still is…" Jan's face dropped. Oh dear. "Is. Can he still be?"

"Yes, providing he picks his sport. I doubt he'll do judo but if he picks his game, he'd be OK."

"Tennis?"

"Seniors' tennis, I'd think, yes."

"Sorry. I stopped you asking about whether he was a sportsman. Why do you ask?"

"Well, if I can get him to Barcelona just for 15 minutes, I'm sure I could keep his attention for the required amount of time."

"What's the bait? Do the Spanish troupe of the Folies Bergère train there?"

"Now, that's another idea! Perhaps that could be arranged. No. Get him there for me and I'll do the rest."

"How long is the required time?"

"About a month."

"I guess he'd settle for about half of that. There's a place in England he's got his eye on – Headley Court in Surrey, where they rehab RAF aircrew and injured militia. Maybe two weeks in Barcelona then two at Headley would fit the bill."

"I could liaise with the UK, I'm sure."

"When would he be ready to be moved?"

"I'd say five days," was the medical opinion.

"Hell. That's as I'm due to go home. What about four days and I'll take him to Barcelona and fly back from there?"

"Are all the Brits dealers? OK. I think it's a day early. Will you be at the hospital there on his first day, his first 15 minutes, even?"

"Yes, I'm sure I can be. Could I drive him there? An ambulance would kill him off."

"That's a most unusual request. I'm not sure that's not too much responsibility for you. Perhaps with a nurse. Yes."

"No nurse. I'll nurse him."

"Do you have experience?"

"Not in nursing. I'm told I'm good with people. He won't need treatment. He'll suffer all the pain the springs of a Seat hire car can inflict. He'll just need man management. I'll do that."

"Miss Roberts," Benito said, standing up. She noticed he'd had a quick glance, somewhat slyly, at his watch.

"Jan… may I call you Jan? It's been an absolute pleasure to meet you. The two of you are forces to be reckoned with. I'll probably not sleep for the next four days, thinking about your proposition and getting Peter to Barcelona. I do apologise but I really must go. I've got a patient round to do." What he didn't say was that he was meeting Gina at 6.30 for an hour or two of what they both expected to be quality time over a drink.

Jan shook his hand. "The feelings are mutual. It's been a joy to meet with you. You'll say yes to the Barcelona hospital and be delighted when we're all delighted when I show up there with Peter. Oh, am I being over-presumptuous? Will you be there?"

"Yes, of course, I want to see his face when all is revealed."

"Do give me a clue."

"I'll give him a zimmer frame and tell him to walk five kilometres."

"Will he ever do that, let alone within three weeks of his, let's say, accident?"

"Fifty pesetas says he will."

"You're on." Jan extended her feminine hand. "Now you really must give time to all your other patients."

When Jan arrived back at the second-floor room, second along the corridor, Peter was sitting out of bed. His day nurse was about to go off duty. Jan obviously must have looked surprised, as the nurse burst into broken English. "Yes! Mr Peter insist," she said, gesticulating as to how he had got out of bed on demand and was sitting in the side chair. "He bad man. Bad in head. He cross. He make me."

"Peter, you shouldn't."

"If you'd been here, I wouldn't have needed to, or wouldn't have wanted to move. Now tell me, Miss Roberts, wherefore hath thou been?"

"I've started to write the report, which is why I'm here."

She stepped close to the chair. Moved his good knee out of the way so that she could step nearer, and then directly in front of him. He looked anxious. She leant forward and offered her outstretched right hand to his left one.

"What was that all about?" Peter said, laughing.

"It's because you're going to be cross with me and I want to shake hands now in case you ask for me to be sent home."

"How do you know? I might not necessarily be cross."

"I know you will be. Well, you might as well know. What's the point not. You'll just have to put up with being cross. I've just spent £5 million."

"That's fine by me," Peter said with a broad smile, as though wanting now to play a part in Jan's childish game. "You can't take it with you, you know. You've obviously won a lottery or something."

"That's it. It wasn't mine."

"Whose was it then?" he said, still smiling.

"Yours."

Peter threw his head back in laughter. "Mine! No girl I know could ever spend that much of my money inside a couple of hours. Besides, if you have, I'd be demanding a bloody sight more out of our relationship beyond it all hinging on another of your business interviews, and me being on my best behaviour."

"OK! Let's start the profile thing, which is what I'm really out here. How do you adjust to being a successful entrepreneur when you tend to debase other people's ideas? By the way, part of that spending is that I've got to get you to Barcelona."

"Barcelona? What, get me out of here? Listen, Jan, what's going on? You can't spend £5 million supposedly in a miracle timespan and get me out of here."

"Well, it's not exactly to get you out of here." She stood up from having perched on the side of his vacated bed, leant forward and brushed his lips again with her forefinger.

"What's that for? Because I'm going to be cross again?"

"No, because this time you should be pleased."

"Riddles, Jan. Riddles! You're really just like any other journalist. Come on, the truth."

"Right. You're going to this specialist rehab hospital in Barcelona. Sñr Alvor has fixed it for you. You're really lucky because it's a very special place. He's allowing me to take you. I'll pop back to England and come out the following weekend, that's if you'd like me to. Then I can take you out to dinner and see how you're getting on."

"Jan," Peter said seriously, "don't interfere. If I'm OK to go to Barcelona, then I'm OK to get back to the UK. There's a place in Headley that'll get me right. So thank you, but no thank you."

"Peter. Can I tell you something from the hip?"

"Providing you're not going to be too much like my mother, yes."

"Now Sñr Alvor has said that with the right rehab, he'll get you to at least seniors' status at tennis."

For once, Peter was speechless. His greatest concern lying there in Palafrugell hospital had been just that. He held his hand out towards Jan's. "So, without prejudice, now tell me about the £5 million."

He looked at her intently. Jan had a way of explaining things and making them interesting, even the way she had used some information about the costings that she had picked up from a previous interview.

She got to the end of the piece. "What do you think, Peter?"

He remained deep in thought for what was probably little more than a couple of minutes. It seemed an eternity.

"You've overlooked one thing."

She was deflated.

"What about the land?"

"Oh, that. You had me frightened the way you said I'd overlooked something. The land is OK. It'll come on a 99 year lease from the local authority at a peppercorn ground rent."

"Who says?"

"Your mother. According to her, your mutual friend Carlos Sanchez has said that will be OK."

"Mother. Carlos. The old team. Jan, I like the idea! We'd need four other similar projects to really make it work, but I guess if we get one off the ground the others would follow. Perhaps an early news conference would act as a catalyst. Why don't we announce the provisional idea on Friday, before we leave for Barcelona? You know, appreciative patient wants to leave his mark on a community into which he was born, which became the cause of his near death, but the life-saver he discovered was in the standard of medical attention available. He now proposes extending the availability of that into a private market, now post-Franco, and to encourage further tourism and external home ownership into retirement in the sun. Have you done news conferences before? You're bound to have done, I suppose. It's good. Really good!"

"Peter, you say 'before we leave for Barcelona'. So, is that on?"

"If I just need a couple of weeks or so of lying on some couch having physio from some young blonde therapist to get me into an acceptable shape, then that's a small penance to pay, surely."

Jan beamed. "Thank you for not being cross."

"Who says I'm not disguising it pretty well, eh!"

She thought she'd best let him have the final say.

"Can you pass me the call button from the head of the bed, please," Peter requested.

"Do you want me to leave?"

"Good God, no!"

The newly attentive night nurse was almost immediately standing in the doorway. "You rang," she said.

"Can you bring me the trolley, please."

"Yes, of course."

She appeared some 30 seconds later with the supper trolley. It had a makeshift tablecloth made from a doubled up sheet. It was laid with two plates and the equivalent cutlery. In the middle was a plate with one of those cheap metal keep-it-warm covers over it. In this case, to keep it cool.

There were two thick utilitarian glasses. Ordinary water tumblers, and standing upright in a dark brown plastic waste-basket was a bottle of champagne, hurriedly acquired, Jan later found out, by the day nurse from the local supermarket as she went off-duty.

"It's not a bouquet, I'm afraid. It's just an 'I'm really so pleased to see you' welcome event." Peter lifted the cover from the centre plate. "Fresh smoked salmon, madam," he announced.

Jan was taking it all in as the night nurse re-appeared. "It's getting dusk. We have these for when there's a power cut," she informed them as she lit two plain hospital candles. Peter had always remembered his and Jan's previous two days together as being full of chat: some serious about his career, other conversation about her life too, her parents, lack of marriage in favour of her career. They had never seemed to struggle for conversation and when silence or quiet reflection was the order of the day, that reigned too.

The night nurse's words were like those of a matron at lights out. "Mr Martinez, I really think you ought to rest now. Señorita, he's usually asleep by now."

"Only because all you nurses keep your coats done up to the neck!"

"Sorry, sir, I no understand."

"Don't worry. You've made your point."

"Sorry, sir, still no understand."

Peter suddenly looked tired but then Jan was too. She'd travelled out that day, had the illuminating first meeting with Maria… and the rest. She too was tired.

"Will you come tomorrow?" Peter enquired.

"Would you like me to?"

"I'd be very cross if you didn't."

"Then I'll come in the afternoon. I'll get networking in the morning with a view to a press conference, as you suggest, on Friday. Then a night with your mother and then I'll drive you to Barcelona on Saturday."

"When will you go home?"

"Probably Sunday."

"I'm missing you already."

"Peter, you're like a big spoof. How many years is it that you've not known me?"

On the other hand, she would have been pleased if he'd meant what he said. She had to take account of the fact, she supposed, that he was still feeling sorry for himself. That apart, she'd be content to pretend he meant it. She was prepared for the time when his entire focus was no longer his sole interest; then he'd be back to Peter Martinez.

The night nurse made herself diplomatically scarce. Jan stood up to leave, leant down and brushed her cheek to his. This time, there was a tenderness about the softness of their skins touching. He had been made to shave, which was a sure sign he was improving.

Her drive to the hotel was full of thought. Her dreams were happy.

The next three days flew by. She was in touch with London, arranging for all her City journalistic mates to have local representation in Palafrugell. Then she had met Carlos with Maria and he introduced her to the local press and a couple of the nationals. She'd invited officials from the Ministry of Health, the police and the senior medical officers from Palafrugell Hospital.

Peter had thrown himself into the new venture as if it was all his idea. He'd contacted his local tailor and together they had designed trousers with one leg, which had the longest zip they could buy, stitched into the inside leg seam, so that he could be seen wearing what would look like regular trousers. He'd wear a white shirt over his heavy bandaging and his mother would look for a suitable tie for him.

He would prefer, he said, to struggle into the conference room on one crutch and a nurse supporting him on his damaged shoulder side, rather than to be in a wheelchair. So they mapped out a route to the hospital lecture theatre, where they were to hold the conference, partially by chair and then avoiding stairs on to the stage from the rear, instead of the side where there were steps to climb.

Three days for three people on individual missions were about to begin.

For Maria, she sensed she had things to do behind the scenes Jan Roberts was setting, apparently to enhance Peter's survival in BCG.

The BCG 'family' never accepted any intruder foisted upon them by Non-Executive Directors or hungry institutional shareholders who fancied backing an outsider to come in and generate an uplift in their financial interests and a higher return than expected on their investment.

Mr William had acted true to form when he heard of Peter's plight, showing an immediate fake concern and compassion for the man, but matched equally by plotting and conniving as to how the family blood could be used as a transfusion to restore them to what they perceived as their rightful place.

Part of their ploy was to send Jan Roberts this time on an impossible mission. The family's inclination was to wonder how one person with a shoulder and knee shot to bits could prove to be anything other than a sacrificial lamb. Jan Roberts was a tough cookie equally hell bent on protecting her career, so faxes and telexes saying this captain of industry was not good for shareholders would be an impossibility. That would not meet with William's requirements and so she'd expect soon to have to fly herself back to interview any other CEO-in-waiting, to keep her network beholden to her important output. The Board knew, however, there was rarely an institutional investor who made a participating decision without first reading Jan's every word, if she had covered the subject matter. So the Chairman and his cronies needed her onside.

There was a call just as she arrived back at the hotel. William no doubt had put somebody on a promise to tip him off when Jan got back.

"What's the news?" came the impatient demands from family head office.

"Good!" was not the reply they expected. Jan was bright, and suspicious, in fact, of all men seeking stardom in industry. She'd met a few, summed up many and barricaded her bedroom door against those who believed bedding her would win her support and promotion. Not so Jan Roberts. The mere attempt would be sufficient for their profile to be lowered by the ball tip of her swathing pen.

That was one of the things she'd liked on her original meeting with Peter. Two whole days went by without a proposition, and he certainly was not gay, nor was he averse to female company, as were some of her more public school-reared interviewees.

"What do you mean by 'good'?" came the almost immediate response.

"Your Chief Executive patient is amazing," she replied. "He's been knocking on death's door, and if not that, certainly permanent disability in the early stages. But his recovery seems amazing. What's more, his nose for a deal hasn't left his senses the whole time he's been cocooned. He's called a press conference for Friday when his plans will be announced. Apparently a paper will be with you Thursday morning to acquaint you with his ideas. Death's door has clearly been slammed shut. Any threats of serious disability with this Spanish bull have to be ruled out. The City needs to know he's working up European ideas here in the heart of the new Europe and I expect he'll produce more results on this accidental stopover than any of his lieutenants sent over on a special mission."

Mr William was absolutely furious. He faxed all Board members, including his mates the Non-Executives.

"Peter Martinez seems out of control. He's doing something, I know not what, without Board consultation. This is what I personally always dreaded, like sending in a number three batsman in a test series without an agenda. Expect, but then it's not a promise, some 'paper' regarding his intentions on Thursday, say am. He's fixed a press conference, without any clearance through Tim Frankman, who is after all the group's tried and tested expert in such matters, for Friday. Suggest we need consult or meet Thursday afternoon to scrutinise intent and to stop it if we feel it's not in the best interests of the group. After all, Martinez is not in the best of health and has nobody with him to keep him in-balance, except a number of Spanish quacks and their nursing staff."

The Non-Execs all knew William well. After all, he'd appointed all of them. Although it had been difficult to strike a balance, they had kept him at the helm, yet had been instrumental in getting the younger, more dynamic Martinez into the powerful role of Chief Executive.

They phoned each other. The consensus view was to confirm back availability for discussion pm but to wait and see quite how intense the Martinez delirium might turn out to be, and how poorly conceived his plans.

At least Jan Roberts is out there to report back, they agreed.

CHAPTER 32

On the Thursday morning, Gina slipped into Peter's room, avoiding the early morning rush of nursing staff he called to his required state of awakening. He'd once clapped his hands to get attention, which brought about a threat of a massive walk-out. The girls on that duty quietly but firmly explained that Peter was not the only patient needing attention and that he would be dealt with in turn... and, "By the way, you're going to be last today."

A couple of boxes of chocolates and 200 Benson and Hedges filter tips soon reversed that procedure and he was back into control mode.

So, today potentially being his last full day, the girls on duty had reckoned they were likely to be on a parting gift. He was first for a morning glass of orange. First for a 'freshen-up' by the pretty young blonde nurse from Poland. He had pole position for blood pressure and temperature and by 7.45 he was dressed and sitting in his side chair ready. More correctly, before he had to face the police press conference.

He was delighted to see Gina. They'd been friends after the first journey on which they met ferrying Bob and Marcia back to England. He'd often wondered what would have happened if it had been Gina and not Marcia who had slipped under the covers with him that first morning. She hadn't generated the appeal factor for him but that need not have ruled out a romp with her, at the height of their adolescence. Even now, he thought she was close to being 'proper' but, with her super slim figure, despite the births of her two girls, had she slipped into bed beside him at this precise moment, he wouldn't have kicked her out, unless he heard either his mother's or Jan's footsteps coming down the corridor, which he now could as they turned off the landing and quickened their steps.

Gina's destiny, on that journey, had been predictable. Almost inevitably, she seemed so straight-laced, bound to marry a boring old banker or other professional type who would run a mile if ever confronted with the expertise somebody like Marcia was able to express in bed. Peter often speculated that such skill could only have come from loads of experience with blokes who could show her how to please. Yet he believed her, that it had been limited to just Bob until she had found Peter's receptiveness to her naturally creative abilities. There was somehow more of a compliment in that than being linked with her possible previous blokes. But who would ever know if there had been any?

He remembered once saying to Marcia, after a physical romp they confessed they had both needed, that if her storyline was true, and he accepted it was, then she was like the scratch golfer who had never had a lesson. "Bloody cheek!" she'd said, sitting up on her haunches. "Nobody has got to practise their putting with me. You're a bastard, Peter Martinez, and the penalty for your cheek and insult is that you're going to have to do another round."

Thereby began another exhausting hour of great physical exertion, at the end of which Peter caved in and said he took back all that he had said for fear of her screwing him to death.

Gina, his morning visitor, was a friend indeed and a part, in fact an integral part, of his life being saved.

"Hey, you look shining bright," was his greeting. *Did she actually blush a little?* he wondered. "What a difference, what have you done?"

"Oh, Peter! You're not meant to notice. Is it that obvious?"

"Yes. But I don't know what it is."

"You men! My husband was the same. I've lost a few pounds. My hair's shorter and I've had highlights."

"Turn around," Peter commanded. She did a little spin. "You've got a boyfriend, you crafty bitch." She did blush. She really did.

"Here!" he said, beckoning her to his chair. "I'm sorry, Gina. I started by joking. This has gone wrong on me."

There was a hint of a tear in the corner of her left eye. She put a hand on his better knee, almost instinctively.

"Does it show that much?" She seemed to pull herself together. Then she laughed as though having satisfactorily pulled off an April Fool's day prank on him. "Well, my dear Peter, you're wrong. At least, you may be," she said with a giggle. "I know you well. Amazingly, although in truth it's only been for a relatively short number of days, because of the long gap and your very occasional letters when you got around to replying, I do feel I know you as well as anybody. So the position's not that I've got a boyfriend, and even if I had, I could never desert my husband and the girls. They, at least, are grown up now but they'd hate me for letting them down.

"What has happened is that I've fallen deeply in love with someone. Actually, someone who's in about the same position as I am in, matrimonially. It's early days." And as she said that, her body secretly squirmed in obvious anticipation of the predictability of something happening at some time over the conference.

"Who knows? It's done one thing for me, though. It's made me realise that I was getting frumpy. Not worried by the odd pound or three. I stripped off secretly and looked in the mirror and didn't like what I saw. So I got to grips with myself. I did yoga through my pregnancies so I got the old prayer mat out again. There's a new hairdresser in Palafrugell so I've given him a try, and we'll just have to see how the refurbished me will make out."

"You'll make out fine," Peter said with reassurance. "Listen, I'll give you a bit of advice... have you made love with each other yet?"

"Goodness, no!" she said indignantly. "That's what I mean. It's early days. That's not quite the point of the agenda. We're just good for each other."

Peter threw his head back with laughter, laughter that was loud enough to bring the early day nurse in to ask if everything was alright. He dismissed her with a wave of his hand and lots of assurance that Gina had said something very funny, but very secret.

"Look Gina. Learn from me. There's a short cut to a man's heart. That's in bed. However deep a relationship is, it's superficial if not, even occasionally, consecrated in bed... and here's the advice... don't give in to your natural shyness... if ever it should come about. Then you won't keep his attention if he's aroused with anticipation and you then start talking about having to pull the curtains, or not do it in the car..."

"I'm not sure I need this advice, Peter."

"Of course you do. Be noisy!"

"Be noisy?"

"Yes, sure. Squeal a little. Then really noisy. Men recognise that as them satisfying you. Once they're in that role, then they'll relax, and you'll get the mutual satisfaction you're probably looking for."

She'd never ever been noisy, as Peter called it. When Marcel and she had first met, the closest they got to sex was heavy petting and then in relative silence so as to not wake his parents upstairs. She would not even allow him more than a hug in her own home, "In case Daddy comes in." Presumably Mummy would understand but on the paternal front, it seemed she had a preconception she'd get beaten and put to bed for a week in disgrace.

Then their first flat had had wafer thin walls. "Shhhh!" Marcel would whisper. "You'll wake the neighbours." Then the concerns turned to waking the children. So noise was not on their agenda. Damn it, Peter might be right.

"Tell you what," Peter said, throwing the single sheet down to expose the bareness of his upper torso. "Close the door. Hop on in and see if you can raise the roof sufficiently to bring in a couple of nurses and a doctor or two. It would be good practice."

Christ, she thought. *He even knows who…*

"Listen, Peter. You're a patient and I can tell you for free it would take more than that invite to get me into bed with you." What had got into her? she thought. Was it overreaction to having been found out or just to challenge what Peter had always offered?

"You certainly know how to put a fellow down. OK, back to your man of the moment if I'm not to get any attention from you. Is he local?"

"Not exactly." She hedged her bets.

"Well, I tell you one thing. He'll like your hair and appreciate the three pounds you've shed in his interests. I'd say you've got a pound or two to go but with all that screaming and shouting going on, he'll be responsible for that. Here!" he said, beckoning for her to come closer. He held up his cheek. "He's bloody lucky."

"Thanks, darling Peter. You're really good for a girl's morale. I actually mean that. I'll give one final shout for you. I hope you'll hear it where you are."

Peter laughed. "Listen, I'm off tomorrow."

"Yes. Had it not been for all the analysis and advice, I would have been able to say by now that's why I came. To say au revoir, and to say not to be so damn stubborn and do what you're told to do for a change."

"Thanks. And thanks for that advice too. I will try. I'm on a promise with my mother and Jan too."

"Do you mind if I ask?"

"Oh hell! What's the question going to be? Ask what?"

"Jan. Well… is she one of your noisy ones?"

Peter nearly burst his sides with laughter this time, enough for the day nurse to re-visit to check if it was mirth or pain again.

"You're a bitch, Gina."

"Why?" she said, somewhat offended.

"You just are. If you were one of the fellows at the bridge club or Max, I'd be bound to say yes and to tell you she goes like a rocket too. In truth, however, I really don't know."

"Don't know! That's not like you, surely. Are you slowing down in your middle age?"

"Look, my love. I've had my bloody shoulder blown to bits. You know, more than anybody, apart from your surgeon friend, what troubles I've had with my leg. So if anybody had lifted the young lady on to my willing but incomplete body, any screams of satisfaction from the lady's direction would have been smothered by mine through pain."

"Sorry, Peter. I presumed you knew each other well in London."

"Well, let's put it this way. In two days, with no intervening overnight stopover, she knows as much about my life as anybody. But we haven't reached bed together."

"I'm sorry again, Peter. But you look such a complete pair. I, and in fact most of the other nurses, thought you were an item."

That made Peter sit up and think. It felt strange hearing it from a third party. Being with Jan recently had indeed made him feel this was 'item' material. He was relaxed with her and quite turned on by the fact that she had announced herself to be a lady-in-waiting, subject to terms. He now intended to get fit in order to meet the challenge.

"You thought what? You and all the other nurses? Is that why they all backed off? Because they saw me spoken for? Bloody over-presumptuous cheek, I'd call it."

"No, darling. Mainly, they'd all worked out that you wouldn't be up to it, and besides, we nurses like to have a real scream if we're going to fool around."

"Touché," he said, matching her broad smile.

"Listen, Peter. I must go. We're operating in about 15 minutes. I'll be here a couple of hours and then I'm off to stock my house with food because I'm going to a conference tomorrow."

"With your boyfriend?"

"Don't be so nosy." She leant forward. "Keep in touch. I'm sure to see you before you head back to London. Take care." She leant forward and kissed him firmly but gently on the lips. As she did, she slid her practised nursing hand under the top sheet and grabbed his testicles hard and squeezed them gently yet firmly.

As Peter wriggled his lips to get out of what seemed to be a plumber's drain suction pad over his mouth and locked over the lower half of his face, he couldn't free himself sufficiently to let out the cry of pain stifled into his now airless throat and lungs.

Gina released her grip and lifted her head.

"CHRISSSST!" Peter bellowed, expelling every last cubic millimetre of breath he had in his body.

The door was thrown open and for the third time, the day nurse was standing in the doorway. "Now that wasn't laughter, Mr Peter. What the hell have you done?"

Gina stood up. "Oh. That's just the way he likes to say au revoir to his entourage of noisy girlfriends. Isn't it, darling?" Gina turned one more time before she left. "Do take care and… oh, seriously, thanks for the advice."

He could hear her laughter right the way down the corridor.

Maria had been put on hold outside Peter's room because he had a senior nurse attending to him, she was told. What was all the screaming about? Once inside, she asked him if he was alright.

"Sure," he said, "she leant on my bad leg."

"Well, at least that made her happy. I don't think I've ever seen her so ebullient. You've certainly made her day."

"Not me, I think," Peter said ruefully, never expecting his private parts ever to recover.

The plan was that Maria would come and pick Peter up after the BCG press conference the next day. She would take him to the hotel for a light lunch with Virginia and Marco and then Jan had said she would run him to Barcelona. That actually was the re-plan, once the two main women currently in Peter's life had given in to male pressure from above.

In Maria's case, she had bowed to Superintendent Santé's pressure for their press conference, originally planned for the Friday, to be brought forward. The deal was that Santé would call the conference for Thursday and announce the facts about the bandit cousins and that they'd got Mr Big, a yet to be identified rebel from southern Spain. That much was politically acceptable to his Catalan masters. It was to be announced that Peter was in no way connected and Jan wrote a piece into the script about how Peter was intending to invest in private medical facilities just, as it happened, as had been precisely forecast to Benito Alvor. That allowed Jan to comply with Sir Richard's request that she should not orchestrate a full-blown press conference without Mr William's sanction.

Peter, too, said to go along with that. It had been his idea for Jan to prepare a press release to be sent to Max in the UK, to then be leaked to the City. That was a very much less prominent way of drawing attention via the quiet approach Peter adopted, as compared to the more razzamatazz one his Chairman followed, whether it was that his horse had a fixed win at a secondary race meeting at Exeter, or the group's appointment to a bought contract in the Sudan.

Thursday's conference also freed Snr Alvor to clear the decks to leave the hospital on the Friday morning and allowed Peter to escape on that same Friday, as opposed to the Saturday. Also, Maria realised Jan and Peter had business to discuss and wanted to see the police press conference was out of the way. She made her apologies on the basis that she had hotel things to catch up on.

The press conference itself had gone well. Even Mr Tovey had put his script of questions back into his briefcase, presumably as there was no mischief to report. That had been abundantly clear once Superintendent Santé, in full

330

dress uniform, had announced the total success of the enquiry, and Peter's complete lack of involvement in the events, beyond being in the wrong place at the wrong time. Peter had intentions to contribute further to the future wellbeing of his native land… all to be revealed the next day, Santé explained.

When Peter and Jan got back to Peter's room, she began work on her paper for release to the Board members, to be faxed to all the members' mail-boxes directly they were on target, to enable the Thursday afternoon discussion and hopefully getting a green light to proceed with the announcement.

Max's little time-bomb was released as a rumour at the same time.

Once all that had been organised, Peter moved on positively towards his release from hospital after the press conference the following day.

He had explained to Jan. "Better let Mother do her thing and get me out of hospital. That's a maternal obligation for her. She'll thank the staff like the UK's Queen Mother, maybe give out medals in the shape of boxes of chocolates, and then have some quality time with me in the car, no doubt to include 'what's the relationship with Jan?'."

"OK with me about the gongs and the lift home. Should we not check out the relationship thing and answer that from common ground?"

"Sure."

"What shall I say? Maria's on the brink of asking me, I'm certain."

"Oh, I think just say you're waiting for me to get my leg better and then we'll screw some time away and just see what develops."

"Fine. I'll use those exact words," she countered with a broad smile. "It's just as well I know you."

Mr William McArthur didn't seem bright enough to have worked out that somebody, in fact three of the Non-Execs, led by Sir Richard, had spoken to the Board members before his own calls. He eventually got round to making those late on the Thursday afternoon, having been sidetracked by his visit to the stables to give his winning horse at Exeter a pat on the back, and by naughty little Jilly, who was also up for a pat on various parts of her body for her role in the win.

He approached the members variously in alphabetical order, with the assistance of his devoted secretary, Vera.

"So do you agree it's a preposterous idea… ?"

"Our man's lost it, hasn't he… ?"

"What is he on, doesn't £5 million of other people's money mean anything to him?"

"I'm outraged… are you too?"

"No. Seems great to me, gives us a foothold in Spain…"

"No. I'm for it. Spain's a really developing country and as Jan Roberts puts it, it'll give us a head start in accessing bidding arrangements for their regional and national road network scheme."

"Sorry, William. I don't agree. It seems a real safe bet."

"I say we go for it…"

It seemed William was alone in doubting the sense of the investment. He had got the message. He muttered under his breath, "Fucked again by the bastard."

He could do nothing other than let Jan Roberts know they had the green light, at least to present the ideas to the planned press conference.

Maria said she'd be there at 10.30, and 10.30 it was. Peter hadn't got back to the ward quite when she arrived, so she busied herself packing Peter's modest collection of clothes and many letters and cards.

Once he was back, she lined the troops up and thanked them profusely. As she was doing that, Sñr Benito Alvor entered the room to find Peter securely propping himself up on forearm crutches. The left one was OK but the right one referred half his weight up into his right shoulder, which was still mending from the gunshot wounds. He could have winced at that pain alone but as he saw Gina in hot pursuit as part of the Alvor entourage, he focussed more on the greater ache in his testicles. In fact, she had administered the torture in such a practised way that the hurt to his pride overruled the physical pain. Gina caught his eye and winked. Peter could not hold back a smile.

Apart from the one day nurse to walk alongside Peter to the hospital main doors, all had now left with their 'thank yous' and variously shaped boxes of chocolates. Maria had forgotten to include Gina and Benito, and whispered to each of them, "There'll be something delivered later."

Peter had practised his crutch-aided walk to the lift. "Chin up, straight shoulders, long strides," as instructed by his favourite physio. "Watch out for the cleaner's sign saying wet surface. The wrong crutch angle on that could break the other leg and put you back ten or twelve weeks," was good advice, so he took extra care. Somehow that sign always spelt special danger to Peter, as he remembered how the dreadful scene had developed with Tania in the past in the hotel.

The automatic sliding doors slid gracefully open out of the hospital. The nurse said that he was on his own now and kissed him affectionately on the cheek, telling him to, "Take care."

Maria had gone ahead and fetched her Mercedes, a symbol of the affluence gained from having run a successful hotel for 20-odd years. Peter slotted in the front alongside his mother. They drove forward at moderate pace and slowed at the mini roundabout, which allowed access to the

Accident and Emergency wing, through which he had entered those weeks before from above, and the service area and staff car park. Maria stopped to let a Mercedes 300SL go through.

"Oh! That's Sñr Alvor," Maria said, in late recognition.

Peter looked up from tuning in the radio away from his mother's favourite 'rubbish' to something he would appreciate slightly more.

"Bloody agony."

"Peter, your language!"

"Well, I'd never have guessed."

"Guessed what?"

Peter was in a degree of shock but reacted quickly. "Oh, guessed he drove a nice car like that."

"Well, it works," Maria said, "he appeared to have a very nice blonde into the bargain."

"Mother, you mustn't say that. It may be his wife."

"I don't somehow think so," she smiled. "He's a very handsome man." At the junction with the main road Benito and Gina, still exchanging excited chatter, took the left turn out through the town and on to the 'A' class road down to the Catalan capital. Maria's car turned almost instinctively in the other direction, towards the sea and home to Calella. It was, of course, the first time out of hospital for Peter. She thought he seemed strangely nervous. She'd got him to herself again, which was now an infrequent occurrence.

"So, what's the plan, chiquito?"

"Mother, that's cheating. I got to play in the first 11, I'm married, got two kids, no, three actually, and apparently have grown up. I'm a bit too much of a man to be called that."

"Peter darling, once a chiquito always a chiquito. Sorry. I'll try not to. But you'll have to understand that's what you'll always be to me. Anyway, what's the plan?"

"Lunch and hi to Marco and Virginia and anyone else who still knows me at the hotel. If you behave, we'll take the rest of the day easy, stay over and then Jan will chauffeur me to purgatory in Barcelona, Hospital de Mar. I'll promise to give them two weeks of my life although they're asking for four, and then back to England, where I might still find I've got a job."

It seemed to have just dawned on Maria what Peter had said. Like a leading counsel in court, she went back to a point he'd established in and earlier cross-examination.

"Married! Peter, you said you're married! Is there something I ought to know about you and Jan?"

Once again in a day fairly full of laughter, Peter burst forth.

"Mother! You're so predictable. I can almost lead you into asking any question I want you to ask. Listen, of course I'm married. Poor Anna died with our wedding ring on and I didn't take her death to mean 'and now I'm free too'. We had a great marriage, which was tragically cut short. A little like yours with Father. Now about Jan…"

"I'm sorry, Peter. Of course, I understand. It's just that I thought you might have just gone off and got married again without telling your doting old mother."

"Now I promise I'd never do that."

"So what about Jan? She's a lovely girl. A bit young, perhaps, but there's a bonus in that if you continue to go around getting yourself into scrapes."

"Well, let's say that the relationship is sufficient for us to have anticipated your question and we've rehearsed the answer."

"Oh, Peter, come on, don't play with me. What's that answer?"

"Ask Jan. She'll tell you. That's a promise."

"You're really a very nasty son to have. Why play with my emotions?"

"Oh, come on. Who was the one in the family having a rampant affair with José without telling us?"

"It wasn't rampant, and besides, that's different. OK, I'll ask her."

Peter was slightly amused by the prospect.

Marco, Peter thought, was really now showing his age. The toil of the last couple of decades, building the hotel into the success it had become, was telling. There had been peaks and troughs in tourism to deal with and many complicated changes in currency rates, which could have swung a predicted profit into a thumping loss. The sister-in-law/brother-in-law relationship had been a good one, Maria balancing out Marco's impetuosity and Marco getting Maria to be a trifle more speculative from time to time.

As for Virginia, she had given up years before and was now fully adjusted to going with the flow, making the most of Marco's enforced holidays, which Maria still reminded him were fundamental to their partnership arrangement. If Marco had not stuck with the drinking embargo, he would have been long gone by now. So all had been well.

Jan appeared about 20 minutes after she had seen Maria's car pull up. She'd tactfully given the family a bit of prime time alone together.

"Hi," she announced on entry.

What's with all the women in my life today? Peter thought. Jan had had her hair done too. She too had a touch of highlights. Perhaps the local coiffeur was giving group discounts. She looked fit and slim, as indeed, Peter reflected, she always did. She held back, not wishing to show too much familiarity to the world outside their budding relationship.

"Hi," Peter responded, "don't I get a welcome-out-of-hospital pat on the head or something?" He rose. Steadied himself on his crutches, and strode towards her. He bent slightly offering her a cheek to peck. She graciously did so.

"Hey! Mother's got a question for you."

Jan blanched. He'd been in a mischievous mood for over a week now. That was really unfair, but she would rise to the bait.

"What's that, Maria?" she asked.

It was Peter's turn now to harbour inward discomfort, which he had in fact brought on himself.

Maria smiled. "Jan, my son is a rebel. It's not a question for here. Later. It's girl talk."

Jan smiled her more competitive smile. "Oh, come on, Maria. I've been around your family for almost a week. Hopefully I know you all well by now. I bet you want to know about our relationship."

Peter was now beginning to hate this little show.

"Bless you, Jan. You've saved me asking the question."

Peter thought: *15-all.*

Jan laughed confidently. Looking towards Peter, she said, "May I?"

Thirty-15, he thought, and he wasn't even playing this game.

"OK by me," he instructed calmly. *Thirty-all.*

"Peter said you'd ask that question. He says apparently any female in his life gets the same interrogation."

Thirty-40.

"Hey, that's not fair. You tell the family the truth."

Deuce.

"OK. Peter's proposed to me..."

No, I bloody haven't, he thought. *I've propositioned her... but that's up to her to say.*

Advantage Jan.

"... And I've said I'll let him know if he's a good boy and sees out the four full weeks of treatment. So I'll be back in a month to let him know... he'll have to wait till then, and only then if he's a lot fitter than he is at this moment."

Game, set, match, tournament, series and one of the classic wins to Jan Masters.

"Well done, Jan. So that serves you right, young man. Let's say you're in for the duration. Good girl, Jan. Perhaps he'll see some sense now."

Maria was openly pleased with that outcome. Poor Peter looked a bit beaten. He was so keen to get back to his job. But if he had real feelings for the ladies in his life, he would stay the one course to accomplish the other.

The five broke into nervous laughter. Virginia took command. "Now… I've organised a light buffet lunch under the awning on the terrace, it's a nice mild day. The air will do you good, Peter. You're looking pasty, dear."

"Aunt, I haven't been out for the best part of… what was it? Two years. I'm bound not to look too much a picture of robust health."

"Oh, don't worry, darling," she countered, "you'll soon get colour back into those Mediterranean cheeks of yours."

Maria disappeared and returned with about 20 envelopes. "There's this post for you, Peter. It all looked a bit formal so I didn't bother you in hospital."

"Oh, Mother, You should have done – who knows, it might have stimulated my brain into action."

"Well, you'll have to leave it for now. Virginia's ready for us. Another hour won't make a great deal of difference."

Virginia's light buffet was not so light, especially for Peter, who had only seen hospital food for ages, apart from the odd treat smuggled in by either Maria or Jan. Marco's wine flowed generously. They were drinking one of his good Montrachets.

"Good God!" Peter exclaimed, once the first sip of the refined juice from the grapes hit his palate. "In all my time in hospital, I hadn't really missed a real drink but now I'm reminded of it, I don't know how I survived without it."

"Santé, everybody."

Jan stood up from the terrace chair and walked across to Peter's side. She leant towards his left ear. The journey was as much a surprise to him as the glimpse of her cleavage.

"Tell them how much you've missed sex," she whispered.

Fifteen-love.

Peter beckoned her ear towards his lips. "I didn't," he whispered back. "There was this night nurse…"

Fifteen -all.

"Male or female?" she countered.

Fifteen-30, he thought.

"Now what on earth are you two children whispering about?" Maria interrupted.

"Tell her, Peter. It's rude to whisper."

Fifteen-40.

"Jan was asking if it would be alright for her to thank you formally for your hospitality and kindness during her stay here." He knew about how she had gone to reception that morning to settle her bill, to be told there was no bill. She had been a welcome guest of the Martinez family.

Thirty-40.

"Jan, it's been a real pleasure." This time, Marco took the honours for not rendering a bill. "You're more than welcome any time." He took care to hold back from saying that her pretty underwear draped across the chairs on her balcony had been as much a welcome sight to him as her actual presence had been.

"Peter said it for me, I'm afraid. I really do appreciate you welcoming me into your home."

"Home," Virginia said succinctly. "That's part of the problem actually, Jan. It all became 'home' and has rather taken over."

"Now don't let's go down that route," Maria chirped in to lighten the conversation. Then quickly: "So, it's from here to Barcelona. Yes? Then is it back to London for you, Jan?"

"That's the plan. Yes. I've managed to convince my agent that I needed time to help Peter on the private hospital funding idea, but that's all been rubber-stamped at amazing speed. Mr William is beginning to soften on the idea and reckons to treat it as a prototype for a UK replication. When I get back, though, I've got some serious interviews to do and a number of booked column inches to honour. I reckon I'll be at it six or seven days a week. I'll give that four weeks and, if I'm invited, I'll of course come back out to see Peter's progress in a month's time."

"I'm sure Peter will be delighted to see you by then."

"Oh, I don't know. He'll have been spoiled silly by the Catalan nurses by then. Male and, I bet, female. So I'll wait for his command to leg it over there for an audience."

Little bitch – game! She's only done it again, he thought. He smiled a smile of great pride and pleasure. He really liked everything about this spirited young lady.

"Jan, darling. Take this as the invite now," he said, and blew her a kiss to where she had now returned to her seat. Small talk, and Marco's recounting of how they came to set up the hotel, passed the time through lunch. An espresso coffee was a real treat to Peter. He checked through the post while the ladies busied themselves clearing dishes and returning with a bowl of fresh fruit. There was nothing too important. A few accountant's letters about Peter's tax position, then a few letters enclosing accounts to be paid for the advice they'd given which, broadly speaking, was not very helpful. One handwritten A5-sized envelope with the crest die-stamped into the back of envelope looked interesting. Peter tore it open.

MR WILLIAM FORRESTER AND MARCIA HUNT
Invite
MR PETER MARTINEZ AND PARTNER
to JOIN THEM IN
CELEBRATION OF THEIR MARRIAGE
at
The PENTHOUSE, ASPECTS HOTEL, LONDON

The date and time were about a month away. It was soon…

The rest was about RSVPs and dress code. Peter, at first, went cold. The thought of Marcia formally out of reach quite shocked him. He had, of course, briefly contemplated taking Marcia as a replacement for his beloved Anna. But he knew she'd only be anything like a wife in bed, and each time his needs had been satisfied, he ruled the prospect out, until the next time.

Marcia, too, had worked out her place. She was under no illusions. So when William Forrester came onto her scene, she jumped at the chance of security, with perhaps the odd furtive visit from Peter should her husband go away and her needs, and those of Peter, come together in the positive/negative magnetism that had always existed between them.

"Hey, Mother!" Peter exclaimed when Maria next came into sight. "Marcia's getting married."

"Married? Good God. How the hell has she done that?" Although she liked Marcia on one level, Maria had never really trusted her presence on this planet, and feared her getting her talons into her treasured son. So, in fact, she was quietly relieved.

"Mother, that's not fair." Peter's point was made. "Jan, have I ever told you about Marcia?"

"Not Marcia. I think, some of the others, yes."

"Well, when we have time to waste, I'll tell you. Despite Mother's vicious insinuations, she and her first husband were good friends to me. In fact, and I've never thought about this before, if it hadn't been for them, I doubt if I would have had the relative success I've enjoyed. Girasol was accidentally down to them, you see. Anyway, can you put 17th November in your diary? I'd like you to come to her wedding. I'll buy you the hat."

Peter had waved goodbye to the Playa and his family many times before. But never, he thought, from the passenger seat of a car. That was a temporary

338

expedient, he reminded himself. He had always rested well at his adopted Spanish home and was always sorry to leave it.

"Take care, both of you," said Maria. "Remember, I'll have the car picked up from the airport. There's a note in the glove pocket where to leave it."

Peter still found it hard to turn due to the muscular restriction in his shoulder. But he turned as far round as possible, to wave fondly to the close and supportive members of his family. His son Alex and daughter Petra phoned regularly, but despite each of their conversations including, he felt sure, a genuine concern and the suggestion that they should fly out from their adopted homes to see him, they seemed to accept the 'really no need' reply a bit too readily. Had the positions been reversed, Peter knew that he wouldn't even ask the question, but would just turn up at their bedside. Maybe, he often reflected, they'd developed a casualness towards family relationships because their mother wasn't around to tie their bonding knots together. He would put that out of his mind again, and thank his blessings for the great matriarch in his life and, he had to acknowledge, Jan's influence at that time.

He turned to her and smiled. "Bitch!"

"Bastard."

They both threw their heads back simultaneously in laughter.

"Well," she said, "you pushed me to the limit."

"Actually, you did very well. You had me really worried. I wasn't sure how liberal you were going to be in front of my relations."

"Now would I let you down?"

"Actually I know you wouldn't." He passed his hand across the gear change and squeezed hers.

They had reached the point of entering the road at that great intersection where he always thought of Tania being thrown off her bike, and Marcia trying to catch him on that first encounter. Then the shopping trip with Marco for Roman remains. This was truly home.

"Which way?" Jan asked.

"Main drag or country route?"

"What time have we got?"

"At least today, into tomorrow if needs be."

"Then, without a doubt, the country route," Jan decided.

"Then equally with no doubt whatsoever, the best way is to the right."

They drove in silence for 20 minutes or so, she following her instincts and trying to turn left or right to keep in a straight line.

"Peter!"

"Yes, Jan."

"I know I'm just a weak-minded female but I've got that distinct feeling I'm heading north… the shadows are falling left to right and…"

"Rubbish. You're fine. Right at the next junction."

"OK."

Fifteen minutes later, she said, "Hey, that's beautiful!" She was referring to a field of tired sunflowers, heads bowed before they faded into winter.

"Do you want to talk to them?" Peter enquired.

"Do they tell horoscopes?"

"Yes. All the time."

"Then yes, please. Providing I can whisper the questions."

"They'll always prefer that," he said.

The ground was soggy and his arm crutches sank a few centimetres into the soil, making crutch-assisted walking difficult. Jan didn't help. She slowed, but walked ahead a little like the hare on the last lap at a greyhound race. Peter held back. *Good,* he thought; he'd witnessed this all once before. What would happen next would be that Jan would say the sunflower had spoken to her. Peter would say, "Of course he did."

She did. He said, "Of course he did." He turned around with difficulty and they jointly manoeuvred back to the waiting car.

"Straight on," Peter advised, and then navigated Jan around the bends and the odd turn.

Jan eventually spoke with authority. "Peter. There's no way this country route is going anywhere near Barcelona."

"I can't lie. You're right. Well, half-right. I wanted to show you Girasol. After I've introduced you, I promise I'll get us back on the right road and in no time we'll get to Barcelona."

"Peter Martinez, you're a cheat. You should have told me…"

"… And you would have said be a good boy and do as you're told. Listen though. I've got to get the fear of Girasol out of the way. I nearly got killed here. I wanted you to be party with me to rediscover it. Just an hour. Then I promise we'll be off and we'll be in Barcelona by about five. Anyway, your matey sunflower didn't say 'turn back', did he?"

"No," she said, "Go on. Trust in Peter. He's passed this way before and never fails to wave." As they moved away, Jan did wave back.

That made Peter go cold. He always waved, but nobody in the world knew that, and now Jan was following suit.

"So it's OK with you to go on?" he said. "It'll be on your terms. You say move and you can take me to the next Institution and bury me away from the rest of the world for a while. Two or three weeks, we'll say."

"You heard what I said during that ridiculous game you set up. You're there for four."

"Suppose I say the prize isn't big enough?"

"Then you'll not see me in Spain again… and I'd be very disappointed if you don't see this rehab as one of the essential steps in your life, if not the biggest."

"You're getting more like my mother every day. OK. It's a four-week aim if I can possibly make it. But you'd better be good."

"You mean noisy?"

Peter paused and went into thought mode. He'd never had that discussion with Jan. How could Jan and Gina have chatted since his consultation earlier that morning? He wasn't going to be able to work that one out alone. "Why did you say noisy?"

"It's got to be confessional time soon. You've been married and, no doubt whatsoever, you've had a relationship or two. I haven't. You know about my time with Richard. Well, when roused, I seem to become noisy naturally. He always found it an embarrassment and would try and suppress it… you know, almost the 'you'll wake the neighbours' syndrome. So really, it was a warning I was giving you. I read that some guys find noise a compliment, so if that's a measure of being good or otherwise, then I just wanted you to know… but I don't know if I can help it."

"OK, it's four weeks, definitely, and then ear muffs."

They drove on for a while in silence, punctuated with the occasional, "Left here,", "Right fork," etc. The giveaway was they passed a sign on the verge: 'Girasol'.

As they turned into the access road to the resort, Jan slowed. She turned to Peter and said, "It really is lovely, Peter. I hope you're very proud of this wonderful creation." She placed a hand on his thigh and patted it. "Really, really beautiful."

Praise from Jan touched Peter greatly. "Thank you, I'd hoped you'd like it. My little place is in the first limb on the left and right at the end, on the water's edge. I'll say when we're there.

"We're there," was the next comment.

Jan eased the car into neutral and applied the handbrake. As of a habit, she looked in the rear-view mirror and patted her hair, as though she might be meeting somebody unexpectedly.

"Stay here," she commanded, "I'll give you a hand out."

That made him feel a bit lame but, on the other hand, it was very comforting.

He had ensured he'd got his house key handy. Ordinarily he'd ring Tania at the hotel and ask her to leave one under the stone on the step. But he wanted a quiet private visit this time. Jan helped him by passing the crutches, which she had laid on the back seat for the journey and allowed him his freedom to get himself out of the car in his own slightly clumsy way. She held his arm lightly as they walked, or in Peter's case crutched, up the short path into the porch of the compact town house. Peter placed the key in the lock and turned it. The door opened freely under the weight of his arm. He placed his crutches gingerly onto the inner door-mat.

In retrospect, a day or so after, when he remembered the moment, he couldn't quite recall if his scream, joined by Jan's, had come during or after the mayhem that accompanied the opening of the door. Shrieking sirens wailed, informing anyone whose eardrums had not already been pierced that there was either extreme danger about, or they were about to be hit by stray American missiles, lamentably off-target.

Peter froze. He knew the war-zone they were now in. Jan had absolutely no idea whether it was something her friendly sunflower had organised or some pre-programmed practical point Peter was making about noise. Peter shouted above the mayhem.

"Shit! I bet it's my bloody mother who's introduced some new security device, and not told me about it."

Somehow they became accustomed to the level of decibels.

"Outside!" Peter commanded.

Jan was happy to obey. She steadied his arm and the two inhibiting crutches as they stepped outside and the door closed shut behind them. In the relatively muted surroundings, Peter allowed himself a smile.

"Jan," he shouted, "I have absolutely no idea what any of that was about!"

On the outside wall, there was a box that simply said 'Securitie Catalonia', to which their eyes were drawn due to a constant clicking noise and a blue flashing light just visible in the softening afternoon sun.

"I'm bloody right, it's my mother providing extra security while I was away... but why the hell not tell me about it?"

At that moment, a female voice came from behind Jan's parked car. "Mr Peter. Thank God, it's you!"

Peter recognised Tania's Romany voice. "Thank God it's me! What the hell do you mean by that? I could be dead with fright. Who the bloody hell turned my house into the nearest thing to a bank?"

"Mrs Maria, sir."

He stopped in his tracks. "Do you know the combination?"

"Yes."

"Well, come on then, Tania, either tell me what it is, or punch it in to stop this deafening noise."

"1234P," she shouted above the din.

"Well go and punch it in!" he shouted back.

She scurried off and within seconds, it seemed, the world became silent. Tania reappeared. Mission accomplished. Her gypsy eyes glistened as the surge of adrenalin began to subside. The three stood in uncomfortable silence while they regrouped their various senses.

"This is an old family employee. Tania. Tania, this is Miss Roberts."

At least it appeared they were not married, Tania thought. She did a small curtsey and bowed her black silk-covered head slightly, instinctively holding out her right hand. Jan took it and lightly squeezed it as they exchanged a traditional greeting.

"Thank you for coming to our rescue," she said. That brought the reality of the situation into Peter's now less demented mind, which had temporarily gone into brainstorming mode.

"Tania. I'm sorry. I haven't thanked you." He, too, took her soft hand into his.

A shiver went up her spine. Being in his presence again was enough; touching him again was a bonus.

"Why the hell do you think my mother didn't tell me about the alarm, do you think?"

Jan introduced reality into the situation. "Because you're cheating. You're meant to be many miles in the opposite direction, checking in to the new hospital." A gentle smile eased over her lips, exposing the teeth her mother had made her clean and polish, promising that, "One day, my dear, you'll thank me," which indeed Jan often did. Likewise with telling her father eventually how much she appreciated, in retrospect, being forced through all the tiresome orthodontic procedures they organised for her, with the comforting forecast that she would be pleased one day to have gone through that.

Mention of 'hospital' had given Tania the opportunity to say, "How is the leg, Mr Peter, oh, and the shoulder?"

"Fine," he said bravely, knowing that he wouldn't have been able to get to the keypad at the same speed as Tania because of his temporary handicap. Tania paused while she thought deeply about whether she should apologise on behalf of her family for what had happened. Peter beat her to the draw.

"Jan. Perhaps it would be better if I explain that it was the bad side of Tania's family who got me tangled up into this mess. It had nothing to do with her. I was just in the wrong place at exactly the wrong time."

Mr Peter was being generous again, like the time he had let it be known he'd walked into a tree, having taken a beating from that wrong side of the family. Like the time, also, she had set him up in the staff changing room in the hotel.

He had always been kind to her. The bicycle, approving Marco's arrangement about where she was now, living and running the small hotel in the complex. Most of all, he had shown – with the benefit, too, of some maturing on her part – that he was not going to be another male in her life who would abuse her, like her father, Toni and then Marco, albeit on a commercial basis. Or accept her open invitation, as more recently those overnight guests had done, for whom she had felt the need. They'd all accepted her invitations as the animal within had decreed.

Her Mr Peter would always be different, yet now, because of her, he had been close to death and being crippled for life.

"Mr Peter. I'm ashamed it was my family who brought this about." She gesticulated towards his two crutches.

The trio were all now slightly more relaxed than in the deafening environment in which they had come together.

"Listen," Peter said, "I bet the larder's bare. Jan, I'm sure you'd like a cup of English tea to restore your nerves. We won't have any milk, though."

"I'll fetch some," Tania said, almost subserviently. "Give me six or seven minutes." And she was off on her mission.

"Well, Jan." Peter turned to his guest.

"Well, Peter," she responded, "aren't you ever going to lead a life without drama? I tell you, much more of this and I'll soon be a frail little grey-haired lady."

"I've never said this before," he said impetuously, "but I'll still love you when you are."

She was stunned. He'd never said anything about their relationship previously. He, too, was surprised but their senses were mutual. They had missed out on the great moment one is meant to experience of love at first sight, and the infatuation stage that follows, which is so often short-lived. They seemed to have graduated straight to a level of contentment and mutual understanding, qualities that characterise longstanding relationships built to last a lifetime, not mere moments of lust that must be satisfied. Maybe those moments, in their case, would develop later, against a backdrop of love.

"So I've got to dye my hair and develop a stoop and fart uncontrollably before you'll love me, have I?"

"No," Peter said, "I just, in fact, said I love you now, and if you weren't being so bloody analytical, you would have come to me, thrown your arms around my neck, and reciprocated my feelings…"

She stepped forward. Put her arms around his neck, looked up into his large open face and said, "Oh, do you know… I think I do love you and…"

Tania was suddenly standing there, pulled up in her tracks at the sight of

Peter and Jan in their clinch. She was carrying a wicker tray on which was a small Thermos of milk and a Tupperware cover over some of her now famous Madeira cake.

"Oh, sorry," she said, with some embarrassment.

"No. OK. Come in," Peter said reassuringly, whispering to Jan, "what was the 'and' going to be?"

All Jan did was to touch his nose with her forefinger. She turned to Tania. "Wow! Tea. That will be welcomed."

"I've brought you some of my Madeira cake."

"She's the queen of that cake. Men come from miles around for that."

Tania dropped her head. Surely there was an innuendo somewhere in that…

"Is there anything else you'll be needing?" she asked.

"How do we reset the frightening alarm when we leave?" Peter asked.

"Just 1234P then E. The 'E' is apparently European for 'exit'."

"Thanks for coming to our assistance. I'll close everything down before we go."

"So that I can check on the lights and look out for robbers, roughly what time will you be leaving?"

"In a couple of…"

Jan interrupted. "We're staying over… leaving in the morning… and I bet Mr Peter didn't check ahead if there were sheets aired." By design, Jan reminded Tania of her service status.

"No, I didn't, to be completely truthful, but I'm sure the hotel have some."

Tania reacted in full co-operation. "They'll be up here in no time. I'll leave you in peace. What are you eating?"

"I'll rustle something up," Peter volunteered.

"How can you do that, darling, on crutches?" Jan turned to Tania. "Do you have what we call a takeaway service?"

"We can do that, but only for special owners. Would you like us to deliver something?"

"Something simple. We had one of Hotel Playa's buffets for lunch."

"Something cold?"

"What do you think, Peter?"

"I'd say yes to that."

"How about some cold salmon and a mixed salad?"

"Great!"

"What time?"

Jan looked at her watch. It was now 4.45pm. "Say, seven. Is that OK, Peter?"

"Absolutely fine. I'm just going to go along with the flow. That seems to be working," he announced with a wry smile.

"So at seven. Would you like to leave the wine to me?" Tania suggested, now with the confidence to do that, given the experience she'd gleaned from Marco over the years, and his words of encouragement.

Peter nodded his agreement.

Tania left. Peter and Jan were stranded back together.

"Here," she said, "this is the first time we'll have been completely alone ever, and then just for two hours or so, when our dinner will be delivered."

She took Peter's elbow and guided him to the French doors that led into the small garden area, and which Tania had opened earlier to give the place a bit of an airing. Not that Jan had yet seen it, but Tania had also done the honours with some windows upstairs in the main bedroom for the same reason. Jan could have found that quite offensive, Tania presuming that they would in fact be just in that one bedroom. But, fair enough. It was a modern stage on which they were the players and she couldn't blame Tania for jumping to that conclusion. She'd have to see how things panned out.

They sat in the wicker loungers, which had yet to be stored away for winter, facing each other. Neither mentioned that Jan had yet to give an answer to Peter's interrupted question. Nor was Peter stupid enough to enquire what exactly had brought on Jan's desire to stay over.

Anna drifted in and out of their conversation, as did Richard, Peter's mother, Jan's parents, Tania... yes, Tania more than once, plus her dreadful cousins, father and forlorn sister. Marco and Virginia did not escape kind analysis.

The bell rang. "Gosh!" they both exclaimed, almost as one. "Can it really be seven already?"

Tania's daughter laid out the dining table at the end of the living area, and her male accompanist attended to some experienced cork-pulling. They checked if everything was OK and then went off, maybe, Peter thought, for their own evening pleasures. They didn't seem just to have a working relationship. Marguerite was, after all, probably a fair way over the 20 year landmark, he thought.

Peter and Jan talked through their supper and sipped the Montrachet, which Peter was sure had been robbed from Marco's cellar. Jan waxed lyrical about her impressions of Girasol. It was 10.15pm when Peter looked at his watch.

"Jan. It's been a memorable day and I can only thank you so much for that. I've been waiting for an answer to the question that remains open. If we're to build on this early beginning to an honest future, I've just got to level with you."

For a fleeting moment, she feared he was going to say that he was gay or infertile or something tragic like that. For Peter to be sufficiently honest to

346

admit that he was absolutely bushwhacked, and would not wish to show failure in their first opportunity to share a bed together was, to her, a strength indeed.

"Peter, darling, we'll sleep together in the absolute sense of the words. We'll hold and comfort each other. That will allow me not to give in and weaken, as I could, until I've got you fit for the intended occasion."

She helped him up the stairs, steadied him out of the bathroom, then drew back the covers and poured him into bed. They had giggled when they realised they had no overnight things, as all her gear was packed for her flight back to the UK and his for his new hospitalisation, though he'd found a pack of travel toothbrushes in the medical cupboard.

She laid him into bed and said she'd be four minutes. "So don't go away."

She slipped in under the covers and found herself next to a silent and mummified body. Peter had crashed into oblivion, little knowing she had been prepared to break her pledge.

CHAPTER 33

Benito and Gina had agreed that, as it was common knowledge, and in fact the envy of a number of Gina's nursing colleagues, that they were both going to the conference, it would be perfectly natural to travel together.

Benito Alvor's determination to turn left at the T-junction was as great as Peter's had been to direct Jan to turn right to take his so-called country route. He and Gina had set out from the hospital with a degree of nervous excitement, expressed as furtive giggling. Now they were 20 minutes or so into the journey, and when they had run out of small talk, Benito's maturity showed through as they had relaxed and played with their own respective thoughts.

"Excited?" he enquired.

"Very."

"Feel guilty?"

"No."

Then she asked him. "Excited?"

"Extremely."

"Feel guilty?"

"Very."

"Actually, so do I." – which enabled them both to laugh naturally.

Benito was the one to introduce some reasoning to the situation. "Gina, let's get it said. In our own ways, we're probably both content with our lot. In many ways we've got what we set out to achieve when we were both a lot younger, as have our other halves, and you've satisfied your maternal desires. We both almost certainly hedged our bets heading for security. You may have been scared by the insecurity you felt from your early travelling, and maybe on those trips you didn't want to get caught up in a relationship within a culture, although it was European, which you didn't fully understand. So when you returned home, you ran for base. How's that?"

"Absolutely right. How on earth do you know me that well? We rarely see each other, other than behind face masks, and then it's not as if we've exchanged life histories."

"Because that's what happened to me too. Behind a mask, you can only read eyes. And the eyes can't lie. They react to emotion and change in light. I've seen your eyes and your emotions over an intense period of time. Through them I know where we're both emotionally balanced and from that I have no hesitation whatsoever in saying our bodies will bond in absolute unison… and that, my sweet…" he laid his right hand on her lower thigh, "… is predicted by a clinical surgeon who dices with odds of between one and 100 per cent failure daily."

"You amaze me, Benito. I thought it was my secret that I could read your every mood and moment. I hope you're right…" She covered his strong hand with her soft one, on which she noticed her wedding ring looking up at her. He had a thin band on the third finger of his other hand.

"Should we take off our rings?" she enquired.

"Will that make any difference to us? I want you to continue to love your Marcel, as I will try to love Alicia. Ours can be… well, just an 'us' thing, nobody else need know about it through the exchange of a crafted band of gold."

"So is it OK for me to say that I 'us' you?"

He roared with laughter. "Yes, of course. I 'us' you too."

Their hands entwined and each went into their silent worlds of thought. He eventually re-opened the conversation. "Gina, I've got a huge favour to ask."

"Go ahead."

"Anything?"

She felt a sudden nausea well up in the pit of her stomach. Was she about to discover he was some sort of deviant, such as it was rumoured the world of academia often created? Or into recreational drugs? After all, his life was full of tension and stress, both at work and at home. But she had to trust him. His eyes had always exuded honesty.

"Anything!" she chanced affirmatively.

"Thanks. From now on, could I possibly not have to hold my stomach in? My ribs are aching."

She roared with laughter, partly in relief, although he was not to know that.

"Of course you can. I need to know what you'll be like when you're old and everything is slipping downwards." She leant forward and peered at his waistline. "Have you let it go?"

"Completely."

"Wow! Then this infatuation I've been trying to hide is with a sylph-like God and not a Buddha!"

He pretended shock. "How dare you!"

She oozed compassion for his reaction by moving her hand so that she was able to pat his thigh, and then gently rubbed the area she had patted as if to say *There, there, there!* to put his hurt right.

"I thought the rule was 'anything'? I'm sorry."

"Not, how dare you touch me. It was how dare you think I would have let myself deteriorate to that extent!"

Mutual laughter abounded. They were having fun.

"Another most important thing," Benito said.

Oh God! she thought. He was going to say he'd got some weakness or other, or worse; something she'd find sordid to kill the fun of early romance.

"Speak, and I will hear," she replied bravely.

"Well, when I was born, my parents, after great research and thought, had me christened as Benito. From about the age of two, I became known as Ben, that is, until my mother disapproved of something. Then I was Benito again. At university I was Ben and then in my early hospital days that continued. Somehow or other, when I became a consultant, I was reverted to Benito. Could I possibly be Ben… unless and until I do something you disapprove of?"

He became Ben and she was very comfortable with that.

The Hotel Pan Europa was particularly geared for large conferences. It was a gamble the Germanic/Swiss ownership had taken with their American connections and interchange flights through Heathrow. Ben had been there before and was aware of their customer parking service but, to Gina's surprise, he drove straight under the large canopied area to where the flunkies were waiting. They were all well-drilled. Out came the light luggage from the trunk and away went the car to allow the next arrivals in without delay.

Ben led the way to check-in, making sure Gina didn't lag behind like a fifth wife in a Saudi Arabian city. He confidently announced himself as Señor Alvor, in which solo name he had booked. It was not of consequence to the management, as they let out rooms on a nightly charge and weren't particularly bothered about how many per room or checking passports. They took the booking and left the question of morality to the conscience of their paying guests, particularly when the organisers of any conference would have agreed to the hotel's terms to indemnify all costs emanating from the event.

Gina was suddenly conscious of her Ben reverting to business mode. There was obviously something wrong with the booking. Perhaps his wife or, oh hell, maybe Marcel, she thought, had checked up and found she was going to be sharing. She actually would have been disappointed not to be, even though she had thought that when she had told her husband she would phone him from the hotel when she arrived, it might be inhibiting if Benito was around.

So what was the problem? she wondered.

The heavy negotiation ended and Ben turned round bearing two keys. He had got separate rooms after all. She surprised herself with the change in her thought process. What a gentleman he was. He'd taken nothing for granted. She supposed if he had booked just the one room, it would have been a bit presumptuous after all. It would have removed the lady's right to respond in her own way to an invite into a fellow's bed. It would have been different the other way round, Gina thought, though what was the difference, really? None. It was the principle.

They moved towards the lift, she with her vanity case she'd picked up in Palafrugell and taken straight to her locker at the hospital so as not to face the barrage of questions from her husband or particularly her two daughters, who would want to borrow it. He had just his flight case with all his conference papers. He had been invited to make the one formal delivery on 'Emergency Surgery – the importance of developing anaesthetics and a supporting team', perhaps intended to bring Gina into prominence.

They alighted at the seventh floor and walked down the plushly carpeted corridor. Ben stopped them both outside 8007, and placed a key in the door. "The lady has first choice," he announced.

Gina entered somewhat gingerly, not really wishing to make any such decision. It was what she had read about in magazines. A very large double bed, which she wouldn't be able to differentiate between king size or queen. It was certainly big. She walked to the window, with an amazing view down to the pool. She looked back inside to the walls, which appeared to be covered in silk. There were panelled wardrobe doors all over the place, it seemed.

She'd noticed a door on the right as they entered, which she went back to and opened. It was a bathroom just like in an advert for a film. The inner glass door concealed a shower. The louvred one shielded the toilet. The bath was adorned with towels and all nice things to make a girl feel clean and smell overpowering. The hand basin was sunk into a marble top and there were enough mirrors to show her that she looked good but even if slightly travel-worn.

Ben seemed to have tactfully held back on entering the bathroom domain and left her to her own discoveries. Was it that he'd been down this route before, or was this all part of his inbred charm? The latter, she felt sure… she hoped.

"Could I test one more thing?" she announced. She'd noticed the room door had closed automatically behind them.

"Sure, what's that?" he said.

"Here. Could we kiss?"

"Kiss?" he said, as though unprepared for such an event.

"Yes," she said, puckering her lips and closing her eyes in anticipation of not being declined.

There was a coolness about Ben's lips. They were soft and gentle. Masculine but not overpowering. They warmed as both their mouths melted together, as though through some chemical reaction. Had she not pulled away, she felt the whole of the remainder of her body would have melted towards his. This was too soon, she resolved. It was broad daylight and no time for melt-down but the embrace was reassuring.

She stood back. "I'll take this one," she said.

"What, without seeing the other?"

"Yes. No problem."

"How come?"

"I feel happy. I feel this is home. I feel lucky in this happy home for our 'us', that's it really."

Ben laughed. "Let's look at mine then."

They went back out into the corridor and stopped outside the next door. Ben produced the second key marked 8008 and led the way in, as if resigned for this to be his room. The bathroom door, this time on the left, was open. That was their first port of call. Gina quickly assessed the shower, toilet cubicle, bath and vanity unit. Then out into the sleeping area. Again a huge bed, across to the window and the same view. The walls again were silk-covered.

"What do you think?" Ben enquired.

"I'm not sure if I should change my mind."

In the front of her mind she had worked out, as they were in transit from hers to his, that, if perchance they eventually shared a bed, it would be better for Benito to have to return to his room than the reverse if, as he had apparently chosen, they were to give the appearance of leading separate lives. *Would that be fair?* she thought. On balance, it would be the decent thing and that surely would be what Ben would prefer.

"Could we do the same test as before please?" she asked.

She puckered her lips and closed her eyes. They experienced again that same melting feeling. She was now more relaxed and, just as she would later wonder what the hell had possessed her to rub his thigh in the car, so she had no idea what made her this time gently run her tongue along his soft lips. He was noticeably aroused, as she was sure he had been in the car; she sensed the soft rounded tissue parting slightly, offering a welcome as she probed her way, feeling a hint of the intimacy beyond.

There was a sudden knock at the door. A private detective sent by one of the opposing team? They parted and Ben went to the peephole.

He looked back over his shoulder. "Baggage," he announced.

"Of course," she said, with relief.

He opened the door. "This one in here. That one into 8007. I'll follow you with the key," he said in a commanding fashion.

The bell-boy obliged and Ben, who had retained the key to Gina's room, walked the short distance to open that door so the case could be delivered. She had followed him without him realising, and so when he turned to leave the room, having put the case in front of one of the wardrobe doors, she startled him.

"Oh, you made me jump!" he said, laughing.

"Well I thought I ought to make tracks too into our lucky room."

"*Our* lucky room? I thought it's *your* lucky room?"

She was sorry she had startled him. Momentarily, he looked exposed and insecure. She had been disappointed by the intrusion of the bell-boy. She'd not been this excited for many a day, if ever, she thought. They were there for each other, blow the conference. Their kisses had been very special.

"It is my lucky room but only when you're in it with me."

His wife had never been that kind, let alone that romantic.

"Come here, you!" he demanded. She did not hesitate. If it had been Marcel, she would have thought he was treating her like some little pet dog. But because it was her Ben, who ordinarily had control over her every action while they were operating, she saw it as more of an invitation than an order. He held both her hands and leant towards her, placing his lips on hers again.

Suddenly a chill of excitement tingled as their tongues this time touched, bridging the otherwise physical barrier between them. She had never realised she had hairs extending from the nape of her neck, down between the muscled mounds protecting her kidneys and along the line of her lower spine, into the crease between the cheeks of her bottom and into the erogenous zones she knew always made her, in her private terms, feel strange. Each hair identified itself as if a fibre optic display in the depths of darkness, and tingled in reaction to the closeness of their bodies. This was night to her but only because her eyes had closed into a dream world.

Suddenly she appeared to freeze as she felt that her body was entering some sort of trembling trauma. Benito was quick to pick up her reactive body language. He pulled back and put both protective arms around her and held her close, reminiscent to them both of their first physical contact.

Gina let out an uncertain laugh and pulled her head away from its comfort zone alongside Benito's. She knew she was trembling and that he had picked that up.

"It's very strange. I've never had it before, and I doubt I ever will again, but nature's reacting on me with volcanic influence."

"What?" Benito exclaimed. "I'm the one who understands bodies. How come?"

"There are earth tremors before the quake. Don't be silly. Just understand.

Now this lady needs her bathroom and you, her man, has had a journey and as much pre-volcanic tension as I know I have. I'm going to use the bathroom. I'd like you to accept the invitation from 2007 to 2008 to rest over. Get under that bed cover and be ready to continue to comfort my embarrassing reverberations. I'll be quick. Very quick."

She pecked him on the lips and pointed to the bed, lifted her overnight case and announced her arrival into her en suite with the clunk of the security lock on the door hitting its keep.

If there had been an Olympic discipline in female undressing, she would have been the winner, in whatever field, on this particular day.

Her blouse was off. Her skirt down. She had invested in new stockings so those were removed more gingerly. She released her bra from its secure clip at the back. As she did she glimpsed her now virtually nude body in the mirror.

OK, she said… *yes, OK, anyway the bedroom is only in a half light and this impulse is going to save Ben a hell of a lot of clumsy fumbling…* Not that he would, but she didn't want him to be the one to show total control from experience.

The bra joined the other clothes on the side of the bath. She put her hands into the elasticated waistband of her new matching knickers and slid them down to the top of her thighs.

No! Keep your dignity, she thought. She pulled them back up.

She'd noticed the hotel's white Turkish towelling beach robe on the back of the door. Well OK, she was not intending to swim just yet but she'd feel less conspicuous in her crowd of two if she was not too exposed.

Benito heard the bolt reversing its journey to the unlocked position.

Her soft voice called out, "Are you asleep yet?"

The reply came, "Yes."

"Then keep your eyes closed, I decided I needed to rest too."

As she appeared at the side of the bed, he opened one eye. He held out a welcoming hand. She took hold of it and moved the other one to join it. It really wasn't planned but on its route, it caught the bow she had tied around the waist of the robe and slowly the front panel parted from the one behind it and she revealed herself as topless.

Benito was by no means disappointed. "You're really beautiful."

She looked down at herself.

"Don't think this is for you. I've got a little strapless number to wear tonight and I didn't want to have strap marks on my shoulders."

"How very correct too," he said as he pulled the hand he still held gently, with Gina on the other end of it. With a little self-motivation she found herself back in his arms and reverting to the interrupted kiss.

She pulled back and spoke. "… And young man. Why no trousers?"

"Oh! You see I'll need to wear them in the morning and I didn't want to crease them."

"Good thinking," she concluded on his behalf.

He was gentle with her. She knew this man could not be otherwise. It was wonderful and arousing. She felt light-headed. Drunk without a drink. Drugged without the pain and suffering of dependency.

Their initial calmness moved on. She was right: the earlier palpitation stimulated state did become volcanic. There were aftershocks of varying readings on any set scale.

Afterwards, as they relaxed, Gina seemed to want to make a confession. "Listen. If I hadn't forced the pace, I think I may have exploded."

"… And how right you were to protect this beautiful body of ours from that fate," Benito said, meaning every word.

Neither would have known how much time had passed since their arrival and unexpected sojourn in Gina's bed. She prised herself away from Ben's sleepy body and slipped into the bathroom, re-appearing minutes later in a cotton hotel robe, which clung to her still warm body. She glided to the window and opened the curtains.

"Goodness me! Look, Ben. It's still light," she said, laughing at the situation. "We'll have to go to bed soon. It'll be getting dark."

"Come here, you bad girl," he commanded.

"You didn't seem to mind me being a bad girl an hour or two ago."

"I've got no complaints," he said, leaning forward and pecking her lips playfully. "We need a serious sad moment."

"Oh," she said, "do we have to?"

"Afraid so. But there's good news to match the bad news."

"Could we have the good news first?"

"Afraid not. Let's get it over with."

"OK. If we have to."

"Right. So, this is how it works. You have to phone Marcel. Tell him we've checked in, and they seem a boring bunch of old farts here. Give him this room number and then there'll be no doubt that we're not sharing. I'll never answer the phone when I'm in here."

"What about your wife?"

"She'll be given room 8008."

"What if I'm in there?"

"You won't be. It's out of bounds to young ladies. But the idea is you can speak to your other half in privacy and I can deal with any moaning sessions in the solitude of my room. That is, the usual ones from Alicia," he said carefully.

Gina was inwardly disappointed. "Supposing I rule that the other room's out of bounds to you too, at least in a sleeping capacity?"

"Then that won't matter."

She was surprised. "Why not?"

"I'll hear the phone from here."

She laughed. "Oh yes. You've got very good hearing then."

"Actually, it'll be easy."

"OK, Superman. We'll see."

Ben got out of bed. "I'll be back in a second."

She was sure she heard the bathroom door close, then the outer one. *Christ!* she thought. *We didn't put out a 'Do not disturb' sign. The chambermaid might have come in and found us.* It did not bear thinking about. Still, she hadn't and it seemed for the only time in Gina's life, sex had been spontaneous. She giggled to herself. Well, she would have been disappointed if they had not indulged at sometime during the stay, but within half an hour of arrival was... well, animal really, but very wonderful.

"Hi!"

"Where the hell did that come from?" she screeched, knowing very well the door to the room had not opened from the corridor.

"Hi. It's me." There he was, standing at the end of the bed.

"Here's the good news. We've got connecting doors so, if invited, this could be our bed and that could be my phone room, and perhaps for dressing in if we're in a hurry. We can leave the door open and if you get a call in the middle of the night because your husband's missing you, you can pack me off and, although I'll hate it, you can bill and coo as much as you need."

"Here," she said, patting the part of the bed next to her. "There are a number of things I want to say. First. You've got a permanent invite. I said it was a lucky room for me, for us. Then I have to say I feel really guilty for both the 'other halves', as you put it. I'm sorry but if they never know, and there's no need for them to, then they, at least, won't be the unhappy ones. Then: thank you. Thank you so much for showing me what real love is like. I thought my head was going to burst... Benito, will you believe me if I let you into a secret?"

"Yes, of course."

"I've never been... well... satisfied before. I thought it was just something men wrote about in magazines under female pseudonyms, to stimulate women into harder at trying to satisfy their men into then satisfying their partners."

356

"You *are* funny. Of course girls climax. It's anatomical. Some apparently die without, and now that modern girls know it's OK, and neither the priest nor God will kill them for such a sinful act, they're at it all the time."

"Go on! All the time!"

"OK, occasionally, but as a right, as opposed to a treat."

"Thirdly," said Gina, "it's getting late and you must make an appearance at the cocktail party."

"So must you."

"Only if I can walk," she said with a giggle.

"Right. So it's time for a shower and a phone call. I'll do the same. Forty-five minutes and we'll regroup and go to the party."

Gina had borrowed a little black number, to be safe, from one of her nursing friends who, she had worked out, was that little bit younger and would have chosen a slightly lower neckline than she herself might have done. At least she had the underwear to go with it, because that was Marcel choice anyway. She had a new white dress for the Saturday night and her smart trouser suit for the Sunday closing event and journey home, as the itinerary reminded delegates that they would have to have booked out before the end-of-term buffet lunch.

There were about 200 people attending the conference, Ben thought. That was apart from the representatives from the pharmaceutical companies who were there to network and try to encourage the use of their new drugs or equipment. Ben had been primed that he would be speaking immediately before the coffee break on the Sunday morning. He had not shown a single nerve about being confronted by 200 people. Most would still be in bed sleeping off the over-exuberance of the night before, or at church, he had forecast.

He entered what they were now calling 'our' room. He'd put on a mid-grey suit with a pale blue shirt and patterned blue tie.

"How do I look?" Gina asked. "Not too indulged, I hope."

"Perfect," he said, assuringly. "Why did you mention being 'indulged'?"

"Because I was."

"Oh, my love. Have I got a shock for you! That was a mere aperitif, leading to a very heavy night of booze."

"Oh sir! You shock me," she said, indicating she was a shy maiden from a previous century, coyly shielding herself from embarrassment with an invisible fan, "… but if that's a promise, I'm certainly very happy to be a part of it. I do think, though, that you ought to ring the management to see if they've got any sound deadening material, because I was hardly raised above 40 decibels the last time."

He saw her as witty, fun, never one to overstep the mark. He knew that in the middle, end, or even as a condition of what they had done, she was not likely to say, "Oh, by the way, the children need new horse-riding gear, or music lessons," or that the house needed painting.

He and Gina were there to give and take equally, without compromise or there being some deal or other at stake.

"We'll see about that. I might just put you into your operating mask. I did bring a couple. That should deaden you vocally, my darling."

It was all smiles into the corridor as they went out, like the weather man and woman, separately, he through 'his' door and she through 'theirs', in case some snoop or other was waiting with camera and divorce papers. That indeed was his joke, but they both knew the reality behind it.

She was ahead of him by the time they got to the lift.

"Hi!" he said as he caught up with her, just as they were joined by another couple waiting for the elevator to arrive. "That was good timing."

They let the other couple into the lift first. He whispered, "Didn't realise what a great butt you've got. Don't often get to see you from behind."

She held back an embarrassed flush.

The four joined another three who were already in the lift. Two of the men greeted Ben like a long-lost friend. That did not surprise Gina. She expected he'd know most people there; he was, after all, one of the most respected surgeons in the country… *and very talented in bed too,* she thought. She held back as they left the lift at the ground floor. She didn't want to burden the three men. Without hesitation, Ben turned back as though he had left something in the lift. He took Gina's arm in a formal way and pushed her gently into the presence of his two acquaintances.

"I'd like you to meet Gina Faro. Gina is my principal theatre sister, she knows the job so well that sometimes she does the whole job – not that the patients ever need to know," he joked.

Gina held out her hand to each and smiled like a well-behaved child.

"… And he's just screwed my butt off…" she wanted to say. "I'm pleased to meet you," she said shyly, thinking of what had been in her mind.

"See you later, Peter," Ben said, and guided Gina towards the signage, which said 'CONFERENCE WELCOME'.

"Ben?" she enquired quietly. "I feel so pleased about our relationship, do you mind, when I meet all your proper friends and acquaintances, if, when you say I sometimes carry out the operations, I then say that's only when I've screwed you off your feet and you need to sit down?"

"Fine with me. Yes. Perfectly OK. I'd quite like you to cap it, though, by saying something like '… I'd give it nine out of ten, for the sheer pleasure I got from it too'. Somehow that would give it more credibility as a talking point."

"OK. But you've got the score wrong. So far, and I know it's early days, you

358

rate at least 11 or 12 on my scale."

"Oh. Sorry, I hadn't realised you work to the Richter scale. I'll be less volcanic if ever there is another occasion."

"Benito," she said firmly, as if she had just heard a ghost. "Tell me you're joking. You didn't mean 'if ever'. Benito, you must tell me there will be many more occasions."

"You're so sweet. Look, of course, I was joking. There will be many more."

She smiled. "Today?" she said, with a wink, adding, "Ben?"

"Incorrigible," he said, as one of the management guided them into the ballroom.

The area was thronging. Gina estimated that most of the 200 attending were already in the ballroom, and she and Ben must have been among the last to arrive. That had the advantage that all the others had already had their warm-up, ice-breaker welcome drink and were all now networking with conviviality. Each time they stopped, Ben went through his meticulous introduction routine. He was good when greeted by those who had known the family from the past and enquired after his wife's wellbeing.

"Fine. Absolutely fine. Totally engrossed in the family, of course, and still hates mixing with 'we cut and repair' merchants, which she sees us as."

"Gina. Oh Gina, how long have we been operating together now?" he'd ask.

"Just a couple of hours or so this afternoon, but I'm promised more when we can move your great intrusive bodies out of the way," she so wanted to say. She was fair to her boss, though. "Seven years now."

"Wow, that's loyalty."

"So why haven't you let the boss bring you out here before to be shown off?" came one question from a greatly overweight orthodontic consultant, ironically with crooked teeth himself.

"Oh, I have family commitments myself and besides, the previous subject matter has been less my field of expertise than this year. So, I'm a bit honoured. Anyway, this isn't the Seville cattle show, so I hope nobody's here to be shown off."

Ben was within earshot of her conversation. "Is this gentleman getting to you, Gina? He does that. Something to do with always having a captive audience who can't answer back in his line of business. So it's a change to hear him get put in his place."

"Juan de Silva, let me formally introduce you two…" Ben announced. So the ice was broken.

Ben suddenly realised neither of them had a drink. "Gina. What would you like to drink?"

"Could I have white wine, please?"

He turned and saw a tray of drinks. Champagne, he ruled, would be the order of the day. He passed her the chilled glass. "I thought this was a little more celebratory," and handed her the gently bubbling nectar.

"Hey! Ben. I'm not very good with this. It usually goes straight to my head."

"Then this evening, I'll ensure it graces the whole of your body... there's John Sewell... he does the equivalent job to the one we do..."

In turn, Ben networked Gina around as many of the people he knew as possible in the time. There weren't any other difficult orthodontists, so it seemed. They were all nice people, not suspecting the truth behind their relationship.

She was right in her forecast. The champagne did go to her head. He was equally correct in saying that the whole of her body would be graced, if not by the wine, then by him.

CHAPTER 34

None of the distant duo parts of the quartet was used to lying in on a Sunday.

In Gina and Ben's case, it was a question of need. As she lay there slowly waking, it was not that she was counting but it seemed they had made love for a lifetime at every opportunity. She hoped this morning they would follow the rule book of each morning shower, he in his room and she in hers, after they had each contacted their other halves and lied their way through the 'of course I'm missing you' chat.

She remembered how they had both awakened, aroused by each other's presence, at about 4am, to find that they were both again, as she had put it, "As horny as a rambling rose." The thought of that had made Ben smile, because he remembered an old mate's joke about his girlfriend, where he had described her as his standard rose. Alright in bed, but no good up against a wall, as in the case of a rambling one.

Now they slumbered on, each with an eye on the time, due to Ben's presentation at 11. He had declared he didn't need a run-through… he knew it… he'd done it before… and anyway, this time, she would be there to inspire him.

In the case of Peter and Jan, they were fairly well awake at the same time as the other couple further south in Barcelona.

The truth of the previous night was, Jan pondered, that despite a token effort, Peter was obviously absolutely whacked by the day's events. The hospital farewells, the family lunch and the tensions caused by Jan's sparring with his mother. Then the journey and the trauma of the alarm, his and Jan's declarations of their relative affections, supper and then bed had all caused him to give up on the idea of any kind of lovemaking.

As he lay asleep, Jan watched his face with fascination as every muscle seemed to relax, allowing each frown, furrow and crease to recede to the point that he looked 20 years younger.

That, in turn, made her relax totally for the first real time in Spain.

At first she was shocked by his condition – not that she should have been, because the newsreel and newspapers had not spared the fact that he was in a very bad way.

Then there was their private funding project and the inane dealings she'd been forced to have with Mr William. She was concerned for Peter by the fact that the family-elected Chairman, who had already proved to the world that he didn't know the meaning of blood ties by sacking his own father for being out of touch and an inhibition to expansion, albeit under the guise of honouring him with the title of 'Life President', was now, in fact, intent on chopping Peter down to size.

Mr William clearly saw everybody as a challenge, not least his own wife, Mrs William the third, who had won the position by being alive (in comparison with the then incumbent), and interested and supportive of William's wellbeing within his own empire. She had been the influence who had advised, though not in so many words, "Top the old man, cocoon yourself with trusted old retainers and when you've got that top barrier of control, and Non-Executive Directors securely in place, buy in new brains that you can expand underneath you. Please the institutions and they'll want to increase their stakes to their own greedy levels. Our shareholders will enhance the overall position and you can put together some rewarding share option deals for yourself and those down the line. Then you'll be getting more out of the business than a good lifestyle: the racehorses... the cars and the plane... you'll have access to cash and an identity to go with all that..."

Hero-worship, it sounded like at the time. There were people who believed that some little stable girl would take Mr William's fancy the next time round and become wife number four, but this Mrs William was sticking it out. After all, 50 per cent of all that advancement would get her any of the available toyboys in Marbella, or Barbados, who were still free of AIDS, so she was happy to perform her wifely duties if that allowed her to continue influencing her husband's business decisions.

Jan had a difficult role. She had been appointed by Mr William, who *was* the company, in reality, and therefore her professional slant would have to ensure she protected the family's position. In accepting Peter as the progressive influence in the organisation and fostering his influence, she reasoned that this would ultimately protect the Board, and William in particular, which they were seeking.

Being in bed with Peter was nothing to do with the group whatsoever. If, in the process, she got Peter back to good health – a test of which would ultimately be whether he could deliver physically without the aid of crutches, a couple of nurses or a great deal of effort on her part – all was in the best interests of the group... and enjoyable in the extreme for her personally.

Jan had thought she'd had a perfectly good relationship with Richard, at the time. But Peter was something else altogether. He'd had the common sense to know that being under crisp cotton sheets was not just an occasion to grope or push for sexual pleasure. He had shown a willingness to be patient and honour the lady's wishes, unlike Richard.

They'd had an undisturbed night. For the first time in a while, Peter had been in normal fresh air, which made sleeping comfortable. Jan, under his direction, had opened the French windows on to the tiny bedroom balcony, which was hardly large enough from which to deliver a Papal blessing. It was certainly not long enough for a table and chairs and a teddy bear's picnic.

But unbeknown to Jan and Peter, the gap in the doors was wide enough to frame their bodies on the bed as Tania's piercing eyes focused through the opening in the fence, which divided Peter's garden from the water's edge to the marina. She'd been watching for an hour or so, waiting patiently for their bedroom light to be put out and the silhouette of Jan's body to rise above his, in the shaft of light given out by the anti-mosquito candles.

It was the very bed, in fact, where Tania had stolen time one furtive night with the young constable shipped in to the site to investigate the shootings and the attempted murder of her dear Peter. He had graduated to receiving her favours occasionally, and had thus unwittingly reported the secrets of the inquiry so far.

Now Tania felt a strange frisson of satisfaction as she watched. The stillness from below the covers was sufficient to bring a smug smile to her face, as she knew the new woman in Peter's life fell far short of her own sexual talents, which she was bound to bestow on him one day.

Tania led her life according to her gypsy aunt's predictions after she had read the cards. "There is a God controlling your difficult life. He will not save you from certain predetermined fates, those cannot be avoided. Expect them to be the Romany sins of incest and tribal interference. But that same God will indirectly provide for you and patience will allow the tenderness and passion you have stored for him to release itself. But beware, those stolen moments will not be without risk and everlasting loneliness."

Being told that, at the age of 15, would influence any impressionable girl. She'd endured the 'Romany sins', but Mr Peter, she was convinced, was the ruling God in her life. Marco was a mere pawn in a game to give her security and continuing contact with his nephew.

Jan was surprised to wake from a dream in which she and Peter were wrapped in each other's arms, rolling down the side of a hill clad in thick soft heather. She didn't ever dream pleasant dreams, it seemed, but this one had been. They had kissed all the way, not allowing the ups and downs over the small hillocks to interfere with their soft, passionate embrace.

She was suddenly shocked into the reality of the situation. Had they rolled down the never-ending incline and finished up still clinging to each other? It appeared they had because, as she looked up, there above her head, laid on its side in the lavender, was Peter, peering down at her through half-closed eyes. His right arm was threaded behind her neck and it held her right shoulder, while his left arm hung between their bodies, holding her right hand into his groin as the back of his hand pressed lightly and encouragingly into the softness of her stomach.

She hadn't been dreaming.

Of course she had. She thought, *God!* We've made love despite the promises. Momentarily, that was real and she was happy with that. She freed her hand and felt between her thighs. They were warm but dry. But then he may have worn a condom. She was now quite awake. Had she been duped?

He was still dead to the world. It was just a very realistic dream after all.

Inevitably, each duo had their new agendas to discuss. Gina and Ben's was about a quick breakfast (she said she'd never been so hungry) and then his presentation.

Jan and Peter's was about getting him back to Barcelona and then Jan going back to London to catch up with her list of outstanding interviews.

None of the four was over-confident about the long term. That was the nature of their relationships. One couple was committed already and cheating on their respective partners for their own self-gratification; the other was scared about the sadness of a break-up, by natural or other causes, of any long-term association and the thought of damaging career ambitions.

Today. It was today that mattered, and then each day as it came.

Jan expressed huge sadness at leaving Girasol. She said it was beautiful and quite understood that she would have to share her love of it with Anna and any others Peter had taken there.

"Hey," Peter replied. "Anna, of course, but she never really liked it and used to send me out alone to recharge while she soaked up the culture of London, or Paris, or Milan. Girasol she always described as a 'dead' place where, whenever she came, even the sunflowers had had it. As for 'the others', there haven't been any. It's a place I'm selfish about. I wouldn't lend it or rent it to anyone. It needs a touch of blonde about it to give it new life."

"You're kind, Peter. Can it be here in a month? Not some seedy hotel or your place or mine, or the toilet on a plane, which I read is very much in vogue."

"You're funny. A toilet on a plane wouldn't be easy."

Their idle chatter continued through getting ready to leave, repacking the car with such few things as they had unpacked. Jan was very happy indeed to say goodbye to Tania. She didn't like the blackness about her, although she could see that the bone structure and small, lithe body would still get her the lead role in Carmen. She distrusted her every move, especially around the hip area, which became pronounced, she noticed, in Peter's company. To be fair, he didn't particularly react, but it was there to capture the attention of any male eye prone to roving, Jan was sure.

The journey down to Barcelona went quickly. The morning roads were clear. Jan drove slowly past her friendly fortune-telling sunflower and waved. "Did you see him smile and wave at us?" she asked Peter.

"Of course. He's a mate of mine anyway."

They had been told to skirt the centre of Barcelona and hug the old coast road down to the fishermen's harbour before getting to the area that was being developed for the liner and container business. They'd find the hospital on the left, immediately overlooking the sea, and there was a car park behind it. Then they should go to the airport, just take the same road south and follow the signs.

All that was sound advice.

Parking at the front of the hospital was unrestricted for an hour for delivering and collecting patients. So Jan took that option as a starter. She felt anything beyond an hour would be an intrusion. She might just as well leave him to his own devices. He was going to be grumpy anyway so she'd best leave him in the care of the professionals.

The nursing staff in the physiotherapy wing to which they were conducted all wore rather trendy white mini-coats, as opposed to formal nursing gear. Jan supposed that was not out of a commitment to fashion but more for practical reasons.

The admissions sister seemed surprised to see Peter. "You're going to be one of our few senior in-patients. We've got quite an intake of young amputees at the moment."

A shiver went up Jan's spine. That was exactly what she didn't want to hear. Peter so needed adult company. He'd been hospitalised for far too long. She sensed he might not be too good surrounded by a bunch of young disableds. Still, he would just have to make the most of it. Perhaps she might fly out for a weekend in the middle of his course to give him a break. She'd keep that idea to herself for now and perhaps surprise him.

The induction procedures were over. He had a room to himself, which Maria and Benito Alvor had managed to arrange. "He's a British VIP," Sñr Alvor had said with authority, and that seemed to do the trick.

Jan now found herself alone with Peter for the first time since parking the car. The physios had done their admission and he was due to see the consultant late that afternoon for an assessment.

"You know what the next bit is about, don't we?"

"You... 'don't we'? What sort of improved English are you trying to teach me? Yes. We're parting... but only for a while and then with a joint ambition in mind. We... that's I... have got to be brave. We'll both get engrossed and then the time will just fly by."

"Right!" Jan said in a determined way. "I'm going to stand up. Kiss you gently. Whisper that I'll miss you, lean down and pat your bad knee, say I hope it all goes well and then turn round and walk without looking back, mainly because I'll be sobbing my heart out."

"Can't I hobble down to the reception with you and wave you off?"

"That would just prolong it."

"I wouldn't mind that. It's got to last a month. It would help. Jan, I've so enjoyed you being with me. You didn't give me the hard time we had when we first met."

"Hard time? You've got a short memory. Who did the rationing of that time together, then?"

"Listen, I thought you were going to be some hard-nosed little bitch who was going to pry into my life and expose everything to the world."

"Oah!" she said, like a little disappointed child who couldn't get her own way. "Was I really not like that? It's my usual style."

"No. You were soft and kind and quite beautiful."

"You didn't make me feel like that."

"You didn't say you'd come into my bed and treat me good on that occasion."

"... And I didn't bloody say I'd do that on this occasion," she responded, half in truth and with a look that showed a mix of hurt and anger. "... And as for treating you..."

He interrupted. "Before you say any more... treating me beautifully, is what I meant to say... beautifully and lovingly, softly... all those things, I'm surprised a hard-nosed interviewer like you can even dream of that in the future..."

"Now you just listen to me, Peter Martinez..."

He had stood up from what was to become the greatest single comfort to him over the course of the treatment: his bedside chair. He placed his arms around Jan's neck as well as he could, and held both shoulders firmly from behind, even though the pain in his shoulder was enormous. His mouth bore down on hers and any next words were stifled.

"Now you just listen to me, Jan Roberts. I'm not sure, and never have been, if there's room for love in my life. I've lived in a tough world and whenever I've softened, it's usually gone wrong. But with you I feel warm and comfortable and I know we can develop and share difficult moments together. If that's love, then I think I've caught it."

Jan had never seen him this soft before. She knew he meant it.

"Listen, baby boy. It's easier for a soft weak girl like me. I actually think I might love you. So thank you for saying what I know was difficult for you to say, when you've hardly got a heart at all."

She was beaming a radiant, happy smile as she seasoned the sentiment with a little gentle mocking. His hands came back from over her shoulders and automatically found both hers, which they entwined together and held between their chests.

"I'll miss you, Jan."

"Not as much as I'll miss you."

"Can I phone you? Will that get in your way?"

"Yes, to the first part. No, it won't, of course, to the second."

They both knew they had reached the moment.

"Listen. What I'm going to do is to turn around after I've kissed you gently, whisper again that I'll miss you, lean down and pat your bad knee, say I hope it all goes well and walk, without looking back… and you'll know why, won't you?"

"I'll know why because you've already warned me and said all that before."

She kissed him gently, whispered that she'd miss him and walked briskly to the door. She stopped, did turn back but with a broad grin on her face.

"Change of plan, dear Peter. Now you work hard on yourself, darling. I… we… want you to be very, very good… oh, and you know why."

She was gone. Like the whirlwind she could be. One step into the corridor and out of his immediate sight, she burst into tears, which positively splashed on to her white cotton blouse she had specially ironed as he shaved that morning.

The physio sister stepped out in front of her halfway down the corridor. She was quick to make her assumption. "Don't worry. He's in safe hands. We'll make him happy."

"You'd better bloody not," Jan said, and stormed on.

The sister put her hand to her mouth and turned to follow the vision of Jan stalking down the corridor.

"Oh! I didn't mean like that!"

Later, as Jan was sitting on the flight from Barcelona to Heathrow, still sobbing, the consultant was making his appraisal.

Initially he was not too forthcoming. Typically, he had his entourage with him, most of whom looked as though they had either been up all night or had bonked just once too often on their weekend break. Those who didn't just looked tired, having had to cover for the 50 per cent who got leave every other weekend. There were three athletic young ladies, a senior houseman, one male medic and another of dubious gender.

Professor Han obviously originated from the Orient. It made Peter wonder how Coco was. She'd phoned from Malaysia as soon as Maria networked her into Peter's condition after the accident, as they now called it. She had wanted to fly out straightaway but Maria had held her back, as well as Alex and Petra – all Peter's 'known about' offspring, in fact. Peter would ring them all once he'd organised a phone in his room.

The professor talked technically at speed while he bent Peter's knee around, testing the pain stress levels to the point beyond the patient's threshold. He seemed to have no regard for reaching the acceptable barrier, and stopping. He obviously knew what he was doing; causing pain, it seemed to Peter, was high on the agenda. Some of the females in the team quietly winced, knowing the pain Peter was enduring. They had had potential patients faint at this level.

Obviously, Han had reached the conclusion to his diagnosis. "So… how much do you want to know?" he eventually asked.

"I'd suggest you level with me. Tell me everything, please."

"Are you sure?"

"Yes."

"Actually, that's the way I prefer it. So you know you've got a bad knee," he said with a smile. "What you also need to know is that Benito Alvor has done an excellent mechanical repair job. I'd say if it was otherwise, as would be my duty if I felt your case was a waste of our time and an abuse of our facilities.

"You see here, time and resources are at a premium. This specialist unit can only take 30 patients. None is allowed to pay for actual treatment. You're being allowed to subsidise your accommodation because I'm told you've got European VIP status of some kind. I'd guess, but I won't hold it against you, that's of the voluminous investment in pesetas type, as opposed to you being a particularly important person."

Most of what Professor Han said came from behind his natural Asian smile, but Peter wasn't sure he liked this chap's cynicism. However, he mustn't form any rash opinions. So he listened on while the professor held court.

"So how bad is this 'bad knee'? On a scale of one to ten, it's better than mid-way. The basic problem is twofold."

What the hell was it, Peter thought, with all so-called specialists – accountants, lawyers, medical consultants – that they always had two options they wanted to tell you about. Take the artisan. He could either do the job, mend the wheel of the tractor, or not. He would rarely offer the 'on the one hand' principle, and then 'on the other'.

Han continued. "Firstly, the mechanics within the knee joint have been restored to about 75 per cent-80 per cent. The cartilages were probably shot to bits and they can't be replaced, nor will they re-form. I suppose Alvor had the decision to make as to whether to replace the knee in stainless steel, but we wouldn't want to see that in such a relatively young man. So on that prognosis, you're always likely to be 20 per cent short on usage.

"However, it's the muscles that have been ripped apart by the shotgun blast, as I have read the history. Now *they* can mend and be enhanced and that, dear Mr Martinez, is, with your help, dedication and perseverance, our specialty. It would appear, on examination, that you have a high pain threshold. If I tell you that you have 60 per cent muscle power and beyond that you show pain, then perhaps you'll appreciate the work we have to do and the pain you'll have to endure. Before we reach that point, I need to know where you yourself want to get to. With the use of a stick and with rebuilt muscles to 70 per cent efficiency, I'd say you could continue to make more pesetas for yourself and family. At 80 per cent and a lot of pain, you'd have very noticeably less of a limp... and so it goes on. Where do you want to be at?"

I'd like to continue to screw very actively, was what Peter thought, but he wasn't sure if he was ready to shock his young audience with such a goal. He thought on.

"Come on, Mr Martinez, if you're a man of great courage, I'd accept a 100 per cent aim. But whether you have the willpower or strength to achieve that, I just do not know."

Bloody cheek, Peter thought, *of course I've got both the willpower and the strength.* He opened up his thoughts to his collected audience.

"As a younger man, I was athletic, actually good at football and tennis particularly. I've managed to ski to a good enough social standard and drive an expensive and suitably fast sports car, as you might expect. So in direct answer to your question, as I'm intending to re-marry, I'd like to reach the point when I can screw vigorously kneeling on an unprotected strip oak floor, and walk to the bathroom without crutches."

The girls screeched with joy. Never had they before heard such an objective. One semi-clapped at the confession. The registrar was suddenly out of the dream in which he'd come to work. Han smiled broadly. The other male nurse/physio seemed a bit nonplussed by such a heterosexual target. As if it mattered, he thought to himself.

Han brought the shocked audience to order.

"So, we've had some objectives before but I don't remember that one. We'll see what we can achieve on a twofold promise basis."

Why the fuck twofold again? Peter thought. Surely it was either he could achieve it or he couldn't.

"Give me both versions," Peter challenged.

"We'll undertake to work hard and push you towards that level of mobility – that's our part. For your part, we all hope to be invited to the christening."

So Han wasn't that bad after all. At least he had a bit of a sense of humour. His job, however, was not about having fun. It was restoring the disabled.

There was a message from Jan the next morning, left with the nursing station as there was no facility yet for Peter to take his own calls. "Got back safely but very lonely. Resolved to keep busy. You too. Miss you. All my love. Jan… and behave and do as you're told." She wouldn't let her resolve for him to make great progress weaken. "Oh, and by the way, keep your eyes off those young physios I noticed were gawping at you on arrival."

Peter, too, was suddenly tinged with loneliness and realised what Jan's presence had meant to him. He was still capable of self-criticism and he could identify exactly where the shooting incident had placed him. It had been déjà vu in many respects. As he had fallen to the ground, shot, flashes had raced through his ever creative brain. It was the taste of death again.

Here in this ward, the majority of patients had yet to reach puberty, and when they did, as long as they laid their crutches outside the bed, they would have already developed such power as they were likely to develop, regardless of any handicaps at birth or accidents in early life.

Peter's immediate inclination was to go and get on a plane and fly home. After all, he could get by on a couple of crutches. He was just working out his escape plan when one of the assessment team entered his room. Fortunately, he had awakened early and found a shower room with a mirror. He'd shaved and put on a regulation hospital pair of shorts, which seemed to fit him. The issued t-shirt bore the simple message 'MAKE STRIDES'. *Did they all have that slogan?* he wondered. What about all the amputees he'd heard about? That hardly seemed appropriate to them.

"Hi!" she said breezily. He detected an Antipodean twang to an otherwise English accent. "We weren't individually introduced yesterday. I'm Sandra. Call me Cas, like everybody else, or on a really bad day, Cassandra. You'll have to take account of the fact that I'm a lazy bitch who'd far rather be bumming it on a beach than being here. I'm your bait."

"Bait?" Peter questioned.

"Yup. Your bait."

What Peter didn't know was that this was all part of Han's set-up. They'd had their meeting after the early reconnaissance of his body.

"What do you think, team?" Han had asked.

One said, "Oh boy. He's the problem case. He'll want out. He can buy independence. He won't make the course."

"Then we'll have to make him," Han insisted. "That's our job. That's our expertise. So who's got the ideas?"

The registrar was the one to speak. "He's obviously sex-driven."

They all laughed. The girls relaxed.

"Well, he's quite dishy." That was Cas's diagnosis and she probably spoke for all of them.

"So what do you suggest, Jonathan?" Han propositioned his number two.

"Bait."

"Bait? That's a new one on me. What do you mean?"

"He needs targets. First of all, we allocate one of the team in the usual way, on a one-to-one basis. I think with this guy, it's got to be one of the girls. You can all get on the treadmill ahead of him and swing arse," he said, including them all in his comment. "He'll think you're available and stride to catch it. You'll be bait. Once he has the idea, we'll appeal to his obvious competitive instincts and put one of the amputees in to play. Get them to compete against each other. With any luck, Peter Martinez will then become their target too."

Han thought. He'd make the ultimate decision. "Don't you girls find Jonathan's idea a bit sexist?" he said.

None did. In fact, one said it would be fun.

"Who'd be the bait?"

"The one with the best arse."

With that, the male with the distinct gene reversal got interested.

"Am I included?" he said with a smile.

"Sure," Han responded, with a reciprocal grin, "I guess all the names go into the hat."

They were all now finding this fun.

Han wrote all the names down on a single A4 sheet of hospital paper. Using a plastic ruler as a guide, he tore the sheet into six equal rectangles, each bearing a name. He folded them and handed the six to Jonathan on a blotter pad from his desk.

"First one out or any other order? What do you think?"

"Shit," said one of the more abrasive nursing staff. "Let's get it over with. The first." They all agreed.

Jonathan picked a piece of folded paper without further ado.

"It's Cas," Jonathan announced.

"Wow! Lucky me. Now, how seriously can I take the bait bit, sir? If he reaches the hook, does he get the rewards?"

If she hadn't giggled, Han might have believed she was serious. "Up to you," he announced, and in deference to the rapport he had built within the team, he followed up by saying, "but only allowing the use of his good knee." They all roared with laughter.

"Well, my boyfriend will at least be pleased by that ruling."

The meeting was over. The goals were set.

"Bait?" Peter repeated.

"Well, you see, we girls had a chat about your target and we guessed you'd need about as much help and encouragement as we can give you. I'm here to swing arse at you to remind you you've got 40 per cent lack of mobility to overcome."

Peter wasn't sure if all this was a set-up or whether she was making a play for him. Either way, it seemed it would pass some time. He'd stay.

Cas explained that the first hour would be manipulation and then some treadmill work. She walked alongside him to the massage room. Whilst he was in her charge, and particularly on crutches, she was responsible. Her training showed through. One would have thought Peter was walking quite unobserved and independently. Then she stopped them both, halfway through their intended journey, and indicated for him to give her the crutches.

"I might fall over."

"If you do, I'll pick you up, but you've got to learn how to balance all over again. You're protecting your bad knee and we've got to stop you doing that."

She slipped her forearm into the grips of the supports and walked seven or eight feet away, still with her back to him. Her coat seemed especially short today, exposing the lower regions of each beautifully sculptured, bronzed and muscular limb. Even in flat regulation plimsolls, she'd got shape, particularly around the rear, he noticed. What the hell would she look like in hot pants and a pair of stilettos?

"Now watch my hips," she said.

"Is that a promise?" he replied.

"Listen, this is work. OK, if you're good, you'll get to play. We work on achievement and reward here. So watch my hips, not in a physical way but in a mechanical one."

She walked four or five paces, lifting herself along on the crutches. She kept her right knee straight and applied a half-weight onto her right foot.

"Now did that look right to you? Mechanically," she added.

"No, I don't think so."

"Can you say what was wrong?"

"It seemed a bit hippy and you're light on your right foot as though you've got a verruca."

"Good. That's you."

"Really?"

"Yes. Now watch this."

This time, she delayed the swing forward of the hip, waiting for the knee to bend and moving the calf forward as opposed to swinging the lower leg with the thigh. She then placed the heel of her right foot firmly onto the ground and rolled with her full weight along the length of it through to the toes, at which point the impetus of the leg supporting and pulling the weight forward produced a rhythm that forced the movement to be repeated.

"See the difference."

"Yes, and that's easy. The difference is I haven't got the middle part of my leg like you have. You try that with what I've got."

She seemed cross. "How's it to be with us?" she said sternly. "Mr Martinez or Peter?"

"Peter."

"OK. Now you just wait there."

"Can I have my crutches please?"

"Get stuffed, Peter. Suffer!"

She made out as though she was storming off into a side room and promptly reappeared carrying a light stool.

"Oh, thanks," Peter said, expecting to be offered the opportunity to sit down.

"Now... wherever you've seen the next part of this act before, they've probably been playing sexy pumping music and, for a few hundred pesetas tucked into the top of the lady's bra, you've probably got to grope whatever took your fancy. But dream on, sir."

Cas placed her right foot on the stool. Her coat pulled tightly around the restriction of the bottom button. She was carefully positioned sideways on to Peter. "So... hum to yourself, but look very carefully."

She undid the bottom two buttons of the coat, oozing sex as she did. She let her carefully cut and shaped blonde hair fall forward and as she slid, the coat up her leg as far as was reasonable.

"Look," she commanded. "Come on, step up closer for the show."

Peter took two petrified steps, with his eyes transfixed on the curvaceous outer thigh she had exposed to him.

"OK," she said in a determined way, and began to run her forefinger along the length of a hint of a light skin tone starting above the knee joint.

It had short intersecting lines along the length, and disappeared without showing any greater fading above the raised hemline of her coat. Even Peter, a mere architect-cum-engineer, could tell that was an operation scar of some magnitude. His stomach heaved with embarrassment. He'd been making such a wimpish fuss and she'd obviously been there herself.

"Christ!"

"So, my dear Mr Peter. You're either going to get up off your butt, or you won't get even the merest chance of putting notes in the top of my stocking – that is, if this bride you're working towards would allow it. Baby!" she added, in a voice laden with sarcasm but also an overtone of fun.

"How on earth did you do that?" he asked.

"Screwing a patient as a reward, but never you mind that. Now, did you want to walk for me or are you going to continue to swing along?"

"I'll walk. But I'd like my crutches."

"OK. You get those for one more day. Then you'll get one stick, that's that. OK?"

"Yes," he said, obediently.

"Oh! By the way, Mr Han keeps a complaint book. If you want to vent any complaints you may have, I'll show you where it's kept."

"I won't need that, thank you. If, and I do say if, I had a complaint, I'd tell you to your face."

"Good."

"So I've got a complaint!" he said impishly.

Somewhat surprised, she asked, "What?"

"I wasn't offered the grope," he replied.

"Here. Do whatever you like with these crutches," she said playfully, as she handed back his friendly supports.

"I'll settle for a walk behind you to watch you swing your backside."

They walked on to the massage room. There Cas worked on Peter expertly, somewhat to his surprise treating each leg equally. She explained that the one leg had been overworked and the bad one, the reverse. She was in work mode now, almost, he thought, on automatic pilot. They both now seemed relaxed with each other.

"So how did you do your leg?" he asked.

"Not as dramatically as yours."

He waited for the response. "So was it really screwing?"

"Well, you could say my fiancé was screwing around with me."

There was a mystique about what she wasn't saying, and a flat innuendo in what she was.

"So come on, Cas. How'd you do it? I'm broadminded." He wasn't going to go away.

"At home in South Africa…"

"Hold on there, I thought you were Aussie or Kiwi?"

"That's the trouble with you poms. I'm always accused of being from Down Under. No. Cape Town. Anyway… that's if I do have to tell you… we used to go out to the dunes, mostly on a Sunday, and instead of buying a wedding ring, I'd agreed that my fiancé Mark could have one last fling and buy a second-hand off-road bike. A whole crowd of friends used to meet up and we'd charge around the humps of sand, racing each other, each driver trying to impress the other guys' pillion passenger more than they themselves were. Mark was good… except his was the second-hand bike. A wheel came off and we both went over the top. I broke my tibia. Well, shattered it really. I came down hard on a rock. The rest is history."

"You didn't get married?"

"I couldn't."

"Sorry. What? Lack of trust?"

She looked away and swallowed hard. "Lack of fiancé. Broke his neck."

They were both now silent, she with her memories, he feeling absolutely dreadful for having pushed the point. His calf muscles were now really hurting. She was clearly being spiteful.

"So now, Mr Martinez. I hope you're satisfied! You've dragged the history out of me. Are you now going to be a big boy and move forward?"

"I'd say so," he uttered with feeling.

"Do you mind if I give you some well-intended advice?"

"I think a girl like you is going to whether I say yes or otherwise."

"I'll take that as a no."

She was bright. His full answer was intended as "No. I don't mind if you give some well-intended advice."

"That's right. Go ahead then."

"OK. First of all, why is a man like you with a brain that's probably huge not acting like a clever fish?"

"Principally because I can't see myself swimming again in a hurry."

"Balls, I'm afraid you will do. But if you concentrate on the bait made available, it's likely to be on a hook. Forget me as bait. Look around you from now on. Look at the other fish around you in the sea we have here. You want to swim again? That may take weeks or months. Build your life around a quick rewarding screw, and that's it. It ends there because we'd all lose respect for you. Got the message? Grow up. Be that successful man again. You're performing like a spoilt kid who's ricked his ankle."

"Cas! How the fuck do you know that?"

"I've been hurt in my life too. Now turn over on your back." He did as he was told. "Give me your bad arm."

Again he was showing signs of being beaten.

"Grip my hand."

"I can't do that very well."

"Look what's important to you, you've had the opportunity to get out. OK?"

"OK."

He gave her his hand, which she put firmly in hers. She shook it hard, taking Peter to the point of, and beyond, excruciating pain in his shoulder.

She smiled. "That's just to say we're friends, OK?"

"Yes! We're friends… but the promise is now more important."

Cas continued in relative silence. Most days she thought about Mark and the tangled mess she had found when she dragged herself over the dunes to see how badly he had been injured, if indeed at all. He and his pals were very macho about their style of riding. It was sissy to wear a crash helmet. Because A) they didn't crash and B) it was more important they spent the money that would have cost on a set of recon tyres.

So Peter had not particularly disturbed her, and in any event, it gave her a greater element of control over her charge.

Suddenly the treatment room became alive. There was the fast, heavy metallic thumping of lightweight aluminium crutches on the regulation linoleum flooring. The hospital itself dated back to before World War II, but had been renovated a serious number of times as the nursing requirements changed from healing the fevers of the day, to TB, then a more general need. It had now been equipped for the rebuilding of limbs and all the paraplegic requirements in Spain, albeit only available for such a limited number of patients.

The staccato drumming of metal against rubber was accompanied by a massive contretemps, represented by a shrieking, demanding girl's voice, an out-of-control teenage boy's one and a softer, genderless one trying to mediate. *What the hell is this tirade all about?* Peter thought, annoyed that his and Cas's thoughts had been interrupted.

The boy was accompanied by one of the female physios and Juan, the effeminate one. The girl was being forceful. Juan looked as though he were there to keep the peace between the obvious clash of personalities.

"I don't need any frigging treatment on the bloody stump!" the boy shouted.

"Yep, you frigging well do!" she screeched back.

Juan said soothingly, "Now come on, be a big boy and see sense."

"I will when I get the limb!" he shouted back.

"You don't get the limb until the thigh can take it."

"My frigging thigh can take anything! It's more than ready."

"Mr Han won't hear of it till he's satisfied by what we report back."

Peter predicted to himself the boy's reply would be something like Han didn't know what he was frigging doing, and that he knew better than the professor anyway.

"What's that frigging professor know? I know I'm ready," was, in fact, the reply.

Peter raised his head and winked at Cas, who was engrossed with Peter's calves. Maybe she'd heard it all before.

The boy was standing at Peter's side, gawping at both his legs.

"Christ!" the boy said. "Which one's the limb? They're good. I bet they don't get such a good match on me."

Peter raised himself up on his elbows and joined the boy in analysing both his own legs. The lad clearly thought he was an amputee too. Peter could now see the young noisy know-it-all patient had one tracksuit trouser with a sports shoe at the end and the other trouser leg was rolled up to about knee height, except there was no knee in sight.

"What's your name?" Peter said.

"Pablito. But what's that got to do with you?"

"Lots. I've always liked to know who I'm competing with."

"Competing with? Who said anything about competing?"

"Well, I've worked it out this way. I've got a knee that won't do what my muscles want it to do. It's a mechanical problem. So if they cut my leg off and fitted a limb, I guess I might get back to running again faster. Is that right, Cas?"

"Let's say there's some truth in it but it's not an option now," she replied cautiously.

"Right, Pablito. So, allowing age for age, injury for injury, let's see how we get to compete. Nurse, how long before Pablito here gets his limb?"

"It could be in the range of three to five days, except his thigh muscles won't take it. They won't develop much more until they're trying to control something on the end of them. You can't fit a foot onto the end of a thigh so, at the moment, Pablito's being his own worst enemy. But he says he knows best. Better even than Mr Han."

"OK, Pab. Do your mates call you Pab?"

"Some do."

"Good. That's what I'll call you. I gather there's a treadmill we both get to practice on. I'll see you on it in four days' time. I'll do ten minutes to your five until you can walk the equivalent of 400 metres to my 800. Who's your football team?"

"Real Madrid."

"OK, mine happens to be Barcelona. They play in ten days' time. So if your time by then is equal or better than mine, I'll take you to the game. If I'm better than you, then we'll have to watch it on TV in this morgue. It's a treat or no treat."

"You're on. I don't know who you are, some plant or other, I expect, but you're the only person to talk any sense to me since the frigging car hit me. That's a challenge. I've never been to a football game. Now listen, you goofs. Why don't you get this frigging thigh of mine working? You haven't got long."

Cas's female colleague walked across to Peter's couch.

"Thanks for your help. Nothing was going to get him on that 'frigging' couch. Thanks very much. By the way, he'll lick you. Be careful of this one. Don't overdo the bets."

"Fine, I'm a good loser. The hard part will be getting the bloody tickets – it's probably sold out. It's the beginning of the season." Peter realised Cas had come to a halt midstream all the shouting and screaming. He turned his head upwards.

"You can get on with your frigging work too. I've got less time than he has, by all accounts," he said with a smile.

The five of them all burst into simultaneous laughter.

"You're on the treadmill in 15 minutes. Then you'll realise what a challenge you've issued against yourself."

Peter patted his mate Pab on the head as he shuffled by. "See you on the circuit," he said, as he left the room with Cas by his side.

Once the boy thought they were out of earshot, he turned to the nurse and Juan and said confidently, "That bloke doesn't know what he's let himself in for. What's the record after a week with a limb?"

Juan looked at Monica, his compatriot. "I'd say 200 metres, wouldn't you?"

"About that," she agreed.

"Well, that's something else about to be smashed. What's his name?"

"Peter. Peter Martinez."

"Is he English?"

"No. He's originally Spanish but lives in England."

"Is he some sort of sports person?"

"No, I don't think so. He's a pretty rich man, we're told."

"Then once the football challenge is done, we'll go for cash. Come on, you guys. I can't really feel a thing yet."

"… And that, dear Pablito, is exactly the point we and Mr Han know from experience," Monica advised firmly.

That silenced the lad.

Peter was standing at the end of the three-metre conveyor belt. There were grab-rails on each side but Cas said that touching those should be a last resort. She had her back to the direction he understood the motorised mat would be moving towards, indicating she'd walk backwards and he would walk towards her. She was obviously expert at this device. She was holding a remote control in her right hand.

"Right, Peter. No heroics, for starters. I've set it on a slow strolling speed. The idea is to develop heel-to-toe technique. You must bend the knee, one swing from the hip and thigh and you'll hear me tell the world about it. Ready? You balanced? OK… steady forward."

She took a slow pace backwards as he matched it going forward. Ten paces along the stationary route, confidence welled up in Peter. He was not finding this the ordeal he had imagined.

"So is the idea if I catch you, I get to squeeze your butt?"

"Yup! Fine by me." She unbuttoned the mini-coat she had buttoned up after the massage and tantalisingly pretended to undo the top one, which he knew would reveal a very pleasant cleavage, because he'd got an advance viewing when he'd raised himself on to his elbows earlier.

She lifted the remote to shoulder height and at arm's length between them.

"OK, are you still up for the bait?" As she said that, she depressed a button, which lifted the speed of the mat up a gear.

Peter stumbled but saved himself from falling by grabbing both rails. His face was panic-stricken.

As Cas stopped the mat, he was able to stop himself from falling backwards by tightening his grip on the rails he had been told not to grab.

"Lesson three, I think it is for today. Peter, we're not looking for over-confidence here. We have to be in control. If we get it wrong through allowing a patient literally to run before they can walk, we would be allowing them to cause themselves long-term damage, particularly those trying out new limbs. So no, you don't get to slap arse or overtake me when we're exercising."

Peter was clearly shaken, but determined to show his resilience.

"Han said part of my rehab, bearing in mind my target, would be some floor work in preparation for my marriage. So how will that work?"

Cas was too alert for him; perhaps age, along with the accident, had crept up on him and slowed him down.

"Why do you think we've got Juan in the team? Of course we'll cater for that… thank God." She smiled a smile of encouragement.

When Peter got back to his room, he found the engineer had connected a phone. He'd also worked out that the routine was early light breakfast, treatment from nine to 11am then 'rest' time till one. Lunch until two, then an open air stroll accompanied by mentor, treatments or weights and gym till 4.30pm, then 'rest' again and the evenings were termed 'recreation'. He hadn't got a clue exactly what that would entail.

He calculated that with a phone at his disposal, he could probably get his personal calls made in the evening, so he'd ring the office and set up a routine to start working again. If the key personnel in the group were given access to him, he'd be back in the loop and not be forgotten, at the risk of dispensability. He knew Mr William's fears about his own abilities and well understood that type of cad would use every opportunity in life to hold on to his own position. If Peter had not been brought in, in pursuance of the acquisition policy, William's dual role of Chairman and Chief Executive would not have been questioned. The CEO handle had been taken from him by the Non-Executives' desires to divide the two positions, more in line with others' policies.

Peter had to mount all the pawns, knights, rooks and bishops in defence of his recently created throne.

When Peter had first called Miss Miles 'Vera', it had seemed to offend her. She had been secretary to William Snr, and now to Mr William, and wanted to hold her position as 'senior barrier to the Chairman's office' by suggesting, if not insisting, that all the minions who wanted time with her boss should address her formally too. Peter had explained he didn't feel comfortable with that and finally charmed his way into being allowed to personalise the association in private. But it was agreed that when in company, he would revert to the more formal type of address.

"Hi, Vera. It's Peter Martinez." Recognising her voice, he addressed her informally now.

The silence at the other end of the line said it all. Obviously, the hierarchy up in Manchester, where the majority of the construction activities were based, had given Peter up for dead. All that was missing was the corporate announcement, which was bound to have involved Jan, in any event.

It was as though Vera had been confronted by a ghost.

"Hi, Vera! Are you there? Don't play around, this is a bloody expensive call from Spain. It's Peter Martinez." Her spine tingled. Although she would not admit it, Peter's style turned her on, if that was at all still possible for her at the age of 57.

"Peter," she responded hesitantly. "It's so good to hear your voice. I…"

Peter interrupted her. "You thought I was dead, hence the artificial condolences."

"Oh, Peter! You're really wicked. Of course we knew you weren't dead. You've got the International Division running round in circles over the private Spanish hospital funding deal."

Perhaps she shouldn't have said that. Maybe that was a giveaway that Mr William wouldn't have wanted. However, she was so surprised that she blurted out the first defence she could think of. So what? It was true.

"How are you?"

"Really good. I'm in this new institution, which may get me walking and running again but it could just send me barmy. So I've got a phone connection and I'm opening my private office from here. Please put a memo round to all on the Executive Board that I can be contacted. And that raises a sub-issue. Shortly before what I'm calling 'my accident', you'll probably know that Jo resigned and we were looking for a replacement in London. We… well… I got a little sidetracked and Jo left before we found a replacement.

"I now have nobody in place who could have done what I've asked you to do. I'll be back shortly and then I'm sure the agency will pull out all the stops and find me somebody, but in the meantime I need a trustworthy temporary PA. I've been wondering if there's anyone within the organisation you think could fill the gap?"

Vera thought for a while.

"Valerie Redmond might fill the gap. She's been with us about five years and she's been PA to a couple of Exec Directors so she at least knows the ropes. She must have been on the receiving end of a lot of your memos and Board reports. She's also relieved for me with Mr William when I've been on holiday. He swears by her ability."

"I think I know her. Mid-20s… isn't she known more normally as Val?"

"Yes. That's right. She's in the divisional offices in London too, so she wouldn't have a location problem. By the way, in case it might help, I'm in touch with Jo. I maybe shouldn't say it, but I think she can see she dropped a clanger by leaving. She hasn't found what she says is 'the right thing' yet. She's also called a few times for an update on you. So… how's your pride, Peter? What about getting her back?"

"My considered, rational view on that is an emphatic no. Once there's a hint of… well, wanting to leave, or whatever, it's always there. It doesn't work to try to patch up and forget. But maybe she could come in for a day or so to show Val the ropes before I get back. Ready to cope with what I know will be a really busy patch.

"Try that. Ask Val if she's up for it, then I'll speak to her on the phone just to break the ice, as it were. You're a brick, Vera. I hope William sees it that way. He's not the best judge of goodness, though."

"Peter, please. Keep me out of your personal opinions. I'm quite satisfied with my role and his level of appreciation. I'll do as you say and come back to you. I gather there's a way of contacting you?"

"Cheers, Vera. Thanks." He gave her his contact number.

Vera sat looking at the phone, contemplating Peter's words.

He was absolutely right. The principal thing missing in her working relationship with her Chairman was that he did not recognise goodness. From the beginning, 15 years before William was going through the beginnings of his second wife, who was wearing him out on an extended all-day, year-round honeymoon, William had interpreted goodness in the affair, which had led to his expensive first divorce without him realising the young lady, of good pedigree and a Roedean education, was an upper-class nymphomaniac who was not oozing the love William had read into the situation. It was just that he was there attempting, through his obsession with sexual pleasures, to satisfy her permanent demands and, as Vera had always thought, providing an equal supply of spending money to fuel her other innate needs.

Peter was still on the line. "Sorry, Vera. Is William there? I forgot I need to speak with him."

"I'm not sure," she replied, clearly protecting her master's arse, to which she had become accustomed.

"Vera, you're a bloody awful liar. Why not just put me through."

She hated lying, particularly to Peter, because she liked him and, who knows, if the group rumours were true, Peter was on course to show William up in his true racing colours and could replace him. If that happened, realistically the organisation would be run from London, but Peter would need the northern link, and a confidante, at least for the three years until she retired.

"I'll see if I can disturb him. He was talking on his private line."

"Come on, Vera, you know as well as I do he'll only be chatting up one of the stable girls, seeing how the horses slept and asking if they were wearing tight jeans or jodhpurs."

How the hell did Peter know these things? She had never told anybody about those calls. She didn't know the whole group knew about it, but then it was fatal for any of the chauffeurs to obtain knowledge; they were bound to pass it around. One of them had been told directly by one such questioned and flirted-with stable girl that any of them could be on a £100 bonus for a roll in the hay with the paunchy Chairman.

"Come on," Peter had challenged when he'd first heard those allegations, "that's schoolgirl make-believe."

"I suppose so is the fact that he's not been circumcised, had a complex appendicitis at boarding school and gets asthmatic after he jacks off?" said Jo, who had passed it up the line to Peter after the driver had networked across the whole garage fraternity, most site managers and everybody in Duke of York Street.

"I'll put you through," Vera eventually gave in, having got clearance to do so. "Take care. Don't go overdoing it."

"I won't. Thanks, you're a darling." Nobody ever said that to her like Peter did.

Peter now retuned his greeting from a normal, "Hi," to a flattering, "Hello, Chairman," which always threw William because he didn't ever know whether Peter was saying that in deference or sarcasm.

"Hello Peter, old chap. So they've got you tied down in another of their institutions, have they?"

"Not exactly, William. I've got myself under treatment."

"How do you see things then?" William asked.

"Sorry. Don't know what you mean."

"You know, old chap. You've had a pasting. Don't worry about us, you understand. Tell us how you want to play it."

Peter could have written this dialogue almost to the letter. Fortunately he'd got friends on the Board who believed that their future was better in the hands of Peter than in Peter and William's, at best, or William's alone at worst. The fact that William had attempted to get the corporate knives out at the previous week's Board Meeting, and that he had lobbied the old stagers and Non-Executives to the view that a disabled man would be better 'retired hurt' than with any vestige of control, at the risk of being savaged by the bright and fit opposition, had reached Peter's ears already.

The outcome of the meeting had not been conclusive, as the level of discussion hadn't given William the confidence to take a resolving vote on the fact that Peter should be retired. He'd merely said he'd have a word with Peter to see what his intentions were.

"Play what?" Peter led him on.

"The Board thinks you must be feeling worried about being sufficiently well to continue in your role. The travelling alone would always knock you back. You can't lead a group like ours if you're dependent on crutches and, who knows, a wheelchair in due time."

"Where do you get your information from, William?"

"Oh, that's a nice thing to ask! You know we're a compassionate company. We've got Bill Sears coming out to see you. Ostensibly over the scatterbrain private hospital deal you think you've set up. What's behind all that? You must think we're daft. What are you going to need most in the next couple of years? Medical help. I'll tell you what… medical help. So you think we don't know what's behind this deal? You've set it up for yourself. Your pension plan… back in your homeland, where at least you'll be nursed in your own mother tongue."

"William, I know you're not recording this information like you sometimes do…" For some reason, Pablito came into Peter's mind momentarily. "… Because you don't know how to work the frigging machine and I kept Vera on the line before being put through to you. So I say with fervour, you're a prat. What do you think my status is currently? Corporately, that is."

William was close to losing it. No, he wasn't recording the call but he knew the whole Board would support him in a defamation case if any employee, even the second in command, called their Chairman a 'prat'.

"Take back what you just called me!" he demanded.

"Take back, William? I reiterate you're a prat. Rise to the challenge, William. Tell me what you think my status is and you'll see I'm the one in touch. You're the one out of it."

"Stop playing games with me, Peter. You're absent. Sick. That's your status and unlikely to improve, so they say."

"Wrong. I'm absent, on leave. I have an annual leave entitlement of five weeks. When I was discharged from Palafrugell, I filed head office, through personnel, with my leave request for three weeks, for this private rehab… which, incidentally, should put me in a physical position to beat you at a five-set tennis match, all served overarm too, and then 18 holes of golf, and even then over a 400-metre sprint, let alone helping you to service your little stock of stable girls and/or boys."

"Peter Martinez. Your brain's gone sour. They said it might. You're hurt, it was the lead shot. I've seen it in the odd pheasant, I've seen them get so demented they devour the heads of their siblings. I'll make some allowance for that. I'll take up the tennis, golf and 400-metre challenge, but you will take back the stable bit."

"No, I frigging won't. Mandy, Emma and Jeremy don't see it any differently from what it is."

Shit! Mr William thought. They would all now be fired, disposed of, even if it would take a few thousand notes. He'd never believed they'd split, it wouldn't have been worth their while.

In fact, they hadn't. All Peter had done was to look up their names in personnel. He'd guessed the rest.

"Now you listen to me. In the next three weeks, and this is really the point of the call, although I'm on leave, and check that out with Glynn Williams, in the 15 working days, I'll make myself available at executive level for three hours per day. I'll review any faxed or telexed information, couriered stuff or phone call conferences. I'll build up 45 hours' bonus time, which I'll then take as a fourth week's leave qualification. Could you fix a Board Meeting for four weeks today? I'll suggest to Vera through Val, who's being seconded to me, the agenda, but be sure the hospital deal will be thrashed out as well as all this waste of group support on the stables. Those facilities are exclusively for your personal pleasures and produce no financial return.

"That's it from me, William. War, you may call it, but I'm not lying down having some overdeveloped prissy English public schoolboy failure stick knives into me. You've picked the wrong bloke, old chap."

Mr William was left holding the phone and was still transfixed when Vera appeared and took it out of her boss's hand and placed it in the cradle.

"He sounded great to me," she said chirpily, which was exactly what William didn't wish to hear.

"I've got six call-backs for you. Two Non-Executives and four principal Executive Divisional Directors."

"Oh! To see how I've agreed Peter's future intentions?"

"No. It would seem they're all totally elated by the fact Peter seems as right as rain, raring to go. He's taken a three-week holiday but wants everyone to know he's on catch-up and wants to go through things with them. Phone, fax or other he says will do. I expect he told you the same." She knew very well he had. She'd listened in. She still had a slight smile about the 'prat' and stable connotations. It had been a more exciting day than she'd had for quite a while.

Cas appeared in Peter's room. "Hey, you're late for lunch."

He hadn't realised the time. The two-hour break had rushed by: chatting to the Divisional Directors, hearing first about their latest golf scores, how their cars were running, then eventually the dual point of the conversation – for Peter to explain he was now on leave, as fit as a fiddle, and would be more so after his intensive physio, which he was now doing in his own time. Then, on hearing William's plans for his future, explaining how wrong the Chairman's appraisal was… and encouraging them to condemn William for underestimating the benefit of the united club Peter was building around himself… oh, and having due regard to the share option deal they were now all involved with, thanks to him.

The Non-Executives were a bit more difficult. The two he had picked out as malleable were worldly chaps. One's background was in banking. He'd been lucky that his father had been Chief Executive of one of the big banks and now there was a family coincidence, which left some of the other public school graduates with their aspirations flailing in the battle to gain rank themselves. It would become apparent they had the wrong fathers to do that. Nevertheless, that Non-Exec was known to change with the wind, Peter thought. He was of an age that his five Non-Exec appointments, at about £20,000 a year, plus his Chairmanship of Rotinda Electronics and his generous bank pension, kept him and his younger bride in reasonable comfort. He'd picked her up, so they said, on his posting to Hong Kong and promoted her from secretary/PA to Chief Executive's wife in one fell swoop, under a light down duvet in his hotel suite.

Peter's second target was a harder chap to read. Peter, in his Spanish upbringing, had not encountered the Jewish fraternity, so he was always a little restricted. Joe Joseph was, fortunately, a nice chap. He was one of the mid-European Jews who'd read the writing on the wall in the mid-30s and just about made Harwich in 1939. In fact he'd had two days to spare before the outbreak of war. So he was allowed into the country but had the territorial restriction put on him that he had to stay within 30 miles of the coastline. Norwich, and its environs, was where he threw away the true benefits of the legal profession he had pursued in his homeland. The only employment needs locally were farming, with its requirements for labourers, with or without legal degrees, a religion or even their own bedroll.

Joseph's brain had locked into gear when the Norfolk farmer who had taken him under his wing explained he was struggling to live as the vegetables then produced all came at once and therefore attracted the lowest possible prices in bulk.

"If," he explained, "I could develop a refrigeration system to hold back the cultures and sell them three months out of season, I'd get two to three times the price."

Joe Joseph stayed awake that night, remembering back to his Hungarian science classes and the device they'd used to store fish for biological analysis. He re-created the end-principle in a metal biscuit box and was elated when he realised he had remembered how to develop frost. He used a water cistern and an improvised lid with a seal to enlarge the process sufficiently to convince his boss that they were then on the brink of producing a vehicle in which to hold back the rotting process in fruit and vegetables.

That small industry became Frost Frozen Foods plc and Joe Joseph got a knighthood into the bargain for services to industry, and as a thank you for donations to the Harold Wilson government.

Sir Joe was very pro-Peter. He was very much a Euro supporter and said having a worldly addition of pure Spanish upbringing was good for the group abroad, as their natural stock was as discoverers well beyond Europe. Most of the Board realised this, as compared to their Chairman, whose knowledge base beyond the shores of Great Britain was confined to summer in Cannes or Juan, racing at Longchamps and winter in Barbados with the jockey set.

The Non-Exec Director was particularly pleased to receive Peter's call and news of his accessibility and rehabilitation. Peter felt secure enough after his morning's dealings.

As Cas said, he was late. He looked around the room for his crutches.

"You don't need them," Cas advised, anticipating what he was looking for. She walked with him to the refectory, where it seemed all 30 inmates were gathered in the high-ceilinged hall. All the food in the buffet looked distinctly healthy stuff.

"Would there be any chance of a beer or glass of wine?" Peter asked gingerly.

The plump Catalan kitchen hand said, "Absolutely no chance," summing up life in this hospital in those three succinct words. Han and all the girls joined the patients for their break, less to eat with them, Peter thought, but more to observe their charges.

He saw a space next to Pablito as he carried his lightly laid tray carefully away from the food bar. "Can I join you?" he asked.

"Of course you friggin' can," the lad replied. "We don't talk limbs, though. Is that alright? We get that crap all the rest of the time."

"Football then?" Peter enquired.

"Yes, but only about Real, not Barcelona."

"That seems a bit narrow."

"Well, it's that or nothing," Pablito informed him.

"OK. Real are going to get whooped by Barcelona on Saturday week, you know."

The lad spent the next ten minutes analysing Barcelona's weaknesses, which players were injured and how they hadn't got a defence to the Real forwards.

"Do you realise you've just spent ten minutes talking about Barcelona?"

The boy looked amazed. "No I friggin' haven't. I've been talking about Real."

Cas smiled gently at the great competition building up between her one man and his challenge.

The weights weren't a strain on Peter. He was used to that sort of exercise. True, the one good leg could accomplish twice the output of the other. But it was OK. His day finished with him being totally exhausted.

The working day shifts ended at seven, having started 12 hours earlier. It appeared the physios' responsibility for the wellbeing of their patients was to see that they were escorted back to their individual or communal wards.

"So are you finished?" Peter asked Cas as they walked along the corridor to his room.

"Sure am," she said with an implied relief.

Peter had a tinge of jealousy as Cas announced she was finished and would see him in the morning.

"Have you got a car?" he enquired.

"No! I don't need one. We live in, except at weekends."

"So what do you do now?"

"There's a pool two blocks down. I go there and do lengths to unwind. Why do you ask about the car?"

"You could have taken me out for a run. Get me out and about. My brain's getting a bit hospitalised."

"Can't do that," she informed him.

"What? Drive?"

"No. Fraternise with the 'guests'."

"Really? What do you do for sex then?"

Cas actually liked his style and persistence, and had not seen through his smokescreen.

Peter, as self-aware as ever, was not too sure he particularly liked his obsession with his physical performance. His whole system remained in shock. Even he could tell now that he'd had a near miss. He felt he was trying too hard to appear young, and without a care in the world. He sensed he was over-reacting to wash away the taste that he was hated, and needed to be loved, something Coco had shown him was a genuine commodity still in supply.

Cas laughed. "I'm inclined to say that for trying to be that personal, you should go swim in the sea with a hook without the bait. It's none of your friggin' business – and another thing, I'm meant to keep a record of everything you say of that nature."

"What, for Professor Han's research?"

"No. For your fiancée. We girls need to stick together when there are sharks like you in the water."

"Go on. I'm all talk. I'd run a mile if I got even the slightest encouragement." He actually meant what he said.

"Oh yes... and tell me, Mr Martinez, has any young fledgling fallen for that line yet?"

"None of your friggin' business, but sincerely, I'd like you to believe that."

They'd all picked up a thing or two from young Pablito.

He held out the hand on his bad arm. Cas responded, took it and shook it gently.

"Friend?" he said.

"Yes friend," came the reply.

They had reached the door to his room. It was an extreme venue, compared to anywhere else he had ever called home in his life.

"Can I invite you in for a night-cap?" he offered.

"Yes, of course…" Peter was surprised. "… Of course you can 'invite', but the corporate answer is no, with gracious thanks. We're not allowed."

"It's that Professor Han again. I suppose."

"No. It's your fiancée again," she said, as she threw her head back with laughter. "Now you be a good patient. Go in and rest."

She turned, leaving him speechless.

As he sat on what he now had to think of as his own bed, he felt puzzled. She didn't wear perfume but he was conscious of her presence all around him. Perhaps it was that she oozed excitement and he was realising, for the first time in his life, that was an essential aspect of the diet on which he needed to live.

ABOUT THE AUTHOR

He said he couldn't bring himself to say it, which is out of character. But I suppose one is bound to be coy when you are unsure as to whether a storyline you have thoroughly enjoyed putting down on paper may appeal equally to others too. Certainly his first enforced attempt at recording a sort of biographic history about him and some friends in early life, *Blokes, Jokes and Forty Stags*, turned out to be quite an epic effort. Principally, it was written for a limited readership of the twenty blokes who were the subject of the book, which was hailed a success by them.

Their message seems to have been that he should go further and so he got round to his first novel *Last Sardana*, its sequel *Sardana Encore*, and it becomes a completed trilogy with its addition of *Sardana Renaissance*.

Personally, I have been gratified by being alongside my husband's very successful business career founded upon his expertise as a Chartered Surveyor. I've loved being able to read books by established authors, taken from the shelves of WHSmith, Waterstones, and the like, and now on my Kindle, in the exotic places dotted around the world where the excuse has been that he writes better on holiday, and in the sun. That's in fact where Last Sardana began. On the Costa Brava, in the 1970s, with him turning to me and saying "What do you think that chap does?" indicating a fellow hotel guest the other side of the pool. It was a few years later we were there to find a sunflower crop to photograph, on which the book covers were to be founded.

His thoughts and inventiveness have, as always, escalated to the now six Sardana novels, and it's not untypical that, because his writing is a hobby, if the books sell, it is intended to commit part of the income to the charities in which we have interest.

Hope you enjoy.

Dean Harwood